Praise for
Wife 22

"Every status update tells a story in this au courant novel of marital crisis, digital-style. . . . Poignant and fresh, [*Wife 22*] is an LOL Instagram about love in a wired world." —*People*

"This modern-day, mixed-media comedy of manners is as up-to-the-minute as your favorite Twitter feed. . . . In the crowded pool of novels about midlife crises, *Wife 22* has the buoyancy of water wings."
—*The Washington Post*

"Gideon's appealing narrator takes part in an online survey about the state of marriage in the twenty-first century, for which she's dubbed Wife 22. She finds the anonymity liberating—and her assigned researcher alarmingly attractive. . . . [*Wife 22*] channels the playful but incisive vibe of Nora Ephron's *You've Got Mail* while exploring questions about how to keep long relationships as compelling as status updates."
—NPR.com

"Gideon's must-read [novel] will make you smile and laugh. Everything is witty and original, especially the dialogue and the chapter layout, some of which consists solely of Alice's answers to an online study. Smart and hilarious, this is definitely not a novel to miss out on!"
—*RT Book Reviews* (Top Pick)

"[A] fresh, funny read." —*Better Homes and Gardens*

"[Gideon] touches on everything from family life in the twenty-first century to Facebook friends and the painful act of 'Googling' yourself. Cleverly she breaks up her chapters with Google searches, Yahoo forums, Facebook postings, along with email and tweet exchanges that read so true it's hard to believe they're fiction. Maybe they aren't. . . . You'll be surprised." —*USA Today*

"Peppered with Facebook updates, email messages, and chat logs, this book is a skillful blend of pop-culture references, acidic humor, and emotional moments. It will take its rightful place . . . alongside Helen Fielding's *Bridget Jones's Diary*, Anna Maxted's *Getting Over It*, and Allison Pearson's *I Don't Know How She Does It*."

—*Library Journal* (starred review)

"Superb . . . Gideon's work is an honest assessment of a woman's struggle to reconcile herself with her desires and responsibilities, as well as a timely treatise on the anonymity and intimacy afforded by digital communiqués. Fully formed supporting characters and a nuanced emotional story line make Gideon's [novel] shimmer."

—*Publishers Weekly* (starred review)

"A domestic romantic fantasy for . . . computer-savvy Bridget Jones fans . . . Breezy fun."   —*Kirkus Reviews*

"A tale sure to please fans of Helen Fielding, Cecelia Ahern, and Sophie Kinsella."   —*Booklist*

"I loved it, loved it, loved it. It's so funny and true and sad and real and clever and of-the-moment. Also so hopeful and wise and ultimately heartwarming."

—MARIAN KEYES, bestselling author of
This Charming Man

"*Wife 22* is not just clever. It is a funny, wise, ultimately tender and revealing portrait of modern family life, of marriage, of a wife and mother and her all-important circle of friends in midlife straits. Every woman who has ever Googled herself, Facebooked her children, or simply wondered *What if?* will come to cheer and adore this particularly winsome wife."

—MARY KAY ANDREWS, *New York Times*
bestselling author of *Summer Rental*

"The delightful, compulsively readable *Wife 22* manages to be both funny and thought-provoking on the eternal question: after many years of marriage, how do two people keep their love vital? Alice Buckle's hilarious search for greater happiness will resonate with readers of all backgrounds."

—GRETCHEN RUBIN, *New York Times* bestselling author of *The Happiness Project*

ALSO BY MELANIE GIDEON

The Slippery Year: A Meditation on Happily Ever After

Wife 22

Wife 22

A Novel

MELANIE GIDEON

BALLANTINE BOOKS TRADE PAPERBACKS • NEW YORK

2013 Ballantine Books Trade Paperback Edition

Copyright © 2012 by Melanie Gideon
Random House reading group guide copyright © 2013 by Random House, Inc.

Published in the United States by Ballantine Books, an imprint of The Random House Publishing Group, a division of Random House, Inc., New York.

BALLANTINE and colophon are registered trademarks of Random House, Inc. RANDOM HOUSE READER'S CIRCLE & Design is a registered trademark of Random House, Inc.

Originally published in hardcover in the United States by Ballantine Books, an imprint of The Random House Publishing Group, a division of Random House, Inc., in 2012.

Chapter-opening photographs for chapters 43, 45, 53, and 64 are by Kerri Arsenault and are copyright © 2012 by Kerri Arsenault. Used by permission.

Library of Congress Cataloging-in-Publication Data
Gideon, Melanie.
Wife 22 : a novel / Melanie Gideon.
p. cm.
ISBN 978-0-345-52796-7
eBook ISBN 978-0-345-52797-4
I. Title. II. Title: Wife twenty-two.
PS3557.I255W54 2012
813'.54—dc23   2012004405

Printed in the United States of America

www.randomhousereaderscircle.com

246897531

Book design by Simon M. Sullivan

FOR BHR—HUSBAND 1

"Only connect."

—E. M. FORSTER

Part 1

1

April 29
5:05 P.M.

GOOGLE SEARCH "Eyelid Drooping"
About 54,300 results (.14 seconds)

Eyelid Drooping: MedlinePlus Medical Encyclopedia
Eyelid drooping is excessive sagging of the upper eyelid . . . Eyelid drooping can make somebody appear sleepy or tired.

Eyelid Drooping . . . Natural Alternatives
Speak from the chin-up position. Try not to furrow your brow, as this will only compound your problems . . .

Droopy Dog . . . eyelid drooping
American cartoon character . . . drooping eyelids. Last name McPoodle. Catchphrase . . . "You know what? That makes me mad."

2

I stare into the bathroom mirror and wonder why nobody has told me my left eyelid has grown a little hood. For a long time I looked younger than I was. And now, suddenly all the years have pooled up and I look my age—forty-four, possibly older. I lift the excess skin with my finger and waggle it about. Is there some cream I can buy? How about some eyelid pushups?

"What's wrong with your eye?"

Peter pokes his head into the bathroom and despite my irritation at being spied on, I am happy to see my son's freckled face. At twelve, his needs are still small and easily fulfilled: Eggos and Fruit of the Loom boxer briefs—the ones with the cotton waistband.

"Why didn't you tell me?" I say.

I depend on Peter. We're close, especially in matters of grooming. We have a deal. His responsibility is my hair. He'll tell me when my roots are showing so I can book an appointment with Lisa, my hairdresser. And in return, my responsibility is his odor. To make sure he doesn't exude one. For some reason, twelve-year-old boys can't smell their underarm funk. He does run-bys in the mornings, arm raised, waving a pit at me so I can get a whiff. "Shower," I almost always say. On rare occasions I lie and say "you're fine." A boy should smell like a boy.

"Tell you what?"

"About my left eyelid."

"What—that it hangs down over your eye?"

I groan.

"Only a tiny bit."

I look in the mirror again. "Why didn't you say something?"

"Well, why didn't you tell me Peter was slang for penis?"

"It is not."

"Yes, apparently it is. A peter and two balls?"

"I swear to you I have never heard that expression before."

"Well, now you understand why I'm changing my name to Pedro."

"What happened to Frost?"

"That was in February. When we were doing that unit on Robert Frost."

"So now the road has diverged and you want to be Pedro?" I ask.

Middle school, I've been told, is all about experimenting with identity. It's our job as parents to let our kids try on different personas, but it's getting hard to keep up. Frost one day, Pedro the next. Thank God Peter is not an EMO, or is it IMO? I have no idea what EMO/IMO stands for—as far as I can tell it's a subset of Goth, a tough kid who dyes his hair black and wears eyeliner, and no, that is not Peter. Peter is a romantic.

"Okay," I say. "But have you considered Peder? It's the Norwegian version of Peter. Your friends could say 'later, Peder.' There's nothing that rhymes with Pedro. Do we have any Scotch tape?"

I want to tape up my eyelid—see what it would look like if I got it fixed.

"Fade-dro," says Peter. "And I like your sagging eyelid. It makes you look like a dog."

My mouth drops open. *You know what? That makes me mad.*

"No, like Jampo," he says.

Peter is referring to our two-year-old mutt, half Tibetan spaniel, half God-knows-what-else: a twelve-pound, high-strung Mussolini of a dog who eats his own poop. Disgusting, yes, but convenient if you think about it. You never have to carry around those plastic bags.

"Drop it, Jampo, you little shit!" Zoe yells from downstairs.

We can hear the dog running manically on the hardwood floors, most likely carting around a roll of toilet paper, which next to poop is his favorite treat. *Jampo* means "gentle" in Tibetan, which of course turned out to be the complete opposite of the dog's personality, but I don't mind; I prefer a spirited dog. The past year and a half has been like having a toddler in the house again and I've loved every minute of it. Jampo is my baby, the third child I'll never have.

"He needs to go out. Honey, will you take him? I have to get ready for tonight."

Peter makes a face.

"Please?"

"Fine."

"Thank you. Hey, wait—before you go, do we have any Scotch tape?"

"I don't think so. I saw some duct tape in the junk drawer, though."

I consider my eyelid. "One more favor?"

"What?" Peter sighs.

"Will you bring up the duct tape after you've walked the dog?"

He nods.

"You are my number-one son," I say.

"Your only son."

"And number one at math," I say, kissing him on the cheek.

Tonight I'm accompanying William to the launch of FiG vodka, an account he and his team at KKM Advertising have been working on for weeks now. I've been looking forward to it. There'll be live music. Some hot new band, three women with electric violins from the Adirondacks or the Ozarks—I can't remember which.

"Business dressy," William said, so I pull out my old crimson Ann Taylor suit. Back in the '90s when I, too, worked in advertising, this was my power suit. I put it on and stand in front of the full-length mirror. The suit looks a little outdated, but maybe if I wear the chunky silver necklace Nedra got me for my birthday last year it will mask the fact that it has seen better days. I met Nedra Rao fifteen years ago at a Mommy and Me playgroup. She's my best friend and also happens to be one of the top divorce lawyers in the state of California whom I can always count on to give very sane, very sophisticated $425-an-hour advice to me for free because she loves me. I try and see the suit through Nedra's eyes. I know just what she'd say: "You can't be bloody serious, darling," in her posh English accent. Too bad. There's nothing else in my closet that qualifies as "business dressy." I slip on my pumps and walk downstairs.

Sitting on the couch, her long brown hair swept back into a messy chignon, is my fifteen-year-old daughter, Zoe. She's an on-and-off vegetarian (currently off), a rabid recycler, and maker of her own organic lip balm (peppermint and ginger). Like most girls her age, she is also a professional ex: ex–ballet dancer, ex-guitarist, and ex-girlfriend of Nedra's son, Jude. Jude is somewhat famous around here. He made it to the Hollywood round of *American Idol* and then was booted off for "sounding like a California eucalyptus tree that was on fire, popping and sizzling and exploding, but in the end not a native species, not native at all."

I was rooting for Jude, we all were, as he made it past the first and second eliminations. But then right before Hollywood he got a swelled head from the instant fame, cheated on Zoe, and then dumped her, thus breaking my girl's heart. The lesson? Never allow your teenager to date the son of your best friend. It took months for me—I mean, Zoe—to recover. I said some horrible things to Nedra—things I probably shouldn't have said, along the lines of *I would have expected more from the son of a feminist and a boy with two moms*. Nedra and I didn't speak for a while. We're fine now, but whenever I go to her house Jude is conveniently out.

Zoe's right hand moves over her cellphone's keypad at top speed.

"You're wearing *that*?" she says.

"What? It's vintage."

Zoe snorts.

"Zoe, sweetheart, will you please look up from that thing? I need your honest opinion." I spread my arms wide. "Is it really that bad?"

Zoe cocks her head. "That depends. How dark is it going to be?"

I sigh. Just a year ago Zoe and I were so close. Now she treats me like she does her brother—as a family member who must be tolerated. I act like I don't notice, but invariably overcompensate, trying to be nice for both of us, and then I end up sounding like a cross between Mary Poppins and Miss Truly Scrumptious from *Chitty Chitty Bang Bang*.

"There's a pizza in the freezer, and please make sure Peter is in bed by ten. We should be home soon after that," I say.

Zoe continues to text. "Dad's waiting for you in the car."

I scurry around the kitchen looking for my purse. "Have a great time. And don't watch *Idol* without me!"

"Already Googled the results. Should I tell you who gets the axe?"

"No!" I shout, running out the door.

• • •

"Alice Buckle. It's been entirely too long. And what a breath of fresh air you are! Why doesn't William drag you to these events more often? But I suppose he's doing you a favor, isn't he? Another night, another vodka launch. Ho-hum, am I right?"

Frank Potter, chief creative officer of KKM Advertising, looks discreetly over my head. "You look wonderful," he says, his eyes darting around. He waves to someone at the back of the room. "That's a lovely suit."

I take a big gulp of wine. "Thanks."

As I look around the room, at all the sheer blouses, strappy sandals, and skinny jeans most of the other women are wearing, I realize that "business dressy" really means "business sexy." At least with this crowd. Everybody looks great. So *of* the moment. I wrap one arm around my waist and hold the wine glass so it hovers near my chin, a poor attempt at camouflaging my jacket.

"Thank you, Frank," I say, as a bead of sweat trickles down the back of my neck.

Sweating is my default response when I feel out of place. My other default response is repeating myself.

"Thank you," I say once more. Oh, God, Alice. A trifecta of thanks?

He pats me on the arm. "So how are things at home? Tell me. Is everything okay? The kids?"

"Everybody's fine."

"You're sure?" he asks, his face screwed up with concern.

"Well, yes, yes, everybody's good."

"Wonderful," he says. "Glad to hear it. And what are you doing these days? Still teaching? What subject was it?"

"Drama."

"Drama. That's right. That must be so—rewarding. But I imagine quite stressful." He lowers his voice. "You are a saint, Alice Buckle. I certainly wouldn't have the patience."

"I'm sure you would if you saw what these kids are capable of. They're so eager. You know, just the other day one of my students—"

Frank Potter looks over my head once again, raises his eyebrows, and nods.

"Alice, forgive me, but I'm afraid I'm being summoned."

"Oh, of course. I'm sorry. I didn't mean to keep you. I'm sure you have other—"

He moves toward me and I lean in, thinking he's going to kiss me on the cheek, but instead he pulls back, takes my hand firmly, and shakes it. "Goodbye, Alice."

I look out into the room, at everyone breezily drinking their lychee FiGtinis. I chuckle softly as if I'm thinking of something funny, trying to look breezy myself. Where is my husband?

"Frank Potter is an ass," a voice whispers in my ear.

Thank God, a friendly face. It's Kelly Cho, a longtime member of William's creative team—long in advertising anyway, where turnover is incredibly fast. She's wearing a suit, not all that different from mine (better lapels), but on her it looks edgy. She's paired it with over-the-knee boots.

"Wow, Kelly, you look fabulous," I say.

Kelly waves my compliment away. "So how come we don't see you more often?"

"Oh, you know. Coming over the bridge is such a hassle. Traffic. And I still don't feel all that comfortable leaving the kids home alone at night. Peter's just twelve, and Zoe's a typical distracted teenager."

"How's work?"

"Great. Other than being up to my neck in details: costumes, wrangling parents, soothing spiders and pigs that haven't learned their lines yet. The third grade is doing *Charlotte's Web* this year."

Kelly smiles. "I love that book! Your job sounds so idyllic."

"It does?"

"Oh, yeah. I would love to get out of the rat race. Every night there's something going on. I know it seems glamorous—the client dinners, box seats for the Giants, passes to concerts—but it's exhausting after a while. Well, you know how it is. You're an advertising widow from way back."

Advertising widow? I didn't know there was name for it. For *me*. But

Kelly's right. Between William's traveling and entertaining clients, I'm basically a single mother. We're lucky if we manage to have a family dinner a few times a week.

I look across the room and catch William's eye. He heads toward us. He's a tall, well-built man, his dark hair graying at just the temples, in that defiant way some men gray (as if to say to hell with the fact that I'm forty-seven—I'm still sexy as hell and the gray makes me look even sexier). I feel a rush of pride as he crosses the room in his charcoal suit and gingham shirt.

"Where did you get your boots?" I ask Kelly.

William joins us.

"Bloomie's. So, William, your wife isn't familiar with the term *advertising widow*. How is that possible when you've made her into one?" asks Kelly, winking at me.

William frowns. "I've been looking all over for you. Where have you been, Alice?"

"She's been right here, suffering Frank Potter, in fact," says Kelly.

"You were talking to Frank Potter?" William asks, alarmed. "Did he approach you or did you approach him?"

"He approached me," I say.

"Did he mention me? The campaign?"

"We didn't talk about you," I say. "We didn't speak for long, actually."

I watch William clenching his jaw. Why is he so stressed? The clients are smiling and drunk. There's a lot of press. The launch is a success as far as I can see.

"Can we get out of here, Alice?" asks William.

"Now? But the band hasn't even started. I was really looking forward to hearing some live music."

"Alice, I'm tired. Let's go, please."

"William!" a trio of attractive young men circles around us—also members of William's team.

After William has introduced me to Joaquin, Harry, and Urminder, Urminder says, "So, I was ego surfing today."

"And the day before," says Joaquin.

"And the day before," says Kelly.

"Will you allow me to finish?" asks Urminder.

"Let me guess," says Harry. "1,234,589 hits."

"Dumb-ass," says Urminder.

"Way to steal his thunder, Har," says Kelly.

"Now 5,881 sounds pathetic," pouts Urminder.

"10,263 definitively does not sound pathetic," says Harry.

"Or 20,534," says Kelly.

"You're all lying," says Joaquin.

"Don't be jealous, Mr. 1,031," says Kelly. "It's unbecoming."

"50,287," says William, silencing everybody.

"*Dude*," says Urminder.

"That's because you won that Clio," says Harry. "How long ago was that, boss? Nineteen eighty—?"

"Keep it up, Harry, and I'll take you off semiconductors and put you on feminine hygiene," says William.

I can't hide the startled look on my face. They're having a competition over how many hits their names bring up. And the hits are all in the thousands?

"Now look what you've done. Alice is appalled," says Kelly. "And I don't blame her. We're a bunch of petty narcissists."

"No, no, no. I wasn't judging. I think it's fun. Ego surfing. Everybody does it, don't they? They're just not brave enough to admit it."

"What about you, Alice? Googled yourself lately?" asks Urminder.

William shakes his head. "There's no need for Alice to Google herself. She doesn't have a public life."

"Really? And what kind of a life do I have?" I ask.

"A good life. A meaningful life. Just a smaller life." William pinches the skin between his eyes. "Sorry, kids, it's been fun, but we've got to go. We have a bridge to cross."

"Do you have to?" asks Kelly. "I hardly ever see Alice."

"He's right," I say. "I promised the kids we'd be home by ten. School night and all."

Kelly and the three young men head for the bar.

"A small life?" I say.

"I didn't mean anything by it. Don't be so sensitive," says William, scanning the room. "Besides, I'm right. When's the last time you Googled yourself?"

"Last week. 128 hits," I lie.

"*Really?*"

"Why do you sound so surprised?"

"Alice, please, I don't have time for this. Help me find Frank. I need to check in with him."

I sigh. "He's over there, by the windows. Come on."

William puts his hand on my shoulder. "Wait here. I'll be right back."

There's no traffic on the bridge and I wish there was. Heading home is usually something I relish: the anticipation of getting into my pajamas, curling up on the couch with the clicker, the kids asleep upstairs (or pretending to be asleep but likely texting and IM'ing away in their beds)—but tonight I'd like to stay in the car and just drive somewhere, anywhere. The evening has been dislocating, and I'm unable to shake the feeling that William is embarrassed by me.

"Why are you so quiet? Did you have too much to drink?" he asks.

"Tired," I mumble.

"Frank Potter is a piece of work."

"I like him."

"You *like* Frank Potter? He's such a player."

"Yes, but he's honest. He doesn't try and hide the fact. And he's always been kind to me."

William taps his fingers on the steering wheel in time to the radio. I close my eyes.

"Alice?"

"What?"

"You seem funny lately."

"Funny how?"

"I don't know. Are you going through some sort of a midlife thing?"

"I don't know. Are *you* going through some sort of a midlife thing?"

William shakes his head and turns up the music. I lean against the window and gaze out at the millions of lights twinkling in the East Bay hills. Oakland looks so festive, almost holidayish—it makes me think of my mother.

My mother died two days before Christmas. I was fifteen. She went out to get a gallon of eggnog and was struck by a man who ran a red light. I like to think she never knew what was happening. There was a screech of metal hitting metal, and then a gentle whooshing, like the sound of a river, and then, a peachy light flooding into the car. That's the end I've imagined for her.

I've recited her death story so many times the details are stripped of their meaning. Sometimes when people ask about my mother I'm filled with a strange, not entirely unpleasant nostalgia. I can vividly summon up the streets of Brockton, Massachusetts, that on that December day must have been garlanded with tinsel and lights. There would have been lines of people at the liquor store, their carts packed with cases of beer and jugs of wine, and the air would have smelled of pine needles from the Christmas tree lot. But that nostalgia for what came immediately *before* is soon vanquished by the opaque *after*. Then my head fills with the cheesy opening soundtrack to *Magnum, P.I.* That's what my father was watching when the phone rang and a woman on the other end gently informed us there had been an accident.

Why am I thinking about this tonight? Is it, as William asks, a midlife thing? The clock is certainly ticking. This September when I turn forty-five, I will be exactly the same age my mother was when she died. This is my tipping-point year.

Up until now I've been able to comfort myself with the fact that even though my mother is dead, she was always out in front of me. I had yet to cross all the thresholds she had crossed and so she was still somehow alive. But what happens when I move past her? When no more of her thresholds exist?

I glance over at William. Would my mother approve of him? Would she approve of my children, my career—my marriage?

"Do you want to stop at 7-Eleven?" asks William.

Ducking into 7-Eleven for a Kit Kat bar after a night out on the town is a tradition for us.

"No. I'm full."

"Thanks for coming to the launch."

Is that his way of apologizing for how dismissive he was tonight?

"Uh-huh."

"Did you have fun?"

"Sure."

William pauses. "You're a very bad liar, Alice Buckle."

3

April 30
1:15 A.M.

GOOGLE SEARCH "Alice Buckle"
About 26 results (.01 seconds)

Alice in Wonderland Belt Buckles
Including the Mad Tea Party buckle, Tweedle Dee, Tweedle Dum buckle, the White Rabbit buckle, Humpty Dumpty buckle . . .

Alice BUCKLE
Boston Globe archive . . . Ms. Buckle's play, *The Barmaid of Great Cranberry Island*, Blue Hill Playhouse "wan, boring, absurd" . . .

Alice BUCKLE
Alice and William Buckle, parents of Zoe and Peter, enjoying the sunset aboard the . . .

GOOGLE SEARCH "Midwife crisis"
About 2,333,000 results (.18 seconds)

Urban Dictionary: Midwife crisis
The act of dropping a newborn on its head shortly after birth.

GOOGLE SEARCH "MidLIFE crisis"
About 3,490,000 results (.15 seconds)

Midlife Crisis—Wikipedia the Free Encyclopedia
Midlife crisis is a term coined in 1965 . . .

Midlife Crisis: Depression or Normal Transition?
Midlife transitions can mark a period of tremendous growth. But what do you do when midlife becomes a crisis that develops into depression?

GOOGLE SEARCH "Zoloft"
About 31,600,000 (.12 seconds)

Zoloft (Sertraline HCl) Drug Information: Uses, Side Effects
Learn about the prescription medication Zoloft (Sertraline HCl), drug uses, dosage, side effects, drug interactions, warnings, and patient labeling . . .

Sertraline . . . Zoloft
Let me tell you about my experience with Zoloft. I was released from the psych ward yesterday afternoon . . .

GOOGLE SEARCH "Keys in refrigerator Alzheimer's"
About 1,410,000 results (.25 seconds)

Alzheimer's Symptoms
The Alzheimer's Association has updated its list of the . . . putting the keys in the egg tray in the door of the refrigerator.

GOOGLE SEARCH "Lose weight fast"
About 30,600,000 results (.19 seconds)

FAT LOSS for Imbeciles
I have lost twenty-five pounds! The fact that I feel like fainting most of the time is a small price . . .

GOOGLE SEARCH "Happy Marriage?"
About 4,120,000 results (.15 seconds)

Hunting for the Secrets of a Happy Marriage—CNN
No one can truly know what goes on inside a marriage except the two people involved, but researchers are getting increasingly good glimpses . . .

Thin Wife Key to Happy Marriage! *Times of India*
Researchers have revealed the secret of a happy marriage—wives weighing less than their hubbies.

INGREDIENTS FOR A HAPPY MARRIAGE
1 cup kindness, 2 cups gratitude, 1 tablespoon daily praise, 1 secret carefully concealed.

4

SPAM Folder (3)

From: Medline
Subject: Cheap, cheap Vicodin, Percocet, Ritalin, Zoloft discreet
Date: May 1, 9:18 AM
To: Alice Buckle <alicebuckle@rocketmail.com>
DELETE

From: Hoodia shop
Subject: New tapeworm diet pills, tiny Asian women
Date: May 1, 9:24 AM
To: Alice Buckle <alicebuckle@rocketmail.com>
DELETE

From: Netherfield Center for the Study of Marriage
Subject: You've been selected to participate in a marriage survey
Date: May 1, 9:29 AM
To: Alice Buckle <alicebuckle@rocketmail.com>
MOVE TO INBOX

5

It occurs to me that I am the Frank Potter of my own small world. Not the social-climbing Frank Potter, but the in-charge Frank Potter—I am the chief drama officer of Kentwood Elementary. The anxious Alice Buckle that showed up at William's vodka launch is not the Alice Buckle who is currently sitting on a bench out on the playground while a fourth-grader stands behind her and attempts in vain to style her hair.

"Sorry, Mrs. Buckle, but I can't do anything with this," says Harriet. "Maybe if you combed it once in a while."

"If you combed my hair it would be nothing but frizz. It'd be a rat's nest."

Harriet gathers up my thick brown hair and then releases it. "I'm sorry to tell you, but it looks like a rat's nest now. Actually, it looks more like a dandelion."

Harriet Morse's bluntness is a typical fourth-grade girl trait. I pray she won't outgrow it by the time she gets to middle school. Most girls do. Myself, I like nothing better than a girl who says what she thinks.

"Maybe you should straighten it," she suggests. "My mother does. She can even go out in the rain without it curling up."

"And that's why she looks so glamorous," I say, as I see Mrs. Morse trotting toward us.

"Alice, I'm sorry I'm late," she says, bending down to give me a hug. Harriet is the fourth of Mrs. Morse's children to have cycled through my drama classes. Her oldest is now at the Oakland School for Performing Arts. I like to think I might have had something to do with that.

"It's only 3:20. You're fine," I say. There are still at least two dozen kids scattered on the playground awaiting their rides.

"The traffic was horrible," says Mrs. Morse. "Harriet, what in the world are you doing to Mrs. Buckle's hair?"

"She's a very good hairdresser, actually. I'm afraid it's my hair that's the problem."

"Sorry," Mrs. Morse mouths silently to me, as she digs in her handbag for a hair tie. She holds it out to Harriet. "Honey, don't you think Mrs. Buckle would look great with a ponytail?"

Harriet comes around from the back of the bench and surveys me solemnly. She lifts my hair back from my temples. "You should wear earrings," she pronounces. "Especially if you put your hair up." She takes the hair tie from her mother and then reassumes her position behind the bench.

"So what can I do to help out this semester?" asks Mrs. Morse. "Do you want me to organize the party? I could help the kids run lines."

Kentwood Elementary is filled with parents like Mrs. Morse: parents who volunteer before they're even asked and who believe fervently in the importance of a drama program. In fact it's the Parents' Association at Kentwood that pays my part-time salary. The Oakland public school system has been on the verge of bankruptcy for years. Art and music programs were the first to go. Without the PA, I wouldn't have a job.

There's always some grade that has a cluster of high-maintenance parents who complain and are unhappy—this year it's the third—but most of the time I consider the parents co-teachers. I couldn't do my job without them.

"That looks lovely," says Mrs. Morse, after a few minutes of Harriet pulling and tugging on my head. "I like the way you've given Mrs. Buckle a little pouf at the crown."

Harriet chews her lip. The pouf was not intentional.

"I feel very *Breakfast at Tiffany's*," I say, as Carisa Norman comes flying across the playground and hurls herself on my lap.

"I've been looking all over for you," she says, stroking my hand.

"What a coincidence. I've been looking all over for you," I say, as she snuggles into my arms.

"Call me," says Mrs. Morse, holding a pretend phone up to her ear as she and Harriet leave.

I take Carisa inside to the teacher's lounge and buy her a granola bar from the vending machine, then we go sit on the bench again and talk about important things like Barbies and the fact that she's embarrassed that she still has training wheels on her bike.

At 4:00 when her mother pulls up to the curb and beeps, I watch with a clenched heart as Carisa runs across the playground. She seems so vulnerable. She's eight years old and small for her age; from the back she could pass for six. Mrs. Norman waves from the car. I wave back. This is our ritual at least a few days every week. Each of us pretending there's nothing out of the ordinary about her being forty-five minutes late to pick up her daughter.

6

love the hours between 4:30 and 6:30. The days are getting longer, and this time of year I usually have the house to myself; Zoe has volleyball practice, Peter, either band or soccer, and William rarely pulls into the driveway before 7:00. As soon as I get home, I do a quick run through the house, de-cluttering, folding clothes, going through the mail—then I get dinner ready. It's Thursday, so it's one-dish-meal night: things like lasagna and shepherd's pie. I'm not a fancy cook. That's William's department. He does the special-occasion dinners, the ones that get lots of oohs and ahs. I'm more of a line chef; my meals aren't flashy and are not very memorable. For instance, nobody has ever said to me, "Oh, Alice, remember that night you made baked ziti?" But I am dependable. I have about eight meals in my repertoire that are quick and easy that I have in constant rotation. Tonight, it's tuna casserole. I slide the pan into the oven and sit down at the kitchen table with my laptop to check my email.

From: Netherfield Center <netherfield@netherfieldcenter.org>
Subject: Marriage Survey
Date: May 4, 5:22 PM
To: alicebuckle <alicebuckle@rocketmail.com>

Dear Alice Buckle,

   Thank you for your interest in our study and for filling out the pre-liminary questionnaire. Congratulations! We're happy to inform you that you have been selected to participate in the Netherfield Center Study—Marriage in the 21st Century. You have successfully met three of the initial criteria for inclusion in this study: married for more than ten years, school-age children, and monogamous.

   As we explained to you in the preliminary questionnaire, this will be an anonymous study. In order to protect your anonymity, this is the last email we will send to you at alicebuckle@rocketmail.com. We've taken the liberty of setting up a Netherfield Center account for your use. Your email address for the purposes of the study is Wife22@netherfield center.org and the password is 12345678. Please log on to our website and change the password at your earliest convenience.

From this point on, all correspondence will be sent to the Wife22 address. We apologize if the pseudonym sounds clinical, but this is done with your best interest in mind. It's only by striking your real name from our records that we can offer you complete confidentiality.

A researcher has been assigned to your case and you will be hearing from him shortly. Rest assured all our researchers are highly credentialed.

The stipend of $1,000 will be paid upon completion of the survey.

Once again, thank you for your participation. You can take pride in the fact that you, along with a carefully selected group of men and women from across the country, are participating in a landmark study that may very well change how the world looks at the institution of marriage.

Sincerely,

The Netherfield Center

I quickly log on to the new Wife 22 account.

From: researcher101 <researcher101@netherfieldcenter.org>
Subject: Re: Marriage Survey
Date: May 4, 5:25 PM
To: Wife 22 <Wife22@netherfieldcenter.org>

Dear Wife 22,

Allow me to introduce myself—I'm Researcher 101 and I will be your point person for the Marriage in the 21st Century Study. First, my credentials. I have a PhD in Social Work and a Master's in Psychology. I have been a researcher in the field of marriage studies for nearly two decades.

I'm sure you're wondering how this works. Basically, I'm on a here-if-you-need-me basis. I'm happy to answer any questions or address any concerns you may have along the way.

Attached is the first questionnaire. The questions will be sent to you in a random order; this is done intentionally. Some of the questions you may find atypical, and some of the questions are not about marriage per se, but of a more general nature (about your background, education, life experiences etc.); please strive to complete all the questions. I suggest you fill out the questionnaire quickly, without thinking too much about it. We've found this kind of rapid-fire response results in the most honest responses. I'm looking forward to working with you.

Sincerely,

Researcher 101

Before I took the preliminary survey, I'd Googled the Netherfield Center website and found out it was affiliated with the UCSF Medical Center. Because of UCSF's stellar reputation, I filled it out and emailed it off with little thought. What could answering a few questions hurt? But now that I've been formally accepted AND assigned a researcher, I'm having second thoughts about participating in an *anonymous* survey. A survey I'm probably not supposed to tell anybody (including my husband) I'm taking part in.

My heart ca-cungs in my chest. Having a secret makes me feel like a teenager. A young woman with everything still in front of her—breasts, strange cities, the unfurling of hundreds of yet-to-be-lived summers, winters, and springs.

I open the attachment before I lose my nerve.

1. Forty-three, no, forty-four.

2. Bored.

3. Once a week.

4. Satisfactory to better than most.

5. Oysters.

6. Three years ago.

7. Sometimes I tell him he's snoring when he's not snoring so he'll sleep in the guest room and I can have the bed all to myself.

8. Ambien (once in a blue moon), fish oil tablets, multi-vitamin, B-Complex, calcium, vitamin D, gingko biloba (for mental sharpness, well, really for memory because people keep saying "That is the third time you asked me that!").

9. A life with surprises. A life without surprises. The clerk at 7-Eleven licking her finger to separate the stack of plastic bags and then touching my salt and vinegar potato chips with her still damp licked finger and then sliding my potato chips into the previously licked plastic bag, thus doubly salivating my purchase.

10. I hope so.

11. I think so.

12. Occasionally, but not because I've ever seriously considered it. I'm the kind of person who likes to imagine the worst, that way the worst can never take me by surprise.

13. The chicken.

14. He makes an amazing vinaigrette. He remembers to change the batteries every six months in the smoke alarms. He can do minor plumbing repairs, so unlike most of my friends I never have to hire somebody to fix a dripping faucet. Also he looks very good in his Carhartt pants. I know I'm avoiding answering the question—I'm not sure why. Let me get back to you on this one.

15. Uncommunicative. Dismissive. Distant.

16. *The Lion, the Witch and the Wardrobe.*

17. We've been together for nineteen years and three hundred and something days, my point is very, very, well.

This is easy. *Too* easy. Who knew that confession could bring on such a dopamine rush?

Suddenly the front door is flung open and Peter yells, "I call the bathroom first."

He has a thing about not using the bathroom at school, so he holds it all day. I close my laptop. This is *also* my favorite time of the day—when the empty house fills back up again and within an hour all of my decluttering is for naught. For some reason this gives me pleasure. The satisfying inevitability of it all.

Zoe walks into the kitchen and makes a face. "Tuna casserole?"

"It'll be ready in fifteen minutes."

"I already ate."

"At volleyball practice?"

"Karen's mother stopped on the way home and got us burritos."

"So Peter's eaten, too?"

Zoe nods and opens the fridge.

I sigh. "What are you looking for? I thought you just ate."

"I don't know. Nothing," she says, closing the door.

"Dang! What did you do to your hair?" asks Peter, walking into the kitchen.

"Oh, God, I forgot. One of my kids was playing hairdresser. I thought it was kind of Audrey Hepburnesque. No?"

"No," says Zoe.

"No," echoes Peter.

I slide the elastic out of my hair and try and smooth it out.

"Maybe if you combed it once in a while," says Zoe.

"Why is everybody so comb crazy? For your information, there are certain types of hair that should never be combed. You should just let it dry naturally."

"Uh-huh," says Zoe, grabbing her backpack. "I've got a ton of homework. See you in 2021."

"Half an hour of Modern Warfare before homework?" asks Peter.

"Ten minutes," I say.

"Twenty."

"Fifteen."

Peter throws his arms around me. Even though he's twelve, I still occasionally get hugs. A few minutes later, the sounds of guns and bombs issue forth from the living room.

My phone chirps. It's a text from William.

Sorry.

Client dinner.

See u 10ish.

I open my laptop, quickly reread my answers, and hit Send.

7

From: researcher101 <researcher101@netherfieldcenter.org>
Subject: #13
Date: May 5, 8:05 AM
To: Wife 22 <Wife22@netherfieldcenter.org>

Dear Wife 22,
   Thanks for your first set of answers and for getting them back to me so quickly. I have one question. In regards to #13, did you mean to write "children," not "chicken"?
   Regards,
   Researcher 101

From: Wife 22 <Wife22@netherfieldcenter.org>
Subject: Re: #13
Date: May 5, 10:15 AM
To: researcher101 <researcher101@netherfieldcenter.org>

Dear Researcher 101,
   I'm sorry about that. I suspect my chickens, I mean children, are to blame. Or more likely auto correct.
   Best,
   Wife 22

   P.S. Is there any significance to our numbers or are they just randomly assigned? I can't believe I'm only the 22nd wife to participate in the survey.

From: researcher101 <researcher101@netherfieldcenter.org>
Subject: Re: #13
Date: May 6, 11:23 AM
To: Wife 22 <Wife22@netherfieldcenter.org>

Dear Wife 22,

   Both of our numbers are randomly assigned, you're right about that.
With each round of the survey we cycle through 500 numbers and then
with the next round we begin at 1 again.

   Regards,

   Researcher 101

From: Wife 22 <Wife22@netherfieldcenter.org>
Subject: #2 upon second thought
Date: May 6, 4:32 PM
To: researcher101 <researcher101@netherfieldcenter.org>

Dear Researcher 101,

   "Bored" is not the reason I'm participating in the study. I'm participating because this year I will turn 45, which is the same age my mother
was when she died. If she were alive I would be talking to her instead of
taking this survey. We would be having the conversation I imagine
mothers have with their daughters when they're in their mid-forties. We
would talk about our sex drives (or lack thereof), about the stubborn
ten pounds that we gain and lose over and over again, and about how
hard it is to find a trustworthy plumber. We would trade tips on the
secret to roasting a perfect chicken, how to turn the gas off when
there's an emergency, how to get stains out of grout. She would ask me
questions like, are you happy, sweetheart? Does he treat you right? Can
you imagine growing old with him?

   My mother will never be a grandmother. Never have a gray eyebrow
hair. Never eat my tuna casserole.

   That's why I'm participating in this study.

   Please revise my answer to #2.

   Best,

   Wife 22

From: researcher101 <researcher101@netherfieldcenter.org>
Subject: Re: #2 upon second thought
Date: May 6, 8:31 PM
To: Wife 22 <Wife22@netherfieldcenter.org>

Dear Wife 22,

Thank you for your honesty. Just so you know, subjects frequently revise their answers or send addendums. I'm very sorry for your loss.

Sincerely,

Researcher 101

8

18. Run, dive, pitch a tent, bake bread, build bonfires, read Stephen King, get up to change the channel, spend hours on the phone talking to friends, kiss strange men, have sex with strange men, flirt, wear bikinis, wake most mornings happy for no good reason (likely due to flat stomach no matter what was eaten night before), drink tequila, hum Paul McCartney's "Silly Love Songs," lie in grass and dream of future, of perfect life and marriage to perfect one true love.

19. Make lunches, suggest to family they are capable of making better choices; alert children to BO, stranger danger, and stray crumbs on corners of lips. Prepare preteen son for onset of hormones. Prepare husband for onset of perimenopause and what that means for him (PMS 30 days of the month rather than the two days he has become accustomed to). Buy perennials. Kill perennials. Text, IM, chat, upload. Discern the fastest-moving line at the grocery store, ignore messages, delete, lose keys, mishear what everybody says (jostling becomes jaw sling, fatwa becomes fuckher), worry—early deafness, early dementia, early Alzheimer's or unhappy with sex and life and marriage and need to do something about it?

20. Burger King cashier, Royal Manor Nursing Home Aide, waitress Friday's, waitress J.C. Hilary's, intern Charles Playhouse, Copywriter Peavey Patterson, playwright, wife, mother, and currently, Kentwood Elementary School drama teacher for grades kindergarten through fifth.

9

"Alice!" William yells from the kitchen. "Alice!" I hear his footsteps coming down the hall.

I quickly close the Netherfield Center questionnaire window and log on to a celebrity gossip website.

"Here you are," he says.

He's dressed for work: khakis and a pale purple dress shirt. I bought him that shirt, knowing how good he'd look in that color with his dark hair and eyes. When I brought it home he'd protested, of course.

"Men don't wear lavender," he told me.

"Yes, but men wear *thistle*," I said.

Sometimes all you need to do to get men to agree with you is call things by another name.

"Nice shirt," I say.

His eyes dart over to my laptop. "Gwen Stefani and the Sisterhood of the Terrible Pants?"

"What do you need?" I ask.

"Oh, those *are* terrible. She looks like Oliver Twist. Yes, I need something but I forgot what."

This is a typical response—one I'm used to. Both of us frequently wander into a room bewildered and ask the other if he or she has any idea what we're doing there.

"What's up with you?" he asks.

My eyes fall on the bill for the motorcycle insurance. "Well. I wish you'd make a decision about the motorcycle. It's been sitting in the driveway forever. You never take it out."

The motorcycle takes up precious space in our small driveway. More than once I've accidentally tapped it while pulling in.

"One of these days I'll start driving it again."

"You've been saying that for years. And every year we keep on paying the excise tax and the insurance."

"Yes, but I mean it now. Soon," he says.

"Soon what?"

"Soon I'll be driving it," he repeats. "More than I have been."

"Mm-hmm," I say, distracted, going back to my computer.

"Wait. That's all you want to talk about? The motorcycle?"

"William, you came looking for me, remember?"

And no, the motorcycle is not all I want to talk about. I want to have a conversation with my husband that goes deeper than insurance policies and taxes and what time will you be home and did you call the guy about the gutters, but we seem to be stuck here floating around on the surface of our lives like kids in a pool propped up on those Styrofoam noodles.

"And there's plenty of things we can talk about," I say.

"Like what?"

Now is my chance to tell him about the marriage study—oh, you wouldn't believe the ridiculous thing I signed up for and they ask the craziest questions but it's for the good of science because you know there is a science to marriage, you may not believe it but it's true—but I don't. Instead I say, "Like how I'm trying, completely unsuccessfully mind you, to convince the third-grade parents that the geese are the most important roles in the school play, even though the geese don't have any lines. Or we could talk about our son, Peter, I mean, Pedro, being gay. Or I could ask you about KKM. Still working on semiconductors?"

"Band-Aids."

"Poor baby. Are you stuck on Band-Aids?" I sing that line. I can't help myself.

"We don't know if Peter is gay," says William, sighing. We've had this conversation many times before.

"He may be."

"He's *twelve*."

"Twelve is not too early to know. I just have a feeling. A sense. A mother knows these sorts of things. I read this article about all these tweens coming out in middle school. It's happening earlier and earlier. I bookmarked it. I'll email it to you."

"No, thank you."

"William, we should educate ourselves. Prepare."

"For what?"

"For the fact that our son might be gay."

"I don't get it, Alice. Why are you so invested in Peter's sexuality? Are you saying you *want* him to be gay?"

"I want him to know we support him no matter what his sexual orientation. No matter who he is."

"Right. Okay. Well, I have a theory. You think if Peter's gay you'll never lose him. There'll be no competition. You'll always be the most important woman in his life."

"That's absurd."

William shakes his head. "It would be a harder life for him."

"You sound like a homophobe."

"I'm not a homophobe, I'm a realist."

"Look at Nedra and Kate. They're one of the happiest couples we know. No one discriminates against them and you love Nedra and Kate."

"Love has nothing to do with not wanting your children to be discriminated against unnecessarily. And Nedra and Kate wouldn't be happy if they didn't live in the Bay Area. The Bay Area is not the real world."

"And being gay is not a choice. Hey, he could be bisexual. I never thought of that. What if he's bisexual?"

"Great idea. Let's shoot for that," says William, leaving my office.

I log on to Facebook once he's gone and check my news feed, scrolling through the status update chaff.

Shonda Perkins
Likes PX-90.
2 minutes ago

Tita De La Reyes
IKEEEEAAAAA!!!! Hell—somebody ran over my foot with their shopping cart.
5 minutes ago

Tita De La Reyes
IKEEEEAAAAA!!!! Heaven—Swedish meatballs and lingonberries for $3.99.
11 minutes ago

William Buckle
Fall, falling . . .
1 hour ago

Wait, *what?* William has a new post and he's not quoting Winston Churchill or the Dalai Lama? Poor William is one of those Facebook posters who has a hard time thinking of anything original to say. Facebook gives him stage fright. But this post has an undeniably ominous ring to it. Is *that* what he came to talk to me about? I have to go ask him what he meant, but first I'll send out a quick post of my own.

> **Alice Buckle** *is educating herself.*
> DELETE

> **Alice Buckle** *is stuck on Band-Aids.*
> DELETE

> **Alice Buckle** *blames her chickens.*
> SHARE

Suddenly my Facebook chat pops up.

> **Phil Archer** *What did the poor chickens do?*

It's my father.

> *Honey, Alice. R u there?*

> **Hi Dad. I'm in a hurry. Have to go find W before he leaves for work. Can we talk tomorrow?**

> *Date tonight.*

> **You have a date?? With who?**

> *I'll let you know who if there's a second date.*

> **Oh. Okay. Well, have a great time!**

> *U not worried about me? STD's 80% increase in people over 70.*

Dad prefer not discuss yr sex life.

WHO ELSE DISCUSS SEX LIFE?

Caps means shouting.

WELL AWARE OF THAT. Thank u for check. It arrived early this month. Gd thing. Property taxes overdue. Stay. Talk 2 me.

Next month I can send more $. This month tight. Zoe lost retainer. *Again.* **Did u change to energy efficient bulbs like I told u?**

Will today. Promise. What's new with u?

Peter may b gay.

Not new.

Zoe embarrassed by me.

Not new either.

Endless to-do list. Can't keep up.

Dad?

Dad?

One day u look back & realize this is the best part of life. Going going going. Always something to do. Someone expecting you to walk in the door.

Oh, Dad. Yr right. I'm sorry.

:)

I'll call tmr. B careful out there.

Love u

U 2

The smell of toast drifts into my office. I shut off my computer and walk into the kitchen in search of William, but everybody's gone. The only sign of my family is a stack of dishes piled high in the sink. *Fall, falling* will have to wait for later.

10

My cell rings. I don't have to pick it up to know it's Nedra. We have this weird telepathic telephone thing. I think of Nedra and Nedra calls.

"I just got my hair cut," she says. "And Kate told me I look like Florence Henderson. And when I asked her who the bloody hell Florence Henderson was she told me I looked like Shirley Jones. A Pakistani Shirley Jones!"

"She said that?" I say, trying not to laugh.

"She certainly did," huffs Nedra.

"That's terrible. You're Indian, not Pakistani."

I adore Kate. Thirteen years ago, when I met her, I knew within five minutes that she was perfect for Nedra. I hate that line *you complete me*, but in Kate's case it was true. She was Nedra's missing half: an earnest, Brooklyn-born, say-it-like-it-is social worker, the person Nedra could count upon not to sugarcoat things. Everybody needs somebody like that in their life. I, unfortunately, have too many people like that in my life.

"Sweetheart," I say. "You got a shag?"

"No, it's not a shag, it's layered. My neck looks ever so long now."

Nedra pauses for a moment. "Oh, fuck me," she says. "It's a shag and I look like a turkey. And now it seems I've grown this little Julia Child hump on the back of my neck. What's next? A wattle? How did this happen? I don't know why I let that slut Lisa talk me into this."

Lisa, our mutual hairdresser, is not a slut, although she has also steered me in the wrong direction several times. There was an unfortunate burgundy henna phase. And bangs—women with thick hair should never have bangs. Now I keep my hair shoulder-length with a few face-framing layers. On a good day people tell me I look like Anne Hathaway's older sister. On a bad day, like Anne Hathaway's mother. *Just do what you did last time* is the instruction I give to Lisa. I find this philosophy works well in many circumstances: sex, ordering a venti soy latte at Starbucks, and helping Peter/Pedro with his algebra homework. However, it's no way to live.

"I did something. I'm doing something. Something I shouldn't be doing," I confess.

"Is there a paper trail?" asks Nedra.

"No. Yes. Maybe. Does email count?"

"Of course email counts."

"I'm taking part in a survey. An anonymous survey. On marriage in the twenty-first century," I whisper into the phone.

"There's no such thing as anonymity. Not in the twenty-first century and certainly not online. Why in God's name are you doing that?"

"I don't know. I thought it would be a lark?"

"Be serious, Alice."

"All right. Okay. Fine. I guess I feel like it's time to take stock."

"Stock of what?"

"Um—my life. Me and William."

"What, are you going through some sort of midlife thing?"

"Why does everyone keep asking me that?"

"Answer the question."

I sigh. "Maybe."

"This can only lead to heartbreak, Alice."

"Well, don't you ever wonder if everything's okay? I mean not just on the surface, but really, deeply okay?"

"No."

"Really?"

"Really, Alice. I *know* everything's okay. You don't feel that way about William?"

"It's just that we're so distracted. I feel like each of us is a line item on the other's list that we're just hurrying to check off. Is that a horrible thing to say?"

"Is it true?"

"Sometimes."

"Come on, Alice. There's something else you're not telling me. What brought all this on?"

I think about explaining to Nedra about my tipping-point year, but honestly, as close as we are, she hasn't lost a parent and she wouldn't understand. She and I don't talk much about my mother. I save that for the Mumble Bumbles, a bereavement support group that I've been a member of for the past fifteen years. Even though I haven't seen them recently, I'm Facebook friends with all of them: Shonda, Tita, and Pat. Yes, I know it's a funny name. We started off being the Mother Bees, then became the Mumble Bees, then somehow it morphed into the Mumble Bumbles.

"I just wonder sometimes if we can make it through another forty years. Forty years is a long time. Don't you think that's worth examining now that we're nearly twenty years in?" I ask.

"Olivia Newton-John!" shouts Kate in the background. "That's who I meant to say you looked like. The *Let's Get Physical* album!"

"In my experience it's the unexamined life that is worth living," says Nedra. "If one wants to live happily ever after, that is—with one's partner. Darling, I've got to go and see if I can do something about this hideous shag. Kate's coming at me with bobby pins."

I can hear Kate singing Olivia Newton-John's "I Honestly Love You" hideously off-key.

"Do me a favor?" says Nedra. "When you see me, do not tell me I look like Rachel from *Friends*. And I promise we'll talk about marriage in the nineteenth century later."

"Twenty-first century."

"No difference whatsoever. Kisses."

11

21. I didn't until I saw that movie about the Hubble telescope in Imax 3-D.

22. Neck.

23. Forearms.

24. *Long.* That's the way I would describe him. His legs barely fit under his desk. This was back before business casual was invented and everybody still dressed for work. I wore a pencil skirt and pumps. He wore a pin-stripe suit and a yellow tie. He was fair, but his straight hair was dark, almost black, and it kept falling in his eyes. He looked like a young Sam Shepard: all coiled up and brooding.

I was completely unnerved and trying not to show it. Why hadn't Henry (Henry is my cousin, the one responsible for landing me the interview; he played in a men's soccer league with William) warned me he was so cute? I wanted him to see me, I mean *really* see me, and yes, I knew he was dangerous, i.e. unreadable, i.e. withholding, i.e. TAKEN— there was a picture of him and some gorgeous blond woman on his desk.

I was in the middle of explaining to him why a theater major with a minor in dramaturgy would want a job as a copywriter, which entailed a great deal of skirting around the truth (because it's a day job and playwrights make no money and I have to do something to support myself while I pursue my ART, and it may as well be writing meaningless copy about dishwashing detergent), when he interrupted me.

"Henry said you got into Brown, but you went to U Mass?"

Damn Henry. I tried to explain. I was giving him my old *I'm a U Mass legacy*, which was a lie; the truth was U Mass gave me a full ride, Brown gave me half a ride, and there was no way my father could afford even half of Brown's tuition. But he interrupted me, waving at me to stop, and I felt ashamed. Like I had disappointed him.

He handed me back my résumé, which I tore up on the way out, sure I had blown the interview. The next day there was a message from him on my machine. "You start Monday, Brown."

12

From: Wife 22 <Wife22@netherfieldcenter.org>
Subject: Answers
Date: May 10, 5:50 AM
To: researcher101 <researcher101@netherfieldcenter.org>

Researcher 101,

I hope I'm doing this right. I'm worried that some of my answers may go on for longer than you'd like and perhaps you'd prefer a subject who just sticks to the subject and says yes, no, sometimes, and maybe. But here's the thing. Nobody has ever asked me these kinds of questions before. These sorts of questions, I mean. Every day I am asked normal questions for a woman my age. Like today when I tried to schedule an appointment at the dermatologist. The first question the receptionist asked was if I had a suspicious mole. Then she told me the first available appointment was in six months and what was the date of my birth? When I told her the year, she asked me if I'd like to have a conversation with the doctor about injectables when I had my moles checked. And if that was the case the doctor could see me next week, and would Thursday do? These are the kinds of questions I am asked, the kinds of questions I would really prefer not to be asked.

I guess what I'm trying to say is that I'm enjoying participating in the survey.

All the best,
Wife 22

From: researcher101 <researcher101@netherfieldcenter.org>
Subject: Re: Answers
Date: May 10, 9:46 AM
To: Wife 22 <Wife22@netherfieldcenter.org>

Wife 22,

I assume you're referring to question #24—as far as your worry that you're giving too lengthy an answer? It was like reading a little scene, actually, with all the dialogue. Was that intentional?

Sincerely,

Researcher 101

From: Wife 22 <Wife22@netherfieldcenter.org>
Subject: Re: Answers
Date: May 10, 10:45 AM
To: researcher101 <researcher101@netherfieldcenter.org>

Researcher 101,

I'm not so sure it was intentional, more like force of habit. I used to be a playwright. I'm afraid I naturally think in scenes. I hope that's all right.

Wife 22

From: researcher101 <researcher101@netherfieldcenter.org>
Subject: Re: Answers
Date: May 10, 11:01 AM
To: Wife 22 <Wife22@netherfieldcenter.org>

Wife 22,

There's no right way or wrong way to answer, just as long as you're answering truthfully. To be honest, I found your #24 to be quite engaging.

Best,

Researcher 101

13

Julie Staggs
Marcy—big girl bed!
32 minutes ago

Pat Guardia
Spending the afternoon with my father. Red Sox. Ahhhh.
46 minutes ago

William Buckle
Fell.
1 hour ago

Fell? Now I'm officially worried. I'm about to text William when I hear the unmistakable sound of the motorcycle being gunned in the driveway. I log off Facebook quickly. The kids are still at school, William has a client dinner, so I jump to the obvious conclusion.

"We're being robbed," I whisper to Nedra on the phone. "Someone's stealing the motorcycle!"

Nedra sighs. "Are you sure?"

"Yes, I'm sure."

"How sure?"

This is not the first time Nedra has received such a call from me.

Once, a few years ago when I was doing laundry down in the basement, the wind blew the front door open and it slammed into the wall with a bang. In my defense, it sounded like a gunshot. I was positive I was about to be robbed while I was musing about whether a load of whites really needed fabric softener. Robberies weren't that unusual in our neighborhood. It's a reality Oaklanders live with, along with earthquakes and $5-a-pound heirloom tomatoes.

Panicked, I stupidly shouted, "I'm calling my lawyer!"

Nobody answered, so I added, "And I have nunchakus!"

I had bought a pair for Peter, who had recently signed up to take tae kwon do, which unbeknownst to me he would be quitting two weeks hence because he didn't realize it was a contact sport. What did he think the nunchakus were for? Oh—he meant tai chi, not tae kwon do. It wasn't his fault so many of the martial arts begin with the same sound.

Still no reply. "Nunchakus are two sticks connected by a chain that people use to hurt each other. By whirling them around. Very fast!" I shouted.

Not a sound from upstairs. Not a footfall, not even a creak from the hardwood floor. Had I imagined the bang? I called Nedra on my cell and made her stay on the line with me for the next half hour, until the wind flung the door shut and I realized what an idiot I had been.

"I swear. It's not a false alarm this time," I tell her.

Nedra is like an ER doc. The scarier the situation, the calmer and more levelheaded she becomes.

"Are you safe?"

"I'm in the house. The doors are locked."

"Where is the robber?"

"Out on the driveway."

"So why are you talking to me? Call 9-1-1!"

"This is Oakland. It'll take the cops forty-five minutes to get here."

Nedra pauses. "Not if you tell them somebody's been shot."

"You can't be serious."

"Trust me, they'll be there in five minutes."

"How do you know that?"

"There's a reason I get paid 425 bucks an hour."

I don't call 9-1-1—I'm a very bad liar, especially when it comes to lying about somebody I love bleeding out—instead I crawl on my hands and knees to the front window and peer out the crack in the curtains, my cell in my hand. My plan is to snap a photo of the perp and email it to the Oakland police. But the perp turns out to be my husband, who peels out of the driveway before I can get to my feet.

He doesn't return until 10:00 that evening, at which point he walks through the front door weaving. Clearly he's been drinking.

"I've been demoted," he says, collapsing onto the couch. "I've got a new job title. Want to know what it is?"

I think of his recent Facebook posts, *Fall, falling, fell*: he sensed this was coming and didn't tell me.

"Ideator." William looks at me expressionlessly.

"*Ideator?* What? Is that even a word? Maybe they changed everybody's titles. Maybe Ideator means creative director."

He picks up the remote and turns on the TV. "No. It means asshole who feeds ideas to the creative director."

"William, shut off the TV. Are you sure? And why aren't you more upset? Maybe you're mistaken."

William presses the mute button. "The new creative director was my ideator until yesterday. Yes, I'm sure. And what good does it do to be upset?"

"So you can do something about it!"

"There's nothing to do. It's decided. It's done. Do we have any Scotch? The good stuff. Single malt?" William looks completely shut down, his face vacant.

"I can't believe it! How could they do this to you after all these years?"

"The Band-Aid account. Conflict of interest. I believe in fresh air, Neosporin, and scabs, not sealing up boo-boos."

"You told them that?"

He rolls his eyes. "Yes, Alice, that's exactly what I told them. There's a cut in pay." William gives me a grim smile. "A rather substantial cut in pay."

I'm panicked, but I try not to change the expression on my face. I need to buoy him up.

"It's happening to everybody, sweetheart," I say.

"Do we have any port?"

"Everybody our age."

"That's extremely comforting, Alice. Grey Goose?"

"How old is the new CD?"

"I don't know. Twenty-nine? Thirty?"

I gasp. "Did he say anything to you?"

"*She.* It's Kelly Cho. She said she was really looking forward to working with me."

"*Kelly?*"

"Don't be so shocked. She's very good. Brilliant, actually. Pot? Weed? Aren't the kids smoking yet? Jesus, they're late-bloomers."

"God, William, I'm so sorry," I say. "This is incredibly unfair." I turn to give him a hug.

He holds up his hand. "Don't," he says. "Just leave me alone. I don't want to be touched right now."

I move away from him on the couch, trying not to take it personally. This is typical William. When he's hurt he becomes even more detached; he makes himself into the proverbial island. I'm the complete opposite. When I'm in pain I want everybody I love on the island with me, sitting around the fire, getting drunk on coconut milk, banging out a plan.

"Jesus, Alice, don't look at me that way. You can't expect me to take care of you right now. Let me just have my feelings."

"No one's asking you to not have your feelings." I stand up. "I heard you in the driveway, you know. Starting the motorcycle. I thought we were being robbed."

I hear the accusatory tone in my voice and hate myself. This happens all the time. William's detachment makes me desperate for connection, which makes me say desperate things, which makes him more detached.

"I'm going to bed," I say, trying not to sound wounded.

A look of relief spreads across William's face. "I'll be up in a while." Then he closes his eyes, blocking me out.

14

I'm not proud of what I do next, but consider it the act of a slightly OCD woman who did budget projections too far into the future and discovered that within one year (at William's reduced salary and what little my job brought in) we'd be tapping into our savings and the kids' college funds. Within two years, our retirement fund and any chance of our children going to college would be nil. We'd have to move back to Brockton and live with my father.

I see no alternative but to call Kelly Cho and beg for William's job back.

"Kelly, hello, this is Alice Buckle. How are you?" I sing into the phone, in my best feel-good, composed drama-teacher voice.

"Alice," Kelly says awkwardly, separating my name into three syllables: Al. Liss. S. She's shocked I'm calling. "I'm fine, how are you?"

"I'm fine. How are you?" I chirp back, my calm drama-teacher voice dropping away. Oh, God.

"What can I do for you? Are you looking for William? I think he stepped out for lunch," she says.

"Actually, I was looking for you. I was hoping we could speak frankly about what happened. William's demotion."

"Oh—okay. But didn't he fill you in?"

"Yes, he did, but, well—I was hoping there's some way we can reverse this thing. Not take away your promotion—that's not what I'm talking about. Of course not, that wouldn't be fair. But maybe there's a way we can make this more of a horizontal move for William."

"I don't know about that."

"Could you maybe put in a good word for him? Just ask around?"

"Ask who?"

"Look, William has been at KKM for more than ten years."

"I'm aware of that. This is really hard. For me too, but I don't think—"

"Jesus, Kelly, it's only Band-Aids."

"*Band-Aids?*"

"The account?"

Kelly is silent for a moment. "Alice, it wasn't Band-Aids. It was *Cialis*."

"*Cialis*. Erectile dysfunction *Cialis?*"

Kelly coughed softly. "That's the one."

"Well, what happened?"

"You need to ask him."

"I'm asking you. Please, Kelly."

"I really shouldn't."

"Please."

"I don't feel okay about—"

"Kelly. Don't make me ask again."

She gives a big sigh. "He lost it."

"Lost it?"

"During the focus group. Alice, I've been wondering if there's something going on at home because honestly, he just hasn't been himself lately. Well, you saw it yourself. How strangely he acted at the FiG launch. For the past couple of months he's been off. Anxious. Short-tempered. Distracted. Like work is the last place on earth he wants to be. Everybody has noticed, not just me. He'd been talked to. He'd been warned. And then this thing with the focus group. It was on video, Alice. The entire team saw it. Frank Potter saw it."

"But he's on the creative side, not strategic. Why was he even running a focus group?"

"Because he insisted. He wanted to be in on the research."

"I don't understand."

"It's probably better if you don't."

"Send me the video," I say.

"That's not a good idea."

"Kelly, I'm begging you."

"Oh, Christ. Hold on a sec. Let me think."

Kelly is silent.

I count to twenty and say, "Still thinking?"

"Fine, Alice," says Kelly. "But you have to swear not to tell anybody I sent it to you. Look, I'm really sorry. I respect William. He's been a mentor to me. I wasn't campaigning for his job. I feel horrible about this. Do you believe me? Please believe me."

"I believe you, Kelly, but now that you're creative director you should probably stop pleading with people to believe you."

"You're right. I've got to work on that. I'll email you the video."

"Thank you."

"And Alice?"

"Uh-huh?"

"Please don't hate me."

"Kelly."

"What?"

"You're doing it again."

"Right, right! I'm sorry. I wasn't prepared for this promotion. It's what I always dreamed about but I didn't think it would happen so abruptly. Between you and me, I feel like such a fake. I don't know what to say. I should go now. I'm really not a bad person. I like you so much, Alice. Please don't hate me. Oh—Christ, goodbye."

From: Wife 22 <Wife22@netherfieldcenter.org>
Subject: New Questions?
Date: May 15, 6:30 AM
To: researcher101 <researcher101@netherfieldcenter.org>

Researcher 101,

   Is the new set of questions coming soon? I don't want to rush you or anything, and you probably have some timetable of when you send the questions out, but I seem to have a lot of anxiety these days and answering the questions calms me down. There's almost a meditative aspect to it. Like confession. Have any other subjects reported feeling this way?

   All the best,
   Wife 22

From: researcher101 <researcher101@netherfieldcenter.org>
Subject: Re: New Questions?
Date: May 15, 7:31 AM
To: Wife 22 <Wife22@netherfieldcenter.org>

Wife 22,

   That's very interesting. I haven't heard quite that response before, but we have heard similar sentiments along the same line. Once a subject described answering the questions as "an unburdening." I believe the anonymity has a lot to do with it. You can expect the next set of questions by the end of the week.

   Best,
   Researcher 101

From: Wife 22 <Wife22@netherfieldcenter.org>
Subject: Re: New Questions?
Date: May 15, 7:35 AM
To: researcher101 <researcher101@netherfieldcenter.org>

I think you're right. Who knew anonymity could be so liberating?

16

Voicemail: *You Have One New Message*
   Alice! Alice, my dear. It's Bunny Kilborn from Blue Hill. It's been a very long time. I hope you've been getting my Christmas cards. I think of you so often. How are you and William? The children? Is Zoe off to college yet? She must be close. Maybe you'll send her back east. Look. I'll get straight to it. I have a favor to ask. Remember our youngest, Caroline? Well, she's moving to the Bay Area and I'm wondering if you'd be willing to help her out a bit? Show her around? She's looking for a job in IT. Maybe you even have some contacts in the tech world? She'll need to find a place to live, a roommate sort of situation, and, of course, a job, but it would be so nice to know she's not completely on her own out there. Besides, you two would hit it off. So how are you otherwise? Still teaching drama? Dare I ask if you ever write plays anymore? I know *The Barmaid of Great Cranberry Island* really took the wind out of your sails, but— I'm on the phone. Jack, I'm ON THE PHONE! Sorry, Alice, have to run, let me know if—
Mailbox Full

Now there's a voice from my past. *Bunny Kilborn:* the renowned founder and artistic director of the Blue Hill Theater in Maine; winner of three Obies, two Guggenheims, and a Bessie Award. She's directed everything from Tennessee Williams's *A Streetcar Named Desire* to Harold Pinter's *The Homecoming*, and in the late nineties, Alice Buckle's *The Barmaid of Great Cranberry Island.* No, I'm not saying I was in the same league as Williams and Pinter. I entered a contest for emerging playwrights and ending up winning first prize, which was the mounting of my play at the

Blue Hill Theater. Everything I had been working for had led to that moment and that win. It felt—well, it felt like destiny.

I had always been a theater rat. I started acting in middle school and then in high school attempted writing my first play. It was horrible, of course (heavily influenced by David Mamet, who to this day is still my favorite playwright, although I can't abide his politics), but I wrote another play and then another and another, and with each play I found my voice a little more.

In college, three of my plays were produced. I became one of the theater department's stars. When I graduated, I took a day job in advertising, which left my nights free to write. When I was twenty-nine I finally got my big break—and I flopped. It's an understatement when Bunny says the play took the wind out of my sails. The reviews were so bad I never wrote another play again.

There was one good review from the *Portland Press Herald*. I can still recite passages by heart: "emotionally generous," "a thought-provoking coming-of-age story, the effect of which is like mainlining Springsteen's 'Jungleland.'" But I can also recite passages from all the other reviews, which were consistently negative: "fails miserably," "clichéd and contrived," "amateurish," and "Act 3? Put us out of our misery already!" The play closed within two weeks.

Bunny made an effort to keep in touch with me all these years, but I didn't reciprocate much. I was too ashamed. I had embarrassed Bunny and her company, as well as blown my one big chance.

Bunny's call has to be more than serendipity. I want to be connected to her; to have her in my life again in some way.

I pick up the phone and nervously dial her number. It rings twice.

"Hello?"

"Bunny—Bunny is that you?"

There's a pause, then . . .

"Oh, Alice, *love*. I hoped you would call."

17

t's taken me a few days to work up the nerve to look at the KKM video. It occurs to me as I sit in front of my laptop, finger about to click the Play arrow, that I am crossing a line. My heart is thrumming in the same way it did when I called Kelly, which, come to think of it, was the real moment I crossed the line—when I started acting like William's mother instead of his wife. If my heart knew Morse code and could tap out a message, it would be saying *Alice, you spying nosy parker, delete this file right now!*, but I don't know Morse code, so I just tuck those thoughts away and click Play.

The camera pans in on a table at which two men and two women are seated.

"One sec," says Kelly Cho. The table becomes blurry, then snaps into focus again. "Ready."

"Cialis," says William. "Elliot Ritter, fifty-six; Avi Schine, twenty-four; Melinda Carver, twenty-three; Sonja Popovich, forty-seven. Thank you all for coming. So you screened the commercial, right? What did you think?"

"I don't get it. Why are they sitting in separate bathtubs if the dude has a four-hour erection?" asks Avi.

"He doesn't have a four-hour erection. If he had a four-hour erection he'd be in an ambulance on the way to the hospital. The precautions have to be clearly stated in the commercial," says William.

Melinda and Avi exchange a lusty look. Under the table, her hand seeks out his thigh and squeezes it.

"Are you a couple?" asks William. "Are they a couple?" he whispers under his breath.

"They didn't say they were a couple," says Kelly.

William must be wearing an earpiece and Kelly must be in the room with the one-way mirror, watching and listening.

"Yeah, well, how did the tubs get on the mountain?" asks Avi. "And who carried them up there? That's what I want to know."

"It's called willing suspension of disbelief. I like the tubs," says Elliot. "My wife likes the tubs."

"Can you tell me why, Elliot?" asks William.

"Some of those other ads are so crude," says Elliot.

"It's better than the one of the man throwing the football or the one with the train. Please. It's insulting. A vagina is not a tire swing. Or a tunnel. Well, maybe a tunnel," says Melinda.

"So your wife prefers the Cialis commercials, Elliot?" asks William.

"She would prefer I didn't have ED," says Elliot, "but since I'm challenged in that department, yes, she finds the bathtub commercials more palatable than the others."

"Sonja, we haven't heard from you yet. What do you think about the commercial?" asks William.

Sonja shrugs.

"Okay, that's all right. I'll circle back to you," says William. "So, Cialis, Avi. You're twenty-four and you're a user. Why?"

"May I suggest you don't refer to him as a 'user'?" says Kelly.

Avi looks at Melinda and she smiles shyly. "Why not?" he says.

"Do you have problems with ED?"

"You mean down there." Avi points at his crotch.

"Yes," sighs William.

"Dude. Do I look like I have problems? It just makes it better."

"Dude. Care to elaborate?" says William.

Avi shrugs, clearly unwilling to share the details.

"Okay, well, how many times a week do you have sex?"

"How many times a *day*," corrects Melinda. "Two. Sometimes three if it's the weekend. But definitely two."

William can't keep the skepticism out of his voice. "Really," he says. "Three times a day?"

Elliot looks flabbergasted. Sonja looks dead. I feel slightly nauseous.

"Draw him out, don't challenge him," suggests Kelly. "We need details."

This doesn't sound crazy to me. When we were in our twenties, William and I sometimes had sex three times a day. On President's Day. And Yom Kippur.

"Yeah, man, three times a day," says Avi, looking irritated. "Why would we lie? You're paying us to tell you the truth."

"Fine. So how many times a week do you take Cialis?"

"Once a week. Usually on Friday afternoons."

"Why Cialis and not Viagra?"

"Four hours. Thirty-six hours. You do the math."

"How did you get the prescription?" asks William.

"Told my doctor I was having problems. *Down there.*"

"And he believed you?"

Avi rocks back in his chair. "Dude, what is wrong with you?"

William pauses and falls back on a stock question. "If Melinda were a car, what kind of a car would she be?"

Something is really off with William. His voice doesn't even sound like him.

Avi says nothing, just stares at the camera confrontationally.

"Back off," says Kelly. "You're losing him."

"Come on. Let me guess," says William. "A Prius. But a fully loaded Prius. Fifty-one miles to the gallon. A smart key system. Bluetooth and seats that fold flat."

"William," warns Kelly.

"So you can fuck Melinda three times a day."

Everybody is shocked into silence. Kelly bursts into the room.

"O-kay. Let's take a break!" she shouts. "Complimentary sodas and cookies out in the hallway." The camera abruptly shuts off, and then a second later pans in on the now empty table.

"I can't believe you said 'fuck,'" says Kelly.

"*He's* a fuck," says William.

"It doesn't matter. He's the customer."

"Yes, and we're paying him to be the customer. Besides, twenty-something males are not our target demographic."

"Wrong. Males twenty to thirty-five account for thirty-six percent of all new users. Maybe I should moderate."

"No, I'll do it. Bring them back in."

The men and women file back into the room, Cokes and Diet Cokes in hand.

"Elliot, how many times a month do you have sex?" asks William.

"With or without Cialis?"

"Take your pick."

"Without, none. With, once a week."

"So would it be fair to say Cialis has improved your sex life?"

"Yes."

"And would you have tried it if you didn't have ED?"

Elliot looks bewildered. "Why would I do that?"

"Well, like Avi here. Would you use it recreationally?"

"Croquet is recreation. Mini-golf is recreation. Making love is not recreation. Love isn't some bottomless Slurpee that magically fills itself up. You have to do the filling up yourself. That's the secret to marriage."

"Yeah man, drive through your wife's 7-Eleven. Get your Slurpee on," says Avi.

Elliot shoots Avi a dirty look. "It's called *making* love for a reason."

Avi rolls his eyes.

"I think that's cute," says Melinda. "Why don't we make love?"

"Get back to Sonja," says Kelly.

Sonja Popovich looks deflated, like she forgot to take her meds. Forty-seven. She's three years older than me. She definitely looks older. No, she looks younger. No, *I* look younger. I play this game all the time. Honestly, I'm incapable of judging anyone's age anymore.

"Can I smoke in here?" asks Sonja.

"I don't think that's a good idea. Some sort of an alarm would probably go off," says William.

Sonja smiles. "I'm not really a smoker. Only occasionally."

"Me, too," says William.

Since when did William become an occasional smoker?

"So are you here because of your husband's ED?"

"No, I'm here because of *my* ED."

"Nod," says Kelly.

"I hate those Cialis commercials. And Viagra. And Levitra."

"Why?"

"When your husband comes home and says, 'Hey, honey, great news, we can have sex for thirty-six hours straight,' believe me, it is not cause for celebration."

"Well, Cialis is not about having sex for thirty-six hours, it's about enhanced blood flow to—" says William.

"Thirty-six seconds, now then you'd have a winner."

"Seriously?" says Avi.

"Yes, seriously," says Sonja. Her face crumples. A big, fat tear rolls down her cheek.

"That's sad," says William.

"Don't say that," hisses Kelly.

"Thirty-six seconds. I'm sorry, but that's very sad," says William. "For your husband, I mean. Sounds like it's good for you."

"Oh, Christ," says Kelly.

Sonja is weeping now.

"Can someone get her some Kleenex? Take your time," William says. "I wasn't trying to make you feel bad. Your answer just surprised me."

"It surprises me, too. Don't you think I'm surprised? I don't know what happened," she says, dabbing her eyes. "I used to love sex. I mean really, really love it. But now the whole thing seems, well, it just seems so silly. Whenever we have sex I feel like an alien watching us having sex thinking, 'Ah, so this is how lower life-forms that only use ten percent of their brain matter procreate. How strange! How messy! How brutish! Look at the ugly faces they make. And all the sounds—the slapping, the flapping, the suction.'"

"We can't use this. Wrap it up," says Kelly. "Change the subject. Ask her what she thinks about the tubs."

"How often do you have sex?" William asks.

Sonja looks up at him with a tear-stained face and says nothing.

"How often would you *like* to have sex?"

"Never."

"This is not a therapy session," says Kelly. "It's a focus group for the *client*. This woman is not our target market. Cut her loose."

"Do you wish you felt differently?"

Sonja nods.

"If you felt differently, how often would you like to have sex? How many times a year?" asks William.

"Twenty-four?" she says.

"Twenty-four. Twice a month?"

"Yeah, twice a month sounds good. That sounds normal to me. Do you think so? Do you think that's normal?"

"Normal? Well, that's one more time a month than *I'm* having it," says William.

"That's it. Shut it down," says Kelly.

I gasp. Did my husband just announce to the entire focus group and his team the frequency with which we have sex?

"My wife and I pretend we have sex every week, just like most other married couples we know who are really only having sex once a month," says William.

"I'm shutting the camera off," warns Kelly.

"I wouldn't call our marriage sexless," William continues. "Sexless would mean sex once every six months, or once a year. It's just the moment used to be right more often than not," says William.

"I'm very sorry to hear that," says Elliot.

"Tell me that's not going to be us in twenty years!" says Melinda.

"Never," says Avi. "That will never happen to us, babe."

"*Anytime* the moment is right. It's the *anytime* that really gets me. That's not freedom. Not for the woman, anyway. It's a threat," says Sonja. "It's an erection Code Orange."

"Can I ask you one more question?" asks William.

"Go ahead," says Sonja.

"Do you think most women your age feel this way?"

Sonja sniffs. "Yes."

I press Pause on the video and rest my head on my desk, wishing I could rewind the last ten minutes of my life. Why, oh why, oh why did I watch that? I feel ashamed for going behind William's back, angry at the brash and unprofessional way he conducted himself (the cardinal rule of conducting focus groups: never, *never* share personal information), humiliated that he publicly outed us as having a sexless marriage (not true, we have sex once a week—okay, once every two or three weeks—okay, *maybe* sometimes it stretches to once a month), worried that *he is* on some sort of new medication that he hasn't told me about, afraid that medication is Cialis and soon he'll be telling me that thanks to modern medicine we now have a thirty-six-hour window in which I will be expected to have sex at least three times a day, but the strongest feeling is grief, because I saw parts of myself in both women. The desire-to-inhale-the-very-air-her-boyfriend-breathes Melinda. And the moment-is-rarely-right Sonja. They were—*are*—both me.

Tell me, Alice Buckle, what car would you be if you were a car right now?

That's easy: a Ford Escape. A hybrid. Base model. Well-used. A scraped-up front bumper. Pings all over the doors. A mysterious rotten-apple smell rising up from the floorboards, but dependable. A car with all-wheel drive that's good in the snow but whose potential is totally wasted because its owner lives in a city where the temperature rarely dips below 40.

And that, right there, is the problem.

18

25. William's girlfriend's name was Helen Davies and she was the VP of Branding. The rumor floating around the firm was that they would be engaged any day. They came in together in the mornings, sipping their coffees. They'd go to Kendall Square for lunch. She'd retrieve him at the end of the day and off they'd zip down to Newbury Street for cocktails. She was always stunningly dressed. I shopped at Filene's Basement.

I was put to work on a toilet paper account. It wasn't as bad as it sounded. I got to go home with rolls of TP samples and think of inventive new ways to say *gets your ass really clean with just one sheet.*

I put him out of my mind. Until one day he sent me an email.

—**Are those running shoes on your desk?**

I emailed him back.

—**Sorry! I know that's a filthy habit. Putting my shoes on working surfaces. It won't happen again.**

And then he emailed me again.

—**Just went by your cubicle. Where are they now?**

—**Where are what now?**

And then a flurry of emails.

—**Your running shoes, Brown.**

—**They're on my feet.**

—**Because you're going home?**

—**Because I'm going running.**

—**When?**

—**At lunch.**

—**Where?**

—**Um—outside.**

—**Yes, Brown. I assumed outside. Where outside?**

—**I start at the Charles Hotel. I do a five-mile loop.**

—**Meet you there in fifteen minutes.**

19

From: Wife 22 <Wife22@netherfieldcenter.org>
Subject: Timing
Date: May 18, 12:50 PM
To: researcher101 <researcher101@netherfieldcenter.org>

Researcher 101,

It might take me a little longer than usual to get the answers back to you, as things are a bit crazy here. I should probably let you know that my husband was demoted. I'm sure we'll figure it out, but it's been stressful on all of us. I have to say it's a strange time to be recounting our courtship. It's hard for me to reconcile the young, vibrant William and Alice with the currently middle-aged us. It makes me kind of sad.

All the best,

Wife 22

From: researcher101 <researcher101@netherfieldcenter.org>
Subject: Re: Timing
Date: May 18, 12:52 PM
To: Wife 22 <Wife22@netherfieldcenter.org>

Wife 22,

I'm very sorry to hear about your husband's job. Please take all the time you need. Going back to the beginning is often difficult and dredges up all sorts of emotions. But in the long run I think you'll find it enlightening to return to the past.

Sincerely,

Researcher 101

From: Wife 22 <Wife22@netherfieldcenter.org>
Subject: Re: Gambling
Date: May 18, 1:05 PM
To: researcher101 <researcher101@netherfieldcenter.org>

Researcher 101,

Sometimes when I log on to my computer I feel like I'm in a casino sitting in front of a slot machine. I have the same shivery feeling of anticipation—that anything is possible and anything can happen. All I have to do is pull the lever, i.e. press Send.

The rewards are immediate. I hear the machine churning. I hear all the lovely chimes and whooshes and pings. And when the symbols come up: "Kate O'Halloran *likes* your comment"; "Kelly Cho wants to be your friend"; "You have been tagged in a photo"—I am a winner.

What I'm trying to say is thanks for such a quick response.

Best,

Wife 22

From: researcher101 <researcher101@netherfieldcenter.org>
Subject: Unreachability
Date: May 18, 1:22 PM
To: Wife 22 <Wife22@netherfieldcenter.org>

Wife 22,

I understand what you're saying completely, and often feel the same way, although I have to admit it worries me. It seems like we've gotten to the point where our experiences, our memories—our entire lives, actually—aren't real unless we post about them online. I wonder if we might miss the days of being unreachable.

All the best,

Researcher 101

From: Wife 22 <Wife22@netherfieldcenter.org>
Subject: Re: Unreachability
Date: May 18, 1:25 PM
To: researcher101 <researcher101@netherfieldcenter.org>

Researcher 101,

    I do not long for the old, unreachable days. When I'm plugged in I can go anywhere, do and learn anything. Today, for instance, I visited a tiny library in Portugal. I learned how the Shakers weave baskets and I discovered my best friend in middle school loves blood-orange sorbet. Okay, I also learned that a certain pop star actually believes she's a fairy, an honest-to-goodness fairy from the fey people, but my point is access. Access to information. I don't even have to look out my window to see what the weather is like. I can have the weather delivered every morning to my phone. What could be better?

    Sincerely,

    Wife 22

From: researcher101 <researcher101@netherfieldcenter.org>
Subject: Weather
Date: May 18, 1:26 PM
To: Wife 22 <Wife22@netherfieldcenter.org>

Wife 22,

    Getting caught in the rain?

    All the best,

    Researcher 101

20

ALERT: Rapidly Developing Class 3 Marital Storm
Saturday AM

Windchill: Cold. Extremely cold. Freezing out husband while trying to pretend nothing is wrong.

Hi: Making it through day without screaming.

Lo: Head in hands. Soft moaning. Constant bouts of shame and mortification imagining KKM employees emailing Cialis video to hundreds of friends and said video then going viral.

Visibility: Limited. Refuse to look above husband's jaw in order to avoid eye contact.

Share Weather: send to nedrar@gmail.com

Instant Message from nedrar@gmail.com

Nedra: *Poor William!*

Alice: *Poor William? Poor me!*

Nedra: *This is what you get for going behind William's back.*

Alice: *Did you even watch the video?*

Nedra: *Want my advice?*

Alice: *That depends. What will it cost me?*

Nedra: *Forget you ever saw it.*

Saturday PM

Heat Index: Very High. Boiling hot.
Hi: Sitting on the couch watching *Masterpiece Theatre*.
Lo: Mentally trying to count the number of times we've had sex in the past twenty years while pretending to watch *Masterpiece Theatre*. Can't do sums in head. Use fingers to add. Estimate 859. What's wrong with that?
Visibility: Poor to none. Dense fog while trying to guess the number of times we'll have sex in the next twenty years.
Share Weather: send to nedrar@gmail.com

> **Instant Message from nedrar@gmail.com**
>
> **Nedra:** *Do not withhold sex.*
>
> **Alice:** *Why not?*
>
> **Nedra:** *This is not about sex.*
>
> **Alice:** *What's it about?*
>
> **Nedra:** *Intimacy. There's a difference.*
>
> **Alice:** *What do you suggest?*
>
> **Nedra:** *Reach out to him.*
>
> **Alice:** *What kind of a divorce lawyer are you?*

Sunday PM

Wind: Calming.
Hi: Horoscope says unexpected romance on its way.
Lo: Viewing Cialis video for the eighth time. In my defense, repeated viewings of video are the best way to desensitize myself to the horrific public humiliation inflicted by my husband. I think I deserve a medal. I tell my family I deserve a medal. For what, they ask.
Drought Conditions: Improving. I sat next to him on the couch.
Share Weather: Send to nedrar@gmail.com

Instant Message from nedrar@gmail.com

Nedra: *Did you delete the bloody video?*

Alice: *Yes.*

Nedra: *Good girl. Now move on.*

Alice: *Horoscope says romance is on the way.*

Nedra: *Sure it is, sweetheart.*

Alice: *I just have to be patient.*

Nedra *You have it good. You know that, don't you?*

Alice: *Being patient is not easy for a Virgo.*

Nedra: *Or a divorce lawyer. CU.*

21

26. Not emptying out the coffee grinds. Pee on the bathroom floor. Not shutting the bathroom door while peeing. Reading over my shoulder. Jeans inside-out in the laundry basket.

27. Three, okay, five.

28. Once a year.

29. In every way. In no way. I can't answer that question.

30. A book of stamps.

31. He was waiting in the courtyard of the Charles Hotel. Wearing his Walkman. He nodded at me, we took off, and he didn't say a word for the entire run. I, on the other hand, didn't shut up—at least in my head. *Asics, huh; must have wide feet. Why isn't he talking? Does he hate me? Are we doing something wrong? Am I supposed to pretend we're not running together? Why doesn't he run with Helen? Helen of Troy? What is he listening to? Is this a date? Jesus, he's cute. What kind of game is he playing? He smells like Coast soap. Are my thighs jiggling? Yep, he just touched my breast with his elbow accidentally. Does he know it was my breast? Was it on purpose? Why isn't he saying anything? Well, screw him, I'm not saying anything either.*

We ran five miles in forty-one minutes. When we got back to Peavey Patterson he nodded once more, then went left, to the executive washroom. I turned right, to the employee bathroom. When I got back to my desk, my hair stuck up in a messy, limp ponytail, there was an email waiting for me. ***You run fast.***

32. That if we weren't careful, it was possible to forget one another.

22

From: Wife 22 <Wife22@netherfieldcenter.org>
Subject: Hello
Date: May 20, 11:50 AM
To: researcher101 <researcher101@netherfieldcenter.org>

Researcher 101,

Sorry it took so long to get back to you. Things haven't been great between my husband and me, which makes it hard to answer the questions. Especially the ones about us falling in love.

All the best,

Wife 22

From: researcher101 <researcher101@netherfieldcenter.org>
Subject: Re: Hello
Date: May 20, 11:53 AM
To: Wife 22 <Wife22@netherfieldcenter.org>

Wife 22,

That's completely understandable given the circumstances, although I have to say you do a wonderful job with the questions. You seem to remember all the details, which, come to think of it, may have something to do with the difficulty you're experiencing. You recall your past so vividly. When I read your #31 I almost felt like I was there. I'm curious. Are you able to experience the present with the same sort of attention to detail?

I hope things have improved with your husband's job situation.

Sincerely,

Researcher 101

From: Wife 22 <Wife22@netherfieldcenter.org>
Subject: Re: Hello
Date: May 20, 11:55 AM
To: researcher101 <researcher101@netherfieldcenter.org>

Researcher 101,

I'm not sure they've improved, but at least I've cut down the time I spend in the grocery store trying to choose between Minute Maid or Tropicana. Now I just grab the SunnyD. And no, I am not capable of experiencing the present with the same sort of attention to detail. But once the present becomes the past I seem to have no problem attending to it obsessively. :)

Wife 22

From: researcher101 <researcher101@netherfieldcenter.org>
Subject: Re: Hello
Date: May 20, 11:57 AM
To: Wife 22 <Wife22@netherfieldcenter.org>

Wife 22,

What ever happened to Tang?

Researcher 101

From: Wife 22 <Wife22@netherfieldcenter.org>
Subject: Re: Hello
Date: May 20, 12:01 PM
To: researcher101 <researcher101@netherfieldcenter.org>

Researcher 101,

You know, I can't help playing "what if" right now. What if I had been a biker, not a runner? What if William had married Helen of Troy instead of me?

Sincerely,

Wife 22

From: researcher101 <researcher101@netherfieldcenter.org>
Subject: Re: Hello
Date: May 21, 1:42 PM
To: Wife 22 <Wife22@netherfieldcenter.org>

Wife 22,
   In my experience "what if" is a very dangerous game.
   All the best,
   Researcher 101

23

I'm sitting on a bench, my phone in my hand, while a hundred or so children run circles around me. I'm on recess duty. Some of the teachers hate recess duty, they say it's exhausting and mind-numbingly tedious, but I don't mind it. I'm excellent at scanning the sea of kids, reading their body language, listening to the pitch of their voices, and getting to them moments before the illegal hair-pulling, Pokémon card trading, or Hello Kitty glitter lip gloss application begins. This kind of intuition can be either a gift or a curse, but I like to think of it as a gift. Recess duty is like driving. The surface is hyper-alert, leaving the rest of me free to process what's going on in my life.

I took Nedra's advice and never told William that I went behind his back and spoke to Kelly Cho. That makes two secrets I'm keeping from him now—the marriage study and my viewing the Cialis focus group tape. I did get a little hysterical while sharing my budget spreadsheets with him and said something along the lines of *you have to try harder.* He says he's investigating openings at other ad agencies in the city, but I'm afraid it's futile. Things are bad everywhere. Shops are closing and ad budgets are shrinking or disappearing altogether. He has to make it work at KKM. As far as the Cialis focus group, I've decided I will never go to another KKM product launch again.

And *my* job? I'm lucky to have one. When the school year ends, I'm going to approach the Parents' Association about the possibility of making my job full-time in the fall. If that doesn't happen, I'll have to look for a higher-paying job. I need to bring in more income.

The bell rings and the kids start running back into the building. I open my Facebook app quickly.

Shonda Perkins ▶ Alice Buckle
Definition of friend: Somebody you've actually had a meal with in the last year.
43 minutes ago

John F. Kennedy Middle School
Suggests you limit your child's screen time to one hour per day, this includes texting, tweeting and Facebooking. This does not include conducting online research for classes.
55 minutes ago

Weight Watchers
Come back! We miss you!
3 hours ago

William Buckle *added Tone Loc and Mahler to favorite music*
4 hours ago

William Buckle *added Deer Hunter, Dr. Strangelove or How I Learned to Stop Worrying and Love the Bomb, and Field of Dreams to favorite movies*
4 hours ago

Tone Loc? "Funky Cold Medina" Tone Loc? And William's favorite movie is *Field of Dreams*? We are decidedly not in a field of dreams. A field of thorns, maybe. William was demoted for telling his entire company how many times a month we have sex, and I'm sneaking around behind my husband's back, telling a total stranger about how he once touched my boob with his elbow. Like my namesake Alice, I've slipped down the rabbit hole, fall, falling, fell.

24

33. If it's a subject that interests him.

34. I was sleeping with a guy named Eddie. I met him at the gym where I swam laps. Eddie was a trainer in the weight room. He was sweet and uncomplicated. He had these red cheeks and perfect teeth. He wasn't my type, but his body—oh, my God. Our relationship was purely physical and the sex was amazing, but I knew it would never go anywhere further than that. Of course I hadn't told him this yet.

"Hey, Al, Allie!"

It was Friday afternoon and I was standing at the counter at Au Bon Pain ordering a chicken salad sandwich and a Diet Coke. I had been in line for fifteen minutes. There were twenty or so people queued up behind me.

" 'Scuse me, 'scuse me. I'm with her."

Eddie pushed his way to the front of the line. "Hi, doll."

I had never been with a man who called me "doll" before, and I have to admit I liked it—until now. In the bedroom it made me feel petite and Bonnie and Clyde-ish, but here in Au Bon Pain it sounded cheap.

He kissed me on the cheek. "Man, it's crowded in here."

He wore a blue bandana tied around his head, Rambo-style. I had seen this bandana in the weight room, which was, as far as I was concerned, where a bandana worn like this belonged. We really hadn't been out in public yet. Normally I went to his apartment or he came to mine; as I said, our relationship was really about sex. But here we were in Au Bon Pain and here he was looking like Sylvester Stallone, and I was mortified.

"Aren't you hot?" I said, staring blatantly at his forehead, trying to silently telegraph *you're in Cambridge, not the North End, take that ridiculous thing off.*

"It *is* kind of hot in here," he said, slipping out of his jeans jacket, stripping down to a wife-beater. He leaned forward, his deltoids flexing, and put a twenty on the counter. "Make it two chicken salads," he said, then turned to me. "I thought I'd surprise you."

"Well, you did! Surprise me, I mean. Um—I think they have a no-tank-top rule in here."

"I was hoping after lunch you might give me a tour of your office. Introduce me. Show me around."

I knew what Eddie was thinking. That I would waltz him through the door and my colleagues at Peavey Patterson would see him and be flabbergasted and ask who is that gorgeous guy with the incredible body (which is exactly what I did when I first saw him at the gym) and whisk him away to be in some major ad campaign. He wasn't completely off about his potential—he was charismatic and could probably have sold anything—paper towels, wet wipes, or dog food. But not in a wife-beater and bandana.

"Wow, that's a great idea. I just wish you had given me some notice. Today's probably not a good day. We have a big client in town. In fact I shouldn't even be out getting my lunch. I should have eaten in. Everybody else in my office is eating in."

"Alice! Alice, I'm so sorry we're late," a woman shouted.

Now Helen pushed her way to the front of the line, dragging an uncomfortable-looking William behind her. He and I were running just thirty minutes before. I'm pretty sure Helen was unaware of the fact that we'd been working out together. Or that I used his sunscreen. Or that even after showering I still smelled of it.

"There's no saving places!" somebody yelled.

"Those people cut to the front of the line!" somebody else yelled.

"We're with her," said Helen. "Sorry about that," she whispered to me. "It was such a huge line. You don't mind, do you? Well, hello!" She broke into a huge smile at the sight of Eddie. Her eyes lingered on his bandana. "Who's your friend, Alice?"

"This is Eddie," I said, suddenly feeling protective, hearing the cat-and-mouse tone in her voice. "Eddie, this is Helen and William."

"Boyfriend," Eddie corrected Helen, leaning in to shake her hand. "I'm her boyfriend."

"Really," said Helen.

"Really?" said William.

"Really," I said, getting irritated now. Did he just assume I was single? Why shouldn't I have a boyfriend, and why shouldn't he look like Mr. Olympia?

"Hey, doll?" said Eddie. He kissed me on the neck.

William raised his eyebrows. His mouth dropped open the tiniest little bit. Was he *jealous*?

"Your sunscreen smells like coconut. Yum," said Eddie.

Helen turned to William. "I thought that was *you*."

25

From: Wife 22 <Wife22@netherfieldcenter.org>
Subject: Maritalscope?
Date: May 25, 7:21 AM
To: researcher101 <researcher101@netherfieldcenter.org>

Researcher 101,

I'm curious. How do you go about interpreting my answers? Is there some sort of a computer program that you feed data into that compiles a profile? A type? Kind of like a horoscope? A maritalscope?

And why don't you just send me all the questions at once? Wouldn't that be easier?

Wife 22

From: researcher101 <researcher101@netherfieldcenter.org>
Subject: Re: Maritalscope?
Date: May 25, 7:45 AM
To: Wife 22 <Wife22@netherfieldcenter.org>

Wife 22,

It's much more complicated than a horoscope, actually. Are you familiar with music streaming services? Where you enter in a song that you like and then a radio station is created just for you based on the song's attributes? Well, how we interpret, code, and assign value to your answers is very similar to that. We strip your answers down to emotional data points. For some of your longer answers there might be fifty data points that will need to be considered and tracked. For shorter answers, perhaps five.

I like to think what we have developed is an algorithm of the heart.

As far as your second query, we've found there's a trust that develops between subject and researcher that slowly builds over time. That's why we parcel out the questions. There's something about the building of anticipation that works to both of our advantages.

Waiting is a dying art. The world moves at a split-second speed now and I happen to think that's a great shame, as we seem to have lost the deeper pleasures of leaving and returning.

Warmly,

Researcher 101

From: Wife 22 <Wife22@netherfieldcenter.org>
Subject: Re: Maritalscope?
Date: May 25, 9:22 AM
To: researcher101 <researcher101@netherfieldcenter.org>

Dear Researcher 101,

The deeper pleasures of leaving and returning. Why, you sound like a poet, Researcher 101. I feel that way sometimes. Like an astronaut looking for a way back into the corporeal world only to discover the corporeal world has ceased to exist while I've been floating around in space. I suspect it has something to do with getting older. I have less access to gravity and so I float through most of my days, untethered.

Once, in ancient times, my husband and I used to lie in bed before we fell asleep every night and give each other our Facebook posts face to face.

Alice had a very bad day. William thinks tomorrow will be better.

I have to say I miss that.

Wife 22

26

The seventh grade is going on a camping trip to Yosemite. Which means I am going on a camping trip—hurray! At least I might as well be going on a camping trip given all the preparation I have to do to get Peter ready.

"Do you have a mess kit?" I ask Peter.

"No, but we have paper plates."

"How many meals?" I start counting on my fingers. "Dinner, breakfast, lunch, dinner, breakfast. The plates are compostable, right?"

Peter's school takes their green very, very seriously. Plastic is forbidden. Cloth napkins encouraged. During spirit week the Parents' Association sells bento boxes alongside mugs and sweatshirts.

Peter shrugs. "I'll probably get some crap."

I do a quick calculation in my head. Drive twelve miles to REI to buy a new mess kit on Spare the Air Day, a day I should be carpooling, or at the very least taking the bus. Arrive at REI to find the only mess kits in stock are made in Japan. Leave defeated, because I will get in trouble (with Zoe) if I buy a mess kit that had to travel over three thousand miles to get to Oakland. Paper plates it is.

"If anybody asks, tell them the carbon cost of getting a new mess kit far outweighs using five of your mother's paper plates, bought in 1998, back when greenhouse gases were a result of gardeners eating too much cabbage for lunch."

"Black beanie or green?" asks Peter. He holds up the green. "Green. And did you remember to get the wet wipes? I want to have a backup in case the showers are disgusting. I hope they let Briana and me share a tent. We told Mr. Solberg that we were like totally platonic, we've been best friends since fourth grade, and why shouldn't tents be co-ed? He said it's under consideration."

"*Under consideration* means no, but I'm going to wait until the very last minute to tell you," I say.

Peter groans. "What if I get stuck with Eric Haber?"

Peter won't shut up about Eric Haber. What a jerk he is. How loudly he chews, what a terrible conversationalist.

"Then offer him the black beanie," I say.

I suspect Peter has a crush on Eric, but is too scared to admit it. I've read the LGBT literature, which says my job is to remain open-minded and wait until my child is ready to come out. To push him into this revelation before he's ready will do nothing but scar him. If only I could come out for him. I've imagined it so many times in my head. *Peter, I have something to tell you and this may come as a surprise. You're gay. Possibly bisexual but I'm pretty sure gay.* And then we would cry with relief and watch *Bonanza* reruns, which is something we already do, but it would feel different now that we had shared the burden of his secret. Instead, I try to subtly broadcast my approval for his pending life choice.

"Eric seems like a cool kid. Maybe you want to invite him over for a playdate."

"Will you stop saying things like 'cool kid' and 'playdate'?"

"Well, what should I call it? When your friends come over?"

"Coming over."

"That's what we used to call it in the 'seventies! Yes, that was thirty-something years ago and things were different then, but what's not different is that it's still hard to be in middle school. Changing bodies. Changing identities. One day you think you're this person. The next day you're somebody else. But don't worry, it's all normal. All a part of—"

Peter's eyes drift up to my head. "What's up with those orange highlights?"

I finger a strand of my hair. "That's what happens when the color fades. Is it really orange?"

"More like rust."

The next morning I drop Peter and Zoe off at school, and on my way to work I notice Peter's pillow in the backseat. I'm going to be late as it is, but Peter will be so uncomfortable sleeping on the ground without his pillow. I race back to his school and get there just in time. The bus transporting the seventh-graders to Yosemite is still in the parking lot, its engine running.

I climb onto the bus, the pillow tucked under my arm. There's a moment before anybody notices I'm standing there when I search frantically through the crowd, thrilled that I have an opportunity to spy on my son in his natural habitat.

I spot him in the middle of the bus, sitting next to Briana. His arm is around her and her head rests on his shoulder. It's a startling sight for a few reasons. One, it's the first time I've seen my son in any sort of intimate position, and he looks disturbingly natural and disturbingly mature. And two—because I know he's faking it. He's trying to pass as straight, which breaks my heart.

"Pedro, your mother's here."

Could there be four more humiliating words whispered on a bus?

"Pedro forgot his *beanie baby*," somebody from the back of the bus sings out.

Yes, yes there could.

"I'll give it to Peter," says Ms. Ward, Peter's English teacher, sitting a few rows back from where I'm standing.

I clutch the pillow tightly—mortified.

"It's okay. Just give it to me," she says.

I hand her the pillow, but remain frozen in place. I can't stop staring at Briana. I know I shouldn't feel threatened, but I do. In the past year she's transformed from a gawky, mouthful-of-braces girl to a very pretty young woman wearing skinny jeans and a camisole. Was William right? Am I that afraid of losing Peter, to the point of feeling competitive with a twelve-year-old?

"You should go now, Mrs. Buckle," Ms. Ward says.

Yes, I should go before *Pedro, your mother's here* turns into *Pedro, your mother is bawling because she can't bear to be away from you for twenty-four hours.* Peter is slumped down in his seat, arms crossed, staring out the window. I get into my car and bang my head softly against the steering wheel while the bus pulls out, then I put on my Susan Boyle CD (the "Wild Horses" track, which always makes me feel plucky and brave) and dial Nedra.

"Peter has a beard," I cry. I don't have to explain to Nedra that I'm not talking about facial hair.

"A beard? Well, good for him! It's practically a rite of passage. If he *is* gay, that is."

Nedra, like William, is still on the fence about Peter's sexuality.

"So this is normal?" I ask.

"It's certainly not *ab*normal. He's young and confused."

"And humiliated. I just completely embarrassed him in front of the entire seventh grade. I was going to ask him to help me color my hair and now he hates me, and I'll be stuck doing it myself."

"Why aren't you going to Lisa?"

"I'm trying to cut back."

"Alice, stop catastrophizing. Things are going to turn around. Does the beard have a name?"

"Briana."

"Lord, I hate that name. It's so—"

"American, yes, I know. But she's a sweet girl. And very pretty," I add guiltily. "They've been friends for years."

"Does she know she's a beard?"

I think of the two of them nestled together. Her eyes half closed.

"Doubtful."

"Unless she's a lesbian and he's her beard, too. Maybe they have some sort of an agreement. Like Tom and Katie."

"Yes, like ToKat!" I say. I hate the thought of Briana being duped. It's almost as sad as Peter faking he's straight.

"Nobody calls them ToKat."

"KatTo?"

Silence.

"Nedra?"

"I'm getting you another subscription to *People*, and this time you'd better damn well start reading it."

27

"You are so sweet to let me stay with you until I get settled," says Caroline Kilborn.

I stand in the doorway, unable to mask my shock. I expected a younger version of Bunny: a blond, elegantly dressed and coiffed young woman. Instead a bare-faced, freckled redhead beams at me, her hair scraped back impatiently into a ponytail. She's wearing a black formfitting skirt and a loose tank that shows off her toned arms.

"You don't remember me, do you?" she says. "You told me I looked like a doll. Like Raggedy Ann."

"I did?"

"Yes, when I was ten."

I shake my head. "I said that? My God, that's so insensitive. I'm sorry!"

She shrugs. "It didn't bother me. It was your debut at the Blue Hill Playhouse. I'm sure you had other things on your mind."

"Right," I say, wincing, trying to shake the unwanted memory of that night from my head.

Caroline smiles and rocks on her heels. "It was a great show. My friends and I loved it."

Her friends, her fellow third-graders.

"Are you a runner?" She points at my dirt-encrusted sneakers, which I've thrown into a planter, which contains nothing but dirt because I can't seem to remember to water anything I plant.

"Uh, yes," I say, meaning twenty years ago I was a runner but now I'm really more of a jogger, okay, a walker, okay, a person who strolls to her computer and counts it as her daily 10,000 steps.

"Me, too," she says.

Fifteen minutes later Caroline Kilborn and I are going for a run.

Five minutes later Caroline Kilborn inquires as to whether I have asthma.

Five seconds later I tell her that wheezing sound I'm making is due to allergies and the fact that the acacia has just bloomed, and perhaps she should run ahead as I don't want to prevent her from getting a good workout on her first day in California.

After Caroline has sprinted out of sight, I step on a pinecone, twist my ankle, and fall, tumbling into a pile of leaves while praying, *please don't let me get run over by a car.*

I needn't have worried. A car does not run over me. A far worse thing happens—a car stops and a kindly old man asks me if I need a ride home. Actually, I'm not really sure what he asks because I am wearing my earphones and desperately trying to wave him on, in the way that you do after you fall, saying things like *I'm fine, I'm fine,* when it's clear you're not. I accept the ride.

When I get home I ice my ankle, then head upstairs, but first make a detour into Zoe's room. I see her latest acquisition from the vintage clothing store, a 1950s crinoline, thrown over the back of a chair, and I remember the pair of striped bell-bottoms I had in high school and wonder why I didn't have the courage to dress like she does, in one-of-a-kind clothes no other high school girl has, because as far as my daughter is concerned following the trends is as bad a sin as saying "plastic" when they ask you what kind of bag you want at the grocery store. I open her closet door and while I'm rifling through her size-4 shift dresses I wonder what is going on in her life, why she won't tell me, how she can be so self-possessed at fifteen, it's unnatural, it's intimidating—is that *my* yellow cardigan?

I have to stand on tiptoes to reach it and when I grab it, a box of Hostess cupcakes, a box of Ding Dongs, and a box of Yodels come tumbling down, as well as three pilled, oniony-smelling cardigan sweaters. One should not buy vintage sweaters: BO never comes out of the wool—I could have told Zoe that had she asked.

"Whoopsie." Caroline stands in the doorway.

"Zoe's door was open," I say.

"Sure," says Caroline.

"I was looking for my sweater," I say, trying to process the fact that Zoe has secreted away boxes of bakery products in her closet.

"Let me help you put those back."

Caroline kneels beside the boxes, her brow furrowed. "Is Zoe a perfectionist? So many girls her age are. Would she have alphabetized them? Cupcakes, Ding Dongs, obviously Yodels go last. Can't hurt to alphabetize just in case."

"She's got an eating disorder," I cry. "How could I have missed it!"

"Whoa," says Caroline, calmly stacking the boxes. "Hold on. I wouldn't jump to that conclusion."

"My daughter has a hundred cupcakes in her closet."

"Uh—that's a bit of an exaggeration."

"How many in a box?"

"Ten. But all of the boxes are opened. Maybe she's got a business. Maybe she sells them at school," says Caroline. "Or maybe she's just got a sweet tooth."

I imagine Zoe cramming Ding Dongs into her mouth at night after we've all gone to bed. At least it's better than cramming Jude's ding dong into her mouth at night after we've all gone to bed. Yes, God help me, this is what I think.

"You don't understand. Zoe would never eat junk food."

"Not in public, anyway. Maybe you should see if she shows any of the signs of an eating disorder before you say anything," she suggests.

There was a time not so long ago when Zoe and I spent every Friday afternoon together. I'd pick her up from school and take her somewhere special: the bead store, Colonial Donuts, to Macy's to try on lip gloss. My heart would seize with happiness the moment she climbed into the car. It still seizes with happiness, but I have to hide it now. I have learned to ignore her blank stares and rolling eyes. I knock when her door is shut and I try not to eavesdrop when she's video chatting. My point is, other than this closet transgression, I am usually very good at letting her have a life—but I miss her terribly. Of course I heard the war stories from parents with older children. I just thought, as every parent smugly does, that we would be the exception; I would never lose her.

"You're probably right," I say. "I'll do some research." I wince. My ankle is throbbing. It's black and blue.

"What did you do to your ankle?" asks Caroline.

"I fell. After you left. Tripped on a pinecone."

"Oh, no! Did you ice it?" asks Caroline.

I nod.

"For how long?"

"Not long enough, apparently."

Caroline jumps to her feet and stacks the boxes in Zoe's closet. Expertly she folds the sweaters—"The Gap, every summer in high school," she explains—and stacks them in front of the boxes. I hand her my yellow sweater. Caroline takes it wordlessly, puts it on the pile, then shuts the closet door. She holds out her hand.

"Now. Let's go get you some more ice."

35. And so we had a secret. Every Monday, Wednesday, and Friday we met in front of the Charles Hotel at lunchtime for a run. In the office we pretended that we didn't work out together every other day. We pretended we didn't know the shape of each other's thighs, or the scars on our ankles and knees, or the brand of each other's running shoes, or who was a pronator and who was not, or that we had matching farmer's tans, which were soon remedied when May turned into June and we peeled off the layers and our shoulders turned the color of walnuts. I pretended that he didn't have a girlfriend. I pretended that I didn't know the mineral smell of his sweat and how exactly he sweated— always the same: a line down his back and vertically across his collar-bone. I pretended I didn't buy new running shorts, and practice running in them in front of the mirror to make sure nothing untoward showed, and that I didn't rub my legs with baby oil so they gleamed. I pretended I didn't obsess about how a running partner should smell, or whether or not to wear perfume and in the end settled on baby powder, which would hopefully convey the message *naturally smells fresh and clean like a woman, not an infant*. He pretended he didn't notice when my breathing turned to small, almost inaudible moans when we sprinted the last quarter mile, the Charles Hotel in sight, and I pretended I didn't have fantasies that one day he would take my hand, lead me up to a room, and into his bed.

36. Having a secret is the most powerful aphrodisiac in the world and, by necessity, exactly what's missing in a marriage.

From: researcher101 <researcher101@netherfieldcenter.org>
Subject: Hope
Date: May 30, 4:45 PM
To: Wife 22 <Wife22@netherfieldcenter.org>

Dear Wife 22,

  I took the liberty of codifying your last email—the emotion data points: longing, sadness, nostalgia, and hope. The last emotion might not seem evident to you, but there's no doubt in my mind. It's *hope.*

  I probably shouldn't tell you this, but what I find most likeable about you is your unpredictability. Just when I think I've gotten a handle on you, you say something that throws me off completely. Sometimes the correspondence between subject and researcher reveals so much more than the answers.

  You are a romantic, Wife 22. I wouldn't have guessed it.

  Researcher 101

From: Wife 22 <Wife22@netherfieldcenter.org>
Subject: Re: Hope
Date: May 30, 9:28 PM
To: researcher101 <researcher101@netherfieldcenter.org>

Researcher 101,

  Takes one to know one. Are you for real?

  Wife 22

From: researcher101 <researcher101@netherfieldcenter.org>
Subject: Re: Hope
Date: May 30, 9:45 PM
To: Wife 22 <Wife22@netherfieldcenter.org>

Wife 22,

I assure you I am very real. I'll take your question as a compliment, and go one further and answer your next question so you needn't ask it—no, I am not a senior citizen. Believe it or not, there are men in your generation who are romantics. Frequently we are disguised as curmudgeons. I look forward to getting your next set of answers.

Researcher 101

From: Wife 22 <Wife22@netherfieldcenter.org>
Subject: Re: Hope
Date: May 30, 10:01 PM
To: researcher101 <researcher101@netherfieldcenter.org>

I took the liberty of codifying *your* last email. The emotion points as I see them are flattered, chagrined, and the last emotion, which may not seem obvious to you, is also hope. What are you hoping for, Researcher 101?

Sincerely,

Wife 22

From: researcher101 <researcher101@netherfieldcenter.org>
Subject: Re: Hope
Date: May 30, 10:38 PM
To: Wife 22 <Wife22@netherfieldcenter.org>

Wife 22,

I suppose it's what everybody hopes for—to be known for who we truly are.

Researcher 101

alicebuckle@rocketmail.com
Bookmarks Bar (242)

nymag.com/news/features/The Science of Gaydar

The Science of Gaydar
If sexual orientation is biological, are the traits that make people *seem* gay
innate, too? The new research on biological indicators, everything from
voice pitch to hair whorl.
EXAMPLE 1: Hair Whorl (Men)
Gay men are more likely than straight men to have a counterclockwise
whorl.

alicebuckle@rocketmail.com
Bookmarks Bar (243)

somethingfishy.org/eatingdisorders/symptoms

1. Hiding food in strange places (closets, cabinets, suitcases, under bed)
to avoid eating (anorexia) or eat at a later time (bulimia).

2. Obsession with continuous exercise.

3. Frequent trips to the bathroom immediately following meals (sometimes accompanied with water running in the bathroom for a long period of time to hide the sound of vomiting).

4. Unusual food rituals such as shifting the food around on the plate to

look eaten; cutting food into tiny pieces; making sure the fork avoids contact with the lips . . .

5. Hair loss. Pale or "gray" appearance to the skin.

6. Complaints of often feeling cold.

7. Bruised or callused knuckles; bloodshot or bleeding eyes; light bruising under the eyes and on the cheeks.

31

"Vegetarian or meat eater today?" I ask Zoe, approaching the table with a platter of roasted chicken and potatoes.

"Carnivore."

"Great. Breast or thigh?"

Zoe raises her eyebrows in disgust. "I said carnivore, not cannibal. *Breast or thigh*. That's exactly why people become vegetarians. They should come up with different words for it so it doesn't sound so human."

I sigh. "Light meat or dark meat?"

"That's racist," says Peter.

"Neither," says Zoe. "I changed my mind."

I put the platter of chicken on the table. "Okay, Mr. and Ms. Politically Correct. What should I call it?"

"How about dry or a little less dry," says Peter, poking at the bird.

"I think it looks delicious," says Caroline.

Zoe shudders and pushes her plate away.

"Are you cold? Sweetheart, you look cold," I say.

"I'm not cold."

"So what *are* you planning to eat then, Zoe?" I ask. "If not chicken boob?"

"Salad," says Zoe. "And roasted potatoes."

"Roasted potat*o*," says Peter, as Zoe puts one measly red potato on her plate. "I guess if you do seven hundred fifty sit-ups a day it basically ruins your appetite, right?"

"Seven hundred fifty sit-ups a day?" My girl has an eating disorder AND an exercise compulsion disorder!

I wish I had an exercise compulsion disorder.

"No wonder why they named you after a penis," says Zoe to Peter.

"Caroline, I can't get over how much you look like your father," says William, trying to change the subject.

He's wearing his weekend uniform, jeans and a faded U Mass T-shirt. Even though he went to Yale, he would never be caught dead advertising it. This is one of the things I've always loved about him. That and the fact that he wears a T-shirt from *my* alma mater.

"She looks like Maureen O'Hara," says Peter.

"Like you know who Maureen O'Hara is, Peter," says Zoe.

"Like *you* do. And it's Pedro. Why won't you call me Pedro? She was in *Rio Grande* with John Wayne," says Peter. "I *know* who Maureen O'Hara is."

Zoe scrapes her chair back and stands up.

"Where are you going?" I ask.

"To the bathroom."

"What, you can't wait until we're finished eating?"

"No, I can't wait," says Zoe. "You're embarrassing me."

"Fine, go." I glance at the clock. 7:31. She'd better not spend more than five minutes in there.

I stand up and hover over Peter's head. "Hey, kiddo, when's the last time they did lice checks in school?" I try and say this as naturally as possible, as if the possibility of lice infestation has suddenly occurred to me.

"I don't know. I think they do them every month."

"That's not enough." I sweep the hair back from his temples.

"Tell me you're not doing a lice check at the dinner table," grunts William.

"I'm not doing a lice check," I say, which is the truth. I'm only pretending to do a lice check.

"That feels good," says Peter, leaning back against me. "I love when people scratch my scalp."

Now, was the *telltale* gay whorl supposed to be clockwise or counterclockwise? The doorbell rings. Damn. I can't remember.

I lift my hands from Peter's head. "Does anybody hear water running?"

Peter starts itching. "I really think you should look some more."

The doorbell rings again. Yes, that is definitely water running in the bathroom. It's been running nonstop. Is she throwing up in there?

"I'll get it." I pass the bathroom as slowly as I can, listening for the *telltale* signs of vomiting—nothing. I walk into the foyer and open the front door.

"Hi," says Jude, nervously. "Is Zoe home?"

What is he doing here? I thought I was over it, but now, seeing him standing on my doorstep, I realize I'm not. I'm still furious at him. Is *he* the reason my daughter has an eating disorder? Did he drive her to it? I gaze at him, this young man who cheated on my daughter, so handsome, six-foot-one, flat-bellied, smelling of Irish Spring. I remember reading him *Heather Has Two Mommies* in Nedra's kitchen when he was in second grade. I was worried he would ask me about his father, about whom I knew nothing except his sperm donor number—128. Nedra and Kate didn't meet until Jude was three.

After we finished reading the book, he'd said, "I'm really lucky. You want to know why?"

"Sure," I said.

"Because if my mommies broke up and then fell in love again, then I'd have four mommies!"

"Zoe's not here," I say.

"Yes, she is," says Zoe, coming to the door.

"We're eating dinner," I say.

"I'm done," says Zoe.

"Sweetheart, your eyes look bloodshot."

"So I'll use Visine." She turns to Jude. "What?" Something private and silent passes between them.

"It's a school night. You haven't even started your homework," I say.

When Zoe was in fifth grade and we finally had the talk about puberty and menstruation, she took it well. She wasn't at all freaked out or disgusted. A few days later, she came home from school and told me she had a plan. When she got her period, she would just carry her pontoons in her backpack.

I had to fight to keep from cracking a smile (or telling her she had it wrong, they were called tampoons, I mean tampons) because I knew laughing in the face of her independence would destroy her. Instead I put on the poker face every mother learns to wear. The poker face every mother then hands down to her daughter, who then turns around and wields it like a weapon against her.

Zoe glares at me.

"Half an hour," I tell them.

My laptop pings as I walk past my office, so I do a quick Facebook check.

Julie Staggs
Marcy—having trouble staying in Marcy's big girl bed!
52 minutes ago

Shonda Perkins
Pretty please, pretty please, pretty please. Don't do this to me. You know who you are.
2 hours ago

Julie teaches at Kentwood, and Shonda is one of the Mumble Bumbles. I hear the sound of a glass shattering in the kitchen.

"Alice!" William shouts.

"Right there," I yell.

I sit down and write two quick messages.

Alice Buckle ▶ Julie Staggs
Don't give up. Maybe try falling asleep with her the first couple of nights? She'll get it eventually!
1 minute ago

Alice Buckle ▶ Shonda Perkins
Egg Shop. Tomorrow lunch. My treat. I want to hear EVERYTHING!
1 minute ago

Then I hurry back to the dinner table where over the course of the next thirty minutes, I proceed to offer up the same platitudes (*Don't give up. I want to hear everything!*). Is everybody living such a double life?

32

From: Wife 22 <Wife22@netherfieldcenter.org>
Subject: Stirring the proverbial pot
Date: June 1, 5:52 AM
To: researcher101 <researcher101@netherfieldcenter.org>

Dear Researcher 101,

I'm finding these questions about my courtship with William to be very pot-stirring. On one hand it's like watching a movie. Who are these actors playing the roles of Alice and William? That's how foreign these younger versions of us feel to me. On the other hand, I can reach back and create scenes in such detail for you. I can remember exactly what it felt like to fantasize about sleeping with him. How delicious the anticipation.

On the subject of not hiding, I have to tell you that to be asked such intimate questions—to be listened to so closely—to have my opinion and my feelings be valued and account for something is profound. I am continually startled at my willingness to disclose such personal information to you.

Sincerely,

Wife 22

From: researcher101 <researcher101@netherfieldcenter.org>
Subject: Re: Stirring the proverbial pot
Date: June 1, 6:01 AM
To: Wife 22 <Wife22@netherfieldcenter.org>

Dear Wife 22,

I've heard similar things from other participants, but I have to reiterate it's precisely because we *are* strangers that you are able to confide in me so easily.

Best,

Researcher 101

33

'm running late as usual. I throw open the door to the Egg Shop and am blasted in the face by the comforting smell of pancakes, bacon, and coffee. I look for Shonda. She's sitting in the back, but she's not alone; all three of the Mumble Bumbles are there in the booth with her. There's Shonda, in her fifties, divorced, no kids, manages the Lancôme counter at Macy's; Tita, who must be in her seventies now, married, grandmother of eight, a retired oncology nurse; and Pat, the youngest of us all, two kids, a stay-at-home mom, and judging by the size of her baby bump, expecting a third any day. They wave cheerily at me and tears well up in my eyes. Even though I haven't seen them in a while, the Mumble Bumbles are my pack, my fellow motherless sisters.

"Don't be mad," shouts Shonda as I wend my way between tables.

I bend down to give her a hug. "You set me up."

"We missed you. It was the only way to get your attention," says Shonda.

"I'm sorry," I say. "I've missed you all, too, but I've been okay, really I have."

They all look at me with scrunched-up, compassionate faces.

"Don't do that. Don't look at me that way. Damn."

"We wanted to make sure you were all right," says Pat.

"Oh, Pat, look at you! You're gorgeous," I say.

"Go ahead, touch it, you might as well—everybody else does."

I put my hands on her belly. "Location, location, location," I whisper. "Hello, baby. You have no idea what a good choice you've made."

Shonda pulls me down onto the seat next to her. "So when is your forty-fifth?" she asks.

All the Mumble Bumbles except me have aged past the year their mother died. I'm the last one. Obviously they have no plans of letting my tipping-point year go by without marking it in some way.

"September fourth." I look around the table. "What's up with the tomato juice?" Each of them has a glass.

"Have a little taste," says Tita, sliding it across the table. "And I brought you lumpia. Don't let me forget to give it to you."

Lumpia is the Filipino version of egg rolls. I adore them. Whenever I see Tita, she brings me a couple dozen.

I take a sip and cough. The juice is laced with vodka. "It's not even noon!"

"Twelve thirty-five, actually," says Shonda, flashing a flask. She waves the waitress over and raises her glass. "She'll have one of these."

"No she won't. She has to go back to work in an hour," I protest.

"All the more reason," says Shonda.

"Mine's a virgin," sighs Pat.

"So," says Tita.

"So," I say.

"So we're all here because we wanted to prepare you for what might be coming," says Tita.

"I know what's coming and it's too late for me. I won't be wearing a bikini this summer. Or the next. Or the summer after that," I say.

"Alice, be serious," says Shonda.

"I went a little bonkers the year I turned the same age my mother was when she died," says Pat. "I was so depressed. I couldn't get out of bed for weeks. My sister-in-law had to come help look after the kids."

"I'm not depressed," I say.

"Well, good, that's good," says Pat.

"I quit working at Lancôme," says Shonda. "And became a sales rep for Dr. Hauschka products. Can you imagine that? Me hawking holistic skin care? My main account was Whole Foods. Have you ever tried to get a parking space at the Whole Foods in Berkeley after nine in the morning? Impossible."

"I'm not going to quit my job," I say. "And even if I wanted to, I can't, because William just got demoted."

The Mumble Bumbles exchange worried, see-I-told-you-so looks.

"It's okay. He's doing some soul searching. It's a midlife thing," I say.

"Alice," says Tita. "The point is—you might start acting a little crazy. Do things that you normally wouldn't do. Does that sound familiar? Anything like that happening to you?"

"No," I say. "Everything's normal. Everything's fine. Except for the fact that Zoe has an eating disorder. And Peter is gay but he doesn't know it yet. And I'm taking part in this secret study on marital satisfaction."

What the Mumble Bumbles knew, what was unspoken between us, what need never be explained or said, was that nobody would ever love us again like our mothers did. Yes, we would be loved, by our fathers, our friends, our siblings, our aunts and uncles and grandparents and spouses—and our children if we chose to have them—but never would we experience that kind of unconditional, nothing-you-can-do-will-turn-me-away-from-you kind of mother love.

We tried to provide it for one another. And when we failed at that, we offered shoulders to lean on, hands to hold, and ears to bend. And when we failed at that, there was lumpia and waterproof mascara samples, links to articles, and yes, vodka-laced tomato juice.

But mostly there was the ease that came from not having to pretend you had ever recovered. The world wanted you to go on. The world *needed* you to go on. But the Mumble Bumbles understood that the loss soundtrack was always playing in the background. Sometimes it was on mute, and sometimes it was blasting away on ten, making you deaf.

"Start from the beginning, honey, and tell us everything," says Tita.

34

37. And then one day, standing in front of the Charles Hotel, he un-plugged my earphones from my Walkman, put them into his Walkman, and for the first time it seemed like we were having a real conversation. It went something like this:

Song 1: De La Soul, "Ha Ha Hey": I'm a white guy who likes watered-down hip-hop. Occasionally if I've had enough to drink I will dance.

Song 2: Til Tuesday, "Voices Carry": It would be best if we spoke to nobody of these lunchtime runs.

Song 3: Nena, "99 Luftballons": I was a punk for three weeks when I was thirteen. Are you impressed?

Song 4: The Police, "Don't Stand So Close to Me": Stand so close to me.

Song 5: Fine Young Cannibals, "Good Thing": You.

Song 6: Men Without Hats, "The Safety Dance": Over.

Song 7: The Knack, "My Sharona": You make my motor run. My motor run.

Song 8: Journey, "Faithfully": An adverb that no longer describes me.

35

From: Wife 22 <Wife22@netherfieldcenter.org>
Subject: Friends
Date: June 4, 4:31 AM
To: researcher101 <researcher101@netherfieldcenter.org>

I think it's time we became friends. What do you think about using Facebook? I'm on Facebook all the time and I love the immediacy of it. And wouldn't it be nice to chat? If we each put up a page and friend only each other we can retain our anonymity. The only problem is that you have to use a real name, so I've set up a page under Lucy Pevensie. Do you know Lucy Pevensie from *The Lion, The Witch and the Wardrobe*? The girl who stumbled through the wardrobe and found herself in Narnia? My children always accuse me of being lost in another world when I'm online, so it makes a strange sort of sense. What do you think?

All the best,

Wife 22

From: researcher101 <researcher101@netherfieldcenter.org>
Subject: Re: Friends
Date: June 4, 6:22 AM
To: Wife 22 <Wife22@netherfieldcenter.org>

Dear Wife 22,

I don't typically communicate with subjects via Facebook due to the obvious privacy issues, but it seems you've found a way to work around that. I will say, for the record, that I don't like Facebook and I don't typically "chat." I find communicating in short bursts both draining and distracting. As did, according to NPR, the teenage girl who fell into an open manhole today while texting. Facebook is another kind of hole—a rabbit hole, in my opinion—but I will check into the feasibility of using it and get back to you.

Sincerely,

Researcher 101

From: Wife 22 <Wife22@netherfieldcenter.org>
Subject: Re: Friends
Date: June 4, 6:26 AM
To: researcher101 <researcher101@netherfieldcenter.org>

What's wrong with rabbit holes? Some of us are quite partial to them. Chagall believed a painting was like a window through which a person could fly into another world. Is that more to your liking?

Wife 22

From: researcher101 <researcher101@netherfieldcenter.org>
Subject: Re: Friends
Date: June 4, 6:27 AM
To: Wife 22 <Wife22@netherfieldcenter.org>

Why, yes it is. How did you know?

Researcher 101

36

"So, what do you want to do?" I ask.

"I don't know. What do you want to do?" says William. "Are you all set for the potluck? What are we supposed to bring?"

"Lamb. Nedra emailed me the recipe. It's been marinating since last night. I have to go to Home Depot—I want to get lemon balm and lemon verbena and that other lemon herby thing—what's it called? From Thailand?"

"Lemongrass. What's with all the lemon?" he asks.

"Lemon is a natural diuretic."

"I didn't know that."

"Didn't you?"

We talk carefully and politely, like strangers making small talk at a party. *How do you know the host? Well, how do you know the host? I love corgis. I love corgis, too!* I know part of this distance is because he's keeping the Cialis debacle secret. And I'm keeping the fact that I know about it secret. And of course there's the fact that I'm emailing total strangers about the intimate particulars of our marriage (just as it seems William is also telling total strangers about the intimate particulars of our marriage). But I can't blame it all on the study or William's demotion. The distance between us has been growing for years. The primary way we converse during the workweek is through text, and we pretty much always have the same conversation:

ETA?

Seven.

Chick or fish?

Chick.

It's Saturday. Caroline's here, but both kids are gone for the day—a rare occurrence in our household. I'm trying not to feel panicked, but I am. In their absence, the day looms without structure. I usually shuttle Peter to piano and soccer and William takes Zoe to volleyball games or Goodwill (where she acquires most of her clothes). I try not to think about the fact that we often operate like roommates, and most of the time roommates is okay, a bit lonely, but comfortable. But a day alone together means stepping out of our parent roles and reverting back to husband and wife, which makes me feel pressured. Kind of like Cialis without the Cialis.

I remember that when the kids were young, an acquaintance confided in me how bereft she and her husband were that their son was leaving for college. I thoughtlessly said to her, "Well, isn't that the point? He's launched. Shouldn't you be happy?" I came home and told William, and the two of us were flummoxed. Deep in the trenches of early parenthood, either one of us would have done anything to have an afternoon to ourselves. We looked forward to our kids becoming independent. Imagine being so attached to your children that you would feel lost when they left, we said to each other. A decade later, I'm just beginning to understand.

"Are the Barbedians coming tonight?" asks William.

"I don't think so. Didn't they say they had Giants tickets?"

"Too bad, I like Bobby," says William.

"Meaning you don't like Linda?"

William shrugs. "She's *your* friend."

"Well, she's your friend, too," I say, irritated that he's trying to pawn Linda off on me.

Nedra and I met Linda when our kids attended the same preschool. Our three families have been doing a monthly potluck for years. All the kids used to come to the potluck but as they got older, one by one they began to drop out, and now it's usually just the adults (and occasionally Peter) who show up. Without the children as a buffer the dynamics of the potluck have changed, by which I mean it's becoming more and more clear we don't have much in common with Linda anymore. Everybody loves Bobby, however.

William sighs.

"Listen, don't feel like you have to hang out with me while I do my errands. Probably the last thing you want to do is traipse around some plant nursery with me."

"I don't mind," says William, looking irritated.

"Really?—well, okay. Should we ask Caroline if she wants to come?"

"Why would we ask Caroline?"

"Well, I just thought—well, maybe if you got bored, the two of you could run laps around Home Depot or something."

After my one failed run with Caroline, William began running with her. It was a rough beginning. He was out of shape, and those first couple of runs were tough. But now they ran five miles a few mornings a week and afterward whipped up spirulina smoothies, which Caroline tried to foist upon me with promises of fewer colds and better bowel function.

"Very funny. What's wrong with just the two of us?" William asks.

What's wrong with "just the two of us" is that these days when we're together, it might as well be "just one of us." I'm the one who starts all the conversations, who brings him up to date on what's happening with the children and the house and finances, and who asks him about what's going on in his life. He rarely reciprocates, and he never voluntarily offers up any information about himself.

"Nothing—of course not. The two of us is great. We can do whatever we want. What fun!" I say, defaulting to my overly enthusiastic Mary Poppins/Miss Truly Scrumptious voice.

I long for a richer life with him. I know it's possible. People out there, like Nedra and Kate, are living richer lives. Couples are making moussaka together while the Oscar Peterson channel plays on Pandora. They're shopping at farmers' markets. Of course they're shopping very slowly (slowness seems to be a key element in living a rich life), visiting all the stalls, sampling stone fruit, sniffing herbs, knowing their lemongrass from their lemon balm, sitting on a stoop and eating vegan scones. I don't mean rich in the sense of money. I mean rich in the ability to feel things as they're happening, to not constantly be thinking of the next thing.

"Hey, Alice." Caroline walks into the kitchen, waving a book.

So far Caroline's had no luck finding a job. She's had lots of interviews (there's no shortage of tech startups in the Bay Area) but few callbacks. I know she's anxious, but I told her not to worry; she could stay with us until she was employed and had banked enough money to pay the security deposit on an apartment. Having Caroline around is not a burden. Besides being great company, she's the most helpful houseguest we've ever had. I'll really miss her when she goes.

"Look what I found. *Creative Playmaking,*" she says in a singsong voice.

She hands the book to me and I let out a little gasp. I haven't seen this book in years. "This used to be my bible," I say.

"It's *still* my mother's bible," she says. "So, you guys have a weekend alone. What fun things do you have planned? Do you want me to *skedaddle?*" She waggles her eyebrows at us.

Caroline often uses old-fashioned terms like *skedaddle*—I think it's charming. I suspect it comes from being a playwright's daughter and seeing too many renditions of *Our Town.* I sigh and randomly flip to page 25 in the book.

1. Have an idea before you start writing.

2. Everything is potential material: the backyard barbecue, a trip to the grocery store, a dinner party. The best characters are frequently modeled after the ones you live with.

I shut the book and press it to my chest. Just holding it fills me with hope.

"*Creative Playmaking? That* used to be your bible?" asks William.

That William has no memory of the book and how important it was to me (even though it sat on my bedside table for five years or so) is not a surprise.

I text William in my mind. *Sorry I ass. But you ass, 2.*

Then I say to Caroline, "We're off to do errands. Want to come?"

37

FESTIVE MOROCCAN POTLUCK AT NEDRA'S HOUSE

7:30: Nedra's kitchen

Me: Hello, Rachel! Where's Ross? Here's the lamb.

Nedra (*peeling back the aluminum foil from roasting dish and frowning*): Did you follow the recipe exactly?

Me: Yes, but with one wonderful twist!

Nedra: No good can come of wonderful twists. Linda and Bobby made it after all.

Me: I thought they were going to the game.

Nedra (*sniffing the lamb and making a face*): They couldn't resist your restaurant-quality dishes. Where are the kids?

Me: Peter's here. Zoe's at home doing sit-ups. Where's Jude?

Jude (*walking into the kitchen*): Wishing he was anywhere but here.

Nedra: Darling, are you going to join us? Alice, wouldn't that be lovely if Jude joined us?

Me: It would. Yes, Nedra. It would be so, so lovely.

Nedra: See, darling. See how wanted you are. Please say you will.

Jude: (*looking down at the floor*)

Me: (*looking down at the floor*)

Nedra (*sighing*): You are big babies, the both of you. Will you please make up?

Jude: I'm going to Fritz's to play Pokémon.

Me: Really?

Jude: No, not really. I'm going to my room.

Nedra: Bye, bye, darling. One of these days the two of you will love each other again. It's my dying wish.

Me: Must you be so melodramatic, Nedra?

Jude: Yes, must you?

Nedra: Melodrama is the language the both of you speak.

7:40: In the living room

Nedra: Men, gather round. The costume portion of the evening will begin. Kate and I brought you each back a fez from our most recent trip to Morocco.

Peter (*unable to wipe stricken look off his face*): I would prefer not to wear a fez as I'm already wearing a trilby.

Nedra: Yes, which is why we got you a fez—to get that damn trilby off your head.

Kate: I think his trilby is cute.

William: I stand with Peter. Being a woman, you may be unfamiliar with the codes of men and hats in the twenty-first century.

Bobby: Yes, it's not like the 1950s, where you take off your hat when you go to dinner. In the twenty-first century you wear your hat throughout dinner.

Me: Or if you are Pedro, throughout the month of June.

William: And if you start off the evening with a hat, you don't switch to another hat. Hats are not like cardigan sweaters.

Nedra: Put on the fez, Pedro, or else.

Me: What about us?

Nedra: Kate, Alice, and Linda, I have not forsaken you. Here are your djellabas!

Me: Fabulous! A long, loose garment with big sleeves that soon I will be dipping accidentally into my mint sauce.

Peter: I'll trade you for my fez.

Nedra (*sighing*): Must you all be so ungrateful?

8:30: At the dinner table

Kate: How was Salzburg, Alice?

William: You were in Salzburg?

Nedra: Yes, eating *palatschinken*. Apparently without you.

Me: I was in Salzburg on Facebook. I took the "Dream Vacation" quiz. I've always wanted to go to Salzburg.

Bobby: Linda and I are on Facebook. It's a fabulous way to stay in touch without really staying in touch. How else would I have known you were going to Joshua Tree this weekend?

Linda: It's a women's weekend, Bobby. Don't sulk. Ladies, you're welcome to come.

Nedra: Will there be drums and burning of things?

Linda: Yes!

Nedra: Then no.

Linda: Hey, did we tell you guys we're renovating? We're redoing the master bedroom. It's the most marvelous thing. We're making it into two master bedrooms!

Me: Why would you need two master bedrooms?

Linda: It's the new trend. It's called a flex suite.

Kate: So you'll be sleeping in separate bedrooms.

Peter: Can I be excused? *Subtext: Can I sneak into your office and play World of Warcraft on your computer, Nedra?*

Nedra: What, you don't want to talk about the intimate sleeping arrangements of your parents and your parents' friends? By all means, Pedro, go!

Linda: Isn't it great? It'll be like we're dating again! Your suite or mine?

Nedra: What about spontaneity? What about waking up in the middle of the night and having wild, half-asleep sex?

Me: Yes, I was wondering about that, too, Linda! What about half-asleep sex?

William: Isn't that called rape?

Linda: I have no desire to have sex at two in the morning. It's a known fact that it gets much harder to share a bed as you get older. Bobby gets up three times a night to pee.

Bobby: Linda wakes up every time I move my middle toe.

Linda: We'll share a bathroom, of course.

Me: Now *that's* the thing I'd like two of.

Linda: Twin suites are going to reignite the mystery and the passion in our marriage. You'll see. God, I miss Daniel. It's the most ridiculous thing. I couldn't wait for him to leave for college and now I can't wait for him to come home.

William: Did I mention that a few weeks ago the dog urinated on my pillow?

Kate: I know a dog psychic you can call.

Nedra: I had a client once who peed in his wife's lingerie drawer.

Bobby: The wife had a lingerie *drawer*? How long had they been married?

Me: Jampo knows you don't like him. He senses that. He's a truth-teller.

William: He's mean. He eats his own shit.

Me: Exactly my point. How much more truthful can you be? Willing to eat your own poop?

Nedra: Why does this lamb taste like face cream?

William: It's the lavender.

Nedra (*putting down her fork*): Alice, is this your idea of a twist? The recipe said rosemary.

Me: In my defense, a rosemary bush looks almost exactly like a lavender bush.

Nedra: Yes, except for the purple lavender-smelling flowers.

9:01: Through the bathroom door

Peter: Can I talk to you in private?

Me: I'm going to the bathroom. Can it wait?

Peter (*sounding teary*): I have something to confess. I did something really bad.

Me: Please don't confess. You don't have to tell me everything. It's good to keep some things private. You know that, right? Everybody has a right to a private life.

Peter: I have to. It's weighing so heavy on me.

Me: How will I react?

Peter: You will be very disappointed and perhaps a little disgusted.

Me: How should I punish you?

Peter: I won't need to be punished. What I saw was punishment enough.

Me (*opening the door*): Jesus, what did you do?

Peter (*crying*): I Googled P-O-R-N.

9:10: In the living room

Linda: I don't understand why "roommate" is such a dirty word. Any couple who've been married for more than ten years are roommates a lot of the time and if they don't cop to that, they're lying.

Nedra: Kate and I are not roommates.

Me: Yes, and you're also not married.

Linda: Lesbians don't count anyway.

Nedra: Gold-star lesbians. There's a difference.

Me: What's a gold-star lesbian?

Kate: A lesbian who's never been with a man.

William: I'm a gold-star heterosexual.

Nedra: Alice, do you ever feel like you and William are roommates?

Me: What? No! Never!

William: Sometimes.

Me: When?

10:10: In Nedra's office

William: I can't believe we're doing this. Why are we doing this?

Me: Because Peter was so traumatized. I have to know what he saw.

William (*sighing*): What's Nedra's password?

Me: *Nedra.* Should you type PORN in caps?

William: I don't think it matters.

Me (*gasping*): Is that a butternut squash?

William: Is that an icicle?

Me: Oh, my poor baby!

William: Clear history.

Me: What?

William: Clear history, Alice. Quick, before Nedra's spam folder is flooded with penis enlargement ads.

Me: I always forget to do that. Stop looking over my shoulder. Go on ahead. I just want to check Facebook.

William: You're being very rude. There's a roomful of people out there.

Me (*waving him away*): I'll be there in a sec.

(*five minutes later*) I have a friend request? John Yossarian wants to be friends? John Yossarian? That name sounds familiar.

GOOGLE SEARCH "John Yossarian"
About 626,000 results (.13 seconds)

Catch-22, **1961 by Joseph Heller, All Time 100 Novels,** *TIME*
Captain John Yossarian is a bomber pilot who is just trying to make it through WWII alive.

John Yossarian . . . Gravatar Profile
I'm John Yossarian. I rowed to Sweden to escape the insanity of war.

Captain John Yossarian: *Catch-22*
John Yossarian spends all his time in the infirmary pretending to be sick so he won't have to fly . . . preservation of life.

Me (*a smile breaking across my face*): Touché, Researcher 101.
(*clicking confirm friend*)
(*sending him a post*) So—*Yossarian lives.*

38

38. "That is *not* a La-Z-Boy."

"Alice, what do you think?"

"That depends. Are we speaking about the chair or the man?" I asked.

William had won a Clio for his La-Z-Boy spot and Peavey Patterson was throwing a party at Michela's in his honor. We'd taken over the entire restaurant. I was stuck sitting at a table full of copywriters.

The chair—of course it was hideous but it did make the firm an awful lot of money, and now I was at this fancy party, so who was I to complain? The man—he was the opposite of lazy: in fact he was the very essence of drive and potential, standing there in his navy Hugo Boss suit.

I watched him surreptitiously. I watched Helen watching me watch him surreptitiously but I didn't care; everybody was staring. People approached William nervously, like he was a god. And he *was* a god, the god of ugly recliners, Peavey Patterson's very own Young Turk. People flitted around him, touching his forearm and shaking his hand. It was exhilarating to be that close to success, because there was always the possibility a bit of that success would rub off on you. William was polite. He listened and nodded but said little. His eyes drifted over to me, and if I didn't know better I'd think he was angry—such was his glowering. But over the course of the evening, his gaze boldly and compulsively sought me out. It was as if I was a glass of wine and every time he glanced at me from across the room, he took a sip.

I looked down at my plate. My *Linguine con Cozze al Sugo Rosso* was delicious but virtually untouched, because all this clandestine staring was making me light-headed.

"Speech, speech!"

Helen leaned in and whispered in William's ear, and a few minutes later William allowed Mort Rich, the art director, to ferry him to the center of the restaurant. He took a piece of paper from his jacket pocket, smoothed it out, and began to read.

"Tips for Giving a Speech.

"Make sure you are not in the bathroom when it's time to make your speech.

"Thank your staff who helped you win this award.

"Pause.

"Never say you are unworthy of winning. This will offend your staff, who did all the work so you could stand up in front of everybody and take the credit for winning this award.

"Don't thank the people who had nothing to do with you winning this award.

"That would be spouses, girlfriends, boyfriends, bosses, waiters and bartenders.

"On second thought, thank the bartender, who had everything to do with you winning this award.

"Pause.

"If you have time, call out each person's name individually and compliment them."

William glanced at his watch. "No pause.

"Smile, look humble and gracious.

"Close your speech with an inspirational comment."

William folded up the paper and slid it into his pocket.

"Inspirational comment."

The room exploded with laughter and applause. When William sat back down at his table, Helen took his face in her hands, looked deeply into his eyes, and then kissed him on the mouth. There were a few hoots and claps. The kiss went on for a good ten seconds. She glanced at me, flashing me a startled but triumphant look, and I turned away, stung, my eyes involuntarily filling with tears.

"Sa-woon. Are they engaged yet?" the woman sitting next to me asked.

"I don't see a ring," said another colleague.

Had I imagined all this? This flirting? It appeared I had, because for the rest of the evening William acted like I wasn't even there. I was such a fool. Invisible. Stupid. I had on flesh-colored stockings, which I could see now weren't flesh-colored at all, but practically orange.

Around midnight, I passed him in the hallway on my way to the bathroom. It was a narrow hallway and our hands brushed as we squeezed by. I was determined not to say a word to him. Our running days were over. I'd ask to be transferred to a different team. But when our knuckles touched, a current of undeniable electricity passed between us. He felt it too, because he froze. We were facing opposite directions. He looked out into the restaurant. I looked toward the bathrooms.

"Alice," he whispered.

It suddenly occurred to me that I'd never heard him say my name. Until this moment he'd only called me Brown.

"Alice," he repeated in a low, gravelly voice.

He said "Alice" not like he was about to ask me a question or tell me something. He said my name like a statement of fact. Like after a very long journey (a journey he hadn't wanted or expected to take) he'd finally arrived at my name, at *me*.

I stared at the bathroom doors. I read *Women, Donne*. I read *Men, Uomini*.

He reached for my fingers, and not accidentally this time. It was the briefest of touches, a private touch not meant for anybody but me to see. I put my other hand on the wall to steady myself, weak-kneed from a combination of too much wine, relief, and desire.

"Yes," I said, then stumbled into the bathroom.

39. Suck it up.

40. I can't remember.

41. We appear to be a couple people envy.

42. Ask me again at a later time.

Lucy Pevensie
Studied at *Oxford College* **Born on** *April 24, 1934* **Current Employer**
Aslan **Family** *Edward, Peter, and Susan* **Work** *Trying to keep from turning
to stone.* **About You** *Years pass like minutes.*

*Yes, I'm afraid the rumor is true, Wife 22. Reports of my death are greatly
exaggerated.*

Rumor is true here also, Researcher 101. There *is* **another world through
the wardrobe. Sightings of fauns and white witches not greatly
exaggerated.**

Enjoyed reading your profile.

Did not enjoy reading your profile, Researcher 101. *Employer:*
Netherfield Center. **That's it? As far as your photo, I despise that little
silhouette. You could have at least used some clip art. A yellow raft,
perhaps?**

We'll see.

**Now that we're friends, we should probably adjust our privacy settings
so people can't search for us.**

*Already locked down. New questions coming soon—via email. I refuse to
chat the questions.*

Thanks for coming down the rabbit hole to find me.

That's my job. Did you think I wouldn't?

**I wasn't sure. I know Facebook is a stretch. But you may surprise
yourself; you may grow to like it. It's immediate in a way email is not.
Soon email may be extinct, gone the way of the letter.**

I sincerely hope not. Email seems civilized compared to texts and posts and Twitter. What's next? Communicating in three words or less?

Great idea. We can call it Twi. Three-word sentences can be very powerful.

No they can't.

Let's find out.

Let us not.

You're not very good at this.

How's your husband holding up? Anything I can do to help?

Get him his old job back.

Anything else?

Can I ask you something?

Sure.

Are you married?

As a rule, I'm not allowed to divulge personal information.

That explains your profile, or lack thereof.

Yes, I'm sorry. But we've learned from experience the less you know about your researcher, the more forthcoming you'll be.

So I should just treat you like the GPS voice?

That's been done before.

By whom, Researcher 101?

By other subjects, of course.

Family members?

I can neither confirm nor deny this.

Are you a computer program? Tell me. Am I writing to a computer?

Cannot answer now. Battery is low.

Look at you. You're Twi-ing. I knew you had it in you.

Should I tell you when I have to go or just type got to go? *I don't want to be rude. What's the protocol?*

It's GTG, not "got to go." And the good thing about chatting is there's no need for long, protracted goodbyes.

A pity, as I tend to be a fan of long, protracted goodbyes.

Wife 22?

Wife 22?

Did you go off-line?

I'm protracting our goodbye.

40

Alice Buckle
Studied at *U Mass* **Born on** *September 4* **Current Employer** *Kentwood Elementary* **Family** *William, Peter, Zoe* **Work** *Trying to keep from turning to stone* **About You** *Minutes pass like years*

Henry Archer ▶ Alice Buckle
Shut up already, cuz—we get that it hasn't rained in California in months!
4 minutes ago

Nedra Rao ▶ Kate O'Halloran
You have captivated me
13 minutes ago

Julie Staggs
Is it considered child abuse to tie your daughter's feet and hands to her bedposts with Little Kitty ribbons? Just kidding!!!
23 minutes ago

William Buckle
Free
1 hour ago

Part 2

41

William has been laid off. Not reprimanded, not warned, not demoted, but laid off. In the middle of a recession. In the middle of our lives.

"What did you do?" I shout.

"What do you mean what did *I* do?"

"To make them lay you off?"

He looks aghast. "Thanks for the sympathy, Alice. I didn't do anything. It was all about redundancies."

Yes, the redundancies of you acting out at work. Of you mouthing yourself right out of a job, I think.

"Call Frank Potter. Tell him you'll work for less. Tell them you're willing to do anything."

"I can't do that, Alice."

"Pride is a luxury we can't afford, William."

"This isn't about pride. I don't belong at KKM. It wasn't a good fit anymore. Maybe this is for the best. Maybe this is the wake-up call I've been needing."

"Are you kidding me? We can't afford waking up, either."

"I don't agree. We can't afford not to."

"Have you been reading Eckhart Tolle?" I cry.

"Of course not," he says. "We specifically made a pact not to live in the moment."

"We've made lots of pacts. Open the window—it's boiling in here."

We're sitting in the car out in the driveway. It's the only place we can talk privately. He starts the car and rolls down the windows. My Susan Boyle CD comes streaming out of the speakers at a high volume— *I dreamed a dream in time gone by.*

"Jesus!" says William, shutting it off.

"It's my car. You're not allowed to censor my music."

I turn the CD back on. *I dreamed that love would never die.* Jesus! I turn it off.

"You're killing me with that shit," groans William.

I want to run to my computer and do more budget projections, projections out to 2040, but I know what they'll reveal—with all of our expenses, including sending both of our fathers checks every month to supplement their paltry Social Security, we have about six months before we are in trouble.

"You're forty-seven," I say.

"You're forty-four," he says. "What's your point?"

"My point? My point is—you're going to have to dye your hair," I say, looking at his graying temples.

"Why the hell would I dye my hair?"

"Because it's going to be incredibly hard to find a job. You're too old. You cost too much. People aren't going to want to hire you. They'll hire a twenty-eight-year-old with no kids and no mortgage for half the salary who knows how to use Facebook and Tumblr and Twitter."

"I have a Facebook page," he says. "I just don't live on it."

"No, you just announce to the world that you got fired on it."

"*Free* can be interpreted in many different ways. Look, Alice, I'm sorry you're scared. But there are times in life that you have to leap. And when you don't have the courage to leap, well then, eventually somebody comes along and pushes you the fuck out the window."

"You *are* reading Eckhart Tolle! What else are you doing behind my back?"

"Nothing," he says dully.

"So, you've been unhappy at work, is that what you're telling me? What is it that you want to do now? Leave advertising altogether?"

"No. I just need a change."

"What sort of a change?"

"I want to work on accounts that mean something to me. I want to sell products that I believe in."

"Well, that sounds lovely. Who wouldn't want that, but in this economy I'm afraid that's a pipe dream."

"It probably is. But who says we shouldn't go after pipe dreams any-more?"

I begin to cry.

"Please don't do that. Please don't cry."

"Why are you crying?" asks Peter, suddenly appearing at my window.

"Go in the house, Peter. This is a private conversation," says William.

"Stay," I say. "He'll find out soon enough. Your father's been laid off."

"Laid off like fired?"

"No, laid off like laid off. There's a difference," says William.

"Does that mean you'll be home more?" asks Peter.

"Yes."

"Can we tell people?" asks Peter.

"What people?" I say.

"Zoe."

"Zoe's not people. She's family," I say.

"No, she's people. We lost her to the people some time ago," says William. "Look, everything's going to be okay. I'm going to find another job. Trust me. Get your sister," he says to Peter. "We're going out to dinner."

"We're celebrating you getting fired?" asks Peter.

"Laid off. And I'd like us to think of this as a beginning, not an end," says William.

I open my car door. "We're not going anywhere. The leftovers need to be eaten or they'll rot."

That night I can't sleep. I wake at 3 a.m. and just for kicks decide to weigh myself. Why not? What else do I have to do? 130 pounds—somehow I've lost eight pounds! I'm shocked. Women my age don't just magically lose eight pounds. I haven't been on a diet, although I am still paying monthly dues for my online Weight Watchers program, which now I really should cancel. And other than my pathetic attempt to run with Caroline, I haven't done any exercise in weeks. However, other people in my household are exercising like mad. Between Zoe's 750-sit-ups-a-day regimen and William's five-mile runs with Caroline, maybe I'm burning calories by osmosis. Or maybe I have cancer of the stomach. Or maybe it's guilt. That's it. I've been on the Guilt Diet and I haven't even known it.

What a brilliant idea for a book! Diet books sell millions of copies. I wonder if anybody else has thought of it.

GOOGLE SEARCH "Guilt . . . Diet"
About 9,850,000 results (.17 seconds)

Gilt Groupe
Luxury designers and fashion brands at up to 70% off . . .

Working Moms . . . Guilt
I may feel a tiny twinge of guilt when the maid is washing my sheets and I'm eating an expensed lunch at Flora . . .

Guilt-Free Sushi
Guilt-free sushi eating may be complicated . . .

I'm not in the market for discount designer clothes and though I am a working mom, I've never felt guilty for having a job, and Zoe doesn't allow me to eat sushi—well, certain kinds of overfished sushi like the common octopus, which is not a hardship for me—but hurrah!—there's no Guilt Diet on Google.

"We're in business!" I relay to Jampo, who is sitting at my feet. I write myself a note to look into the Guilt Diet in more depth once it's morning, when I'm pretty sure it will reveal itself to be the most ridiculous idea ever, but you never know.

I log on to Facebook and go to William's wall. He has no new update, which oddly disappoints me. What did I expect him to post?

William Buckle
Wife forced me to listen to Susan Boyle, but I got myself fired so I deserve it.

William Buckle

Wife looks mysteriously skinnier—suspect she's ingesting tapeworms.

Or more likely something along the lines of—

William Buckle

"The past has no power over the present moment." Eckhart Tolle

42

43. After that night celebrating William's Clio, a torturous three weeks went by. Three weeks in which William ignored me. Our lunchtime runs abruptly stopped. If he had to talk to me he avoided eye contact and looked at my forehead, which was deeply unsettling and made me blurt out stupid things like *according to our focus groups what people (women) really want to know about toilet paper is that it doesn't tear while you're in the middle of using it due to the fact that men wash their hands far less than women and if they do wash them most of the time they don't use soap.* He also reverted to calling me Brown, and so I could only conclude he (like me) was drunk that evening and had absolutely no memory of the knuckle-grazing incident outside the bathroom. Or after sobering up was totally embarrassed having stared at me all night long and was doing everything he could to pretend it never happened.

Meanwhile, he and Helen were inseparable. At least three times a day she flounced into his office and shut the door, and every night she collected him and off they went for Rob Roys at the Copley Hotel, or to attend some fancy event at the Isabella Gardner Museum.

And then, just when I'd accepted an invitation from a friend to be set up on a blind date, I got this email.

From: williamb <williamb@peaveypatterson.com>
Subject: Tom Kah Gai
Date: August 4, 10:01 AM
To: alicea <alicea@peaveypatterson.com>

As you've probably noticed, I've been home sick for the past two days. I'm craving Tom Kah Gai. Would you bring me some? Make sure it's from King and Me, not King of Siam. Once a mouse ran across my feet while eating at King of Siam. Thanks very much. 54 Acorn Street. 2nd Floor. Apt. 203

From: alicea <alicea@peaveypatterson.com>
Subject: Re: Tom KHA Gai
Date: August 4, 10:05 AM
To: williamb <williamb@peaveypatterson.com>

Bangkok Princess has the best Tom KHA Gai on Beacon Hill. King and Me a far second. I can forward your craving for soup to Helen, who surely said request was meant for.

From: williamb <williamb@peaveypatterson.com>
Subject: Re: Tom KHA Gai
Date: August 4, 10:06 AM
To: alicea <alicea@peaveypatterson.com>

The request was meant for you.

From: alicea <alicea@peaveypatterson.com>
Subject: Re: Tom KHA Gai
Date: August 4, 10:10 AM
To: williamb <williamb@peaveypatterson.com>

So let me get this straight. Because you have a craving for Tom Kha Gai, I'm to leave work in the middle of the day, traipse across the bridge, and hand-deliver your soup?

From: williamb <williamb@peaveypatterson.com>
Subject: Re: Tom KHA Gai
Date: August 4, 10:11 AM
To: alicea <alicea@peaveypatterson.com>

Yes.

From: alicea <alicea@peaveypatterson.com>
Subject: Re: Tom KHA Gai
Date: August 4, 11:23 AM
To: williamb <williamb@peaveypatterson.com>

Why would I do that?

He didn't answer and he didn't have to. *Why* was very clear to both of us.

Forty-five minutes later, I knocked on his door.

"Come on in," he called out.

I nudged the door open with my foot, clutching a paper bag filled with two plastic containers of Tom Yung Goong. He was sitting on his couch, hair wet, barefoot, wearing a white T-shirt and jeans. I'd never seen him in anything but a suit or running shorts, and in casual attire he looked younger and somehow cockier. Had he showered for me?

"I have a fever," he said.

"Yes, and I have Tom."

"Tom?"

"Tom Yung Goong."

"Tom Kha Gai couldn't make it?"

"Stop complaining. It's a Thai soup that begins with Tom that I walked over half a mile to bring you. Where are your utensils?" I asked.

I brushed past him on the way to the kitchen and suddenly he grabbed my arm and pulled me down on the couch next to him. Startled (he seemed just as startled), we both looked intently forward as if we were attending a lecture.

"I don't want to get sick," I said.

"I've broken it off with Helen," he said.

He moved his leg slightly and our knees bumped together. Was that intentional? Then he moved his thigh so it was pressing up against mine. Yes, it was.

"It doesn't look like you've broken it off," I said. "She's practically been living in your office."

"We've been negotiating the terms of our breakup."

"What terms?"

"She didn't want to break up. I did."

"We can't do this," I said, by which I meant *press your thigh harder against mine.*

"Why?"

"You're my boss."

"And—"

"And there's a power differential."

He laughed. "Right. A power differential—between *us.* You're such a weak, submissive little creature. Tiptoeing around the office."

"Oh, Jesus."

"Tell me to stop and I'll stop."

"Stop."

He put his hand on my thigh and a shiver went through me.

"Alice."

"Don't screw with me. Don't say my name unless you mean it. What happened to Brown?"

"That was to keep me safe."

"Safe?"

"Safely away from you. You, Alice. Goddammit. You."

Then he turned and leaned in to kiss me and I could feel his fever and I thought *no no no no no* until I thought *yes, you son-of-a-bitch, yes.*

It was at that precise moment that the door opened and Helen walked in carrying a plastic bag of takeout from the King of Siam; apparently she hadn't gotten the message about the restaurant's rodent problem. I was so surprised, I gave a little shriek and jumped to the other side of the couch.

Helen looked just as surprised.

"You son-of-a-bitch," she said.

I was confused. Had I called William a son-of-a-bitch out loud? Had she heard me?

"Is she talking about me?" I asked.

"No, she's talking about me," said William, rising to his feet.

"Your assistant said you were sick. I brought you Pad Thai," said Helen, her face contorted with anger.

"You told me you had broken up," I said to William.

"He told me you had broken up," I said to Helen.

"Yesterday!" yelled Helen. "Not even twenty-four hours ago."

"Look—Helen," said William.

"You slut," said Helen.

"Is she talking about me?" I asked.

"Yes, now she's talking about you," sighed William.

I'd never been called a slut before.

"That's not very nice, Helen," he said.

"I'm so sorry, Helen," I said.

"Shut up. You went after him like a dog in heat."

"I told you it was an accident. Neither one of us was looking for this," said William.

"That's supposed to make me feel better? We were practically engaged," shouted Helen. "There's a code between women. You don't steal another woman's man, you whore," she hissed at me.

"I think I'd better go," I said.

"You're making a big mistake, William," said Helen. "You think she's so strong, so sure of herself. But that won't last. It's all an act. She'll hit one bad patch and she'll run away. She'll disappear."

I had no idea what Helen was talking about. Running away and disappearing was something drug addicts or people going through midlife crises did—not twenty-three-year-old women. But later I would look back on this moment and realize Helen's words were eerily prescient.

"Please come sit down," said William. "Let's talk."

Helen's eyes filled with tears. William walked to Helen, put his arm around her shoulder, and led her to the couch. *Come back tonight,* he mouthed to me.

I quietly slipped out the door.

44. Plucking eyebrows. Flossing teeth. Picking things out of teeth. Paying bills. Talking about money. Talking about sex. Talking about your kid having sex.

45. Grief.

46. Of course I do. Doesn't everybody? You want particulars, I know. Okay, that I changed the sheets (when really I've just changed the pillowcases). That I wasn't the one who put the nice knives in the dishwasher instead of hand-washing them and by the way, I don't need anybody to tell me the nice knives are the knives with black handles— I'm not a dolt, just somebody who's in a hurry. That I'm not hungry for dinner (if I'm not hungry it's because I ate an entire package of Keebler Fudge Stripes an hour before everybody came home). That it took me five nights to finish that bottle of wine (then why are there two bottles in the recycling bin?). That somebody must have sideswiped my side mirror when I parked at Lucky's—those inconsiderate jerks—it did not happen when I was backing out of the garage. But no, not the obvious one. We've never had a problem there.

43

 John Yossarian *added his profile picture*

You bear a striking resemblance to a yeti, Researcher 101.

Why thank you, Wife 22. I was hoping you'd say that.

However, it looks like you have a very un-yeti-like ear hanging from your head.

That's not an ear.

Actually, it's more like a bunny ear.

Actually, it's a hat.

I'm revising my opinion. You bear a striking resemblance to Donnie Darko. Has anybody ever told you that?

This is precisely why I didn't post a photo in the first place.

Can we talk about the orange pants?

No, we may not.

Okay, let's talk about #45. I can't stop thinking about it. This was a tough one.

Tell me more.

Well, at first I thought it would be easy. The answer would be grief, of course. But upon further reflection, I'm wondering if stasis isn't the correct answer.

You might be interested to know that subjects often answer in much the same way you did, first stating the obvious and then struggling to come up with something more nuanced. Why stasis?

Because in some ways stasis is a cousin of grief, but rather than dying all at once, you die a tiny bit every day.

Hello?

I'm here. Just thinking. That makes sense to me, especially given your answer to #3—once a week—and to #28—once a year.

You've memorized my answers?

Of course not, I have your file here in front of me. Would you like me to go ahead and change your answer to stasis?

Yes, please change my answer. It's more truthful, unlike your profile photo.

I don't know about that. In my experience, the truth is frequently blurry.

Wife 22?

Sorry—my son's calling me. GTG.

44

Alice Buckle
Sick boy.
1 minute ago

Caroline Kilborn
Arches hurt. 35 mile week!!
2 minutes ago

Phil Archer
Wishes his daughter would SLOW DOWN and text him once in awhile.
4 minutes ago

John F. Kennedy Middle School
Also keep in mind that what fit last year might be indecent this year due to exponential physical growth.
3 hours ago

John F. Kennedy Middle School
*Parents: please make sure your child's private parts and undergarments aren't visible when leaving the house. This is **your** responsibility.*
4 hours ago

William Buckle
"The dangers in life are infinite and among them is safety."—Goethe
One day ago

Some of my best memories as a kid are of being sick. I'd go from the bed to the couch, my pillow in hand. My mother would cover me with an afghan. First I'd watch back-to-back episodes of *Love, American Style*, then *The Lucy Show*, then *Mary Tyler Moore*, and finally *The Price Is*

Right. For lunch my mother would bring me toast with butter, ginger ale with no bubbles, and cold apple slices. In between shows I'd throw up in a pail my mother conveniently put beside the couch in case I couldn't make it to the bathroom.

Thanks to modern medicine, a flu now usually passes in twenty-four hours, so when Peter wakes with a fever it's like I've been granted a snow day. Just as we're snuggling in on the couch, William wanders into the living room in his sweats.

"I don't feel so good, either," he says.

I sigh. "You can't be sick, Pedro's sick."

"Which is probably why I'm sick."

"Maybe you gave it to me," says Peter.

I put my hand on Peter's forehead. "You're burning up."

William grabs my other hand and puts it on his forehead.

"Ninety-nine degrees. One hundred, tops," I say.

"If Dad's sick does this mean we have to watch the cooking channel?" asks Peter.

"First one sick gets the clicker," I say.

"I'm too sick to watch anyway," says William. "I have vertigo. Wonder if it's an inner-ear thing. I'm going to take a nap. Wake me when *Barefoot Contessa* comes on."

I have a vision of the way the days will soon be passing. William sitting on the couch. Me thinking up reasons to leave the house without him, which all have something to do with lady parts. In desperate need of sanitary pads. Going for a Pap smear. Attending a lecture on bio-identical hormones.

"Could you bring me some toast in about half an hour?" William calls out as he's walking up the stairs.

"Would you like some orange juice, too?" I yell, feeling guilty.

"That would be very nice," comes the disembodied voice.

The Sixth Sense is one of my absolute favorite movies. I don't like horror movies, but I do love psychological thrillers. I am a big fan of the twist. Unfortunately, until this very moment there was nobody in my household who was willing to watch them with me. So when Peter was in fourth grade and reading the Captain Underpants series for the eleventh time I started a mother-son short-story club, which was really in my mind a mother-groom-your-son-to-watch-creepy-thrillers-with-you club. First I had him read Shirley Jackson's "The Lottery."

" 'The Lottery' is about small-town politics," I explained to William.

"It's also about a mother getting stoned to death in front of her children," said William.

"Let's let Peter decide," I said. "Reading is such a subjective experience."

Peter read the last line of the story aloud—"and then they were upon her"—shrugged, and went back to *The Big, Bad Battle of Bionic Booger Boy*. That's when I knew he had real potential. In fifth grade I had him read Ursula Le Guin's "The Ones Who Walk Away from Omelas" and in sixth, Flannery O'Connor's "A Good Man Is Hard to Find." With each short story he grew a thicker skin and now, in the spring of his twelfth year, my son is finally ready for *The Sixth Sense*!

I begin downloading the movie from Netflix.

"You'll love it. The kid is so creepy. And there's this unbelievable twist at the end," I say.

"It's not a horror movie, right?"

"No, it's what's called a psychological thriller," I tell him.

Half an hour later I say, "Isn't that cool? He sees dead people."

"I'm not sure I like this movie," says Peter.

"Wait—it gets even better," I tell him.

Forty-five minutes later Peter asks, "Why is that boy missing the back of his head?"

Twenty minutes later he says, "The mother is poisoning her daughter by putting floor wax into her soup. You told me this wasn't a horror movie."

"It isn't. I promise. Besides, you read 'A Good Man Is Hard to Find.' The Misfit murders the family one by one. That was much worse than this."

"That's different. It's a short story. There are no visuals or scary soundtracks. I don't want to watch this anymore," he says.

"You've made it this far. You have to watch the rest. Besides, you haven't seen the twist yet. The twist redeems everything."

Fifteen minutes later, after the big twist is revealed (with much clapping of my hands and exclamations of "Isn't that incredible, do you get it? You don't get it—let me explain it to you. *I see dead people*? Bruce Willis is actually dead and has been dead the entire time!").

Peter says, "I can't believe you forced me to watch that movie. I should report you."

"To who?"

"To *whom*. Dad."

It's a very bad beginning to my mother-son short-story book club.

"I'm going to sleep on the couch," says William that night. "I may be contagious. I don't want you to get it."

"That's very considerate of you," I say.

William coughs. Coughs again. "Could be a cold, but could be something more."

"Better to be safe," I say.

"Which one are you reading?" he asks, pointing to the stack of books on my bedside table.

"All of them."

"At once?"

I nod. "They're my Ambien. I can't afford to become a sleep-eater."

I read one page of one book and fall asleep. I'm awakened a few hours later by Peter shaking my shoulder.

"Can I sleep in your bed? I'm scared," he snuffles.

I switch on the light. "*I see alive people*," I whisper.

"That's not funny." He's near tears.

"Oh, sweetheart. I'm sorry." I flip back the covers on William's side of the bed, feeling surprisingly sad that he isn't there. "Climb in."

45

 John Yossarian *changed his profile picture*

John Yossarian *added Relationship Status*
It's Complicated

John Yossarian *added Interests*
Piña Coladas

You're still being blurry, Researcher 101.

I thought you'd be pleased. I'm filling in my profile.

It's complicated is a given in any relationship.

Facebook only gives you so many options. I had to choose one, Wife 22.

If you could write your own Relationship Status, what would it be? I suggest you answer this question without thinking about it too much. I've found this kind of rapid-fire response results in the most honest answers.

Married, questioning, hopeful.

I knew you were married! And I believe all of those adjectives fall under the category It's Complicated.

If you could write your own Relationship Status, what would it be?

Married. Questioning.

Not hopeful?

Well, that's the strange thing. I am hopeful. But I'm not sure the hope is directed toward my husband. For the moment, anyway.

What's it directed toward?

I don't know. It's sort of a free-floating hope.

Ah—free-floating hope.

You're not going to lecture me about redirecting my hope toward my husband?

Hope isn't something you can redirect. It lands where it lands.

True. But it's nice you feel hopeful about your marriage.

I didn't say that, exactly.

What did you say?

I'm not sure.

What did you mean?

I meant that I'm hoping to have hope. Sometime in the future.

So you don't have it now?

It's a little up in the air.

I see. Up in the air like you in your profile photo?

I hope we can have more of these conversations.

I thought you didn't like chatting.

I like chatting with you. And I'm getting used to it. My thoughts come faster, but at a price.

What's that?

With speed comes disinhibition: i.e. see first sentence in previous comment.

And that worries you.

Well, yes.

With speed comes truth, as well.

A certain sort of truth.

You have a need to be very precise, don't you, Researcher 101?

That is a researcher's nature.

I don't like to think of you as being a fan of sickly sweet frozen drinks.

A lost opportunity for you, Wife 22.

46

"Is that Jude?" I ask.

"Where?"

"In the hair products aisle?"

"I doubt it," says Zoe. "He doesn't pay any attention to his hair. It's part of his singer-songwriter vibe."

Zoe and I are in Rite-Aid. Zoe needs pontoons and I'm trying to find this perfume I wore when I was a teenager. There's a flirtatious undertone to my Researcher 101 chats that's making me feel twenty years younger. I've been fantasizing about what he looks like. So far he's a cross between a young Tommy Lee Jones and Colin Firth—in other words, a weathered, slightly banged-up, profane Colin Firth.

"Excuse me," I say to a clerk who's restocking a shelf. "Do you carry a perfume called Love's Musky Jasmine?"

"We have Love's Baby Soft," she says. "Aisle seven."

"No, I'm not looking for Baby Soft. I want Musky Jasmine."

She shrugs. "We have Circus Fantasy."

"What kind of an idiot would name a perfume Circus Fantasy?" asks Zoe. "Who would want to smell like peanuts and horse poop?"

"Britney Spears," says the clerk.

"You shouldn't wear that synthetic stuff anyway, Mom. It's selfish. Air pollution. What about people with MCS? Have you given any thought to them?" says Zoe.

"I like that synthetic stuff, it reminds me of when I was in high school, but apparently they don't make it anymore," I say. "What's MCS?"

"Multiple chemical sensitivity."

I roll my eyes at Zoe.

"What? It's a real affliction," says Zoe.

"How about Gee Your Hair Smells Terrific?" I ask the clerk. "Do you carry that?"

When did tampons get so expensive? It's a good thing I have a coupon. I look at the fine print and squint, then hand it to Zoe. "I can't read this. How many boxes do we have to buy?"

"Four."

"There were only two boxes on the shelf," I say to the clerk when we get to the counter. "But your coupon is for four."

"Then you need four," he says.

"But I just told you there were only two."

"Mom, it's okay. Just get the two," whispers Zoe. "There's a line."

"It's two dollars off a box. It's *not* okay. We're using the coupon. We are a coupon-using family now."

To the clerk I say, "Can I get a rain check?"

The clerk snaps his gum and then gets on the loudspeaker. "I need a rain-check coupon," he says. "Tampax." He picks up a box of tampons and studies it. "Are there sizes on these things? Where does it say it? Oh—okay. There it is. 'Tampax, super plus. Four boxes,'" he announces to the entire store.

"Two," I whisper.

Zoe groans with embarrassment. I turn around and see Jude a few people back. It *was* him. He holds up his hand sheepishly and waves.

After the clerk has tallied up our purchase and given me a rain-check coupon, Zoe practically sprints out of the store.

"I bet your mother never did anything like that to *you*," she hisses, walking five feet in front of me. "Cheap plastic bags. They're practically see-through. Everybody knows exactly what you've bought."

"Nobody is even looking," I say as we reach the car, thinking how I would give anything to have had my mother around to humiliate me by buying too many boxes of tampons at the drugstore when I was Zoe's age.

"Hi, Zo," says Jude, catching up with us.

Zoe ignores him. Jude's face falls and I feel sorry for him.

"It's a bad time, Jude," I say.

"Unlock the car," says Zoe.

"I heard about your father's job," says Jude. "I just wanted to say I'm sorry."

I'm going to kill Nedra. I made her swear she wouldn't tell anybody but Kate about William getting laid off.

"We're in a hurry, Jude. Zoe and I are going to lunch," I say, tossing my bag into the backseat.

"Oh—nice," says Jude. "Kind of a mother-daughter thing."

"Yup, a mother-daughter thing," I say, climbing into the car. Even though the daughter wants nothing to do with the mother.

Once I get into my seat, I adjust my rearview mirror and watch Jude walking back to the drugstore. His shoulder blades jut poignantly through his T-shirt. He's always been bony. He looks like a six-foot-tall boy. Oh, Jude.

"I'm not hungry," says daughter.

"You'll be hungry when we get there," says mother.

"We can't afford to eat out," says daughter. "We are a coupon-using family."

"Yes, let's just go home and eat crackers," says mother. "Or bread crumbs."

Ten minutes later we're sitting in a booth at the Rockridge Diner.

"Does it bother you? Jude acting like nothing ever happened. Following you around. Can I have a sip of your tea?" I ask.

Zoe hands me her mug. "Don't blow on it. I hate when you blow on my tea when it's already cool. You don't get to have an opinion on me and Jude."

"Hair gel and tweezers."

"What?"

"That's what was in his bag."

Zoe snorts.

"Grilled ham and cheese and PB and J," says the waitress, putting down our plates, smiling at Zoe. "Never too old for a good PB and J. You want a glass of milk, too, honey?"

Zoe looks up at the waitress, who looks to be in her mid-sixties. We've been coming to the Rockridge Diner forever, and she always waits on us. She's seen Zoe at every stage of her life: milk-drugged infant, french-fry-smashing toddler, Lego-building preschooler, Harry Potter–reading fifth grader, dour adolescent, and now thrift-shop-attired teenager.

"That would be really nice, Evie," says Zoe.

"Sure," says the waitress, touching her on the shoulder.

"You know her name?" I ask, once Evie has disappeared behind the counter.

"She's been waiting on us for years."

"Yes, but she's never told us her name."

"You never asked her." Zoe's eyes suddenly fill with tears.

"You're crying, Zoe. Why are you crying? Over Jude? That's ridiculous."

"Shut up, Mom."

"That's one. You get one shut-up a month and that's it. You've used it up. I can't believe you're crying over that boy. In fact, I'm furious you're crying over him. He hurt you," I say.

"You know what, Mom," she snaps. "You think you know everything about me. I know you think you do, but you know what? You don't."

My phone chimes. Is it a new message from Researcher 101? I try and mask the hopeful look on my face.

Zoe shakes her head. "What's wrong with you?"

"Nothing's wrong," I say, reaching into my bag and grabbing the phone. I glance at the screen quickly. It's a Facebook notification alerting me that I've been tagged in a photo. Oh, goodie. I'm probably wearing a djellaba.

"Sorry." I shut my phone off.

"You're so jumpy," says Zoe. "It's like you're hiding something." She stares plaintively at my phone.

"Well, I'm not, but why shouldn't I be? I'm allowed to have a private life. I'm sure you've got secrets, too," I say, looking plaintively at her sandwich. Two bites, maybe three—that's what I'm betting she'll eat.

"Yes, but I'm fifteen. I *should* have secrets."

"Of course you're allowed to have secrets, Zoe. But not everything has to be a secret. You can still confide in me, you know."

"*You* shouldn't have secrets," says Zoe. "You're way too old. That's disgusting."

I sigh. I'm not going to get anything out of her.

"Here's your milk," says Evie, returning to the table.

"Thanks, Evie," whispers Zoe, her eyes still moist.

"Is everything okay?" Evie asks.

Zoe shoots a dirty look across the table at me.

"Evie, I owe you an apology. I never asked you your name. I should have. It's a terribly rude thing that I never did and I'm really, really sorry."

"Are you saying you'd like a glass of milk, too, sweetheart?" she asks me gently.

I look down into my plate. "Yes, please."

John Yossarian *added Favorite Quotations*
Omit needless words.—E. B. White

Just saying hello, Researcher 101.

Hello.

Lunchtime—grilled ham and cheese.

Grilled ham & cheese. Never use "and" when an ampersand will do. 2nd Favorite Quotation: Omit adverbial dialogue tags.*—Researcher 101*

Sunny here, she said sunnily.

Cloudy here.

I'm a bad mother.

No you aren't.

I'm a tired mother.

Understandable.

I'm a tired wife.

And I'm a tired husband.

You are?

Sometimes, he said, disinhibitingly.

"Omit invented words." —Wife 22

47. Ages: 19–27: Three plus days a week (the plus being active sex life, actually a bit of a slut). Ages 28–35: Two minus days a week (the minus being pregnancy, infants, no sleep=no libido). Ages 36–40: Seven plus days a week (the plus being desperate, the big 4-0 looming, making an effort to have active sex life so don't feel like sex life is over). Ages: 41–44: One minus days a month (the minus being when asked by doctor say five days a week, even doctor not fooled, she says five days a week doing what? Chair dancing?).

48. This is an utterly annoying question—pass!!!

49. Shah Jahan and Mumtaz Mahal, Abigail and John Adams, Paul Newman and Joanne Woodward.

50. Ben Harper. Ed Harris (I have a thing for bald men with beautifully shaped heads). Christopher Plummer.

51. Marion Cotillard (but not in Edith Piaf movie where she shaved her hairline). Halle Berry. Cate Blanchett (*especially* in Queen Elizabeth movie). Helen Mirren.

52. Frequently.

53. I put my key in the lock and opened the door. William was working. He held up his hand. "Don't move," he said. He picked up his pad of paper and began to read out loud.

PEAVEY PATTERSON BRAINSTORMING SESSION
CLIENT: ALICE A
CREATIVE: WILLIAM B
TOPIC: THINGS ALICE SHOULD NEVER WORRY ABOUT

1. If her hair is too long (only too long if down to ankles and impedes ability to walk)

2. If she forgot to put on lipstick (doesn't need lipstick—lips a perfectly lovely shade of raspberry)

3. If you can see through her dress (Yes)

4. If she should have worn a slip to work today (No)

"You ass! I've been walking around all day with my underwear showing? Why didn't anybody tell me?"

"I just told you."

"You should have told me earlier. I'm so embarrassed."

"Don't be. It was the highlight of my day. Come here," William said.

"No," I said, pouting.

He dramatically swept the table clean of all his papers. Who did he think he was? Mickey Rourke in *9½ Weeks*? God, I loved that movie. After I saw it I bought a garter belt and stockings. I wore them for a few days, feeling very sexy, until I experienced a garter malfunction. Have you ever had a stocking suddenly pool around your ankle while you're in the process of boarding a bus? There is no quicker path to feeling like an old lady.

"Alice."

"What?"

"Come here *now*."

"I've always fantasized about having sex on a table but I'm not sure I'd recommend it," William said half an hour later.

"I concur, Mr. B."

"What did you think about the pitch?"

"I'm not sure the client will go for it."

"Why not?"

"The client thinks it's a bit too on-the-nose. Can we move this into the bedroom now?" In order to lie next to each other on the table, each of us had a leg and an arm dangling off.

"I've changed my mind. I like the table."

"Well," I said. "It's hard. I'll give you that." My hand traveled down his chest to his waist.

"That's the nature of a table," he said, covering my hand with his own, guiding it south.

"Always have to be in charge, don't you."

He groaned softly when I touched him. "I'll come up with a new pitch, Ms. A. I promise."

"Don't be stingy. Five new pitches. The client would like some choices."

In deference to Helen, not wanting to rub it in her face (this was my idea), we'd decided it was best if our relationship stayed secret at work. Keeping up the masquerade was both thrilling and exhausting. William passed by my cubicle at least ten times a day, and because I could see directly into his office (and whenever I looked, he was looking right back at me) I was in a constant state of arousal. Nights, I came home and collapsed from the effort of having to sublimate my desire all day. Then I sat around and thought about his Levi's. And how he looked in those Levi's. And when we did venture out, for a walk in the Public Garden or to a Red Sox game, or to the hinterlands of Allston to hear some alternative band, it was like we'd never done any of those things before. Boston was a new city with him by my side.

I'm sure we were extremely annoying. Especially to older couples that did not walk down the sidewalk hand in hand, who often didn't even seem to be speaking, a three-foot distance between them. I was incapable of understanding that their silence might be a comfortable, hard-won silence, a benefit that came from years of being together; I just thought how sad it was they had nothing to say to one another.

But never mind them. William kissed me deeply on the sidewalk, fed me bites of his pizza, and sometimes when nobody was looking, copped a quick feel. Outside of work we were either arm in arm or hands in each other's back pockets. I see these couples now, so smug, appearing to need nobody but one another, and it hurts to look at them. It's hard for me to believe that we were once one of those couples looking at people like us, thinking *if you're so damn unhappy why don't you just get divorced?*

49

Lucy Pevensie
Not a fan of Turkish Delight.
38 minutes ago

John Yossarian
Has a pain in his liver.
39 minutes ago

So sorry to hear you're feeling unwell, Researcher 101.

Thank you. I've been spending a lot of time in the infirmary.

I assume you'll still be in the infirmary tomorrow?

Yes, and the next day and the next and the next until this damn war is over.

But not so ill that—

I can't read your surveys—no. Never that ill.

Are you saying you like reading my answers, Researcher 101?

You describe things so colorfully.

I can't help it. I was a playwright once.

You're still a playwright.

No, I'm wan, boring, and absurd.

You're funny, too.

I'm quite certain my family would not agree.

Regarding #49. I'm curious. Have you ever been to the Taj Mahal?

I was there just last week. Courtesy of Google Earth. Have you ever been?

No, but it's on my list.

What else is on your list—and please don't say seeing the *Mona Lisa* at the Louvre.

Tying a cherry stem with my tongue.

Suggest you set the bar a little higher.

Standing atop an iceberg.

Higher.

Saving somebody's marriage.

Too high. Good luck on that.

So listen, I have to press you a bit further on your refusal to answer #48. Resistance of this sort usually indicates we've touched upon a hot-button topic.

You sound like the Borg.

I would guess your aversion has something to do with the way the question was posed?

Honestly I can't remember how it was posed.

It was posed in an entirely clichéd way.

Now I remember.

You're insulted by a question that has been so clearly designed for the masses. To be lumped into a group is an affront for you.

Now you sound like an astrologer. Or a human resources manager.

Perhaps I can ask #48 in a way that you might find more palatable.

Go right ahead, Researcher 101.

Describe the last time you felt cared for by your husband.

Come to think of it, I prefer the original question.

50

Alice Buckle
Bloated
24 minutes ago

Daniel Barbedian ▶ Linda Barbedian
You do realize posting on Facebook is not the same as texting, Mom.
34 minutes ago

Bobby Barbedian ▶ Daniel Barbedian
Check no longer in the mail. Tell Mom.
42 minutes ago

Linda Barbedian ▶ Daniel Barbedian
Check in the mail. Don't tell Dad.
48 minutes ago

Bobby Barbedian ▶ Daniel Barbedian
Tired of funding your social life. Get a job.
1 hour ago

William Buckle
Ina Garten—really? Golden raisins in classic gingerbread?
Yesterday

"I saw a mouse yesterday," says Caroline, unpacking vegetables from a canvas bag. "It ran under the fridge. I don't want to freak you out but that makes two this week, Alice. Maybe you should get a cat."

"We don't need a cat. We have Zoe. She's an expert mouse catcher," I say.

"Too bad she's still in school all day," says William.

"Well, maybe you can fill in for her," I say. "I'm sure she wouldn't mind."

"This rainbow chard looks amazing!" says Caroline.

"Except for those little bugs," I say. "Are those mites?"

William paws through the chard. "That's dirt, Alice, not mites."

William and Caroline are just back from an early-morning trip to the farmers' market.

"Was the bluegrass band there?" I ask him.

"No, but there was somebody playing 'It Had to Be You' on a suit-case."

"It's pretty," I say, fingering the yellow and magenta stalks, "but it seems like the color would leech out once you cook it."

"Maybe we should put it in a salad," suggests Caroline.

William snaps his fingers. "I've got it. Let's do Lidia's *strangozzi* with chard and almond sauce. Ina's gingerbread will be perfect for dessert."

"I vote for salad," I say, because if I am forced to eat another heavy meal I will *strangozzi* William. He's found a new hobby, or should I say reignited an old passion—cooking. Every night for the past week, we've sat down to elaborate meals that William and his sous-chef, yet-to-be-employed Caroline, have dreamed up. I'm not sure what I feel about this. A part of me is relieved to not have to shop, plan meals, and cook, but another part of me feels uprooted at the sudden shift in William's and my roles.

"I hope we have durum semolina," says William.

"Lidia uses half durum, half white flour," says Caroline.

Neither of them notices when I leave the kitchen to get ready for work.

There are only three weeks left before school ends, and these are the most stressful weeks of the year for me. I'm mounting six different plays—one for every grade. Yes, each play is only twenty minutes long, but believe me, that twenty-minute performance takes weeks of casting, staging, de-signing sets, and rehearsal.

When I walk into the classroom that morning, Carisa Norman is waiting for me. She begins crying as soon as she sees me. I know why she's crying—it's because I made her a goose. The third-grade play this semester is *Charlotte's Web*. I look at her tear-stained face and wonder why didn't I give her the role of Charlotte. She would have been perfect for it. Instead I made her one of three geese, and unfortunately geese have no lines. To make up for this, I told the geese they could honk whenever they wanted to. Trust themselves. They'd know when the honking moment was right. This was a mistake, because the honking moment turned out to be every moment of the play.

"Carisa, what's wrong, sweetheart? Why aren't you at recess?"

She hands me a plastic baggie. It looks like it's filled with oregano. I open the bag and sniff—it's marijuana.

"Carisa, where did you find this!"

Carisa shakes her head, distraught.

"Carisa, sweetheart, you have to tell me," I say, trying to hide the fact that I'm horrified. Kids are smoking pot in elementary school? Are they dealing, too?

"You're not going to get in trouble."

"My parents," she says.

"This belongs to your parents?" I ask.

I think her mother is on the board of the Parents' Association. Oh, this is not good.

She nods. "Will you give it to the police? That's what you're supposed to do if you're a kid and find drugs."

"And how do you know that?"

"*CSI Miami*," she says solemnly.

"Carisa, I want you to go enjoy recess and don't give this another thought. I'll take care of it."

She throws her arms around me. Her barrette is about to fall off. I re-clip it, pulling the hair back from her eyes.

"Shut the worry switch off, okay?" This is something I used to say to my kids before they went to bed. When did I stop doing this? Maybe I should reinstitute the ritual. I wish somebody would switch off my worry.

· · ·

In between classes I fight with myself over the proper course of action. I should take the pot directly to the principal and tell her exactly what happened—that sweet Carisa Norman narced on her parents. But if I do, there's a possibility the principal might call the police. I don't want that, of course, but doing nothing is not an option either, given Carisa's emotionally labile state. If there's one thing I know about third-graders, it's that most of them are incapable of hiding anything—eventually they will confess. Carisa can't take back what she knows.

At lunch, I lock the classroom door and Google "medical marijuana" on my laptop. Maybe the Normans have a medical marijuana card. But if they did, surely the marijuana would be dispensed in a prescription bottle—not a ziplock baggie. Maybe I could ask a professional how they typically dispense their wares. I click on *Find a Dispensary Near You* and am about to choose between Foggy Daze and the Green Cross when my cell rings.

"Can you do me a favor and pick Jude up from school today? This bloody deposition is running late," says Nedra.

"Nedra—perfect timing. Remember you said that thing about not informing on kids to their parents when we went to *How to Keep Your Kids from Turning into Meth Addicts* night at school? That I should learn to keep my mouth shut?"

"It depends on the circumstances. Is it about sex?" says Nedra.

"Yes, I'll pick up Jude and no, it's not about sex."

"STDs?"

"No."

"General all-around sluttiness?"

"No."

"Plagiarism?"

"No."

"Drugs?"

"Yes."

"Hard drugs?"

"Is pot classified as a hard drug?"

"What happened," sighs Nedra. "Is it Zoe or Peter?"

"Neither—it's a third-grader. She narced on her parents, and my question is should I narc on her narc back to her parents?"

Nedra pauses. "Well, my advice is still no, stay out of it. But trust your intuition, darling. You've got good instincts."

Nedra's wrong about that. My instincts are like my memory—they both started fizzling out after forty or so years.

Please go to voice mail, please go to voice mail, please go to voice mail.

"Hello."

"Oh, hi. Hiiiiii. Is this Mrs. Norman?"

"This is she."

I ramble. "How are you? Hope I haven't caught you at a bad time. Sounds like you're in the car. Hope the traffic isn't bad. But jeez, it's always bad. This is the Bay Area after all. But a small price to pay for all this abundance, right?"

"Who is this?"

"Oh—sorry! This is Alice Buckle, Carisa's drama teacher?"

"Yes."

I've been teaching drama long enough to know when I'm talking to a mother who's nursing a grudge over me casting her child as a goose in the third-grade play.

"Ah, well, it seems we have a situation."

"Oh—is Carisa having a problem learning her lines?"

See?

"So listen. Carisa came into school quite upset today."

"Uh-huh."

The brusqueness of her voice throws me off. "You allow her to watch *CSI Miami*?" I ask.

Oh, God, Alice.

"Is that why you're calling me? She has an older brother. I can't possibly be expected to screen everything Carisa sees."

"That's not why I'm calling. Carisa brought in a baggie full of pot. *Your* pot."

Silence. More silence. Did she hear what I said? Has she put me on mute? Is she crying?

"Mrs. Norman?"

"That's simply out of the question. My daughter did not bring in a bag of pot."

"Yes, well, I understand this is a delicate situation, but she did bring in a bag of pot because I'm holding it in my hands right now."

"Impossible," she says.

This is the grown woman's version of putting her hands over her ears and humming so she doesn't have to hear what you're saying.

"Are you saying I'm lying?"

"I'm saying you must be mistaken."

"You know, I'm doing you a favor. I could lose my job over this. I could have brought this to the principal. But I didn't because of Carisa. And the fact that you might have some medical condition for which you have a medical marijuana card."

"A medical condition?"

Doesn't she understand I'm trying to give her an out?

"Yes—plenty of people use marijuana for medical reasons; it's nothing to be embarrassed about. Minor things, like anxiety or depression."

"I am neither anxious nor depressed, Ms. Buckle, and I appreciate your concern—but if you insist on continuing to harass me I'll have to do something about it."

Mrs. Norman hangs up.

After work I drive to McDonald's and throw the baggie full of pot into the Dumpster behind the restaurant. Then I drive away like a fugitive, by which I mean obsessively looking into my rearview mirror and driving twenty miles an hour in a forty-mile-an-hour zone, praying there wasn't a video camera in the McDonald's parking lot. Why is everybody so rude? Why won't we help each other? And when *was* the last time I felt truly cared for by my husband?

51

**KED3 (Kentwood Elementary Third Grade Drama Parents' Forum)
Digest #129**
KED3ParentsForum@yahoogroups.com

<u>Messages in this digest (5)</u>

1. Was it fair of Alice Buckle to give the geese no lines? Weigh in, people!
Posted by: Queenbeebeebee

2. RE: Was it fair of Alice Buckle to give the geese no lines? Look, I know
this will likely be an unpopular position, but I'm just going to come right out
and say it. It's not realistic to think that every kid in the play will have a line.
It's just not possible. Not with thirty kids in the class. Some years your kids
will get lucky and get a good role. And some years they won't. It all bal-
ances out in the end. **Posted by: Farmymommy**

3. RE: Was it fair of Alice Buckle to give the geese no lines? No! It's not fair.
And it doesn't all balance out. Alice Buckle is a hypocrite! Do you think she
ever cast her children as geese? I think not and I can prove it. I have all the
school play programs dating back ten years. Her daughter Zoe was Mrs.
Squash, Narrator #1, Lion Tamer with Arm in Cast and Lazy Bee. Her son
Peter was Fractious Elf, Slightly Overweight Troll, Bovine Buffoon (everybody wanted that role) and Walnut. Alice Buckle has just gotten lazy. How
hard can it be to make sure each child has at least one line? Perhaps Mrs.
Buckle has been teaching drama for too long. Perhaps she should think of
retiring. **Posted by: Helicopmama**

4. RE: Was it fair of Alice Buckle to give the geese no lines? I have to agree
with Helicopmama. Something is very off with Mrs. Buckle. Shouldn't she be

keeping track of each class? The plays they've done and the roles each kid has performed over the years? That way she could make sure everything was equitable. If your child had a one-line role last year, well, then this year they should have a lead. And if they have no lines—well, don't even get me started. That is simply unacceptable. My daughter is heartbroken. *Heartbroken.* **Posted by: Storminnormandy**

5. RE: Was it fair of Alice Buckle to give the geese no lines? May I make an observation? I'm pretty sure that how many lines your child has in his or her third-grade play will have no bearing on his future. Absolutely none. And if, in fact, I'm wrong, and it does, I would ask you this: consider the possibility that a small role might be a good thing. Perhaps those children who had only one-line roles (or perhaps, no lines at all) will end up with higher self-esteem. Why? Because they will have learned from an early age to deal with disappointment and to make the best of a situation and to not quit or throw a tantrum when something doesn't go their way. There are plenty of things going on in this world right now that are worthy of being heartbroken over. The third-grade play is not one of them. **Posted by: Davidmametlurve182**

52

54. "Hi, Mama," she shouted cheerfully, when we pulled up to the curb. It was nearly midnight, and William and I were picking her up from the last dance of the school year.

She stuck her head in my window and giggled. "Can we give Jew a ride home?"

"Who?" I said.

"Jew!"

"Jude," interpreted William. "Goddammit, she's wasted."

William quickly rolled the car windows up, just seconds before she threw up on the passenger-seat door.

"Got your phone?" asked William.

We knew this moment would come, we had discussed our plan, and now we sprung into action. I bolted out of the car, my iPhone in hand, and started taking photos. I got some classic shots. Zoe, leaning against the car door, her fleur-de-lys crinoline splattered in vomit. Zoe, climbing into the backseat, shoeless, her sweaty hair stuck to the back of her neck. Zoe on the drive home, her head lolling on the seat; her mouth wide open. And the saddest one: her father carrying her into the house.

We had gotten this advice from friends. When she got wasted—and she *would* get wasted, it wasn't a matter of *if*, but *when*—we should document the whole thing because she'd be too drunk to remember any of the details.

It may sound hard core but it worked. The next morning when we showed her the photos she was so horrified that, to the best of my knowledge, she hasn't ever gotten drunk again.

55. I had William all wrong. He wasn't some blue-blood, entitled, silver-spoon, Ivy League elitist. Everything he had he'd worked his ass off for, including a full scholarship to Yale.

"Beer?" his father, Hal, said to me, holding the refrigerator door open.

"Would you like Bud Light, Bud Light, or Bud Light?" asked William.

"I'll take a Bud Light," I said.

"I like her," said Hal. "The last one drank water. No ice." Hal gave me a huge grin. "Helen. She didn't stand a chance once you came into the picture, right, slim? You don't mind if I call you slim?"

"Only if you called Helen that, too."

"Helen was not slim. Zaftig, maybe."

I was in love with Hal already.

"I see where William gets his charm."

"William is lots of things," said Hal. "Driven, ambitious, smart, arrogant, but charming he is not."

"I'm working on that," I said.

"What are you making for dinner?" asked Hal.

"Beef stroganoff," said William, unpacking the bag of groceries we'd brought.

"My favorite," said Hal. "I'm sorry Fiona couldn't make it."

"Don't apologize for Mom. It's not your fault," said William.

"She wanted to come," said Hal.

"Right," said William.

William's parents divorced when he was ten and his mother, Fiona, very quickly remarried a man with two other children. Hal and Fiona had a split custody agreement at first, but by the time William was twelve he was living with his dad full-time. William and Fiona weren't close and he saw her infrequently, on holidays and special occasions. Another surprise. Both of us un-mothered.

56. I saved you an egg.

57. Don't worry. I'll take care of that.

53

John Yossarian *changed his profile picture*

So cute, Researcher 101! What's her name?

I'm sorry but I can't divulge that information.

Okay. Can you divulge what you like most about her?

Him. The way he touches his cold nose to my hand at six every morning. Just once. Then sits at attention by the side of the bed waiting patiently for me to wake.

So sweet—what else?

Well, right now he's pushing his snout under my arm as I attempt to chat with yousdfsfd. Sorry. He gets jealous when I'm on the computer.

You're very lucky. He sounds like a dream dog.

Oh, he is.

I do not have a dream dog. In fact, our dog is so ill behaved my husband wants to give him away.

It can't be that bad.

He peed on my husband's pillow. I'm afraid to have guests come over.

You should do some training.

Training is not the issue.

Of your husband.

Ha!

I'm not kidding. Loving an animal doesn't come naturally to everybody. Some people have to be taught.

I don't agree. You shouldn't have to teach love.

Spoken by somebody to whom love comes easily.

What makes you say that, Researcher 101?

I can read between the lines.

The lines of my answers?

Yes.

Well, I'm not sure love comes easily, but I will say it is my default setting.

I've got to go. I'll be emailing the next survey in a few days.

Wait—before you leave I wanted to ask you. Is everything okay? This is the first time you've been on Facebook in days.

Nothing's wrong, just busy.

I was worried you might be angry.

This is what I hate about communicating online. There's no way to judge tone.

So you're not angry.

Why would I be angry?

I thought I might have offended you in some way.

By doing what?

Not answering your revised #48.

You're allowed to take a pass on any question.

So I haven't offended you?

You've done nothing to offend me—quite the opposite, actually—that's the problem.

54

Shonda Perkins
PX90 30 days in!!
12 minutes ago

William Buckle
Dog. Yours for free. Must like being bitten.
One day ago

William Buckle
Recent Activity
William Buckle and Helen Davies are now friends
Two days ago

"Mail," announces Peter, dropping an *AARP* magazine on my desk. He peers over my shoulder. "What's with all the Dad postings? And who's Helen Davies?"

"Somebody we used to work with."

"Did she friend you, too?"

No, Helen Davies, *Helen of Troy*, did not friend me, too. She only friended my husband. Or he friended her. Does it matter who friended whom? Yes, it probably does.

I glare at the silver-haired couple on the cover of the *AARP* magazine. Damn it! I do not want to take advantage of a special offer for cataract drops, nor do I care to consider my line of sight above the steering wheel because I am NOT fifty and I won't be fifty for another six years. Why do they keep sending me copies of their magazine? I thought I had taken care of this. Just last month I called AARP to explain that the Alice Buckle who recently turned fifty lived in Charleston, South Carolina, in a lovely old house with a huge wraparound porch. "And how did I know this?" they asked. "Because I Google Earthed her," I told them. "Google Earth Alice Buckle in Oakland, California, and you will find a woman standing in her driveway hurling an *AARP* magazine back at her mailman."

Old girlfriends resurfacing. Getting retirement magazines before your time. This is not a good way to start off my Saturday. I Google Monkey Yoga. There's a class in twenty minutes. If I hurry I can make it.

"And—*shavasana*, everybody."

Finally, corpse pose! My favorite part of yoga. I roll over onto my back. Usually by the end of the class I'm nearly asleep. Not today. Even my fingertips are pulsing with energy. I should be running with Caroline—not doing sun salutations.

"Eyes shut," says the teacher, walking around the room.

I stare up at the ceiling.

"Empty your mind."

What the hell is happening to me?

"For those of you that want a mantra, try *Ong So Hung*."

How can she say that with a straight face?

"This means 'Creator, I am Thou.'"

I don't need a mantra. I have a mantra that I've been repeating obsessively for the past twenty-four hours. *You've done nothing to offend me— quite the opposite, actually—that's the problem.*

"Alice, try to stop fidgeting," the teacher whispers, stopping at my mat. I close my eyes. She squats and puts the palm of her hand on my solar plexus.

That's the problem? Let's tease that sentence apart for the fiftieth time. The problem is I don't offend him. The problem is he wishes I would offend him. The problem is he wishes I would offend him because I'm doing the opposite. What's the opposite of offend? To please. To give pleasure. The problem is I'm giving him pleasure. Too much pleasure. Oh, God.

"Breathe, Alice, breathe."

My eyes snap open.

• • •

I'm in the dressing room, changing out of my yoga gear, when a naked woman walks by on her way to the shower. Nudity is not something I'm comfortable with. Of course I might feel differently if I had a fabulous body like this woman, perfectly groomed, manicured, pedicured, her pubic hair completely waxed off.

I stare for a moment—I can't help it; I've never seen an actual live woman with a Brazilian. Is this what men like? Is this what gives them *pleasure*?

After my yoga class, Nedra and I meet for lunch. Just as she's biting into her burrito I ask, "Do you wax down there?"

Nedra puts down her burrito and sighs.

"Of course it's fine if you don't. There might be different pubic-hair rules for lesbians."

"I wax, darling," says Nedra.

"How much?"

"All of it."

"You've been getting Brazilians?" I cry. "And you didn't tell me I should be getting them, too?"

"Technically, it's called a Hollywood if you take everything off. You want the number of the place I go? Ask for Hilary. She's the best and she's quick; it barely hurts. Now can we talk about something else? Perhaps a topic more suitable for daylight?"

"Okay. What's an antonym for 'offend'?"

Nedra stares at me suspiciously. "Have you lost weight?"

"Why, do I look like I have?"

"Your face is skinnier. Are you working out?"

"I'm working too much to work out. School ends in two weeks. I'm juggling six plays."

"Well, you look good," says Nedra. "And you're not wearing fleece for once. I can actually see your body. I like the tank-and-cardi look. It suits you. You have a very sexy neck, Alice."

"A sexy neck?" I think of Researcher 101. I think I should show Nedra Lucy Pevensie's Facebook page.

Nedra picks up her cellphone. "I'm going to call Hilary and make you an appointment because I know you'll never do it." She punches in the number, has a quick conversation, utters a *thank you darling*, and snaps her cell shut. "She had a cancellation. She can take you in an hour. My treat."

"Nedra said you're quick. And painless."

"I do my best. Have you considered *vajazzling*? Or *vatooing*?" asks Hilary.

Does this woman really expect me to have a conversation about *vajazzes* when she's about to apply hot wax to my *vatoo*?

Hilary stirs the pot of wax with a tongue depressor. "Let's take a look, shall we?" She lifts the paper thong and *tsk*s. "Someone hasn't been keeping up with their waxing."

"It's been a while," I say.

"How long?"

"Forty-four years."

Hilary's eyes widen. "Wow—a waxing virgin. We don't get too many of those. Never even had the bikini line waxed?"

"Well, I keep things tidy. I shave."

"Doesn't count. Why don't we start with a Brazilian with a two-inch strip? More of an American, really. We'll ease you into it."

"No—I want a Hollywood. That's what everybody does these days, right?"

"A lot of younger people do. But most women your age tend to just neaten things up."

"I want it all off," I say.

"All right," says Hilary.

She folds one side of the paper thong back and I close my eyes. The hot wax drips onto my skin. I tense up, expecting it to burn, but surprisingly it feels good. This isn't so bad. Hilary lays down a cloth strip and smooths it.

"I'm going to count to three," she says.

I grab her wrist, suddenly panicked. "I'm not ready."

She looks at me calmly.

"No, please. Okay, wait, wait, just give me a sec—I'm almost ready."

"One," she says and rips off the strip.

I shriek. "What happened to 'two'?"

"It's better to be surprised," she says, surveying the area, frowning. "You don't use retinol products, do you?"

On my *vatoo*, no.

"The first time is the worst. Each time it will be easier." She hands me a mirror.

"I don't need to see," I say, tears springing to my eyes. "Just finish it."

"Are you sure?" she asks. "Do you want to take a break?"

"No," I practically shout.

She raises her eyebrows at me.

"I'm sorry. What I meant to say is please keep going before I lose my nerve, and I'll do my very best not to cry."

"It's all right if you do. You wouldn't be the first," she says.

I waltz out of Hilary's shop with a half-off coupon for my next wax and an aftercare admonition (DO NOT take any Dead Sea salt baths for at least twenty-four hours—no problem there, Hilary) and a sexy little secret that nobody knows but me. I smile at other women I pass on the street, feeling like I've joined the tribe of impeccably groomed women, women who are taking care of business *down there*. I feel so lighthearted (and relieved I don't have to endure that pain for another month) that I stop at Green Light Books to look at magazines, something I rarely do because I'm always in such a hurry.

Michelle Williams is on the cover of *Vogue*. Apparently, according to *Vogue*, MiWi is the new it-girl. There's a two-page spread of MiWi's Night on the Town in Austin. Here's the lovely MiWi taking a dip at Barton Springs. Here she is sitting at the bar at Fado, drinking a Green Flash Le Freak. And here she is an hour later trying on the skinniest, hottest jeans at Luxe Apothetique. Wasn't Michelle the it-girl two years ago, too? Do they recycle it-girls? That doesn't seem fair. Shouldn't they give other it-girls like me a chance?

IT-GIRL ALICE BUCKLE'S NIGHT OUT FROM ANSWERING THE PHONE TO PARKING, TO SINGING HORRIBLY OFF KEY IN THE CAR. FOUR HOURS WITH ALBU ON A FRIDAY NIGHT

6:01 P.M.: Answering her cellphone (something she will later regret)

"Yes, of course I want to go to a movie about a beautiful French woman who owns a banana plantation in the Congo who is eventually macheted to death by the men she used to employ," says Alice Buckle, a forty-four-year-old mother and wife who unfortunately *still* doesn't have a bikini body even though she's lost eight pounds recently (the truth is, 130 pounds at forty-four looks very different from 130 pounds at twenty-four). "I'm looking forward to having a man with extremely long legs knee my chair for the entire show," says Alice.

6:45 P.M.: AlBu spotted hyperventilating

It-girl Alice Buckle circles around and around the mall parking lot looking for a spot, muttering "get the hell out of my way, cow," to all the people who are also circling around the mall parking lot looking for a spot. "What the hell, I'll just park illegally," cries Alice. "It could be worse," she laughs gaily, as she runs to the theater. "This could be opening night for *Toy Story 8*."

6:55 P.M: AlBu in enormous line at ticket counter

"It's opening night for *Toy Story 8*," reports Alice Buckle.

7:20 P.M.: It-Girl Alice Buckle crawling over a bunch of old people in her not-ready-for-bikini body to get to the seat her best friend, Nedra, saved for her

"You just missed the best part—where the son was conscripted into the Hutu army," says Nedra.

7:25 P.M.: AlBu fast asleep

9:32 P.M.: AlBu spotted pulling into neighbor's driveway mistaking it for her own

AlBu's night vision is impaired. Her mood darkens, worrying about early-onset macular degeneration. Mood improves after listening to "Dance with Me" by Orleans in the car. "This reminds me so much of high school," she cries, then she really begins to cry. "It's so unfair. How come French women look so good without makeup? Maybe if every woman in America stopped wearing makeup we'd all look good, too. After a few months, that is."

10:51 P.M.: AlBu goes to bed without washing off her makeup

"It was a magical night, but I won't lie. Being an it-girl is exhausting," admits Alice as she crawls into bed. "Roll over, darling, you're snoring," she says, tapping her husband on the shoulder, who promptly licks her on the face. "Jampo!" Alice cries, gathering up her tiny dog in her arms. "I thought you were William!" It's hard to be angry at the dog for kicking her husband out of bed when he's so cute and spirited to boot. The two snuggle up together and in a few hours, Alice wakes to find the nice present Jampo has left on her husband's pillow.

· · ·

"Excuse me, but are you planning on buying that magazine?" interrupts a young saleswoman.

"Oh—sorry." I close the *Vogue*, smoothing out the cover. "Why, do you want to look at it?"

She points to a handwritten sign. "You're not allowed to read the magazines. We try and keep them pristine for people who are actually buying them."

"Really? Then how are you supposed to know if you want to buy them?"

"Look on the cover. The cover tells you everything that's inside." She gives me a dirty look.

I put the magazine back on the rack. "This is exactly why magazines are dying," I say.

That night, while the kids are cleaning up after dinner, I announce to William that something about cookies is wrong with my computer and will he please come help me. This is a lie. I'm perfectly capable of getting rid of my own cookies.

"Peter can help you," he says.

"It's easy, Mom. All you do is go to preferences and—"

"I've already tried that," I interrupt. "It's more complicated. William, I need you to take a look."

I follow him into my office and shut the door.

"It's no big deal," he says, walking to my desk. "You click on the apple, then go—"

I unbutton my jeans and slip them off.

"To preferences," he finishes.

"William," I say, stepping out of my panties.

He turns around and stares at me and says nothing.

"Ta-da."

He has a strange look on his face. I can't tell if he's appalled or turned on.

"I did this for you," I say.

"You did not," he says.

"Who else would I do it for?"

What was I thinking? This is completely backfiring. Isn't sudden bikini-line grooming one of the sure signs that your spouse is cheating on you? I'm not cheating, but I am flirting with a man who is not my husband who has just admitted I bring him pleasure, which has brought me pleasure, which has resulted in a sudden surge in my libido, which has led to the first bikini wax of my life. Does that count? Is it possible he knows?

William makes a strange sound in the back of his throat. "You did it for you. Admit it."

I begin to shake. The tiniest little bit.

"Come here, Alice."

I hesitate.

"*Now*," he whispers.

We proceed to have the hottest sex we've had in months.

55

58. *Planet of the Apes.*

59. Not much. Well, hardly ever. I don't really see the point. We have to live with each other, so what's the use and honestly, who's got the energy? We used to, in the early years. Our biggest argument happened before we were even married, and it was over me wanting to invite Helen to the wedding. I told him it would be a nice conciliatory gesture—she probably wouldn't come, but inviting her was the right thing to do, especially since we were inviting almost all of our colleagues from Peavey Patterson. When he told me he had no intention of inviting a woman who called me a whore (and who seemed to hate him vehemently) to his wedding, I reminded him that technically I *was* the other woman when she called me that name, and could we blame her for hating us? Wasn't it time to forgive and forget? After I said that, he told me I could afford to be generous because I'd won. Well, that so infuriated me that I took off my engagement ring and threw it out the window.

Now, this wasn't a ring from Zales, this was my mother's engagement ring that had been in her family for years, brought over by her mother from Ireland. It wasn't worth much—it was one small diamond flanked by two tiny emeralds. What *was* priceless about the ring was its history and the fact that my father had given it to William to give to me. There was an engraving inside the band. Something terribly sweet, probably bordering on saccharine, that I can't recall. All I can remember is the word "heart."

The problem was we were in the car when I threw the ring out of the window. We had just left my father's house and were driving past the park in Brockton when William made the comment about me having *won*. I just wanted to scare him. I hurled the ring out the window into the park and we proceeded to speed by, both of us in shock. We drove back and tried to pinpoint the spot where I had thrown it, but even though we searched through the grass methodically we couldn't find it. I was devastated. Each of us secretly blamed the other. He blamed me, of course, for throwing the ring. I blamed him for being so coldhearted. The loss of the ring deeply unsettled both of us. Losing, or in my case, throwing away, something so priceless before we had even started our lives together—was this a bad omen?

I couldn't bear to tell my father the truth, so we lied and told him our apartment was robbed and the ring stolen. We even planned what to say if he asked why I hadn't been wearing it at the time. I took it off because I was giving myself a facial and didn't want to get the green gunk caught in the delicate filigree setting, which I would then have to root out with a toothpick or a dental probe. I have since learned that when lying, it's best not to offer up any details. It's the details that do you in.

60. "Lo-lee-ta: the tip of the tongue taking a trip of three steps down the palate to tap, at three, on the teeth. Lo. Lee. Ta."

61. Long, tapered fingers. Big palms. Cuticles that never needed to be pushed back. Chet Baker on the tape player. He was cutting peppers for the salad. I looked at those hands and thought, I am going to have this man's children.

62. What would you do if you ever stopped communicating? I wrote "That would NEVER EVER happen. William and I talk about everything. That won't be our problem." And no, it does not hold true today.

63. In the backyard of my cousin Henry's apartment in the North End, which overlooked Boston Harbor. It was in the evening. The air smelled of the sea and garlic. Our wedding bands were simple and plain, which felt right after the engagement ring debacle. If my father was upset about the ring, he didn't say anything. In fact, he said very little that night, he was so overcome with emotion. Every five minutes or so before the ceremony started he would clasp my shoulders vigorously and nod. When it was time to give me away, he walked me to the arbor, lifted my veil, and kissed me on the cheek. "Off you go, honey," he said, and that's when I began to cry. I proceeded to cry through the entire ceremony, which understandably threw William off. "It's all right," he kept mouthing to me while the priest did his part. "I know," I kept mouthing back to him. I wasn't crying because I was getting married, I was crying because my history with my father had come down to those four, perfectly chosen words. He could only say something that appeared to be so mundane precisely because our life together had been the opposite.

Did u read article advising everybody eat more cheese, Alice?

Why you ignore my texts, Alice?

HonE?

Sorry Dad. End of the school year. 2 busy 2 text. 2 busy to read. 2 busy to eat.

I worry u not eating enuf cheese. Women yr age need protein and calcium. Hope you not turn vegan out there Cali.

Trust me. U needn't worry about my cheese intake.

News. Think might B falling in love.

What??? With who??

Conchita.

Conchita Martinez, our neighbor Conchita whose son Jeff I dated and then dumped my senior year?

Yes! That the one. She remember you fondly. Jeff, no so much. He harbor long grudge.

Why you sound like Indian in *The Great Sioux Uprising*? Are u spending a lot of time together?

Ever night. Hr house or mine. Mostly mine due to fact Jeff still live at home. Loser.

Oh, Dad—so happy for u.

Happy u, too. U hippily married all these years. Very proud. All turned out okay, for us, but do me favor—eat wheel of Brie today. Afraid u will collapse. U delicate flower u.

John Yossarian
Speaking plainly is underrated.
23 minutes ago

Okay, I'm worried that I'm becoming a problem for you, Researcher 101.

How so, Wife 22?

I'm not offending you enough.

I can't disagree with that.

Fine. I'll do my best to offend you more in the future because according to antonym.com pleasure is the opposite of offense, and I wouldn't inadvertently want to give you pleasure.

One cannot be held responsible for the way one is received.

To give you pleasure was never my intention.

Is this your idea of speaking plainly, Wife 22?

You know it's strange. The way our conversations go on and on. It's like a river. We just keep jumping in and diving under the water. When we surface we may find we've drifted miles from where we were last time we spoke but it doesn't matter. It's still the same river. I tap you on the shoulder. You turn around. You call out. I answer.

I'm sorry you lost your engagement ring. It sounds like a very traumatic event. Did you ever tell your father the truth?

No, and I've always regretted it.

Why not tell him now?

Too many years have passed. What's the point? It will just upset him.

Did you know that according to synonym.net, the definition of problem *is a state of difficulty that needs to be resolved.*

Is this *your* idea of speaking plainly, Researcher 101?

After communicating with you all these weeks I can definitively say you, Wife 22, are in need of some resolution.

I can't disagree with that.

I can also say (a little less definitively for fear of putting you off) I would like to be the one that resolves you.

58

64. Three months into my pregnancy with Zoe, I was wretchedly sick but doing a good job of hiding it. I had actually lost five pounds from morning sickness, so nobody at the theater could tell I was pregnant—except of course for laser-eyed Bunny, who guessed my secret the instant she saw me. We had only met once before in Boston after she contacted me with the incredible news that *The Barmaid* won the contest. She immediately let me know that even though my script had won, it needed work. She asked if I was willing to do some rewriting. I said I was, of course, but assumed the changes would be minor.

I arrived in Blue Hill on a September afternoon. The past few weeks hadn't been easy. William did not want me to go—certainly not when I was so sick. We had a fight over breakfast and I had stormed out, accusing him of trying to sabotage my career. I felt awful for the entire ride, but now that I stood in the doorway of the theater looking down at the stage I was light-headed with excitement. Here it was, spread out before me; my life as a real playwright was about to begin. The Blue Hill Theater smelled exactly the way a theater should smell, the top notes of dust and paper, the base notes of popcorn and cheap wine. I hugged my script to my chest and walked down the aisle to greet Bunny.

"Alice! You're pregnant," she said. "Congratulations! Hungry?" She held out a box of Little Debbie snack cakes.

"How did you know? I'm only twelve weeks along. I'm not even showing."

"Your nose. It's swollen."

"It is?" I said, touching it.

"Not hideously. Just the eensiest bit. Happens to most women, but they don't notice because the membranes swell over the course of the pregnancy, just not all at once."

"Look, I'd appreciate if you didn't tell anybody—"

The cloyingly sweet smell of Bunny's open snack cake drifted into my nostrils and I clapped my hand over my mouth.

"Lobby, take a right," Bunny instructed, and I ran back up the aisle and to the bathroom to throw up.

Those weeks of rehearsal were intense. Day after day I sat beside Bunny in the darkened theater, where she tried to mentor me. At first, most of Bunny's suggestions were along the lines of encouraging me to move beyond cliché. "I just don't believe it, Alice," she'd often say of a scene. "People don't talk this way in real life." As the rehearsals went on, she got tougher and more insistent, because it was clear to her something was not working. She kept pushing me to find the nuance and shading she believed the characters were missing. But I didn't agree. I thought the depth was there; she just wasn't seeing it yet.

One week before opening night, the lead quit. The first dress rehearsal was a disaster; the second just a little bit better, and finally, in the eleventh hour I saw *The Barmaid* through Bunny's eyes and was horrified. She was right. The play was a caricature. A bold, shiny surface, but little substance beneath. All curtain but no stage.

At that point it was too late to make any changes. I had to let the play go. It would catch a stiff wind or founder all on its own.

Opening night went well. The theater was packed. I prayed it would all come miraculously together that evening and judging by the enthusiastic crowd, that appeared to be the case. William was by my side the entire night. I had a small baby bump now, which brought out his protective instincts; his hand was a constant presence on the small of my back. The next morning came a rave review from the *Portland Press Herald*. The entire cast celebrated by taking a cruise on a lobster boat. Some of us got drunk. Others of us (me) threw up. None of us knew this was the single moment in the sun *The Barmaid* would get, but does anybody ever suspect that the magic is about to end just when the magical thing is unfolding?

I won't say that William was happy that the play flopped, but I will say he was happy to have me home, getting ready for the baby. He didn't go so far as to say I told you so, but anytime Bunny emailed me another bad review (she was not one of those directors who believed in ignoring your reviews—quite the opposite, she was in the you-get-enough-bad-reviews-you-become-inoculated camp) he got this grim look on his face that I could only read as embarrassment. Somehow my public failure had become his. He didn't have to advise me not to write another play; I came to that decision all on my own. I convinced myself there was a three-act structure to pregnancy, a beginning, middle, and end. I was in essence a living play, and for now that would have to be enough.

65. I know "roommate" is a taboo word, but here's a thought: what if being roommates is the natural stage of the middle part of marriage? What if that's the way it's supposed to be? The *only* way we *can* be while getting through the long, hard slog of raising kids and trying to save money for retirement and coming to terms with the fact that there is no such thing as retirement anymore and we'll be working until the day we die?

66. Fifteen minutes ago.

59

"Yum," says Caroline.

"That hits the spot," says William.

"Is it supposed to taste like soil?" I ask, looking down into my smoothie.

"Oh, Alice," says Caroline. "You're such a truth-teller."

"You mean she's got no filter," says William.

"You should really run with us," says Caroline.

"Yes, why don't you?" asks William, sounding completely disingenuous.

"Because somebody has to work," I say.

"See, no filter," says William.

"Okay—well, I've got to take a shower and get ready. I've got a second interview at Tipi this afternoon. It's an intern position, but at least it's a foot in the door," says Caroline.

"Wait, what's Tipi?" I ask.

"Microfinance. It's this amazing company, Alice. They've only been around for a year but they've already given out over 200 million dollars in loans to women in third-world countries."

"Have you told your mom you're going on a second interview? She must be thrilled."

"I haven't told her. And believe me, she'll be far from thrilled," says Caroline. "She thinks I'm wasting my computer science degree. Now if it were Paypal or Facebook or Google, she'd be doing cartwheels."

"That doesn't sound like your mother."

Caroline shrugs. "That *is* my mother. Just not a part of my mother most people ever see. I'm off." She pops a strawberry into her mouth and leaves the kitchen.

"Well, good for her. She's out there hustling," I say.

"Meaning I'm *not* out there hustling?" says William. "I've been on ten interviews. I just don't talk about it."

"You've been on *ten* interviews?"

"Yes, and not one callback."

"Oh—William, God, *ten* interviews? Why haven't you told me? I could have helped you. This is overwhelming. It's bad out there. It's not just you. Let me help. I can help you. *Please.*"

"There's nothing to help with."

"Well, let me support you. Behind the scenes. I'm a good commiser-ater. Top-notch, in fact—"

He cuts me off. "I don't need commiseration, Alice. I need a plan. And I need you to leave me alone while I come up with it. I'll figure it out. I always do."

I bring my glass to the sink and rinse it out. "Fine," I say slowly. "Well, here's my plan. I sent off that letter to the Parents' Association asking if they'd consider making my position full-time in the fall. Six plays every semester should be a full-time job."

"You *want* to be a drama teacher full-time?" asks William.

"I want us to be able to send our kids to college."

William crosses his arms in front of his chest. "Caroline's right. You should start running again. It would be good for you."

"You seem to be doing okay with Caroline."

"I'd rather run with you," he says.

He's lying. I wonder if Researcher 101 is a runner.

"What?" he asks.

"What do you mean 'what'?"

"You had this strange look on your face."

I stack my glass in the dishwasher and slam the door shut. "That's just the way I look when I'm leaving you alone so you can figure things out."

"California geese, we're unforgettable. Goslings, gaggles, ganders on top. White feathers so soft you'll want to pet us. Honk, honk, honk honk. Honk, honk, honk honk."

Ganders on top. You'll want to pet us? What was I thinking? I'm stand-ing in the wings of the stage at Kentwood Elementary, second-guessing my decision to have the geese do a parody of Katy Perry's "California Gurls" as the closing number for *Charlotte's Web*. The lavender wigs I got at the costume store make the geese look slutty (as does their prancing and hip-wiggling) and judging by the jealous faces of Wilbur and Charlotte and the rest of the cast, I'm pretty sure I went too far in my attempt to make up for the geese having no lines. It seemed like such a brilliant idea at three in the morning when I was mucking around on YouTube and convinced myself that Katy Perry naked, draped in nothing but a cloud covering her ass, was a post-postfeminist statement.

I start thinking up excuses for why I have to leave before the play is over. For some reason, they are all tooth-related. I was eating caramels and my crown just fell off. I was eating a bagel and a piece of crust impaled my gum.

I can hear twitters and whispers coming from the parents as the geese wind up their number, which includes lining up like the Rockettes, arms slung around each other and seductively blowing kisses to the audience. The geese finish their song, adding a cheeky little butt swivel. Limp applause and the geese prance off the stage. Oh, Jesus, God. Helicopmama is right; I have been doing this for far too long. Then I see the boy who played Wilbur holding a bouquet of carnations. Next I am pushed onstage, where the bouquet is shoved in my arms. I turn to face an audience of mostly disapproving faces, except for three: the mothers of the geese, one of whom is a beaming Mrs. Norman, who seems to have forgiven me for accusing her of being a pothead.

"Well," I say, "*Charlotte's Web*. Always a favorite. And didn't we have a wonderful Charlotte this year? You might think *Charlotte's Web* is a bit inappropriate—Charlotte dying in the end and all—but in my experience the theater is a safe place to experiment with difficult issues like death. And what it feels like. What death feels like."

It feels like this.

"I want to thank you for trusting me to look after your children. It's not always easy being a drama teacher. Life isn't fair. We aren't all equal. Somebody has to have the bit part. And somebody has to be the star. I know we live in a time where we try and pretend this isn't true."

Parents are packing up their video cameras and leaving.

"We try and shield our kids from disappointment. From seeing things they shouldn't see before their time. But we must be realistic. There are bad things out there. Especially on the Internet. Why, just the other day my son—my point is you can't let them watch a movie and then fast-forward through the scary parts. Am I right?"

The auditorium is nearly empty now. Mrs. Norman waves at me from the front row.

"Okay, so thank you all for coming. Um—have a great summer and see you next year!"

"When will the DVD be available?" asks Mrs. Norman. "We're so proud of Carisa. Who knew she was such a little dancer? I'd like to order three copies."

"The DVD?" I ask.

"Of the play," she says. "You did have it professionally taped, didn't you?"

She can't be serious. "I saw lots of parents taping the performance. I'm sure somebody will be happy to send you a copy of the tape."

She shakes her head gravely. "Carisa, go get your backpack. I'll meet you out front."

We both watch as Carisa sashays away.

"That wig was a mistake, I'm sorry."

"What are you talking about? The geese stole the show," says Mrs. Norman. "The wigs were brilliant. As was the song choice."

"You didn't think it was a bit—mature?"

Mrs. Norman shrugs. "It's a new world. Eight is the new thirteen. Girls are getting breasts in fourth grade. She's already begging me for a bra. They make them in very small sizes, you know. Tiny. Padded. So cute. So, look, I want to apologize for what happened the other week. You took me by surprise. I wanted to thank you. I'm very grateful you did what you did."

Finally, some gratitude!

"You're very welcome. I'm sure any mother would have done the same thing had they been in my shoes."

"So where and when can I meet you? I know we shouldn't do this at school."

"I think we're okay," I say. The auditorium is empty. "Nobody can hear us."

"You want to do this now? You've been carrying it around? In your purse," she points to my shoulder bag. "Great!" She holds out her hand and then retracts it quickly. "Maybe we should go backstage."

This woman thinks I still have her pot? "Uh, Mrs. Norman? I don't have your—*stuff*. I got rid of it. The day I called you about it, in fact."

"You threw it away? That was nearly a thousand dollars' worth!"

I look at her indignant, entitled moon face and I think of Researcher 101, which gives me confidence to *speak plainly*.

"Mrs. Norman, I've had a very difficult day. It was wrong of me to have the girls perform 'California Geese.' I apologize for that and really, really hope you don't buy Carisa a bra. She's far too young and as far as I can see has no breasts whatsoever. Perhaps you should have a conversation with your daughter about the trauma she incurred in finding your stash of illicit drugs instead of talking with me about how you can get it back. She's a really sweet kid, and she's confused."

"What gives you the right?" Mrs. Norman hisses.

"Tell her something. Anything. Just address it. She won't forget about it. Believe me."

Honk, honk, honk, honk, honk, says Mrs. Norman, meaning "you piece-of-crap teacher."

Honk, honk, honk, honk, honk, I say, meaning "you pothead mother, goodbye."

I play my music at top volume in the car to calm myself down, but *I dream a dream of days gone by* doesn't work today. When I get home I'm still amped up from the afternoon's events, so I do something I know will likely only add to my anxiety: I steal into Zoe's room to check the Hostess product inventory, something I do every week in hopes it will bring me some understanding as to how my daughter can consume thousands of Ding Dong calories a week and never gain an ounce.

"I don't think she's bulimic," says Caroline, poking her head into the room. "You'd know if she were purging."

"Yes, well, there are two Yodels missing," I say.

"You've been counting them?"

"And I always hear the water running in the bathroom when she's in there."

"That doesn't mean she's throwing up. She probably doesn't like people to hear her pee. I've been watching her. She's not a puker. I don't think she's bingeing on Yodels, I really don't, Alice. She just doesn't fit the profile."

I give Caroline a hug. I love having her here. She's smart, funny, brave, creative, and kind: exactly the sort of young woman I hope Zoe will grow up to be.

"Ever had a Yodel?" I ask.

Caroline shakes her head. Of course she hasn't.

I toss her one.

"I'll save it for later," says Caroline, frowning at the packaging.

"Give it back. I know you're not going to eat it."

Caroline wrinkles her nose. "You're right, I'm not going to eat it, but my mother will—you know how she loves junk food. She and my dad are coming to visit. Yodels have no expiration date, right?"

"Bunny's coming to Oakland?"

"We spoke this morning. They just decided."

"Where are they staying?"

"I think they're planning on renting a house."

"Absolutely not. That's too expensive. They can stay here. You can sleep in Zoe's room and they can have the guest room."

"Oh, no, she won't want to impose. You're already putting me up."

"It's no imposition. Actually, it's selfish on my part—I want to see her."

"But don't you need to ask William first?"

"William will be fine with it, I promise."

"Okay. Well, if you're sure, I'll tell her. She'd love that. So Alice, I had a thought. What about if you and I went running? We could do it secretly. Take it slowly. Run at your pace. And eventually get you to the point where you and William could run together again."

"I don't think William is interested in running with me."

"You're wrong. He misses you."

"He told you that?"

"No, but I can tell. He talks about you all the time when we're running."

"You mean he's complaining."

"No! He just talks about you. Stuff you've said."

"*Really?*"

Caroline nods.

"Well—that's nice, I guess."

Actually, it irritates me. Why can't William act like he misses me to my face?

I take the Yodel out of Caroline's hands. "Your mother's favorite is Sno Balls."

I can just see Bunny sitting in the back of the Blue Hill Theater, peeling the pink marshmallow skin off the chocolate cake while instructing an actor to *go deeeeeeper*. There's something about the theater and simple carbohydrates.

"When I was a kid these used to come wrapped in foil," I say. "Packaged up like it was a surprise. A gift that you didn't know was coming."

Like the Yodel, Bunny's visit feels like fate.

Three days later, summer officially arrives. The kids are out of school and I am, too. Because of our finances we're not doing much of anything this summer (except going on a camping trip to the Sierras in a few weeks). Everybody will be home all the time, except Caroline, who scored a part-time intern position at Tipi.

I take Caroline up on her offer to train with me and am now standing in the middle of the street, panting, bent over like an old lady, my hands on my knees, deeply regretting my decision.

"That's a twelve-minute mile," says Caroline, looking at her watch. "Good, Alice."

"Twelve minutes? That's pathetic. I can walk faster," I gasp. "Tell me again why we're doing this."

"Because you'll feel great afterwards."

"And during I'll feel like dying and curse the day I ever let you come stay with us?"

"That's about right," she says, bouncing on her toes. "Come on, keep moving. You don't want the lactic acid building up in your calves."

"No, noooo lactic acid for me. Just give me a second to catch my breath."

Caroline squints distractedly into the distance.

"What's wrong?" I ask.

"Nothing," she says.

"Are you looking forward to your parents coming?"

Caroline shrugs.

"Did you tell Bunny about Tipi?"

"Uh-huh." Caroline does a quick stretch and then takes off at a trot. I groan and stagger after her. She spins around and runs backwards. "William told me you used to run a nine-minute mile. We'll get you back there again. Pump your arms. No, not like a chicken, Alice. Tucked under your shoulders."

I catch up to her, and after a few minutes she looks at her watch and frowns. "Do you mind if I sprint the last quarter mile?"

"Go, go," I huff, waving her away.

As soon as she's out of sight, I slow to a walk and take out my cell. I click on the Facebook app.

Kelly Cho
Thanks for the add, Alice!
5 minutes ago

Nedra Rao
Prenups, people. Prenups!!
10 minutes ago

Bobby Barbedian
Robert Bly says it's all right if you grow your wings on the way down.
2 hours ago

Pat Guardia
Is dreaming of Tita's lumpia. Hint-hint.
4 hours ago

Phil Archer
I read my daily fortune cookie!
The sensitivity you show to others will return to you.
5 hours ago

Boring. Nothing exciting.
Then I check Lucy Pevensie's account.

John Yossarian
Likes barmaids.
5 hours ago

I give a little squeal.

60

John Yossarian
Why not?
1 hour ago

Okay I'm just going to ask. Are you flirting with me, Researcher 101?

I don't know. Are you flirting with me?

Let me be the researcher for once. Answer my question.

Yes.

You should probably stop.

Really?

No.

61

FESTIVE SWEDISH POTLUCK AT NEDRA'S HOUSE

7:30: Standing in Nedra's kitchen

Me: Here's the meatballs!
Nedra (*peeling back the aluminum foil and making a face*): Are these homemade?
Me: And here's the lingonberry jam to go with them.
Nedra: *Now* I understand why you chose Swedish. Because you ran out of cheap candles. Alice, the whole point of these internationally themed potlucks is to step outside our comfort zones and make new foods, not buy them at Ikea.
William: *Blåbärsplåt* (*handing her a casserole dish*).
Nedra (*peeling back the aluminum foil, her face aglow with delight*): You brought something, too?
William: I made it. It's a traditional Swedish delicacy.
Nedra: William, darling, I'm so impressed. Alice, put the lingonberry jam on the table, will you? The Styrofoam cup is a nice touch, by the way.

7:48: Still standing in the kitchen

Linda: Wait until you have to move your kid to college. It's like childbirth, or marriage; nobody tells you the truth about how hard it is.
Kate: Come on, it can't be that bad.
Bobby: Did we tell you the twin master suites are finished?
Linda: First I had to get up at five in the morning to log on to get Dan-

iel's scheduled move-in time. It's first come first served, and everybody wants the 7-to-9 a.m. slot. If you don't get that slot you're screwed.

Nedra: Why didn't you make Daniel get up at five in the morning?

Linda (*waving her hand, dismissing the idea that an eighteen-year-old boy could possibly be counted upon to set an alarm clock correctly*): I got the 7-to-9 a.m. slot. We arrived on campus at 6:45 and already there were huge lines of parents and kids waiting for the four elevators that serviced the entire dorm. Clearly there was a 5-to-7 a.m. the-rules-don't-apply-to-me-because-I'm-paying-$50,000-a-year slot that I was not made aware of.

Bobby: I've been sleeping like a baby. Linda, too. And our sex life—I won't go into details, but let's just say it's an extreme turn-on to feel like strangers in your own home.

Linda: So each of us dragged a fifty-pound suitcase up five flights of stairs to Daniel's room. A Sisyphean feat, given the fact that every couple of minutes we were pushed aside by the happy-go-lucky parents who got there early enough to use the elevator to haul their kids' stuff up to their rooms, who said stupid things like "looks like you got your hands full" and "moving-in day—aren't you glad to be rid of them!" And when we got to Daniel's room—horror!—his roommate was already there and almost completely moved in. When the roommate's mother saw us she didn't even say hello; she was frantically unpacking and hoarding as much floor space as she could. Apparently the roommate had that syndrome where one leg is shorter than the other and had been given special dispensation to move in super-duper early—the 3-to-5 a.m. slot.

Me: William, just think of all the money we're going to save now that the kids won't be going to college so that we can avoid moving-in day.

Bobby: My only question is, why did we wait so long? We could have been this happy years ago. Our contractor told us that's what all the people who get twin master suites say.

Linda: At least the roommate had the decency to seem embarrassed by the quantity of stuff he'd brought: a microwave, hot plate, fridge, a bike. We left Daniel's suitcases in the hallway and told them we'd be back later.

Bobby: Pop over and I'll give you a tour.

Linda: So we're leaving and the roommate says, "Guess what? I have a sno-cone maker." My heart sank. I'd bought Daniel a sno-cone maker, too. I read on some blog it was one of the top things you should bring to college to make you popular. Now they would have two sno-cone makers in one ten-by-ten room, which would be one sno-cone maker too many to make them popular. Instead people would be wondering what's up with those tools in 507 with the two sno-cone makers? All those years of subtle social manipulation, making sure he got invited to the popular kids' parties, making helpful suggestions like if you don't feel comfortable "freaking" at the dance, just say it's against your religion or that your parents forbid you to do it. That's when I started to cry.

Me: What's "freaking"?

Kate: Dry humping. Basically, simulating sex on the dance floor.

Bobby: I told her she should save the tears for later when all the parents said goodbye to their kids in the hallways—the one officially sanctioned location for farewells—but did she listen?

Linda: I cried then. I cried when we came back that evening and the roommate's goddamn mother was still there organizing and rearranging knickknacks and I couldn't in good conscience say *what the fuck, lady* to a mother whose kid's left leg is three inches shorter than his right, and I cried once more in the hallway at the designated crying time.

Me: Isn't it nice none of the children are here?

Linda (*sobbing*): And now I'm going to have to do it all over again in August with Nick. And then the kids are gone. We'll officially be empty-nesters. I'm not sure I can bear it.

Bobby: I'll bet there are services that will move your kid into college for you.

William: Great idea. Subcontract the job.

Nedra: No mother wants some stranger moving her kid into college, you bloody idiots.

Me: I'd love to hear more about the twin master suites. Do you have photos? Is this pink stuff gravlox?

Nedra: *Lax. Lox* is Jewish.

Me: How do you know?

Nedra: Hebfaq.com.

8:30: On the patio, eating dinner

Nedra: Believe it or not, there *is* such a thing as a good divorce.

Me: What makes a good divorce?

Nedra: You keep the house, I'll keep the cabin in Tahoe. We'll share the condo in Maui.

William: In other words, money.

Nedra: It helps.

Kate: And respect for one another. And wanting to do right by the kids. Not hiding assets.

William: In other words, trust.

Me (*not looking at William*): So tell us what it's like, Linda—having two masters. How does it work?

Linda: We watch TV in his or my bedroom, we have our snuggle time, and it's only when we're ready to sleep that we each go to our suites.

Bobby: The suites are purely for sleep.

Linda: Sleep is so important.

Bobby: Lack of sleep leads to binge eating.

Linda: And memory loss.

Me: And repressed anger.

William: What about sex?

Linda: What do you mean, what about it?

Nedra: When do you have it?

Linda: When we normally have it.

Nedra: Which is when?

Bobby: Are you asking how often?

Nedra: I've always wondered how many times a week straight married couples have sex.

William: I imagine that has something to do with how long they've been married.

Nedra: That does not sound like an endorsement for marriage, William.

Me: What color did you paint the walls, Linda?

Nedra: A couple married for more than ten years—I'd guess once every two weeks.

Me: What about carpets? Can you believe shag is back in style?

Linda: Way more.

Me: Well—*I'm* not going to lie.

Linda: You're saying I'm lying?

Me: I'm saying you might be stretching the truth.

William: Pass the *Blåbärsplåt*.

Me: Once a month.

William: (*coughs*)

9:38: In the kitchen, putting leftover food into Tupperware containers

Nedra: My forehead is shiny. I'm stuffed. I'm drunk. Put away your phone, Alice. I don't want my photo taken.

Me: You'll thank me one day.

Nedra: You do not have my permission to post this on Facebook. I have plenty of enemies. I would prefer they not know where I live.

Me: Calm down. It's not like I'm posting your address.

Nedra (*grabbing my phone out of my hand, her thumbs working the screen*): It *is* like you're posting my address. If your phone has a GPS, your photos have geotags embedded in them. Those tags provide the exact longitude and latitude of where the photo was taken. Most people don't know that geotags even exist, which let me tell you has worked to many of my clients' advantages. There. I've shut off the location services setting on your camera. Now you may take my picture.

Me: Forget it. You've taken all the fun out of it.

Nedra: So you were exaggerating, right? You have sex more than once a month.

Me (*sighing*): No, I was telling the truth. At least lately that's how it is.

Nedra: It may feel like once a month, but I'm sure it's more. Why don't you keep track of it? There's probably some phone app created just for that purpose.

Me: Have you seen the *Why Am I Such a Bitch* app? It's free. Tells you what day you are in your cycle. There's a version for men, too, only it's $3.99. It's the *Why Is My Lady Such a Bitch* app. And for $4.99 you can upgrade to the *Never Ask Your Lady if She's About to Get Her Period* app.

Nedra: What does that do?

Me: It charges you $4.99 every time you're stupid enough to ask your lady if she's about to get her period.

Nedra (*a look of horror on her face*): What are you doing? Don't toss the *Blåbärsplåt*!

10:46: Through the bathroom door

Me: Anybody in there?

William (*opening door*): No.

Me (*shuffling from one side to the other, trying to get by William and into the bathroom*): Pick a side, William. Left or right?

William: Alice?

Me: What? (*trying to squish past him*) I have to go to the bathroom.

William: Look at me.

Me: After I pee.

William: No, look at me now. Please.

Me (*looking at the floor*): Okay, I'm sorry, I shouldn't have told EVERY-BODY we only have sex once a month.

William: I don't care about that.

Me: You *should* care. That's private information.

William: It doesn't mean anything.

Me: It means something to me. Besides, it's probably more than once a month. We should keep track of it.

William: It's once a month lately.

Me: See—you care. (*Pause.*) Why are you looking at me like that? Say something. (*Pause.*) William, if you don't move out of my way I'm going to have an accident. Now, left or right?

William (*long pause*): I loved that night in your office.

Me (*longer pause*): Me, too.

10:52: Wandering through the garden

Bobby: I sense you're interested in the master suites idea.

Me: The lanterns are magical. It's like Narnia back here.

Bobby: I can email you the name of my contractor.

Me: If we made two master suites out of our bedroom, we'd each be in a room the dimensions of a prison cell.

Bobby: It's changed our lives. I'm not lying.

Me (*touching his cheek with the palm of my hand*): I'm happy for you, Bobby. I really am. But I don't think separate bedrooms is going to fix us.

Bobby: I knew it! You guys *are* having problems.

Me: Do you think Aslan could be waiting for us on the other side of that hedge?

Bobby: Sorry. I didn't mean to sound so enthusiastic about your struggles.

Me: I'm not struggling, Bobby. I'm waking up. This is me waking up (*lying down on the grass*).

Bobby (*staring down at me*): You waking up looks remarkably similar to you after five glasses of wine.

Me (*gasp*): Bobby B! There's so many stars! When did there get to be so many stars? This is what happens when we forget to look up.

Bobby: Nobody's called me Bobby B in a long time.

Me: Bobby B, are you crying?

11:48: Walking upstairs to our bedroom

Me: It would appear I'm a little drunk.

William: Take my arm.

Me: I suppose now would be a good time to have sex.

William: You're more than a little drunk, Alice.

Me (*slurring*): Am I unbecomingly drunk or becomingly drunk?

William (*escorting me into the bedroom*): Get undressed.

Me: I don't think I'm capable of that at the moment. You undress me. I'll just close my eyes and have a little rest while you take advantage of me. That will still count, won't it? In our monthly total? If I fall asleep while we're doing it? Hopefully I won't vomit.

William (*unbuttoning my shirt and taking it off*): Sit down, Alice.

Me: Wait, I'm unprepared. Give me a second to hold in my stomach.

William (*sliding my pajama top over my head, pushing me back into the pillows, and covering me with a blanket*): I've seen your stomach before. Besides, it's completely dark.

Me: Well, since it's completely dark you're welcome to pretend I'm Angelina Jolie. Pax! Zahara! Eat your whole-wheat pasta or else. And all six of you scram out of the family bed—NOW! Hey, why don't you be Brad?

William: I am not a role-playing sort of man.

Me (*bolting up*): I forgot to buy candles at Ikea. Now I have to go back. I hate Ikea.

William: Jesus, Alice. Go to sleep.

62

wake in the late morning with a terrible headache. William's side of the bed is empty. I check his Facebook status.

William Buckle
52,800 feet
One hour ago

Either he's on his way to Paris or he's gone for a ten-mile run. I lift my head from the pillow and the room tilts. I'm still drunk. Bad wife. Bad mother. I think about what embarrassing things I did last night at the potluck and cringe. Did I really try and pass Ikea meatballs off as my own? Did I really crawl through a hedge in Nedra's garden looking for a portal into Narnia? Did I really admit to our friends that we have sex only once a month?

I fall back to sleep. Two hours later, I wake and weakly call out "Peter," then "Caroline," then "Zoe." I can't bring myself to call for William—I'm too humiliated, plus I don't want to admit to him I've got a hangover. Finally, in desperation, I yell "Jampo" and am rewarded with the immediate frantic pitter-pat of tiny feet. He rushes into the bedroom and hurls himself up on the bed, panting at me as if to say "you are the only thing in this world I love, the only thing I care about, the one thing I live for." Then he proceeds to pee all over the sheets in excitement.

"Bad boy, bad boy!" I shout but it's useless, he can't stop in midstream, so I just watch him dribble. His bottom lip has somehow gotten stuck on his teeth, giving him a pathetic, unintentional Elvis sort of sneer that could be read as hostility but I know is shame. "It's all right," I tell him. When he's done, I drag myself out of bed, strip off my clothes, the duvet, sheets, and mattress cover, and make a mental list of things I will do today to set myself right.

1. Drink room-temperature water with lemon.
2. Knit a scarf. A long, thin scarf. No, a short, thin scarf. No, a coaster, i.e. an extremely short, short scarf.
3. Take Jampo on a brisk walk outside: 30 to 45 minutes minimum without sunglasses, perhaps in a low-cut V-neck, so I can fully absorb optimal daily dose of vitamin D through my retinas and the delicate skin at the tops of my breasts.
4. Plant lemon verbena in the yard so I can start drinking tisanes and feeling organic and cleansed and elegant (providing 1. lemon verbena is still alive after buying at Home Depot a month ago and then forgetting to water or repot AND 2. if able to dip head below waist without puking).
5. Laundry.
6. Make Bolognese sauce, simmer on the stove all day so the family comes home to homey smell of cooking.
7. Sing, or if I'm too nauseous to sing, watch *The Sound of Music* and pretend I am Liesl.
8. Remember what it felt like to be sixteen going on seventeen.

It's a good to-do list—too bad I don't do a thing on it. Instead, I make another mental list of things I absolutely should NOT do and proceed to knock off every single item:

1. Load the washer but forget to turn it on.
2. Eat eight bite-sized Reese's peanut butter cups while telling myself they only add up to half of a regular-sized cup.
3. Eat eight more.
4. Put a bay leaf (because lemon verbena very clearly dead) in some boiling-hot water and force myself to drink entire mugful.
5. Feel great because I picked that bay leaf while taking a hike in Tilden Park and then dried it in the sun (okay, in the dryer, but I would have dried it in the sun if I hadn't left it in the pocket of my fleece and then stuck it in the wash).

6. Feel really great because I am now officially a forager.

7. Contemplate a new career as a bay leaf forager/supplier to Bay Area's best restaurants. Fantasize about being featured in the annual food issue of the *New Yorker* wearing a bandana on my head while holding a woven basket full of fresh bay leaves.

8. Google California bay leaf and discover it's the Mediterranean bay leaf that is used for cooking and while the California bay leaf is not poisonous, ingestion is not recommended.

9. Go online and reread all the communication between me and Researcher 101 until I've read between all his lines and sucked every bit of titillation out of his words.

10. Exhausted, fall asleep on the chaise in the sun, Jampo curled up beside me.

"You smell like booze. It's oozing out of your pores."

I open my eyes slowly to see William looking down at me.

"It's customary to give a person some warning when a person is sound asleep," I say.

"A person shouldn't be sound asleep at four in the afternoon," William counters.

"Would now be a good time to tell you I'd like to change schools and enroll at the Pacific Boychoir Academy in the fall?" asks Peter, he and Zoe strolling out onto the deck.

I raise my eyebrows at William, giving him my see-I-told-you-our-son-was-gay look.

"Since when do you like to sing?" asks William.

"Are you getting bullied?" I ask, cortisol flooding through my body at the thought of him being picked on.

"God, Mom, you stink," says Zoe. She waves her hand at me.

"Yes, your father already informed me of that. Where have you been all day?"

"Zoe and I hung out on Telegraph Avenue," says Peter.

"Telegraph Avenue? The two of you? *Together*?"

Zoe and Peter exchange a furtive look. Zoe shrugs. "So."

"So—it's not safe there," I say.

"Why, because of all the homeless people?" asks Zoe. "I'll have you know our generation is post-homeless."

"What does that mean?" I ask.

"It means we're not afraid of them. We've been brought up to look homeless people in the eye."

"And help them panhandle," adds Peter.

"And where were you while our children were begging on Telegraph Avenue?" I ask William.

"It's not my fault. I dropped them off at Market Hall in Rockridge. They took the bus to Berkeley," says William.

"Pedro sang 'Ode to Joy' in German. We made some guy twenty bucks!" says Zoe.

"*You* know 'Ode to Joy'?" I ask.

"There's a 'You Can Sing Ludwig van Beethoven in German' channel on YouTube," says Peter.

"William, should I start with the potatoes?" Caroline shouts from the kitchen.

"I'll help," I say, hauling myself out of the chaise.

"No need. Stay here. We've got it under control," says William, disappearing into the house.

As I watch everyone bustling around the kitchen, it occurs to me that Sunday afternoon is the loneliest time of the week. With a sigh, I open my laptop.

John Yossarian *likes Sweden*
3 hours ago

Lucy Pevensie
Is in need of her magic cordial but seems to have misplaced it.
3 hours ago

There you are. Have you looked under the backseat of the car, Wife 22?

No, but I looked under the backseat of the White Witch's sled.

What does the cordial do?

Heals all illnesses.

Ah—of course. Are you ill?

I have a hangover.

I'm sorry to hear that.

Are you of Swedish descent?

I can't divulge that information.

Well, can you tell me what you *like* about Sweden?

Its neutrality. It's a safe place to wait out a war, if one is in a war, that is.

Are you in a war?

Possibly.

How can somebody "possibly" be in a war? Wouldn't it be obvious?

War is not always obvious, particularly when one is in a war with oneself.

What kind of war does one typically have with oneself?

A war in which one side of him thinks he may be crossing a line, and the other side of him thinks it's a line that was begging to be crossed.

Researcher 101? Are you calling me a beggar?

Absolutely not, Wife 22.

Well, are you calling me a line?

Perhaps.

A line you are in the process of stepping over?

Tell me to stop.

Wife 22?

You're Swedish.

What makes you think that?

Based on the fact that you use the word "ah" sometimes.

I'm not Swedish.

Okay, you're Canadian.

Better.

You grew up on a cattle ranch in Southern Alberta. You learned to ride when you were three; home-schooled in the mornings with your four siblings, afternoons spent poaching cows with the Hutterite children who lived in the Colony next door.

How I miss my friends, the Hutterites.

You were the oldest, so much was expected out of you, not the least of which was to grow up and run the ranch. Instead you went to college in New York and only came home once a year to help with branding. An event to which you brought all your girlfriends to impress and shock the hell out of them. Also so they could see how good you look in chaps.

I still have those chaps.

Your wife fell in love with you when she saw you mount a horse.

Are you psychic?

You've been married a long time. It could be she is no longer as interested in seeing you mount a horse, although I would imagine that would never get old.

You'll get no disagreement from me on that.

You are not: pasty, a gamer, a golfer, a dullard, somebody who corrects other people's malapropisms, somebody who despises dogs.

No disagreement there either.

Don't stop.

Don't stop what, Wife 22?

Crossing my line.

63

67. To want the people you love to be happy. To look homeless people in the eye. To not want what you don't have. What you *can't* have. What you *shouldn't* have. To not text while driving. To control your appetite. To want to be where you are.

68. Once I got past the morning sickness with Zoe, I loved being pregnant. It changed the dynamics between William and me utterly. I let myself be vulnerable and he let himself be the protector, and every day this stunned, primal, bumper-stickerish voice inside of me whispered *this is the way it should be. This is how you were meant to live. This is what your whole life has been for.* William was gallant. He opened doors and jars of spaghetti sauce. He heated up the car before I got in and held my elbow as we navigated rainy sidewalks. We were whole, the three of us, a trinity way before Zoe was born—I could have happily stayed pregnant for years.

And then Zoe arrived, a colicky, drooling, aggressively unhappy baby. William fled to the sanity of the office each day. I stayed home on maternity leave and divided hours into fifteen-minute increments: breastfeed, burp, lie on couch with screaming baby, attempt to sing screaming baby to sleep.

This was when I felt the loss of my mother most acutely. She never would have let me go through those disorienting early months alone. She would have moved right in and taught me the things a mother teaches her daughter: how to give a baby a bath, how to get rid of cradle cap, how long you should stay mad at your husband when he straps your baby into the swing haphazardly and she slides out.

And most importantly, my mother would have filled me in about time. She would have said, "Honey, it's a paradox. For the first half of your life each minute feels like a year, but for the second half, each year feels like a minute." She would have assured me this was normal and it would do no good to fight it. That's the price we pay for the privilege of growing old.

My mother never got that privilege.

Eleven months later, I woke one morning and the disorientation was gone. I picked my baby up out of her crib, she made the sweetest dolphin squeal, and I fell instantly in love.

69. Dear Zoe,

Here is the story of the beginning of your life. It can be summed up in one sentence. I loved you and then I got really scared and then I loved you more than I ever thought it was possible for one person to love another. I think we are not so dissimilar, although I'm sure it feels like we are right now.

Things you may not know or remember:

1. You have always been a trendsetter. When you were two, you stood up on Santa's lap and belted out "Do, a Deer" to the hundred irritated people who had been standing in line for an hour. Everybody started singing with you. You were flash-mobbing before anybody even knew what flash-mobbing was.

2. The first vacation your father and I took without you kids was to Costa Rica. You know how some girls go through a horse stage? Well, you were going through a primate stage. You convinced yourself I'd agreed to bring you home a white-faced capuchin. When we returned and I gave you your gift, a stuffed chimp named Milo, you said thank you very much, then went into your room, opened your window, and threw it into the branches of the redwood tree in the backyard, where to this day it still lives. Occasionally, when there's a big storm, and the tree sways from side to side, I get a glimpse of Milo's face, his faded red mouth smiling sadly at me.

3. Often I wish I were more like you.

Zoe, my baby—I am in the still-in-your-camp-even-though-you-can-barely-stand-to-look-at-me-most-of-the-time-right-now stage. It's difficult, but I'm muddling through. Soy venti lattes help the time pass, as does watching *Gone with the Wind*.

Your loving Mama

64

John Yossarian *changed his profile picture*

Do you like walking in circles, Researcher 101?

Sometimes walking in circles can be very helpful.

I suppose—as long as the circle walking is intentional.

I've been imagining what you look like, Wife 22.

I can't divulge that information; however, I can tell you I'm not a Hutterite.

You have chestnut-colored hair.

I do?

Yes, but you would likely describe it as mouse brown because you tend to underestimate yourself, but you have the kind of hair women envy.

That's why I always get such dirty looks.

Eyes, brown as well. Possibly hazel.

Or possibly blue. Or possibly green.

You're pretty, and I mean this as a compliment. Pretty is what lies between beautiful and plain, and in my experience pretty is the best place to be.

I think I'd rather be beautiful.

Beautiful makes evolving into any sort of a person with morals and character very difficult.

I think I'd rather be plain.

Plain—what can I say about that? So much of life is a lottery.

So you think of me when we're not chatting online?

Yes.

In your regular life? Your *civilian* life?

Frequently I'll find myself in the middle of doing something mundane, emptying the dishwasher or listening to the radio, and something you said will pop into my head and I'll get this amused look on my face and my wife will ask me what's so funny.

What do you tell her?

That I met this woman online.

You do not.

No, but soon I may have to.

65

Kelly Cho
Loves being in charge.
5 minutes ago

Caroline Kilborn
Is full.
32 minutes ago

Phil Archer
Cleaning house.
52 minutes ago

William Buckle
Gimme Shelter
3 hours ago

"Could you please stop checking Facebook, Alice? For one bloody minute?" asks Nedra.

I set my phone on vibrate and slip it into my purse.

"So, as I was just saying but will repeat for your benefit—I have some
big news. I'm going to ask Kate to marry me."

Nedra and I are browsing in a jewelry store on College Ave.

"And what's your opinion on moonstones?" she adds.

"Oh, dear," I say.

"Did you hear what I just said?"

"I heard."

"And all you have to say is 'Oh, dear'? May I see that one, please," says
Nedra, pointing to an oval moonstone set in eighteen-karat gold.

The saleswoman hands it to her and she slips it on her finger.

"Let me see," I say, grabbing her arm. "I don't get it. Is there something about moonstones and lesbians? Some Sapphic thing that I'm missing?"

"For God's sake," says Nedra. "Why am I asking you? You have no taste in jewelry. In fact, you never wear jewelry and you really should, darling. It would perk you up a bit." She studies my face worriedly. "Still having insomnia?"

"I'm going for the French no-makeup look."

"I'm sorry to tell you, but the French no-makeup look only works in France. The light is different there. Kinder. American light is so crude."

"Why do you want to get married now? You've been together thirteen years. You never wanted to get married before. What's changed?"

Nedra shrugs. "I'm not sure. We just woke up one morning and solidifying our relationship felt right. It's the strangest thing. I don't know if it's my age or something—the big five-oh looming. But suddenly I want tradition."

"The big five-oh is not looming. You won't be fifty for another nine years. Besides, things are great with you and Kate. If you get married you'll be all screwed up like the rest of us."

"Does this mean you don't want to be my maid of honor?"

"You're going to do the whole thing? Bridesmaids, too?" I say.

"You and William are screwed up? Since when?"

"We're not screwed up. We're just—distant. It's been incredibly stressful. Him losing his job."

"Mmm. Can I try that one?" Nedra asks the saleswoman, gesturing to a marquise-cut diamond ring.

She puts it on her finger, extends her arm, and admires her hand.

"It's a bit Cinderella-ey, but I like it. The question is, will Kate? Alice, you're in a rather bad mood today. Let's forget we ever had this conversation. Here's what's going to happen. I'm going to call you tomorrow. You're going to say, 'Hello, Nedra, what's new?' I'm going to say, 'I have news; I've asked Kate to marry me!' You're going to say, 'Goodness—about time! When can we go out shopping for dresses? And can I accompany you to the cake tasting?'" Nedra hands the ring back to the saleswoman. "Too flashy. I need something more subtle. I'm a divorce lawyer."

"Yes, and it would look unseemly for her wife to be sporting a two-carat diamond engagement ring. Bought on the proceeds of other people's failed marriages," I say.

Nedra gives me a dirty look.

"Sorry," I say.

"Look, Alice, it's as simple as this. I've found the person I want to spend the rest of my life with. And she's passed the spectacular test."

"The spectacular test?"

"When I first met Kate she was spectacular. And a decade later she is still the most spectacular woman I've ever known. Besides you, of course. Don't you feel that way about William?"

I want to feel that way about William.

"Well, why shouldn't I have what you have?" Nedra asks.

"You should. Of course you should. It's just that everything in your life is changing so fast. I can't keep up. And now you're getting married."

"Alice." Nedra puts her arm around me. "This isn't going to change anything between us. We'll always be best friends. I hate married people who say ridiculous things like 'I married my best friend.' Is there any clearer path to a sexless marriage? That won't be me. I am marrying my lover."

"I'm so happy for you," I squeak. "And your lu-va. It's just super-terrific news."

Nedra frowns. "Things will get better with William. You're just going through a rough patch. Ride it out, darling. Good things are ahead. I promise you. Let me ask you something. Why don't you want to be my maid of honor? Is it the word *maid* you object to?"

No. I have absolutely no problem with *maid*. It's the word *honor*. Honor is something I said goodbye to in my last two chats with Researcher 101.

"May I see the emerald ring?" asks Nedra.

"Lovely choice. Emeralds are a symbol of hope and faith," says the saleswoman, handing her the ring.

"Ah—" says Nedra. "It's bloody gorgeous. Here, Alice, try it on."

She slides the ring onto my finger.

"That looks stunning on you," says the saleswoman.

"What do you think?" Nedra asks.

I think the gleaming green stone looks like it was flown by hot-air balloon directly from Oz to Oakland, and it's the perfect symbol of Nedra's sparkling life.

"Spectacular Kate will love it," I sniff.

"But do you love it?" asks Nedra.

"Why does it matter if I love it?"

Nedra pulls the ring off my finger and hands it back to the saleswoman with a sigh.

Watching my best friend read my private emails and Facebook chats is not typically an activity I indulge in. But for the last half hour, that's precisely what I've been doing. I've finally confided in Nedra about Researcher 101 and judging by the look of contempt on her face, I'm starting to think this was a very bad idea.

Nedra flings my cellphone across the kitchen table.

"I can't believe you."

"What?"

"What the hell are you doing, Alice?"

"I can't help it. You read them. Our chats are like a drug. I'm addicted."

"He is witty, I'll give him that, but you're married! Married as in 'I will love you and only you until the end of my days.'"

"I know. I'm a terrible wife. That's why I told you. You have to tell me what to do."

"Well, that's easy. You have to sever all ties with him. Nothing's happened yet. You haven't crossed any line except in your mind. Just stop chatting with him."

"I can't just stop," I say, horrified. "He'll worry. He'll think something's happened to me."

"Something *has* happened to you. You've come to your senses, Alice. Right now. Today."

"I don't think I can do that. Just quit the study without saying anything."

"You must," says Nedra. "Now, I'm not a prude, you know that. I think a little bit of flirting is good for a marriage, as long as you redirect that sexual energy back into your relationship, but you've gone way beyond the flirting stage."

She picks up my phone and scrolls through my chats. "'A war in which one side of him thinks he may be crossing a line, and the other side of him thinks it's a line that was begging to be crossed.' Alice, this isn't innocent anymore."

Hearing her read Researcher 101's words out loud makes me shudder—in a good way. And although I know Nedra is absolutely right, I also know I'm not capable of letting him go. At least not yet. Not without a proper goodbye. Or finding out his intentions—if he has intentions, that is.

"You're right," I lie. "You're absolutely right."

"Good," says Nedra, softening. "So you'll stop chatting with him? You'll quit the study?"

"Yes," I say, my eyes filling with tears.

"Oh, Alice, come on, it can't be that bad."

"It's just that I was lonely. I didn't realize how lonely I was until we started emailing. He listens to me. He asks me things. Important things, and what I say matters," I say, suddenly sobbing.

Nedra reaches across the table and takes my hand. "Darling, here are the facts. Yes, William is an idiot sometimes. Yes, he's flawed. Yes, the two of you may be going through a dry spell. But this—" she picks up my phone and shakes it. "This isn't real. You know that, don't you?"

I nod.

"So do you want me to refer you to a great couples counselor? She's wonderful. She's actually helped some of my clients get back together."

"You send your clients to a couples counselor?"

"When I think there's something worth saving, yes."

Later that afternoon, when I'm sitting in the school bleachers pretending I'm watching Zoe play volleyball (every five minutes I shout out "Go Trojans," and she glances up in the bleachers and gives me a withering look), I think about William and me. Some of the blame for my emotional straying has to fall on him; his being so uncommunicative. I want to be with somebody who listens to me. Who says, *Start from the beginning, tell me everything, and don't leave out a thing.*

"Hi, Alice." Jude plops down beside me. "Zo's playing well."

I watch him watching Zoe and can't help but feel a little jealous. It's been so long since I've been gazed at like that. I remember the feeling as a teenager. The absolute surety that the boy was not in control of his gaze—that I was, simply by existing. No words needed to be spoken. A gaze like that needed no translation. Its meaning was obvious. *I can't stop looking at you, I wish I could but I can't, I can't, I can't.*

"You've got to stop stalking her, Jude."

"Tic Tac?" He shakes three mints into the palm of my hand. "I can't help it," he says.

Didn't I just say the same thing to his mother not more than an hour ago?

"Jude, sweetheart, I've known you since you were a toddler, so trust me that this is said with love. Move the hell on."

"I wish I could," he says.

Zoe looks up into the bleachers and her mouth drops open when she sees the two of us together.

I leap to my feet. "Go Trojans! Go Zoe! Nice spike!" I shout.

"She's a setter, not a spiker," says Jude.

"Nice set, Zoe!" I shout, sitting down.

Jude snorts.

"She's going to kill me," I say.

"Yep," says Jude, as Zoe's cheeks flush pink with embarrassment.

"I have news," I say to William that evening.

"Hold on, I'm just finishing the onions. Did you prep the carrots, Caroline?" asks William.

"I forgot," says Caroline, hustling to the refrigerator. "Do you want them julienned or diced?"

"Diced. Alice, please get out of the way. You're blocking the sink."

"I have news," I repeat. "About Nedra and Kate."

"There's nothing like the smell of caramelized onions," says William, sticking the pan under Caroline's nose.

"Mmmm," she says.

I think about the way Jude looked at Zoe. With such longing. With such desire. The same exact way my husband is looking at a pile of limp onions.

"How much tarragon?" asks William.

"Two teaspoons, a tablespoon? I forgot," says Caroline. "Although it might not be tarragon. It might be marjoram. Look on Epicurious."

I sigh and grab my laptop. William glances at me. "Don't go. I want to hear your news. I just have to check the recipe."

I give him an exaggerated thumbs-up and walk into the living room.

I log on to Lucy's Facebook page. Researcher 101 is online. I look up at William. He's busy, frowning at his iPhone.

"Is it tarragon or marjoram?" asks Caroline.

"Hold on," says William. "I can't find the recipe on Epicurious. Was it Food.com?"

I click on Chat and quickly type:

What's happening?

It takes Researcher 101 just a few seconds to respond:

Besides our brains being flooded with phenylethylamine?

I shudder. Researcher 101's voice sounds remarkably similar to George Clooney's—at least in my head. I write:

Should we put a stop to this?

No.

Should I ask that my case be transferred to another researcher?

Absolutely not.

Have you ever flirted like this with another of your subjects?

I have never flirted with another woman besides my wife.

Jesus! I feel a sudden pulsing heat in my groin and I cross my legs as if to hide it, as if somebody could see.

"Did you find it?" asks Caroline.

"Food.com. Two teaspoons of tarragon," replies William, waving his phone at her. "You were right."

I sit there on the couch, trying to persuade my heart rate to go back to its resting state. I breathe though my mouth. Is this what it feels like to have a panic attack? William looks at me from across the room.

"So what's your news, Alice?" he asks.

"Nedra and Kate are getting married."

"Are they?"

"You don't sound surprised."

He pauses and smiles. "I'm only surprised it took them this long."

66

70. That sometimes, when I'm alone and in a place where nobody knows me, I speak with a pretend British accent.

71. Worry. Ask Peter when's the last time he flossed. Fight off the urge to push the hair out of Zoe's eyes so I can see her pretty face.

72. How stunning it would be to see his features in my children's faces.

67

 John Yossarian *changed his profile picture*

It's my 20th anniversary tomorrow.

And how are you feeling about that, Wife 22?

Ambivalent.

I'm sorry. I didn't mean for this to happen.

"This" meaning me?

I remember when I first went to college. It was in a city. I won't say where. But I remember after I had said goodbye to my parents, I walked down the streets feeling exhilarated that nobody knew me. For the first time in my life I was completely disconnected from everybody I loved.

I remember that feeling, too. I found the disconnection terrifying.

You realize future generations will never experience this. We are reachable every minute of the day.

And your point is?

Your reachability is highly addictive, Wife 22.

Is that your hand in your new profile photo?

Yes.

Why did you post a photo of your hand?

Because I wanted you to imagine it on the back of your neck.

68

"We have to get potstickers," says Peter.

"We always get potstickers. Let's get lettuce wraps," says Zoe. "The vegetarian ones."

"Are you guys sure you're okay with us crashing your anniversary dinner?" asks Caroline. "It's not very romantic."

"Alice and I have had twenty years to be romantic," William says. "Besides, it's nice to go out and celebrate. Did you know the traditional wedding gift for the twentieth anniversary is china? That's why I made the reservation at P.F. Chang's." He taps his finger on the menu. "Cheng-du Spiced Lamb. China."

China, yes. This morning I gave William a commemorative photo plate that I ordered back in December. The photo was taken of us twenty years ago standing in front of Fenway Park. He's behind me, his arms draped around my neck. We look breathtakingly young. I'm not sure he liked the gift. The plate came with a display easel, but he just stuffed it back into the box.

William looks around the dining room stiffly. "Where's the waiter? I need a drink."

"So, twenty years," says Zoe. "What's it like?"

"Oh, Zoe, what kind of a question is that?" I say.

"The kind you're supposed to ask on an anniversary. A serious kind. A taking-stock kind," she says.

What were we thinking asking them to come to our anniversary dinner? If it was just William and me we'd talk about safe subjects like the bond market, or the sticky garage door. Instead we're going to be interrogated as to how we feel about our marriage.

"What's it like *how*?" asks William. "You must be more specific, Zoe. I hate the way your generation asks such vague questions. You expect everybody else to do all the work, including clarifying what you meant to ask in the first place."

"Shit, Dad," says Peter. "She was just asking to be nice."

"Peter Buckle—this is our anniversary dinner. I would appreciate it if you didn't say *shit*," I say.

"Well, what am I allowed to say?"

" 'Dang.' 'Rats.' Or how about 'bananas'?" I suggest.

"As in, *Bananas, Dad? She was just asking to be nice*?" says Peter. "Are you bananas?"

William nods at me from across the table and for a moment I feel united. Which causes me even more duress as I think of Researcher 101 asking me to imagine his hand on the back of my neck.

"How about I take Peter and Zoe to California Pizza Kitchen?" asks Caroline. "We can meet up with you afterwards. What kind of food are you in the mood for, Zoe?" Caroline raises her eyebrows at me. She and I are still debating as to whether Zoe has an eating disorder.

"Vegetarian lettuce wraps," says Zoe, shooting William a questioning look.

"It's okay. I want you all to stay," I say. "And your father does, too. Right, William?"

"Alice, would you like your present now or later?" William says.

"I thought P.F. Chang's was my present."

"It's only part one of your present. Zoe?" says William.

Zoe rummages around in her purse and pulls out a smallish rectangular package wrapped in dark green paper.

"Did you know that emerald is the official twentieth-anniversary color?" asks William.

Emerald? I flash back to the day in the jewelry store with Nedra. Her making me try on that emerald ring. Oh, God. Had William solicited her to help him pick out a ring for our twentieth anniversary? An emerald ring like the one that belonged to my mother that I threw out the car window the week before we got married?

Zoe hands me the package. "Open it," she says.

I stare at William, shocked. His gifts are usually last minute, like fancy jams or a gift certificate for a pedicure. Last year, he gave me a book of forever stamps.

"Now?" I ask. "Wouldn't it be better to wait until we're home? Anniversary gifts are kind of private, aren't they?"

"Just open it, Mom," says Peter. "We all know what it is."

"You do? You told them?"

"I had some help with this one," he admits.

I shake the package. "We're on a budget. I hope you didn't do anything crazy." But I really, really hope he did.

I rip open the paper excitedly to reveal a white cardboard box that says Kindle.

"Wow," I say.

"Isn't it cool?" says Peter, grabbing the box out of my hands. "Look, the box opens like a book. And Dad preloaded it for you."

"I ordered it a month ago," says William, by which he means *I want you to know I put some thought into this.*

"He got you *The Stand.* Said it was your favorite book when you were in high school. And the Twilight series—apparently many mothers are into the books," says Zoe. "I think it's gross, but whatever." She looks at me suspiciously, as a fifteen-year-old daughter is apt to look at her mother. I nod as innocently as possible while simultaneously trying to look delighted.

"The latest Miranda July, *You Are She Who Knows Something I Used To but Forgot,*" says Zoe, "or something like that. You'll love her. She's awesome."

"And *Pride and Prejudice,*" says Peter.

"Wow," I say. "Just wow. I've never read *Pride and Prejudice.* This is so unexpected."

I put the Kindle back in its box carefully.

"You're disappointed," says William.

"No, of course not! I just don't want to scratch it. It's a very thoughtful gift."

I glance around the table. Everything seems out of plumb. Who is this man? I barely recognize him. His face is lean because of all the running. His jaw firm. He hasn't shaved in days and he's sporting a light stubble. If I didn't know him, I'd think he was hot. I reach across the table and pat William's arm awkwardly.

"That means she loves it," translates Peter.

I look down at the menu. "I do," I say. "I really do."

"Great," says William.

"I was twelve when I started to work," says Caroline. "After school I'd sweep the theater while Mom was in rehearsals."

"Hear that, kiddos?" I say, spooning a second helping of Kung Pao chicken onto my plate. "She was *twelve*. That's the way they do it in Maine. You kids need to contribute. You need to get a job. Raking lawns. Delivering newspapers. Babysitting."

"We're okay," says William.

"Well, actually we're kind of not," I say. "Pass the chow mein, please."

"Should I be scared? Is this something I should be scared about? I have fifty-three dollars in my savings account. Birthday money. You can have it," says Peter.

"Nobody has to give up their birthday money," says William. "We all just have to be more frugal."

I look at my Kindle guiltily.

"Starting tomorrow," says William. He raises his glass. "To twenty years," he toasts.

Everybody raises his or her glass but me. I'd already pounded down my Asian pear mojito.

"I only have water," I say.

"So toast with your water," says William.

"Isn't it considered bad luck to toast with water?"

"If you're in the Coast Guard," says William.

I raise my water glass and say what's expected. "To twenty more."

Zoe studies my conflicted face. "You've answered my question about what twenty years of marriage is like."

She looks at William. "And without any further clarification from me."

An hour later, back at home, William sinks into his chair with a sigh, remote control in hand, and then leaps to his feet. "Alice!" he shouts, his hand on his ass.

I look at where he's been sitting. There's a huge wet stain on the cushion. Oh, Jampo!

"I dropped a glass of water this afternoon," I say.

William smells his fingers. "It's piss."

Jampo comes running into the living room and jumps on my lap. He buries his head in my armpit. "He can't help it. He's just a puppy," I say.

"He's two years old!" shouts William.

"Twenty-four months. No child is toilet-trained at twenty-four months. He didn't do it on purpose."

"He most certainly did," William says. "First my pillow and now my chair. He knows all my places."

"You're being ridiculous," I say.

Jampo peeks out of my armpit and growls at William.

"Bad boy," I whisper.

He growls some more. I feel like we're in a cartoon. I can't help it. I start to laugh. William looks at me in shock.

"I can't believe you're laughing."

"I'm sorry, I'm sorry, I'm really sorry," I say, still laughing.

He glares at me.

"Think I'll go to bed now," I say, tucking Jampo under my arm.

"You're bringing him with you?"

"Only until you come to bed and then I'll kick him out," I say. "I promise."

I wave my Kindle at him.

"What are you going to read first?" William asks.

"*The Stand*. I can't believe you remembered how much I loved it. I want to see if it's as good as it was when I first read it."

"You're setting yourself up for disappointment," says William. "I suggest you don't hold it to the same standard."

"What—I should make a new standard?"

"You're not seventeen. The things that were relevant then aren't anymore."

"I disagree. If it was gripping then, it should be gripping now. That's how you know something is a classic. A keeper."

William shrugs. "The dog's ruined my chair."

"It's just pee."

"It's soaked through the entire cushion and into the frame."

I sigh. "Happy anniversary, William."

"Twenty years. That's something, Alice."

William pushes the hair back from his eyes, a gesture I know so well, and for a moment I see the young man that he was, the day I first met him, when I was interviewing for the job. Everything is colliding, past and present and future. I grip Jampo so tightly he squeals. I want to say something to William. Something so he knows to reach out and pull me back from the edge.

"Don't be too long."

"I won't," says William, the remote control back in his hand.

That night he sleeps on the couch.

69

John Yossarian *added Games*
Clue

Lucy Pevensie *added Lives in*
Spare Oom

How was your anniversary, Wife 22?

Confusing.

Is that my fault?

Yes.

What can I do?

Tell me your name.

I can't.

I imagine you have an old-fashioned sort of name. Like Charles or James. Or maybe something a bit more modern, like Walker.

You do realize everything changes once we know each other's names. It's easy to reveal our true selves to strangers. Far harder to reveal those truths to those we know.

Tell me your name.

Not yet.

When?

Soon—I promise.

70

73. Yes, it was different with Peter. After the delivery, after I had slept for a few hours, they brought him to me. It was the middle of the night. William had gone home to be with Zoe.

I peeled back the swaddling blanket. He was one of those babies who looked like a grizzled old man, by which I mean he was the most beautiful baby I had ever seen (although the size of his forehead worried me).

"I already hate his wife," I told the nurse.

74. Bliss. Exhaustion. Coming-home party. Too tired to clean. Too tired to have sex. Too tired to greet William when he comes in the door after work. Zoe tries to smother Peter. Peter adores Zoe even though daily she thinks of inventive new ways to try and knock him off. Forty-plus diapers a week. Is three years old too young for a sister to change her baby brother's diaper? Afternoons on the couch, Peter sleeping on my stomach. Zoe watching inappropriate TV for four hours. Fight with husband over whether *Oprah* inappropriate TV. Shirts soaked in spit-up. Family of three, hours of 6 a.m. to 7 p.m. Family of four, hours of 7 p.m. to 10 p.m. Family of two (me and Peter), hours of 10 p.m. to 6 a.m. Don't worry, say all the books. Distance between you and husband is only temporary. Once baby is four months old, sleeping through the night, eating solids, a year old, past the terrible twos, in kindergarten, reading, getting more pee in the toilet than on the floor, recovered from the poison oak that got everywhere including under his foreskin, has learned to do the backstroke, had his tetanus shot, stopped biting girls, is capable of putting on his socks, no longer lies to you about brushing his teeth, no longer requires lullabies, goes to middle school, enters puberty, comes out as a proud gay tween—then you and William will get back to normal. Then the distance will miraculously disappear.

75. Dear Peter,

The truth—I was upset when I found out you were going to be a boy. Mostly because I had no idea how to mother a boy. I thought it would be much more difficult than being a mother to a girl because of course I knew all about being a girl due to the fact that I was one. Actually still am. The girl inside me lives. I think you've seen her from time to time. She's the one who understands the pleasure of a good nose pick—just do it in private, please, and wash your hands afterward.

Some things you might not know or remember:

1. When you were two and had a horrible ear infection and wouldn't stop crying, I was so distraught at seeing you in pain that I climbed into your crib and held you until you fell asleep. You didn't wake for ten hours, not even when the crib broke.

2. When you were three, you had only two things on your Christmas list: a potato and a carrot.

3. Funny thing you once said upon me giving you ravioli with butter for dinner (we'd run out of tomato sauce): I can't eat this. This ravioli has no heart.

4. Unanswerable thing you once said while helping me fold laundry: Where was I when you were a little girl?

5. Thing you said that broke my heart: Even when I die I'll still be your boy.

It has given me unbelievable pleasure to be your mother. You are my funniest, dearest, brightest star.

Your loving Mama

76. First part of question: I don't know; second part of question: to some degree.

71

"Oh, darling, this is nice. Isn't this nice? Why don't we do this more often?" asks Nedra.

Nedra is taking me to the M·A·C store on 4th Street in Berkeley to buy makeup, her treat. She says she's tried to adjust to my French no-makeup look, but after weeks of me bearing no increasing resemblance to Marion Cotillard (Marie Curie, maybe), something must be done. I don't bother telling Nedra that I'll wear the makeup for two days, maybe three, and then forget about it. She knows this is the case, but it doesn't matter to her. The real reason she's taking me is to guilt me into being her maid of honor. I'm sure we'll find our way over to Anthropologie, where I'll be forced to try on dresses.

It's right after rush hour and the streets are still busy. As we pull up to the intersection of University and San Pablo, I see two kids standing in the median holding up a sign scrawled on a piece of cardboard.

"That's so sad," I say, trying to read the sign, but we're too far away. "Can you read that, Nedra?"

She squints. "I really wish you would get some reading glasses. I'm tired of being your interpreter. *Father lost job. Please help. Songs for free. Requests taken.* Oh, Jesus, God, Alice, don't freak out," she says as we pull closer and those two kids metamorphose into Peter and Zoe.

I inhale sharply and roll down the window. Peter is singing Neil Young's "After the Gold Rush." The driver of a Toyota three cars in front of me holds out a five-dollar bill. "You got a nice voice, kid," I hear him say. "Sorry about your dad."

Despite my confusion, the sound of Peter's angelic voice makes me want to cry. He *does* have a nice voice. He didn't get that from William or me.

I stick my head out the car window. "What the hell are you doing?"

They stare at me in total shock.

"Leave 'em alone, lady. Better yet, give them a twenty," yells the woman in the car behind me. "You look like you can afford it."

I'm sitting in the passenger seat of Nedra's Lexus. "This isn't my car," I yell back at her. "For your information, I drive a Ford!"

"You told us to find work," yells Zoe.

"Babysitting!"

"It's a recession, in case you haven't heard. Unemployment is twelve percent. There's no applying for jobs anymore. You have to invent them," yells Zoe.

"She's right," says Nedra.

"This is an awesome spot," adds Peter. "We've already made over a hundred dollars."

We pull up next to them and stop. The light turns green and the air buzzes with angry horns. I stick my hand out the window and wave the cars on.

"A hundred dollars for whom? You're donating that money to a food shelter. I couldn't be more embarrassed," I hiss.

And terrified—some lunatic could have coaxed them into his car. For all their grown-up posturing, Peter and Zoe are both sheltered, naïve kids. A refresher course on stranger danger is in order.

"You enterprising little things," says Nedra. "I didn't know you had it in you."

"Get in the car," I say. "RIGHT NOW."

Zoe looks at her watch. She's wearing a vintage Pucci dress and ballet flats. "Our shift doesn't end until noon."

"What, you punched in for panhandling?" I say.

"It's important to have structure and keep regular hours," says Peter. "I read that in Dad's book: *100 Ways to Motivate Yourself: Change Your Life Forever.*"

"Climb in, kids," says Nedra. "Do as your mother says or I'll have to look at her pale, blotchy face forever and that will be your fault."

Peter and Zoe climb into the backseat.

"You don't smell homeless," says Nedra.

"Homeless people can't help the way they smell," says Peter. "It's not like they can knock on somebody's door and ask to take a shower."

"That's very compassionate of you," says Nedra.

"That was fun, Pedro," says Zoe, bumping fists with Peter.

I knew the day would come when I'd lose Peter to Zoe, when they'd begin to confide in one another and keep each other's secrets, but I had no idea it would happen this soon or like this.

"Can we please go home?" I say.

Nedra keeps driving up San Pablo.

"Is anybody listening to me?" I cry.

Nedra takes a left onto Hearst and a few minutes later parks on 4th Street. She turns around. "Get lost, darlings. Meet us back here at one."

"You look tired, Mom." Peter pokes his head into the front seat.

"Yeah, what's up with the dark circles?" asks Zoe.

"I'm going to take care of that," says Nedra. "Now scram, you two."

"It's not like you caught them smoking crack," says Nedra, as we're walking into M·A·C.

"You sided with them. Why do you always have to be the cool one?"

"Alice, what's wrong?"

I shake my head.

"What?" she repeats.

"Everything," I say. "You wouldn't understand. You're fiancéed. You're happy. Everything good is ahead of you."

"I hate it when people make nouns into verbs," says Nedra. "And plenty of good things are ahead of you, too."

"What if you're wrong? What if my best days are behind me?"

"Don't tell me this is about that ridiculous marriage survey. You stopped writing to that researcher, right?"

I pick up a tube of eggplant-colored lip gloss.

"So what's this about?" she asks, putting the lip gloss back. "Not your color."

"I think Zoe's got an eating disorder."

Nedra rolls her eyes. "Alice, this happens every summer when school gets out. You get paranoid. You become morose. You're a person who needs to stay occupied." I nod and let myself be led to the foundation counter. "A tinted moisturizer—not too heavy. A little mascara and a pop of blush. And after that we'll take the teensiest, quickest trip through Anthropologie, shall we?" says Nedra.

That night Peter crawls into bed with me.

"Poor Mom," he says, wrapping his arms around me. "You had a hard day. Watching your children begging on the streets."

"Aren't you too old for snuggling?" I say, pushing him away, wanting to punish him a little.

"Never," he says, snuggling in closer.

"How much do you weigh?"

"A hundred pounds."

"How tall are you?"

"Five one."

"You may snuggle for another five pounds or another inch, whichever comes first."

"Why only five pounds and an inch?"

"Because after that it will be unseemly."

Peter is quiet for a moment. "Oh," he says softly, his hand patting my arm the exact same way he used to when he was a toddler.

He was so tuned into me when he was younger; it was exhausting. If any sort of a worried look broke over my face he'd run over. *It's okay, Mama. It's okay,* he would say solemnly. *Would you like a song?*

"I'll miss it, too, sweetheart," I say. "But it will be time."

"Can we still watch movies together on the couch?"

"Of course. I've got our next one lined up. *The Omen.* You're going to love the part at the zoo where all the animals go wild."

We lie quietly together for a while.

Something is nearly over. I put my hand over my heart as if I can keep its contents from spilling out.

72

Lucy Pevensie *added her profile picture*

Nice dress, Wife 22.

You think so? I'm wearing it for my coronation. The rumor floating around here is that soon I'm to be crowned Queen Lucy the Valiant.

Will I be invited to your coronation?

That depends.

On what?

Do you have the proper coronation attire? A velvet cape, preferably royal blue?

I have a velvet cape, but it's puce. Will that do?

I suppose. My best friend wants me to be her maid of honor.

Ah—so this is a maid of honor dress.

Well, this is what she'd *like* me to wear. Well, not exactly this dress, but something similar.

Is it possible you're exaggerating a bit?

Has it ever occurred to you that marriage is a sort of Catch-22? The very things that you first found so attractive in your spouse—his darkness, his brooding, his lack of communication, his silence—those things that you found so charming in the beginning are the very things that twenty years later drive you mad?

I've heard similar sentiments from other subjects.

Have you ever felt this way?

I can't divulge that information.

Please. Divulge something, Researcher 101. Anything.

I can't stop thinking about you, Wife 22.

73

77. A dictatorship where the dictator changes every day. Not sure if democracy is possible.

78. Well, many people here on earth in the twenty-first century believe in the concept of the *one true love*, and when they believe in the *one true love* this often leads to marriage. It may seem to you like a silly institution. Your species might be so advanced you have different partners for different stages of your life: first crush, marriage, breeding, child-raising, empty nest, and slow, but hopefully not painful, death. If that's the case, maybe the *one true love* doesn't enter into it—but I doubt it. You probably just call it something else.

79. It seems to me that everyone takes their turn: behind the curtain managing props, being a bit player, then in the chorus, then center stage, then, at last, all of us end up in the audience, watching, one of the faceless appreciators in the dark.

80. Days and weeks and months of glances, of unrequited lust.

81. Living on the top of a mountain in a house with a quilt on the bed and fresh flowers on the table every day. I would wear long white lace dresses and Stevie Nicks–style boots. He would play the guitar. We would have a garden, a dog, and four lovely kids who built towers out of blocks on the floor while I made chicken in a pot.

82. You need it, like air.

83. Kids. Companionship. Can't imagine life without them.

84. Can imagine life without them.

85. You know the answer to that.

86. Yes.

87. Of course!

88. In some ways, yes. Other ways, no.

89. Cheat. Lie. Forget about me.

90. Dear William,

Do you remember that time we went camping in the White Mountains? We did most of the hike the first day. Our plan was to spend the night and then get up early and climb to the top of Tuckerman Ravine. But you drank too much and the next morning you had a killer hangover, the kind of hangover one can only sleep off. So you crawled back inside your sleeping bag and I went up Tuckerman without you.

You didn't wake until late afternoon. You looked at your watch and knew immediately something was very wrong; it was a hike that should have taken me two hours, but I had been gone close to six and you had a pretty good idea why—I had gone off trail. I was always going off trail. *You*, on the other hand always stayed on the trail, but without you there walking beside me, I drifted, and became helplessly lost.

Now, this was a long time ago. Before AOL. Before cellphones. We were still years away from searching and clicking and browsing and friending. So you came after me the old-fashioned way. You rang your bear bell, you called out my name, and you ran. And at dusk, when you finally found me, sobbing at the base of a pine tree, you made me a promise I'll never forget. *No matter where I went, no matter how far I drifted, no matter how long I was gone, you would come after me and bring me home.* It was the most romantic thing a man had ever said to me. Which makes it all the more difficult for me to come to terms with the fact that twenty years later we've drifted from one another again. Profligate drifting. Senseless drifting. As if we had all the daylight left in the world to make it to the top of Tuckerman.

If this sounds like a goodbye letter, I'm sorry. I'm not sure it's goodbye. It's more of a warning. You should probably look at your watch. You should probably say to yourself, Alice has been gone a very long time. You should probably come and find me. AB

wake to the clatter of aluminum tent poles skittering over the hardwood floor.

"Where the hell is your mother?" I hear William shout from downstairs.

I just want to stay in bed. However, thanks to me, sleep will have to be shelved because we're going camping in the Sierras. I made the reservation a few months ago. It sounded so idyllic then: sleeping under the stars surrounded by sugar pines and firs—a little family bonding. Caroline and Jampo will have the house to themselves for a few days.

"Goddammit!" William shouts. "Is there anybody here capable of packing a tent properly?"

I climb out of bed. Not nearly so idyllic a vision now.

An hour later we are on the road and our family bonding looks like this: William listening to the latest John le Carré novel on his iPhone (which, by the way, is exactly what I'm listening to on the car's CD player, but William says he's unable to concentrate unless he's read to privately), Peter playing Angry Birds on his phone, every so often shouting *bananas* and *dang it*, and Zoe furiously texting—God knows to whom. It's like this for two and a half hours until we begin driving over the pass and cell reception cuts out. Then it's like they've awoken from a dream.

"Whoa, trees," says Peter.

"Is that where those people ate those people?" asks Zoe, peering down at the lake.

"You mean the Donner Party," says William.

"Breast or thigh, Zoe?" asks Peter.

"Hil-ar-ious, Pedro. How long is this camping trip anyway?" asks Zoe.

"Our reservation is for three nights," I say. "And it's not like it's work. It's car camping. Nobody *has* to do anything. We're here to have fun and relax."

"Yes, this morning was extremely relaxing, Alice," says William, staring out the window. He's as unenthusiastic as the children.

"Does this mean there'll be no cell service?" asks Zoe.

"Nah, we're just in a dead zone. Dad said there'd be Wi-Fi at the campground," says Peter.

"Uh—he's wrong, sorry. There's no Wi-Fi," I tell them.

I just found out this fact myself yesterday when I confirmed our reservation. Then I went into my bedroom and had a nice, private panic attack at the thought of being incommunicado with Researcher 101 for seventy-two hours. Now I'm resigned to it.

Gasps issue forth from the backseat.

"Alice, you didn't tell me that," says William.

"No, I didn't tell any of you that because if I did, you wouldn't have come."

"I can't believe *you* are going to unplug," says Zoe to me.

"Well, believe it," I say. I reach over William and pop my cellphone into the glove box. "Hand your phones over, kiddos. You, too, William."

"What if there's an emergency?" says William.

"I brought a first-aid kit."

"An emergency of a different sort," he says.

"Like what?"

"Like having to get in touch with somebody," he says.

"That's the whole point. To get in touch with each other," I say. "IRL."

"IRL?" asks William.

"In real life," I say.

"It really disgusts me that you know that acronym," says Zoe.

Fifteen minutes later, apparently incapable of doing anything— daydreaming, conversing, or having one original thought without the aid of their devices—the kids are asleep in the backseat. They stay asleep until we roll into the campground.

. . .

"Now what?" says Peter, after we finish setting up the campsite.

"Now what? *This* is what," I say, spreading my arms wide. "Getting away from it all. The woods, the trees, the river."

"The bears," says Zoe. "I have my period. I'm staying in my tent. Blood is like catnip to them."

"Disgusting," says Peter.

"That's an old wives' tale," says William.

"No, it's not. They can smell it miles off," says Zoe.

"I'm going to throw up now," says Peter.

"Let's play cards," I say.

Zoe holds up a finger. "Too windy."

"Charades," I suggest.

"What? No! It's not dark yet. People will be able to see us," she says.

"Fine. How about we go find some firewood?" I ask.

"You look mad, Mom," says Peter.

"I'm not mad, I'm thinking."

"It's strange how your thinking face looks like your mad face," says Peter.

"I'm going to take a nap," says Zoe.

"Me, too," says Peter. "All this nature makes me sleepy."

"I'm a little tired, too," says William.

"Do what you want. I'm going down to the river," I say.

"Take a compass," says William.

"It's fifty feet from here," I say.

"Where?" asks Peter.

"Through the trees. There. See? Where all those people are swimming."

"That's a river? It looks like a stream," says Zoe.

"Tucker, you are not allowed to do dead man's float in the water!" we hear a woman scream.

"Why not?" a boy yells back.

"Because people will think you're dead!" the woman screams back.

"We drove all this way so you could swim in a stream with hundreds of other people? We could have just gone to the town pool," says Peter.

"You people are pathetic," I huff, stomping off.

"When are you coming back, Alice?" William calls after me.

"Never!" I shout.

Two hours later, sunburned and happy, I pick up my shoes and head back. I'm exhausted, but it's a good exhausted, the kind that comes from submersing yourself in a glacial river on a July afternoon. I walk slowly, not wanting to break the spell. Occasionally I have this sort of out-of-body experience where I feel all my previous incarnations simultaneously: the ten-year-old, the twenty-year-old, the thirty-year-old, and the forty-something-year-old—they're all breathing and looking out of my eyes at the same time. The pine needle path crunches under my bare feet. The smell of hamburgers grilling makes my stomach growl. I hear the faint sounds of a radio—Todd Rundgren's "Hello It's Me"?

It feels strange not to have my phone with me. It feels even stranger not to be on constant alert, waiting for my next hit: an email or post from Researcher 101. What I feel instead is emptiness. Not a yearning emptiness, but a lovely, blissed-out emptiness that I know will be obliterated the moment I set foot in our campsite.

But that's not what happens. Instead I find my family sitting around the picnic table, talking. TALKING. Without a device, or a game, or even a book in sight.

"Mama," cries Peter. "Are you okay?"

He hasn't called me Mama in at least a year, maybe two.

"You went swimming," said William, noting my wet hair. "In your shorts?"

"Without me?" says Zoe.

"I didn't think you'd want to go. You spent half an hour blow-drying your hair this morning."

"If you had asked I would have gone," Zoe sniffs.

"We can swim again after dinner. It will still be light."

"Let's go for a hike," says Peter.

"Now?" I say. "I was thinking I'd take a little nap."

"We've been waiting for you," says William.

"You have?"

The three of them exchange looks.

"Fine. Great. Let me change and we'll go."

"We're not making enough noise," says Zoe. "Bears only attack when they're surprised. Or smell you. *Woo-hoo. Woo-hoo, bear!*"

We've been hiking for over forty-five minutes. Forty-five mosquito-slapping, horse-fly-buzzing, children-whining, no-breeze-to-be-found-anywhere minutes.

"I thought this was a loop. Shouldn't we be back already?" says Peter. "And why didn't anybody bring a water bottle? Who goes hiking without a water bottle?"

"Run up the trail, Pedro," I say. "Scout ahead. This is all looking very familiar to me. I'm sure we're almost at the end. In fact, I think I hear the river."

This is a lie. I don't hear anything but droning insects.

Peter takes off and William yells after him, "Not too far ahead! I want you to stay in singing range. That's the rule."

"I beg you. Please don't do this to me," says Zoe.

"*Right, right, turn off the lights, we're gonna lose our minds tonight,*" we hear Peter crooning.

Zoe rolls her eyes.

"It's better than *woo-hoo, bear,*" I tell her.

"Do you really think we're almost there?" asks William.

"*Party crasher, penny snatcher.*"

"Oh, my God. Is penny snatcher a *you-know-what*?" I ask.

"What?" says William.

"You know. Something you put pennies in? A bank. A slot. A euphemism for—"

He looks at me perplexed.

"A purse?" I whisper.

"Oh my God, mother, a *vagina*, just say it," says Zoe. "And it's *panty* snatcher, not penny snatcher."

"*Call me up if you a gangsta—*" Peter's voice suddenly breaks off.

We walk for another couple of minutes.

"Is there anything more ridiculous than a twelve-year-old white boy using the word 'gangsta'?" asks Zoe.

"Zoe, shush!"

"What?"

We all stop and listen.

"I don't hear anything," says Zoe.

"Exactly," I say.

William cups his hands to his mouth and yells, "We asked you to sing!"

Silence.

"Peter!"

Nothing.

William tears down the path, Zoe and me on his heels. We round the corner and find Peter frozen in place, standing not more than five feet away from a mule deer. Now, this is not a run-of-the-mill mule deer. It's an enormous trophy buck, well over two hundred pounds, antlers as long as baguettes, and he and Peter seem to be engaged in some sort of staring contest.

"Back away slowly," whispers William to Peter.

"Do mule deer charge?" I whisper to William.

"Slowly," repeats William.

The buck snorts and takes a few steps toward Peter and I let out a little gasp. Peter looks like he's under a spell: he has a half-smile on his face. Suddenly I understand what I'm witnessing. It's a rite of passage. The kind Peter's gone through hundreds of times in his video games, battling otherworldly creature of all sorts, ogres and sorcerers and woolly mammoths, but rarely does a twenty-first-century boy have such an opportunity in real life—to have actual physical contact with the wild thing; to lock eyes with it. Peter extends his hand as if to touch the buck's antlers, and his sudden movement seems to wake the buck up and it darts away into the brush.

"That was unbelievable," says Peter, turning to us, his eyes gleaming. "Did you see him looking at me?"

"You weren't scared?" breathes Zoe.

"He smelled like grass," Peter says. "Like rocks."

William looks at me and shakes his head in wonder.

On the way back, we hike through the woods single-file. Peter leads the way, then Zoe, then me, then William bringing up the rear. Occasionally the setting sun pierces through the trees—magenta, then bright orange. I tip my face up to receive the warmth. The light feels like a benediction.

William reaches for my hand.

75

I wake in the middle of the night to the sound of Zoe screaming. William and I bolt up and look at each other.

"It *is* an old wives' tale," he says, "isn't it?"

In the few seconds it takes to untangle ourselves from our sleeping bags and unzip the tent, we hear three more very disconcerting sounds: Peter roaring, the sound of feet pounding across the dirt, and then Peter screaming, too.

"Oh God, oh God, oh God," I cry. "Hurry up, get out!"

"Give me that flashlight!" yells William.

"What are you going to do with it?"

"I'm going to brain the bear with it, what do you think I'm going to do with it?"

"Make lots of noise. Scream. Wave your arms about," I say, but William is gone.

I take a few deep breaths, then crawl out after him, and here's what I see: Zoe in her nightgown and bare feet, brandishing a guitar like a bat. Jude kneeling, his head bowed, as if he's on the chopping block. Peter sprawled on the ground, and William beside him.

"He's okay," William yells to me.

A few people from neighboring campsites have run over and stand on the perimeter of our campsite. All of them are wearing headlamps. They look like miners, except for their pajamas.

"Everything's okay," William tells them. "Go back to your tents. We've got it under control."

"What happened!" I shout.

"I'm so sorry, Alice," says Jude.

"Are you crying, Jude?" asks Zoe, lowering the guitar, her face softening.

"Where's the bear?" I shout. "Did it run off?"

"No bear," moans Peter.

"It was Jude," says Zoe.

"Jude attacked Peter?"

"I just wanted to surprise Zoe," says Jude. "I wrote her a song."

I run to Peter's side. His shirt is rolled up and I see a gash in his stomach. I cover my mouth with my hand.

"Pedro heard me scream and was trying to save me," says Zoe. "With his marshmallow roasting stick."

"He was running with it," says Jude. "It got stuck in the ground."

"Then he impaled himself," says Zoe.

"Screw you," groans Peter. "I fell on my sword for you."

"There's hardly any blood. That's not good," says William, shining the flashlight on the wound.

"What's that yellow stuff that's curling out?" I ask. "Pus?"

"I think it's fat," says William.

Peter squeals.

"That's okay, that's fine, nothing to worry about," I say, trying to sound like fat poking out of a wound is an ordinary thing. "Everybody has fat."

"It means it's pretty deep, Alice," whispers William. "He's going to need stitches. We need to bring him to the ER."

"I just saw that movie *Say Anything* with John Cusack and I got inspired," explains Jude.

"'In Your Eyes.' I love Peter Gabriel," grunts Peter. "Your song better be worth it."

"You wrote me a song?" asks Zoe.

"Is that your car, Jude?" asks William, referring to the Toyota parked in front of our campsite.

Jude nods.

William helps Peter to his feet. "Let's go, you're driving. Peter can stretch out in the backseat. Alice, you and Zoe follow in our car."

"You're driving like a crazy person. You don't have to tailgate them," snaps Zoe.

"Did you know Jude was coming?"

"No! Of course not."

"Who were you texting on the way down here?"

Zoe crosses her arms and looks out the window.

"What's going on between the two of you?"

"Nothing."

"And 'nothing' is why he drove four hundred miles in the middle of the night to serenade you?"

Even though I'm furious at Jude—why couldn't he have made his surprise appearance in daylight?—I think what he did was incredibly romantic. I loved *Say Anything*. Especially the iconic scene where John Cusack is standing on his car holding up his boom box in that trench coat with the huge shoulder pads—*I see the doorway to a thousand churches in your eyes*. Eleven words that pretty much sum up what it was like to be a teenager in the 1980s.

"It's not my fault he keeps stalking me."

"He wrote you a song, Zoe."

"Not my fault either."

"I saw the way you were looking at him. Obviously you still have feelings for him. Finally!" I say as we drive off the dirt onto a paved road and Jude picks up speed.

"I don't want to talk about it," says Zoe, covering her face with her arm.

We drive down an empty road, past meadows and fields. The moon looks like it's sitting on a fence post.

"Where the hell is the hospital!" I cry after ten minutes. Finally on my right I see a set of buildings, ablaze in lights.

The parking lot is practically deserted. I say a silent prayer of thanks that we're in the middle of nowhere. If this were Children's Hospital in Oakland, we'd be waiting five hours to be seen.

I forgot about stitches. Actually, I forgot about the lidocaine shots that come before the actual stitches.

"You may want to look the other way," suggests the ER doc, the needle in his hand.

Whenever we watch movies or TV that has any bit of sex in it, Peter asks me, "Should I look away?" Depending on the content, if it's just rolling around on the bed fully clothed or kissing or a little bit of dry humping, I tell him no. If there's any sign body parts might be making an appearance, I tell him yes. I know he's seen breasts on the Internet, but he hasn't seen them with his mother sitting beside him on the couch. I don't know who would be more uncomfortable in that situation—him or me. He's not ready. He's not ready to see himself get injected with lidocaine, either.

"Look away," I say to Peter.

"I was talking to you, actually," says the doctor.

"I don't have a problem with needles," I say.

Peter has a death grip on my hand. "I'm going to distract myself now. By having a meaningless conversation with you."

His eyes stare intently into mine, but my eyes skitter involuntarily toward the needle.

"Mom, I have something to tell you and it may come as a surprise."

"Uh-huh," I say, watching the doctor begin to make injections all around the wound.

"I'm straight."

"That's good, honey," I say, as the doctor now begins to inject the lidocaine *inside* the wound.

"You're doing great, Peter," says the doctor. "Almost done."

"Mrs. Buckle," says the doctor. "Are you okay?"

I feel dizzy. I grab onto the side of the bed.

"This always happens," says the doctor to William. "We tell the parents not to look but they can't help it—they look. I had a father in here the other day who suddenly collapsed when I was stitching up his daughter's lip. Pitched right over. Big guy. Two hundred pounds. Chipped three teeth."

"Let's go, Alice," says William, taking my elbow.

"Mom, did you hear me?"

"Yes, sweetheart, you're straight."

William forces me to my feet.

"Your son is straight. And would you please stop shaking?" I say to William. "It's making me nauseous."

"I'm not shaking," says William, holding me up. "You are."

"There's a gurney out in the hallway," says the doctor.

Those are the last words I hear before I faint.

76

The next day, after a six-hour drive home (two of those hours being stuck in stop-and-go traffic), I go straight upstairs to bed. I'm exhausted.

Zoe and Peter follow me into my room. Peter hurls himself onto the bed next to me, fluffs a pillow, and grabs the remote. "Netflix?" he says.

Zoe looks at me with concern.

"What's wrong?" I ask. I can't remember the last time she looked at me kindly.

"Maybe you fainted because you were getting sick," she says.

"That's very generous of you, but I fainted because I watched the doctor stick a needle into an open wound in Pedro's belly."

"Six stitches," Peter says proudly, pulling up his shirt to expose the bandage.

"Aren't you overdoing it a little? The doctor said you'd be fine by today," says Zoe.

"Six stitches," Peter repeats.

"I know, Pedro, you were very brave."

"So are we watching *When Barry Met Wally* or what?" asks Peter.

After Peter admitted to me he had no desire to see *The Omen*, I put an end to the mother-son creepy thrillers club. Peter and I are now the sole members of the mother-son romantic comedy club, and I promised when we got home that we'd begin the Nora Ephron series. First we'll watch the classic *When Harry Met Sally*, then *Sleepless in Seattle*, and finally, *You've Got Mail*. I do not expect these movies to result in any nightmares for Peter, other than the horror of realizing how often and comprehensively men and women misunderstand one another.

"I hate romantic comedies," Zoe says. "They're so predictable."

"Is that your way of saying you want to join the club?" asks Peter.

"Dream on, gangsta," she says, leaving the room.

"Should I look away?" Peter asks one minute into the movie, when Billy Crystal is kissing his girlfriend outside Meg Ryan's car.

"Should I look away?" he asks again during the famous fake orgasm scene in Katz's deli. "Or maybe just plug my ears?"

"Should I look away?" he asks when—

"Oh, for God's sake, Pedro. People have sex, okay. People love sex. People talk about sex. People simulate sex. Women have vaginas. Men have penises." I wave my hand. "Blah, blah, blah."

"I've decided I don't want to be Pedro anymore," he says.

I mute the movie. "Really? Everyone's gotten the hang of it."

"I just don't."

"Okay. Well, what do you want to be called?"

Please don't let him say Pedro 3000 or Dr. P-Dro or Archibald.

"I was thinking—Peter."

"Peter?"

"Uh-huh."

"Well, that's a lovely name. I like Peter. It suits you. Should I be the one to break it to your father or should you?"

Peter unmutes the movie.

Billy Crystal: There are two kinds of women: high maintenance and low maintenance.

Meg Ryan: Which one am I?

Billy Crystal: You're the worst kind. You're high maintenance but you think you're low maintenance.

Peter mutes the movie again. "Why did you think I was gay?"

"I didn't think you were gay."

Peter gives me a skeptical look.

"Okay, I thought there might be a possibility."

"Why, Mom?"

"You just gave off—a vibe."

"Examples?"

"Well. You changed your name to Pedro."

"Right—there are so many gay Pedros. Go on."

"You hated Eric Haber. Too much."

"That's because he liked Briana too. He was my competition. But he and Pippa Klein are going out, so now he's cool."

"Um—your hair swirls counterclockwise."

Peter shakes his head at me. "You are a kook."

"And because you use words like 'kook.'"

"Because *you* use words like 'kook'! I'm straight, Mom."

"I know, Peter."

"Wow, I haven't heard 'Peter' in a long time."

"Sounds good, doesn't it?"

"Don't think I've forgotten that it's slang for penis."

"Of course not. But doesn't that give it a sort of edge?" I poke him.

"Ow!"

I sigh. "I'm going to miss my gay son who would never leave me for another woman. I know *that's* homophobic—thinking you'll stay unnaturally attached to me because you're gay. Either way, you're leaving me eventually."

"If it makes you feel better, you could still think of me as your gay son in private. Besides, what kind of a straight twelve-year-old would agree to watch *When Harry Met Sally* with his mother?" asks Peter.

He unmutes the movie and chuckles.

"That's exactly the vibe I was talking about," I say.

"What? Precocious? Smart? Funny? Straight people can be those things, too. You're so heterophobic."

After the movie (both of us tear up at the ending), Peter goes in search of something to eat and I log on to Facebook. There's nothing from Researcher 101, which is not really a surprise: I did tell him I was going to be off-line for a few days. There is, however, no shortage of postings on my wall.

Pat Guardia ▶ Alice Buckle

Braxton Hicks—FOR NOW.

30 minutes ago

Shonda Perkins ▶ Alice Buckle

New samples: Waterproof Defencils. Juicy Tubes.

32 minutes ago

Tita De La Reyes ▶ Alice Buckle

Five dozen lumpia looking for a good home.

34 minutes ago

Weight Watchers

Amnesty Day!! Rejoin the program. First two months free!

4 hours ago

Alice Buckle

Has been tagged in a photo by Helen Davies

4 hours ago

Within minutes of logging on, I feel sick, for two reasons. One—the Mumble Bumbles, Pat, Tita, and Shonda, are stalking me through the ethers. If I don't agree to breakfast at the Egg Shop soon, they'll ring my doorbell, throw me in the car, and drive me there. And two—because falling down a rabbit hole into the past frequently has this effect on me. Helen's posted a load of photos from our Peavey Patterson days. The one I can't stop looking at was taken the night William won his Clio. It's of him and Helen sitting at the table, heads tipped toward one another, as if in deep conversation. And there in the background, sitting at another table, is me, staring at them hungrily like a madwoman. Helen's posted this embarrassing photo on purpose.

Helen friended me right after she friended William, with only one intention as far as I can see: to let me know that losing William didn't ruin her life. She married a man named Parminder, and she and her husband started their own ad agency, which, according to her profile on LinkedIn, has offices in Boston, New York, and San Francisco, and had over $10 million in billings last year. She's on Facebook all the time; she makes me look like a Luddite. She is no longer zaftig—she golfs, does the tango, and spins, and as of today, weighs a svelte 122 pounds. She uploads photos constantly. Here are her three children sitting at the table making homemade valentines. Here is her cutting garden. And here she is with her new haircut. Do you *Like*? And although I know her page is curated meticulously, I can't help falling for her pitch. She has an enviable life. Perhaps she even won, if the markers for winning are a toned body, highlights, and an estate in Brookline.

At least Weight Watchers won't make me feel envious. I log on and open up my Plan Manager. I scroll back to February 10, the last day I used it.

Weightwatchers.com
Plan Manager for Alice Buckle

PointsPlus Values: 29   **Daily Used** 32   **Daily Remaining** 0   **Activity Earned** 0

Favorites (recently added)

Egg	Point Value	2
Yoplait yogurt	Point Value	3
Gummy Bears (30)	Point Value	14
Krispy Kreme glazed donut	Point Value	20

Don't know PointsPlus Value?

Enter Food	Marshmallow Fluff
Enter Fiber	0
Enter Fat	5
Enter Carbohydrates	30
Enter Protein	0
Calculating PointsPlus Values NOW!	33

Now I remember why I stopped Weight Watchers. Counting every morsel of food made me feel incredibly hopeful for the first half of the day, then when one tablespoon of Fluff turned into five an hour before dinner, utterly guilty. Hey, whatever happened to my idea for a Guilt Diet? The same template would work beautifully, with just a few little tweaks.

Guiltdiet.com
Plan Manager for Alice Buckle

GuiltPlus Values: 29 **Daily Used** 102 **Daily Remaining** 0 **Penance Earned** 0

Favorites (recently added)

Used last piece of toilet paper and did not replace roll	Guilt Value 1.5
Said I read *Anna Karenina*	Guilt Value 3
Denied I read *The Unauthorized Biography of Katy Perry*	Guilt Value 7
I am not bilingual.	Guilt Value 8
I am American.	Guilt Value 10
I do not know the difference between Shias and Sunnis.	Guilt Value 11
I secretly believe in the Law of Attraction.	Guilt Value 20
I didn't call back my best friend after she called four times and left scary messages in her divorce lawyer voice saying, "Alice Buckle, call me back immediately, there's something we have to talk about."	Guilt Value 8

Don't know Guilt Value?

Enter Guilt	Excessive flirting and nearly constant fantasizing about a man who is not my husband
How many people were hurt?	None yet.
How many people could be hurt?	3 to 10
Cost to make it up?	?
Time to make it up?	??
Unmakeupable?	I'm afraid so.

CALCULATE GuiltPlus Value NOW: 8942

WARNING: This exceeds (by 44.04 weeks) weekly allotment of GuiltPlus points.

RECOMMENDED ALTERNATIVE: Pee on the seat in a public toilet instead (Guilt Value 5).

I am a very bad person. Helen of Troy is a very put-together person. Even though I stole her boyfriend, she went on to have a fine life. A better life, perhaps, than mine.

I slide off the bed and walk to the top of the stairs.

"William!" I shout. I feel a pressing need to talk to him. I don't know about what. I just want to hear his voice.

No answer.

"William?"

Jampo comes tearing up the stairs.

"Your name is not William," I say, and he cocks his head forlornly.

I think about the way William reached out for my hand when we were in the woods, right after Peter saw the deer. I think about Peter's accident and how that unlikely event—its marshmallow roasting sticks and pus and ER confessions of sexual identity—have bonded us all together. I think about Zoe looking at me with kindness and worrying I might be getting sick and I know what I have to do. The past twenty-four hours have just solidified it. I log on to Lucy's Facebook page before I lose my nerve and send a message to Researcher 101.

This has gone too far. I'm sorry, but I have to quit the study.

As soon as I press Send, I feel a rush of sweet relief, not unlike the relief I used to feel on a Monday when I entered "eggs" on my Weight Watchers Plan Manager.

The next day I decide to unplug. I'm scared to see Researcher 101's reply (or worse, his silence) and I don't want to spend the day obsessively checking my Facebook messages, so I shut off my phone and computer and leave them in my office. It's not easy. My fingers involuntarily tap and circle all day as if browsing an invisible page. And even though I don't have my phone, I react as if I do. I'm in a state of hypervigilance—waiting to be summoned by a bell that will not be ringing.

I try and embed myself in the day. I run with Caroline; Peter and I bake blueberry muffins; I take Zoe to Goodwill; but even though my body is there, my brain is not. I'm no better than Helen. I, too, treat my life as something to be mined and then packaged up for public consumption. Every post, every upload, every *Like*, every *Interest*, every *Comment* is a performance. But what happens to the performer when she's playing to an empty stage? And when did the real world become so empty? When everybody abandoned it for the Internet?

My digital diet lasts until after dinner, when I can't bear it any longer and I break my fast. By the time I log on to Lucy Pevensie's Facebook page, I'm breathless.

John Yossarian *invited you to the event "Coffee"*
Tea & Circumstances, July 28, 7 p.m.
You can't quit yet. There are things I need to tell you now that can only be said in person.
RSVP Yes No Maybe

Relief floods through me again, but there's nothing sweet about it this time. It's relief of the desperate, addictive, I-may-never-have-an-opportunity-like-this-again sort, and it hits me like I've mainlined a drug. Before I can stop myself, God help me, I click *Yes*.

$$77$$

**Exercise: Write a breakup scene where the characters
speak almost entirely in clichés.**

" I 'm coming over there right now," says Nedra.

"I'm in the middle of coloring my hair—you can't," I say, looking into the bathroom mirror with dismay. "Hold on, I'm putting you on speaker."

I place the phone on the counter and start scrubbing my forehead with a dry washcloth. "I've got dye all over my face and it's not coming off!" I cry.

"Are you using soap and water?"

"Of course I am," I say, squirting the washcloth with three pumps of liquid soap and then running it under the tap.

"Alice. This is crazy. I'm begging you, don't go meet him," says Nedra.

"You don't understand."

"Oh, really? Okay. Let's see—your needs weren't being met. Could you be any less original, Alice?"

"Researcher 101 sees me for who I really am," I say. A woman in her underwear with dye dripping down her temples. "And he's a mystery. And I feel like if I don't do this now, there'll never be another chance." I throw the washcloth in the sink and check the time. "I didn't mean for this to happen."

Nedra pauses. "That's what they all say. Researcher 101 is an invention, you know that, don't you? You've invented him. You think you know him, but you don't. It's a one-way relationship. You've revealed everything to him, all your secrets, your confessions, your hopes and your dreams, and he hasn't told you anything about himself," says Nedra.

"That's not true," I say, combing my hair. "He's told me things."

"What, that he likes piña coladas? What kind of a man likes piña coladas?"

"He told me he can't stop thinking about me," I say softly.

"Oh, Alice. And you believed him? William is real. *William*. Okay, you've grown apart. Okay, you're going through a dry spell, but you have a marriage worth saving. I've heard every iteration of this story a thousand times, from every angle, from every perspective—an affair is never worth it. Go to counseling. Do everything you can to fix this."

"Jesus, Nedra, I'm just meeting him for coffee." I peer in the mirror. Is my part *supposed* to be orange?

"If you agree to meet him for coffee, you are crossing a threshold, and you know it."

I open the cupboard under the sink and rummage around for the hair dryer. "I thought you'd support me. Out of all the people in the world, I thought you'd at least try and understand what I'm going through. I didn't go looking for this. It came looking for me. Literally. The invitation showed up in my Spam folder. It just happened."

"Bloody hell, Alice, it didn't just happen. You were complicit in making it happen."

I find the hair dryer, but the cord is hopelessly tangled. Can't anything be easy? Suddenly I feel so tired. "I'm lonely. I've been lonely for a long time. Isn't that worth something? Don't I deserve to be happy?" I whisper.

"Of course you do. But that's no reason to abandon your life."

"I'm not abandoning it. I'm just meeting him for coffee."

"Yes, but what do you want out of this? *Why* are you meeting him for coffee?"

Why indeed, when I look like this? There are circles the color of, yes, thistles, under my eyes. With concealer, maybe I could lighten them to lavender. "I don't know, exactly," I admit.

I can hear Nedra breathing. "I have no idea who you are anymore," she says.

"How can you say that? I'm the same person I've always been. Maybe *you've* changed."

"Well, I guess the apple doesn't fall far from the tree."

"Meaning what?" I ask.

"Like mother, like daughter."

"I have no idea what you're talking about, Nedra."

"If you had returned any of my last four phone calls you would."

"I told you I was in the mountains. There was no cell reception."

"Well, you may be interested to know Jude and I had a little heart-to-heart about Zoe."

"Good. Did you tell him to move on? She's not going to take him back."

"She'd be lucky to get him back. He finally told me what really happened. I knew something didn't feel right. It was Zoe who cheated on Jude."

"No, Jude cheated on Zoe," I say slowly.

"No, Jude *let* Zoe tell everybody he cheated on her in order to protect her reputation but she cheated on him, and despite her cheating ways, and for the life of me I don't know why, he's still madly in love with her, the little sap."

Could this be true?

"Jude's lying. Zoe would have told me," I say, but I know in my heart it *is* true. It explains so much. Oh, Zoe.

"Your daughter has issues; lying is the least of them."

"I know about my daughter's issues. Don't you dare throw information I've shared with you in confidence in my face."

"Alice, you've been so busy carrying on with Researcher 101 that you have no idea what's happening with your own daughter. She doesn't have an eating disorder; she's got a Twitter account. With over five hundred followers. Would you like to know her user name? It's Ho-Girl."

"*Ho-Girl?*"

"Short for Hostess Girl. She reviews bakery products, but her reviews can be interpreted in a few different ways, if you know what I mean. The point is your daughter is in trouble, but you haven't noticed as you've been so busy living your double life. She's obviously working something out."

"Yes, whether she prefers Twinkies or fruit pies. Why do you always have to exaggerate? And why are you treating me this way? I'm your best friend, not your client. I expected to you to be on my side, not William's."

"I *am* on your side, Alice. This is me being on your side. *Don't go meet him.*"

"I don't have a choice."

"Fine. Don't expect me to be waiting here when you come back. I can't be your confidante. Not on this front. I won't lie for you. For the record, I think you're making a huge mistake."

"Yes, you've made that very clear. I assume you'll be finding a new maid of honor? One who isn't such a whore?"

Nedra inhales sharply.

I fantasize about throwing the phone against the wall in lieu of hanging up, but I can't afford to buy a new one, and I am *not* in some Nora Ephron movie (as much as I would like to be because if I were, I'd know no matter how horrible things got, there would be a happy ending on New Year's Eve), so instead I stab Off on the phone with my finger, leaving a permanent smudge of Clairol Nice 'n Easy Medium Golden Brown on the screen.

78

FROM *CREATIVE PLAYMAKING*

Exercise: Now write that same breakup scene in two sentences.

"Don't do it," says the best friend.
    "I have to," says the protagonist.

79

July 28th is a perfect summer day. No humidity and a temp of 75. I spend an hour upstairs in my bedroom agonizing over what to wear to meet Researcher 101. A skirt and sandals? Too schoolgirlish. A sundress? Trying too hard. In the end I settle on jeans and a peasant shirt, but I put on some of the new makeup Nedra bought for me: mascara and a quick swipe of blush. This is the real me and it will have to do. If he doesn't like it, tough. The conversation I had with Nedra has completely shaken me up. I almost want to disappoint 101. To turn him off, so I don't have to make any decision and he can make it for me.

Downstairs, Caroline and William are making a salad. When I walk into the kitchen William looks up, startled. "You look nice," he says. "Are you going somewhere?"

"Meeting Nedra for a cup of tea after dinner, so I'll have to eat quickly."

"Since when does Nedra drink tea in the evening?"

"She says she has something to talk to me about."

"That sounds ominous."

"You know Nedra."

I'm stunned by my ability to lie so effortlessly.

The doorbell rings and I look at my watch. 6:00.

"Are the kids expecting anybody?"

William shrugs.

I walk to the door in my espadrilles, taking the opportunity to practice a sexier gait. I put a little sway into it, dip my head to the side coquettishly. I swivel around to make sure William hasn't seen me. He's standing in front of a cupboard, studying its contents. I open the front door.

"Alice," cries Bunny. "It's been so long!"

• • •

The next few hours pass like this.

6:01: I try and wipe the stunned look off my face. We've gotten the dates messed up. We thought Bunny and Jack were arriving tomorrow night, but here they are, a day early, standing on the doorstep.

6:03: Jampo comes racing to the door, barking furiously.

6:04: Jampo bites Bunny on the leg, drawing blood. Bunny cries out in pain.

6:05: Hearing the scream, William, Caroline, Zoe, and Peter run into the hallway.

6:07: Triage in the kitchen in the form of me babbling on endlessly. It's just a nip, not a bite. Where are the Band-Aids? Do we have Neosporin? That's not Neosporin, it's Krazy Glue.

6:09: William grits his teeth as he cleans Bunny's wound.

6:10: I check the time.

6:15: William asks who would like a drink.

6:17: I open a bottle of pinot noir and pour the adults a glass.

6:19: I drain my glass and pour another glug.

6:20: William suggests I slow down.

6:30: The buzzer goes off and William takes the macaroni and cheese out of the oven.

6:31: Everybody exclaims how good it smells and how they can't wait to eat it.

6:35: The pros and cons of using Gruyère over the more traditional cheddar when making homemade macaroni and cheese are discussed and parsed.

6:40: I tell Bunny and Jack how thrilled I am to have them come stay with us.

6:45: Bunny inquires as to whether I'm feeling well. I say I'm feeling fine, why does she ask? She says something about the beads of sweat that are popping out on my forehead.

6:48: Bunny asks Caroline how her job search is going.

6:49: Caroline tells her "great!"; she's been appointed the new CEO of Google.

6:51: I tell everybody that I'm very, very sorry but I have a previous engagement that I can't miss and I can't call to cancel because Nedra dropped her cellphone in the toilet yesterday and therefore I have no way to reach her.

6:51: William pulls me aside and says he can't believe I'm still going—Bunny and Jack have just arrived.

6:52: I tell him I'm sorry, but I have to go.

6:52: William reminds me that having Bunny and Jack come stay with us was my idea. It's not fair to make him play host alone. He asks me please not to go.

6:53: I go.

7:05: High on adrenaline, I arrive at Tea & Circumstances and grab a table. Researcher 101 is late, too.

7:12: I check the time.

7:20: I open the Facebook app on my phone. No new posts and he's not online.

7:25: I order a lemon tea. I'd rather have coffee, but I don't want to risk the bad breath.

7:26. I check Facebook.

7:27: I check Facebook again.

7:28: I turn my phone off and on.

7:42: I feel middle-aged.

7:48. I send him a Facebook message. *Did we say seven or eight? Maybe we said eight. Anyway, I'm here!*

8:15: You stupid, stupid woman.

I look down at my espadrilles, and at the lip gloss smeared on the rim of my mug. My body shudders, starting from my toes and working all the way up to my shoulders.

"Are you okay?" asks the waitress gently, a minute later.

"I'm fine, I'm fine," I mumble.

"You're sure?"

"I just got some bad news."

"Oh—gosh. I'm so sorry. Can I help?"

"No, thank you."

"Okay. Well, please don't hesitate to let me know if you need anything. Anything at all." She hurries off.

I sit at the table, my head buried in my arms. Suddenly my phone chimes. It's a Facebook message from John Yossarian.

I'm so sorry. Something unexpected came up.

I look at the words in shock. Okay, okay, okay. There's a reason he didn't come. But who does he think he is, standing me up? I swing between wanting desperately to believe him and wanting to tell him to fuck off, but before I can stop myself I type *I was worried something had happened to you.*

My phone chimes again almost instantly.

Thank you so much for understanding. I'm not playing games. I wanted to be there more than anything. You have to believe me.

I glance up from my phone. Tea & Circumstances is deserted. Apparently nobody wants Tea & Circumstances after 8 p.m. I read and reread his last two messages. Although he's saying all the right things, I don't think I've ever felt lonelier. Did something *really* come up? Was he even planning on coming to meet me? Or did he change his mind at the last minute? Did he decide he liked me better at a distance? That meeting the real me would ruin his fantasy? And what about *my* fantasy? That there was a real man out there who saw me. A man who couldn't stop thinking about me. A man who made me feel like a woman worthy of being obsessed about. What if the truth is that Researcher 101 is just some stupid jerk who gets off on leading pathetic, lonely, middle-aged women on?

I'm too heartbroken to lie. I type *I wanted you to be here more than anything, too.*

8:28: I get in my car.
8:29: I drive home.
8:40: I pull into the driveway.

8:41: I unlock the front door.

8:42: "Alice?" William shouts. "We've been waiting for you. Come join us."

8:44: Flooded with guilt at the sound of William's voice, I force a smile on my face and walk down the hallway to the living room.

Part 3

80

"Perfect timing, Alice will settle the argument," says Bunny, smiling at me as I enter the room.

Bunny sits on the chaise, looking as if she's been sitting there for a hundred years. Her bandaged leg is propped up on a pillow, her feet are bare, and her toenails are painted a cheerful shade of tangerine. Even injured, she's a veritable poster girl for aging gracefully. She must be in her sixties now and she's more beautiful than ever.

"Bunny, I'm so sorry about your leg," I say.

"Pah," says Bunny. "We're practically friends now, aren't we, Jampo?"

Jampo is curled up on his dog bed in the corner of the room. When he hears his name he lifts his head.

"Bad, stinky dog," I admonish him.

He growls softly and then lays his head back down on his crossed paws.

Jack stands, all limbs and freckles and a full head of ginger hair. He has the coloring of a tabby cat; peaches and cream, just like Caroline. I never got to know him as well as I did Bunny, even though he practically lived at the Blue Hill Theater when I was mounting my play (he liked to refer to himself as Bunny's personal *jack*-of-all-trades), but he was always very kind to me.

"Take my seat, Alice," he says.

"There's plenty of room here, too," says William, patting the cushion of the couch.

I can't bring myself to look at him. "I'm fine. I'll sit on the floor."

Jack raises his eyebrows.

"Really, the floor is my favorite place."

"It's true, she prefers it," says William. "Frequently she sits on the floor even when there are chairs available."

"I used to like the floor, too. Until my hips stopped preferring it," says Jack.

"Did you take your baby aspirin today?" asks Bunny.

"Baby aspirin has nothing to do with hips," says Jack.

"Yes, but it has something to do with hearts, my love," says Bunny.

I had forgotten how Bunny called Jack "my love." That term of endearment always struck me as so romantic. After the *Barmaid* run was over, when I went home to Boston I tried calling William "my love," but it just felt too much like an affectation. "My love" was something you had to earn, or be born into. I glance at William, who smiles pleasantly back at me, and I feel nauseous.

"Jack had a thing with his heart a few months ago," explains Bunny.

"Oh, no—was it serious?" I ask.

"No," says Jack. "Bunny worries unnecessarily."

"That's called looking out for you," says Bunny.

" 'Looking out for me' means she took all the Rihanna off my iPod and replaced it with Verdi."

"*You* listen to Rihanna?" I ask.

"He was playing his music too loud," says Bunny. "Deaf and a bad heart are too much for me to be expected to bear."

"A shame," says Jack. "A little deafness isn't the worst thing for a marriage." He winks at me.

"Alice," exclaims Bunny. "Look at you. You're glowing! The forties are such a wonderful decade. Before you get too comfortable, come here and give me a proper hello."

I cross the room, sit down on the edge of the chaise, and sink into her arms. She smells exactly the way I remembered—of freesia and magnolia.

"Everything okay?" she whispers.

"Just life," I mumble back.

"Ah—life. We'll talk later, hmmm?" she says softly into my ear.

I nod, embrace her once more, and slip onto the floor beside her. "So what's the argument?" I ask.

"Christiane Amanpour or Katie Couric?" says Bunny.

"Well, I like them both but if I had to choose," I say, "Christiane."

"We're arguing about who's more attractive," says William, "not who's a better reporter."

"What does it matter how attractive they are?" I say. "These are women who talk to presidents, prime ministers, and dignitaries."

"That was exactly my response," says Bunny.

"How's Nedra?" asks William.

"I—uh."

"You—uh," he says.

"Sorry. I'm just tired. She's wonderful. We had a lot to catch up on."

"Really?" he says. "Didn't you just talk to her yesterday?"

Stay calm, Alice. Keep it simple. Whatever you do, don't look up and to the right when you talk to him. That's a sure sign somebody is lying. And don't blink. Absolutely no blinking. "Well, yes, on the phone, but we rarely get a chance to talk in person. Without anybody else there. You know how it is," I say, my eyes boring into his.

William gives me a bug-eyed look in return. I try and soften my gaze.

"Nedra's Alice's best friend. She's getting married," says William.

"How wonderful! Who's the lucky man?" asks Bunny.

"Lucky woman. Her name's Kate O'Halloran," I say.

"Well. All right. Nedra and Kate. I can't wait to meet them," says Bunny.

"Alice is the maid of honor," says William.

"Actually, I haven't quite agreed to that yet."

"I can see why. *Maid* is so medieval. Why not *woman*? Woman of honor," asks Bunny.

I bob my head agreeably. Why the hell not? I'm a woman of honor—at least I used to be, before tonight.

"Well," says Jack, looking at his watch. "I'm beat. Let's hit it, Bunny. It's nearly one in the morning our time."

"I'm sorry," I say, leaping to my feet. "I'm being so rude. Has anybody shown you to your room?"

I hear the TV blaring from the den and the sound of the kids talking over it.

"Yes, yes. William already brought our luggage up," says Bunny. "And, Alice, you must promise to tell us when you become sick of us. Our return tickets are three weeks from now, but like Mark Twain says, visitors and fishes start to stink after . . ."

"I'll never be sick of you," I say. "You can stay here as long as you like. So you're between shows?"

Bunny nods, following Jack up the stairs. "I've got a pile of scripts. I'm trying to decide what to do next. I'm hoping you'll help me. Read through some of them?"

"I'd be honored. I think I'll go to bed, too. It's been a long day," I say, faking a yawn. I plan to pretend to be asleep when William comes up.

"I'll check on the kids," says William once Bunny and Jack have disappeared into the guest room.

"Make sure that you tell them to shut off all the lights when they're done with their show." I head up the stairs.

"Alice?"

"What?"

"Should I bring you up some tea?"

I spin around, paranoid. Does he know something? "Why would I want tea? I just spent all evening drinking tea with Nedra."

"Oh—right. Sorry, I just thought you might want something warm."

"I do want something warm," I say.

"You do?" he asks.

Is that eagerness in his voice? Does he think the *something warm* I'm talking about is him?

"My laptop," I say.

His face falls.

I wake at four the next morning and shuffle downstairs, a raggedy mess. I walk into the kitchen only to find Bunny already there. She's standing at the stove. The kettle is on and two mugs are lined up on the counter.

She smiles at me. "I had a feeling you might join me."

"What are you doing up?"

"It's seven for me. The question is, what are *you* doing up?"

"I don't know. I couldn't sleep." I hug my ribs.

"Alice, what is it?"

I groan. "I've done something really bad, Bunny."

"How bad?"

"Bad."

"Addicted to painkillers *bad*?"

"Bunny! No, of course not!"

"Then it's not that bad."

I pause. "I think I've fallen in love with another man."

Bunny slides into a kitchen chair slowly. "Oh."

"I told you it was bad."

"Are you sure, Alice?"

"I'm sure. And wait—it gets worse. I've never even met him."

And so I tell Bunny the entire story. She doesn't say one word while I'm speaking, but her face tells me everything I need to know. She's an amazing, responsive audience. Her eyes widen and narrow as I show her the emails and Facebook chats. She murmurs and clucks and coos as I read her my answers to the survey. But mostly what she does is receive me—with every bit of her body.

"You must be heartbroken," she finally says when I'm done.

I sigh. "Yes. But I feel so much more than that. It's complicated."

"It seems simple enough to me. This man, this researcher—he listened to you. He told you exactly what you wanted to hear. I'm sorry to say you're probably not the first woman he's done this to."

"I know, I know. Wait. Do you really think that? God, I don't think so. I really don't. It seemed we had something kind of special, something just between me and—"

Bunny shakes her head.

"You think I'm a fool."

"Not a fool, just vulnerable," says Bunny.

"I feel so humiliated."

Bunny waves my words away. "Humiliation is a choice. Don't choose it."

"I'm angry," I add.

"Better. Anger is useful."

"At William."

"You're angry at *William*? What about this Researcher?"

"No, William. *He* drove me to this."

"Now, that's not fair, Alice. It just isn't. Listen. I'm no saint and I'm not sitting here in judgment. There was a time with Jack and me—we went through a rocky patch. We actually separated for a while, when Caroline left for college. Well, look, I don't need to go into the details, but my point is no marriage is perfect and if it looks perfect, the one thing you can be damn sure of is that it isn't. But don't blame this on William. Don't be so passive. You need to take responsibility for what you've done. What you *almost* did. Whether you end up staying with William is not the point. The point is don't just *let* this happen to you."

"This?"

"Life. Not to be morbid, but honestly, Alice, you don't have enough years left to just fritter away. None of us does. God knows I don't." Bunny gets up and puts the kettle back on. The sun has just risen, and the kitchen momentarily fills with an apricot light. "By the way, do you have any idea what a natural storyteller you are? You've held me enraptured for the past two hours."

"Storyteller?" William walks into the kitchen. He surveys the mugs. The dried-up teabags.

"How long have you two been up," he asks, *"storytelling?"*

"Since four," says Bunny. "We've had a lot of catching up to do."

"Fifteen years' worth," I say.

"It was a beautiful sunrise," says Bunny. "The backyard was the color of a peach. For a moment there, anyway."

William peers out the window. "Yes, well, now it's the color of a Q-tip."

"That must be the legendary Bay Area fog everybody always talks about," says Bunny.

"Clear one minute, can't see a thing the next," says William.

"Just like marriage," I say under my breath.

81

John Yossarian *added Games*
Sorry

Lucy Pevensie *added Activities*
Looking for the lamppost

Please tell me you had a very good reason for not coming last night, Researcher 101.

I'm sorry, I really am. I know this sounds clichéd, but something unexpected came up. Something unavoidable.

Let me guess. Your wife?

You could say that.

Did she find out about us?

No.

Did you think she would?

Yes, I did.

Why?

Because I was going to tell her about us after I met with you last night.

You were? So what happened?

I can't say. I wish I could. But I can't. You're looking for the lamppost?

That's what I said.

You're saying you want to go home, then? You want to leave this world. Our world?

We have a world?

I've been thinking that maybe things worked out for the best. Maybe it was fate that we couldn't meet.

It wasn't that we *couldn't* meet. I was there. You stood me up.

I would have been there if I could, I promise you. But let me ask you something, Wife 22. Didn't you feel the least bit relieved that I didn't show?

No. I felt toyed with. I felt ridiculous. I felt sad. Do *you* feel relieved?

Does it help to know I've thought about you nearly every minute since?

And what about your wife? Have you thought about her nearly every minute since, too?

Please forgive me. The man who doesn't show is not the man I want to be.

Who's the man you want to be?

Someone other than who I am.

IRL?

What?

In real life?

Oh. Yes.

Are you trying?

Yes.

Are you succeeding?

No.

And would your wife agree with that assessment?

I'm working very hard not to hurt either one of you.

I need to ask you a question now and I need you to tell me the truth. Can you do that?

I'll do my best.

Have you done this with other women? Been like this. The way you are with me.

No, never. You are the first. Stay here. Just a little while longer. Until we figure this out.

Are you telling me I should stop looking for the lamppost?

For now, yes.

82

"And that, my dear, is material," says Bunny, nudging me. "I could definitely work that into a scene."

Standing under the Tasty Salted Pig Parts sign at Boccalone is a line, at least twenty men long. Down the aisle, standing under the pastel blue Miette sign is another line, at least twenty women long. The men are buying salumi, the women petits fours.

"Actually, that's a play unto itself," she amends.

"Do you think women are afraid of mortadella?" asks Jack.

"Intimidated, maybe," I say.

"Disgusted more like it," says Zoe.

It's 9:00 on a Saturday morning and the Ferry Building is already packed. Whenever we have out-of-town visitors this is one of the first places we take them. It's one of San Francisco's most impressive tourist attractions—a farmers' market on steroids.

"It makes you yearn for a different kind of life, doesn't it?" says William as we wander outside onto the wharf, strolling past bundles of gleaming red radishes and perfectly stacked pyramids of leeks. He snaps photos of the vegetables with his iPhone. He can't help himself. He's addicted to food porn.

"What kind of a life is that?" I ask.

"One where you wear your hair in braids," pipes up Peter, referring to the pink-cheeked girl working the Two Girls and a Plow booth. "Like your apron," he says to her.

"Muslin," says the girl. "Holds its shape better than cotton. Twenty-five bucks."

"When you're under thirty, aprons are sexy," says Bunny. "Over thirty you tend to look like one of the Merry Wives of Windsor. Caroline, would you like one? My treat?"

"Tempting, seeing that I only have four good apron-wearing years left. But I'll pass."

"That's a good girl," says William. "Real cooks aren't afraid of stains."

Bunny and Jack stroll just ahead of us, holding hands. Watching the two of them together is difficult: they're so openly affectionate. My husband and I walk on opposite sides of the aisle. It occurs to me we've become one of those couples I wrote about in the survey. The ones who have nothing to say to each other. William has a grim, closed look on his face. I turn my back to him and open my Facebook App on my phone. John Yossarian is online.

Do you ever see other couples and feel envious, Researcher 101?

In what way?

That they're so close.

Sometimes.

So what do you do?

When?

When that happens?

I look away. I'm an expert compartmentalizer.

William calls to me from across the aisle. "Should we buy some corn for tonight?"

"Okay."

"Do you want to pick it out?"

"No, you go right ahead."

William drifts over to the Full Belly Farm booth. He looks forlorn. His job search isn't going well. Every week that passes wears him down a little more. I hate to see him like this. Despite the fact that his hijinks were a contributing factor toward his being laid off, they're not the only reason. What happened to William is happening to so many of our friends: they're being replaced by younger, cheaper models. I feel for him. I really do. I duck behind a towering display of beeswax hand creams.

Could it be as easy as holding his hand, Researcher 101?

Could what be?

Connecting with my husband.

I don't think so.

I haven't done that in a long time.

Maybe you should.

You *want* me to hold my husband's hand?

"Is a dozen enough?" William shouts.
"That's perfect, honey," I answer.
I never call him honey. "Honey" is for Bunny and Jack's benefit.
Bunny turns around, smiles, and nods at me approvingly.

Uh—not really.

Why not?

He doesn't deserve it.

Oh, God.
"What?" Bunny mouths when she sees my startled face.
Suddenly I feel protective of William. What does Researcher 101 know about what William deserves?

That was mean. I don't think I can do this anymore, Researcher 101.

I understand.

You do?

I was thinking the same thing.

Wait. He's going to give up that easily? He's giving me such mixed messages. Or maybe I'm giving him mixed messages.
"Do you have a five, Alice?" asks William. I look across the aisle. His face has suddenly gone the color of milk. I think about Jack and his

heart. I think I should start buying baby aspirin and forcing William to take it.

"Are you okay?" I ask, approaching the stall.

"Of course. I'm fine," says William, looking completely un-fine.

I glance at the corn. "Those are puny ears. Better make it another half dozen."

"Will you help me?" he says.

"What's wrong?"

He shakes his head. "I feel dizzy."

He really does look sick. I take his hand. His fingers lace automatically through mine. We make our way over to a bench and sit there quietly for a few minutes. Peter and Caroline are sampling almonds. Zoe is sniffing a bottle of lavender oil. Bunny and Jack are standing in line at Rose Pistola to buy one of their famous egg sandwiches.

"Do you want an egg sandwich?" I ask. "I'll go get you one. Maybe your blood sugar is low."

"My blood sugar is fine. I miss this," he says.

He looks straight ahead. His thigh touches mine ever so slightly. We sit stiffly next to each other like strangers. I'm reminded of the time I brought soup to his apartment on Beacon Hill. The first time he kissed me.

"You miss what?"

"Us."

Seriously? He's picking *today*, the day after I sneaked out to have an assignation with another man, to tell me that he misses us? Emotionally, William always arrives at the table just as the plates are being cleared. It's infuriating.

"I've got to find a bathroom," I say.

"Wait. Did you hear what I said?"

"I heard."

"And all you have to say is you have to go to the bathroom?"

"Sorry—it's an emergency." I run into the Ferry Building, find a seat at Peet's, and pull out my phone.

What the hell, Researcher 101?

I know. You're angry.

Why did you even suggest meeting me?

I shouldn't have.

Did you even plan on coming?

Of course I did.

You didn't change your mind at the last minute? Decide the fantasy was better than the real thing?

No. It's the real you that's so appealing. I'm not interested in fantasies.

The damn survey. It's completely changed my life.

Why?

Because now I realize how unhappy I've been.

Subjects frequently—

Don't talk to me about subjects. Don't insult me. I'm more than a subject to you.

You're right.

I'm thinking of leaving my husband.

You are?

Researcher 101's shock buzzes right through the phone; I feel it like a Taser. That's not what he wanted to hear, neither is it true. I haven't contemplated leaving William. I just said it to get a response. I look up and see Bunny walking briskly toward me. I slip down into my seat. She grabs the phone out of my hand, quickly reading the last lines of our chat. She shakes her head, kneels by my chair, and begins typing.

Let me ask you a question, Researcher 101.

Okay.

Tell me one thing you love about your wife.

I'm not sure that's a good idea.

I've told you everything about my husband. Surely you can tell me one thing about your wife.

Okay, she is the most stubborn, proud, opinionated, stick-to-her-guns, loyal-to-the-death person I know. The weird thing is I think you'd like her. I think you'd be friends.

Oh. I'm not sure what I'm supposed to do with that information.

I'm sorry—but you asked.

It's okay. Actually it makes me feel better.

It does? Why?

Because it shows me you're not a cad. That you have nice things to say about your wife.

"Cad? Who the hell uses words like 'cad'?"
"Quiet!" says Bunny, elbowing me aside.

Thank you, I guess.

So what are we supposed to do now, Researcher 101?

I don't know. I think things will become clear. I never thought any of this would happen. You've got to believe me.

What did you think would happen?

That you would just answer the questions and we would go our separate ways and it would be over.

What did you think wouldn't happen?

That I would fall for you.

I grab the phone out of Bunny's hand and type *GTG,* then I log off Facebook.

"Don't want to answer him, hmm?" she asks.

"No, Cyrano, I don't."

Bunny sniffs. "He seems rather genuine. In his feelings for you."

"I told you."

"Something to drink?"

"No."

We sit there for a moment, eavesdropping on people placing their orders for coffee.

"Alice?"

"What?"

"Listen to me. Every good director knows that even with the darkest of subject matter there have to be moments of grace. There have to be places where the light streams in. And if those places aren't there, your job is to put them there. To write them in. Do you understand, Alice?"

I shake my head.

Bunny reaches across the table and squeezes my hand. "It's a misstep many playwrights make. They mistake darkness for meaning. They think light is easy. They think light will find a way through the crack in the door by itself. But it doesn't, Alice. You have to open the door and let it in."

83

"Nedra."

"Alice."

"How are you?"

"I'm fine, how are you?"

"Been biking, have you?"

"Yes, Alice. That would explain the shorts. And the biking shoes. And the helmet."

"And the bike."

"So."

"So."

"So what happened?"

"With what?"

"With Researcher 101?"

"Nothing happened."

"Don't lie to me."

"It's over."

"It's over? Just like that, it's over?"

"Yes. Happy now?"

"Oh, this is ridiculous, Alice. Are you going to invite me in or not?"

I open the door wide and Nedra wheels her bike in.

"I didn't know Brits perspired. Do you want a towel?"

Nedra props the bike against the wall, then rubs her sweaty face on the sleeve of my T-shirt. "No need, darling. Is William here?"

"What do you want with William?"

"It's a business matter," she says. "I have a proposition for him."

"He's in the kitchen."

"Are we still not talking?"

"Yes."

"Fine. You'll let me know when we are?"

"Yes."

"Via phone or text?"

"Smoke signals."

"Have you spoken to Zoe about Ho-Girl?"

No, I haven't spoken to Zoe yet and I feel terrible about that. But the truth is, Ho-Girl and Zoe's betrayal of Jude are on the back burner as I try and make sense of what's happening between Researcher 101 and me.

"You're making too big a deal of it. We're talking cupcakes, Nedra."

"Don't put it off, Alice. I really think there's something there you should look at."

"Nedra?" William calls from the kitchen. "Is that you?"

"Ta, darling. At least somebody in this house is happy to see me," says Nedra, walking away, leaving me alone in the foyer.

Shonda Perkins
PX90 DVD's for sale. Cheap.
5 minutes ago

Julie Staggs
Marcy—too small for Marcy's big girl bed.
33 minutes ago

Linda Barbedian
Insomnia
4 hours ago

Bobby Barbedian
Have been sleeping like a baby
5 hours ago

I'm trying to distract myself from the sound of laughter coming from the kitchen by reading my Facebook feeds, when my computer makes a submarine sound. A Skype message flashes on my screen.

Beautiful Russian Ladies

Are European and American women too arrogant for you? Are you looking for a sweet lady that will be caring and understanding? Then you come to the right place. Here you find a Russian lady that will love you with all her heart.

www.russiansexywoman.com

Please excuse if you are not interested.

For some reason I find this solicitation touching and sad. Is there anyone in the world who is not looking for somebody who will love them with all their heart?

There's a sudden rap on my door. William walks into my office. "So that was interesting. Nedra asked me to cook for her wedding."

"Cook what?"

"Dinner. Appetizers. Dessert. The entire meal."

"You're kidding!"

"It's a small crowd, only twenty-five or so people. I've asked Caroline to help me."

"You want to do this?"

"I think it'll be fun. Plus she's paying me. Quite well, I might add."

"You know Nedra and I aren't speaking."

"I gathered that. What are you not speaking about?"

"The maid-of-honor dress she wants me to wear. It's horrible. Empire waist. Puffy sleeves. I'll look like Queen Victoria."

"She's your best friend, Alice. You're going to miss her wedding over a dress?"

I frown. He's completely right, of course.

"Alice? Are you okay?"

"I'm fine. Why?" It's so hard to keep this up. To continually hide my distracted state.

"You just seem—funny," he says.

"Well, you seem funny, too."

"Yup. Although I'm trying not to be."

He looks at me a moment too long, and I turn away. "So have you thought about the menu?" I croak.

"Anything but oysters. That's the only requirement. Nedra thinks they're too obvious. Like roses or champagne on Valentine's Day."

"I love oysters."

"I know you do."

"I haven't had them in a long time."

William shakes his head. "I don't know why you insist on keeping yourself from the things you love."

84

After William leaves, I go upstairs to my bedroom and shut the door. I set the timer on my phone for fifteen minutes. Then I let myself feel all the anticipation and heartbreak of the past few days. William's comment about "missing us" ticker-tapes though my head, a constant loop. Ten minutes later, I'm sitting in the middle of the bed with a pile of used Kleenex in front of me, when I hear footsteps coming down the hallway. I can tell by the light tread that it's Bunny. I try and compose myself, but it's useless.

"Is everything okay?" she asks, opening the door.

"It's fine. It's really fine. I'm really very fine," I say, the tears streaming down my cheeks.

"Can I do anything?"

"No, don't worry. It's just—" I burst into tears. "I'm sorry. I'm so embarrassed."

Bunny enters the room, pulls out a starched hankie from her pants pocket, and hands it to me.

I stare at it blankly. "Oh, I couldn't. It's clean. I'm going to get it all dirty."

"It's a handkerchief. That's what it's for, Alice."

"Really? That's so nice," I say, and then I start crying again, the full-blown ugly cry, hiccupping and gulping and trying to stop and not being able to.

Bunny sits beside me on the bed. "You've been holding that in a long time, haven't you?"

"You don't know how long!"

"Well, you just let it out now. I'll stay here with you until you're done."

"It's just that I don't know if I'm a good person or a bad person. I'm thinking right now I'm a bad person. A cold person. I can be very cold, you know."

"Everybody can," she says.

"Especially to my husband."

"Ah—it's easiest to be cold to those we love."

"I know. But why?" I sob.

Bunny sits with me until I arrive at that exhausted, washed-out, clear place on the other side of shame, where the air smells of late summer, of chlorine with a rising note of back-to-school supplies, and I feel for the first time in a very long time—hope.

"Better?" asks Bunny.

I nod. "I'm ridiculous."

"No," she says. "Just a little lost, like all of us."

"I've been writing, you know."

"You have?"

"Yes. Little scenes. About my life. Me and William—when we first met. Dinner parties. Conversations. Nothing interesting. But it's a start."

"Wonderful! I'd love to look at what you've got."

"You would?"

"Of course. I've been waiting for you to ask."

"Really?"

"Oh, Alice. Why are you so surprised?"

I look at the handkerchief balled up in my hand. "I've ruined your hankie."

"Pah. Give me that."

"No! It's disgusting."

"Give it!" she orders.

I drop it into her waiting hand.

"Don't you understand, Alice? Nothing you do can disgust me."

"That's what I say to my kids."

"That's what I say to my kids, too," she says softly, stroking my hair.

I start to sob again. She presses the handkerchief back into my hand. "It appears I took this prematurely."

85

Lucy Pevensie *added her Favorite Quotation*
"Is—is he a man?" asked Lucy.

Well, is he, Researcher 101?

I'm not sure what you're asking, Wife 22.

Does a real man leave his wife?

A real man looks for his wife.

And then what?

I'm not sure. Why are you asking?

I haven't been the best of wives.

I haven't been the best of husbands.

So maybe you should look for your wife.

Maybe you should look for your husband, too.

Why should I look for him?

He may be lost.

He's not lost. He's in the garage building shelves.

In his Carhartt pants?

You don't forget anything, do you?

I forget plenty of things; however, the Internet does not.

He's got a cute ass in those pants.

What makes a cute ass?

An ass that's bigger than mine.

I'm going to the movies today with my wife.

You know, Researcher 101, I'm getting very mixed messages from you.

I know. I'm sorry. But that's precisely why I'm going to the movies with my wife. I've been thinking about this a lot. I've reread all your answers from the survey and I'm convinced there is some spark left in your marriage. If there wasn't, you wouldn't be able to write about your courtship the way that you did. It's not over between you and him. It's not over between my wife and me, either. I'm making an effort. I think you should do the same with your husband.

And if it doesn't work out with our spouses?

Then six months from now we'll meet at Tea & Circumstances.

Let me ask you something.

Anything.

If we had met? If you had showed up that night? What do you think would have happened?

I think you would have been disappointed.

Why? What are you keeping from me? Do you have scales? Do you weigh 600 pounds? Do you have a comb-over?

Let's just say I would not be what you had expected.

Are you sure about that?

The meeting was premature. It would have been disastrous. I'm convinced of that.

How so?

Each of us would have lost everything.

And now?

We lose only one thing.

What's that?

The fantasy.

What are you going to see?

The new Daniel Craig movie. My wife likes Daniel Craig.

My husband likes Daniel Craig, too. Maybe your wife and my husband should get together.

86

I find William out in the garage standing on a ladder, wearing, yes, his Carhartt pants.

"I heard there's a great new Daniel Craig movie out. Want to go see it?" I ask.

"Hold on," William mumbles and quickly finishes mounting a bracket on the wall. "I thought you hated Daniel Craig."

"He's growing on me."

"Hand me that shelf," says William. I give it to him and he slides the shelf into place. "Damn. It's crooked. I should have used the level."

"Why didn't you?"

"Sloppy," he says. "Thought I could eyeball it."

"It's not that bad. Nobody's going to see it."

"That's beside the point, Alice. Not a word, you," says William to Jampo, who is sitting beside the ladder obediently. Jampo gives a mournful *errrr*, never taking his eyes off William.

"So you're hanging out with Jampo? *Voluntarily*?"

"He followed me out here," he says, climbing down the ladder.

Jampo sniffs his boots excitedly. William watches him with a half-smile. "He thinks I'm going to take him on a run."

"You've been running with him?"

"Once in a while. Hey, do you know what 'sexiled' means?"

"'Sexiled'? No. Why?"

"I overheard Zoe discussing it with one of her friends. They were talking about college. It's a term for being kicked out of your room when your roommate wants to have sex."

"Must they coin a word for everything? What happened to hanging a sock on the door?" I ask.

"It's a different generation."

"She's going to be gone soon. A blink and she'll be gone. Another blink and there goes Peter. Blink, blink. Our progeny—poof. Do you think she's having sex?"

"Do I think she *had* sex? With Jude? Probably."

"Really?"

"Alice, I know about Ho-Girl. Nedra told me."

"Oh, God. *Ho-Girl.* I can't believe I haven't spoken to her about it. It's just been—so crazy around here. With Bunny and Jack coming and everything," I add.

"Uh-huh."

"Did Nedra tell you she cheated on Jude, too, not the other way around?"

"Yes, she did. And you haven't checked out her Twitter account?"

"I was kind of hoping it would just go away."

William pulls out his phone. "Let's get it over with. It can't be that bad." He goes to his Google browser and types in *Twitter Ho-Girl.* His scent washes over me—Tide detergent and oranges. I love his smell. I've missed it. I breathe it in quietly.

"There she is," I whisper, leaning into him.

Ho-Girl

Name Ho-Girl
Location California
Bio Creamy, filling, sugary, moist
Followers 552

You get a big delight in every bite. About 2 hours ago

@ **boooboobear** *Yes indeed, Ho-Girl. I can attest to that.*

@**Fox123** *Sexy, sexy, girl. How about posting a photo? Of your delight?*

@**Lemonyfine** *Okay, Okay. I get that u love cupcakes. But can we talk about Yodels?*

@**Harbormast50** *You have a bit of frosting on the corner of your lip. I'd be happy to wipe it off.*

"Jesus! Nedra was right."

"When is Nedra ever wrong? We're signing up to get short, timely messages from Ho-Girl right now," William barks.

"What—no! You can't do that. She'll know it's us."

"Give me some credit. I'm not going to sign up as @ma&pabuckle."

"You're going to use a fake handle?"

"Do you have a problem with that?"

"Well—yes. Don't you? Shouldn't we?" I try to keep a straight face.

"Not when it comes to our daughter. Let's keep it in the Hostess family so she won't suspect. How about @snoball?" he asks.

"Ug—that pink marshmallow skin makes me sick. How about @dingdong?" I suggest.

"I hate Ding Dongs. How about @hohos?"

"Too close to Ho-Girl. How about @nuttyhohos? Remember those? When they added peanuts?" I say.

"Fine. Done."

We turn to each other and begin laughing.

"Quiet, you Nutty Ho Ho," whispers William.

"I can't believe we're doing this."

"She just tweeted again," he says.

I peer at his screen and we read the Tweet out loud together.

There is no better way to start the day than sucking the cream out of a Twinkie. About 1 minute ago

"What the hell, Zoe!" I gasp. "Does she have any idea how dangerous this is?"

William's fingers fly over the touch screen.

@**nuttyhohos** *What the hell, Zoe? Do you have any idea how dangerous this is?*

"You weren't supposed to type that! Now those sickos are going to know her real name," I yell at William. "And so much for our fake handle."

Stop following me, J. I can tell it's u. About 1 minute ago

"She thinks we're Jude," says William.

*@**booboobear** Ho-Girl is a queen. She should be treated as thus. I am here to serve you, my queen. Is it a Ding Dong Day?*

William growls.

*@**nuttyhohos** Ho-Girl is not a queen. She's a fifteen-year-old girl, you sick predator.*

I mean it, J. Stop it. About 1 minute ago

*@**Lemonyfine** Listen to the fine lady, J, or I'll have to go all diggity do on your ass.*

Stop fighting, all of you. There's still some cream left in my Twinkie :)
About 1 minute ago

I grab the phone out of William's hand.

*@**nuttyhohos** OMG, Zoe, why can't you be like a normal girl and have an eating disorder?*

R u implying I'm fat? I'm not fat, J. About 1 minute ago

*@**nuttyhohos** This is not J. This is your mother. I know all about the Hostess cupcakes in your closet.*

*@**Fox123** BFN.*

William grabs the phone back.

*@**nuttyhohos** This is your father. Deactivate this account right now, Zoe Buckle!*

"Now you've given them her last name!" I shout.

@**booboobear** *WTF. BFN.*

@**nuttyhohos** *Deactivate your account NOW, Ho-Girl!*

Suddenly the garage door begins to open. William and I stand there, blinking, huddled together, as Zoe materializes in front of us. She holds her phone in one hand, the garage door opener in the other. She's so furious she can't speak. She tweets instead.

I can't believe u guys. This is a total invasion of privacy! I'll never forgive you. About 1 minute ago

"Zoe, please—" I say.

I'm not talking to you. About 1 minute ago

@**nuttyhohos** *We can see that.*

I'm never talking to you again. About 1 minute ago

@**nuttyhohos** *This is not okay, sweetheart. Ho-Girl is really not okay. You could have gotten yourself into serious trouble.*

Zoe looks at me and begins to cry. Then she starts tweeting again.

How could you wish I had an eating disorder? About 1 minute ago

"Baby," I say.
"I am so not your baby. You have absolutely no idea who I am!" she yells.
Zoe holds the garage door opener up over her head and clicks it aggressively like she's firing a weapon, and the door slowly begins to lower on us.
"William—"
"Just let her be," he says, as our daughter's head, then her torso, then her legs disappear.
I give a little cry and he pulls me under his arm, where the scent of detergent is the strongest. It's nice there, a nest. We stay like that for a few minutes.
"Well," he finally says. "What now?"
"Lock her in her room for a thousand years?"

"Force her to eat skirt steak?"

"Are we terrible?"

"At what?"

"Being parents?"

"No, but we suck at Twitter."

"*You* suck at Twitter," I say.

"That's because you made me nervous. I had stage fright."

"Oh, if I hadn't been there you would have been much wittier?" I ask.

"**@nuttyhohos** Apricots are ripe, vegan daughter," he says.

"**@nuttyhohos** Saved them all for you, please consider eating instead of Ding Dongs."

"**@nuttyhohos** Not that I don't like Ding Dongs. There is a time and place for Ding Dongs. When you're thirty and live in your own apartment and can pay your own rent."

"**@nuttyhohos** Not kidding. If you don't eat the apricots today they'll rot."

"**@nuttyhohos** FYI apricots six dollars a pound. EAT THEM OR ELSE."

"**@nuttyhohos** and try not to swallow pits."

"**@nuttyhohos** swallowing bad idea in general."

"**@nuttyhohos** says surgeon general."

"**@nuttyhohos** and your father."

"Well?" says William.

"Not bad."

"Yes, all my followers think so."

"All *one* of them."

"All you need is one, Alice."

"I have to go talk to her."

"No, I think what you need to do is give her a little time."

"And then what?"

William lifts my chin. "Look at me."

Jesus, you smell so good, how could I have forgotten you smelled like this?

"Let her come to you," he says.

Then he abruptly lets go of me and turns back toward the shelves, frowning. "I'm going to have to do it again," he says. "Now where's the damn level?"

87

"Mom! Help! I need a bigger Tupperware!" Zoe shrieks from the kitchen.

These are the first words Zoe has uttered to me in two days. Both William and I have been getting the silent treatment since the Twitter incident.

"Could this be interpreted as 'her coming to me'?" I ask William, who is sitting on the couch.

William sighs. "Damn dog door."

"Well?"

He puts down the paper. "Beggars can't be choosers."

I leap to my feet.

"I've been calling you for ages!" Zoe's crouched by the stove, holding a pint-sized Tupperware container, her eyes darting around wildly.

"That's not big enough."

"No shit, Mom. All the Tupperware has disappeared."

I open the fridge. "Leftovers."

"There it is!" yells Zoe and I whirl around just in time to see the mouse barreling toward me from across the room.

"Eek!" I shout.

"Do you think you could come up with something more original?" grunts Zoe as she chases after the mouse, who skitters like a drunk, ears flapping, a tiny Dumbo.

"Eek, eek!" I cry again as the mouse runs between my legs and disappears under the fridge.

Zoe stands up. "That's your fault," she says.

"What's my fault?"

"That it went under the fridge."

"Why is it *my* fault?"

"You seduced it."

"How?"

"By opening the door and letting all that nice cool air out."

"Really, Zoe? Well, let me open it again and maybe the mouse will reappear."

I take out a large Tupperware container full of lasagna. I empty the lasagna onto a plate, wash the Tupperware, and hand it to her. "Here you go."

"Thanks."

"Now what?"

Zoe shrugs, sitting down at the table. "We wait."

We sit in silence for a few minutes.

"I'm very glad you are not the kind of girl who is scared of mice," I say.

"No thanks to you."

We hear the mouse scrabbling around under the fridge.

"Should I get a broom?" I ask.

"No! That will traumatize it. Let it come out on its own."

We sit in silence for another five minutes. We hear more scratching sounds, louder this time. "The elephant in the room," I say.

Zoe's eyes suddenly well up and she bows her head. "I didn't want you to be ashamed of me," she whispers.

"Zoe. Why would I be ashamed?"

"It just happened. I didn't mean it to. Jude was in Hollywood. He was getting all this attention. And there was this boy. He kissed me. I didn't kiss him first. And then I couldn't stop kissing him. I'm a slut!" she cries. "I don't deserve Jude."

"You're not a slut. Don't you ever let me hear you use that word again when describing yourself! Zoe, you're fifteen. So you made a mistake. You had a lapse in judgment. Why didn't you just explain it to Jude? He adores you. Don't you think he would have understood? Eventually?"

"I told him. Right away."

"And what happened?"

"He forgave me."

"But you didn't forgive yourself. And that explains Ho-Girl?"

Zoe nods.

"Okay, okay. But Zoe, there's something I don't understand. The kiss matters far less to me than why you've been so mean to Jude. He follows you around like a puppy. He'd do anything for you."

"He's smothering me."

"So your solution is to just run away?"

"I learned it from you," she mumbles.

"You learned what from me?"

"Running away."

"You think *I'm* running away? From what?"

"From *everything*."

I register that hit in my belly. "Really? That's *really* what you think?" I ask.

"Kind of," whispers Zoe.

"Zoe. Oh, God," I trail off.

At that moment the mouse runs under the table.

I lift my feet and we look at each other, wide-eyed. Zoe puts her finger up to her lips. "Don't make a sound," she mouths.

"Eek!" I mouth back.

Zoe fights off a smile as she very slowly slides off the chair and crouches on the floor, Tupperware in hand. Next I hear the sound of the plastic slapping the floor.

"Got it!" she yells, crawling out from under the table, pushing the Tupperware in front of her.

The mouse isn't moving. "Did you kill it?" I ask.

"Of course not," says Zoe, flicking the plastic with her fingers. "It's playing dead. It's scared to death."

"Where should we release it?"

"You're coming with me?" asks Zoe. "You never come with me. You're scared of mice."

"Yes, I'm coming with you," I say, getting a piece of cardboard from the recycling bin. "Ready?" I slide the cardboard underneath the Tupperware and the two of us lift the container and slip out the back door, Zoe with her hand on top of the plastic container, me with my hand beneath, supporting the cardboard. We walk that ungainly way for a while, up the hill to a grove of eucalyptus trees. Then we bend as one, lowering the Tupperware to the ground. I slide the cardboard out.

"Bye, little mouse," croons Zoe as she lifts the plastic.

A second later the mouse is gone.

"I don't know why, but I always feel sad when I let them go," says Zoe.

"Because you had to trap them?"

"No, because I worry that they won't ever find their way home," says Zoe, her eyes filling with tears again.

It occurs to me in that moment that Zoe is the same exact age I was when my mother died. She looks mostly like a Buckle, not an Archer. She has good hair, by which I mean hair she doesn't have to fight with. She has lovely clear skin, and lucky girl, she's got William's height: she's nearly five foot seven. But where I see myself, where I see the Archer side of the family, is around her eyes. The resemblance is especially pronounced when she's sad. The way she bats the tears away with those inky dark lashes. The way her iris lightens from a navy to a sort of stormy blue-gray. That's me. That's my mother. Right there.

"Oh, Zoe. Sweetheart. You have such a big heart. You always have. Even as a little girl." I put my arm tentatively around her.

"I shouldn't have said those things to you. It's not true. You're not running away," she says.

"It might be true. A little true."

"I'm sorry."

"I know that."

"I'm an ass."

"I know that, too," I say, punching her playfully on the shoulder. Zoe makes a face.

"Zoe, honey, look at me."

She turns and bites her lower lip.

"Do you love Jude?"

"I think so."

"Then do me a favor?"

"What?"

I put my hand on her cheek. "Don't wait any longer, for God's sake. Tell him how you feel."

88

"Who's the understudy for the lead?" asks Jack, squinting at his theater program. "I can't read it. Alice, can you read this?"

I squint at the program. "How is anybody supposed to read this? The print is minuscule."

"Here." Bunny hands me a pair of reading glasses. They're very hip—square and gunmetal gray.

"No, thanks," I say.

"I bought them for you."

"You did? Why?"

"Because you can no longer read small print and it's time you faced up to that fact."

"I can no longer read *minuscule* print. That's very nice of you, but I don't need them." I hand the glasses back to her.

"God, I love the theater," I say, watching the people around us filing into their seats. "Berkeley Rep is in our backyard. Why don't we do this more often?"

The lights dim and a hush descends upon the theater as a few last-minute stragglers find their seats. This is my favorite part. Right before the curtain opens, when all the promise of the evening is ahead of you. I glance over at William. He's wearing khakis, flat-front and slim-cut, which accentuate his muscular legs. I look at his thighs and a little shiver goes through me. All his running is paying off.

"Here we go," whispers Bunny as the curtain parts.

"Thank you for taking us," I say, squeezing her arm.

"Tweeting with Ho-Girl would have been more pleasurable," says William, forty-five minutes later.

It's intermission. We're waiting in line at the bar along with dozens of other people.

"I can't believe that made it to the stage," says Jack. "It wasn't ready."

"And it was the playwright's debut," says Bunny. "I hope she's got some thick skin."

Everybody suddenly looks at me.

"Oh, I'm sorry, Alice. That was terribly insensitive," says Bunny.

"Pah, is that what you say, Bunny? It was wan, boring, and absurd, just like *The Barmaid*, I'm afraid."

Bunny's eyes light up with pleasure. "Why, Alice, brava! It's about time you faced up to that smelly fish of a review. Haul it into the boat instead of letting it swim circles around you over and over again for years on end. That's how it loses its power."

She winks at me. This morning I finally got up the courage to give her some of my pages. I've been setting aside time to write every day now. I'm starting to get into a rhythm.

"How old is the playwright?" I ask.

"Early thirties, I'd guess by her photo," says William, looking through the program.

"Poor baby," I say.

"Not necessarily," says Bunny. "It's only excruciating because for most of us the devastations happen in private, behind closed doors. When you're a playwright, it all happens out in the open. But there's a real opportunity there, you see? To take that ride publicly? Everybody gets to see you fall, but everyone also gets to see you rise. There's nothing like a comeback."

"What if you just fall and fall and fall?" I ask, thinking of William's Facebook postings.

"Not possible; not if you stay with it. Eventually you'll stand."

We're only three people away from the bar. I'm desperate for a drink. What's taking so long? I hear the woman at the front of the line admonishing the bartender for not stocking Grey Goose and I freeze. That voice sounds familiar. When I hear the woman asking if they have grüner veltliner and the bartender suggesting perhaps she consider going with the house chardonnay, I groan. It's Mrs. Norman, the druggie mother.

I have the sudden urge to dart behind a pillar and hide, then I think, why should I hide? I haven't done anything wrong. *Stand erect, Alice.* I hear my father's voice in my head. My slumping gets especially pronounced when I'm nervous.

"Sutter Creek, can you believe it?" Mrs. Norman says, as she turns around and catches sight of me.

I give her a half-smile and nod while standing perfectly erect.

"Well, hello," she says sweetly. "Darling, look, it's the draaama teacher. From Carisa's school."

Mr. Norman stands about a foot shorter than Mrs. Norman.

He extends his hand. "Chet Norman," he says nervously.

"Alice Buckle," I say. I quickly introduce Bunny, Jack, and William, and then step out of line to talk to them.

"I'm sorry I missed *Charlotte's Web.* I heard it was quite the performance," says Mr. Norman.

"Um—I guess it was," I say, trying not to wince. I still feel as though that production was a major miscalculation on my part.

"So," says Mrs. Norman. "Attend the theater often?"

"Oh, yes. All the time. It's part of my work, isn't it? To see plays."

"How nice for you," says Mrs. Norman.

The lights flicker on and off.

"Well," I say.

"Carisa just loves you," Mr. Norman says, his voice breaking.

"Really?" I say, locking eyes with Mrs. Norman.

The lights flicker again, a little faster this time.

"I'm sorry," he says, sticking out his hand again. "I'm really very sorry."

"Chet," warns Mrs. Norman.

"We've held you up," he says.

"Oh, dear. I'm afraid you'll have to swig your wine," says Mrs. Norman as William walks toward us with my drink.

I look at her, all arch and glitter and condescension, and honest to God have to hold myself back from pinching a pretend joint between my thumb and index finger and pretend-puffing away on it.

"Carisa is a wonderful girl," I say to Mr. Norman. "I'm very fond of her, too."

"This play is crap, Chet," says Mrs. Norman, considering her glass of wine. "As is this swill. Let's skip the second half."

"But that would be rude, honey," whispers Mr. Norman. "You just don't walk out at intermission at the theater, do you?" he asks me. "Is that—done?"

Oh, I like Chet Norman. William joins us and hands me a glass of wine.

"I don't think there are any hard-and-fast rules," I say.

"Are you having a nice summer, Mrs. Buckle?" asks Mrs. Norman.

"Lovely, thank you."

"That's nice," says Mrs. Norman.

Then she abruptly turns away and walks toward the exit.

"A pleasure to meet you," Mr. Norman calls out as he trots after her.

The second half of the play is even worse than the first, but I'm glad we stick it out. For me it's desensitization therapy—where you gradually inject the patient with a bit of the substance the person has an allergy to, in my case, public failure, so the person learns to tolerate the substance without the body overreacting. I feel deeply for the playwright. I'm sure she's here, sitting in the wings or maybe even in the back of the theater. I wish I knew who she was. If I did, I would find her. I would tell her to let it wash over her, to feel it all, to not run from it. I would tell her that people would eventually forget. It might feel like the experience would kill her, but it wouldn't. And one morning, maybe a month, or six months, or a year, or five years from now, she'd wake up and notice the way the light streamed through the curtains and the smell of coffee descended upon the house, like a blanket. And on that morning she'd sit down and confront the blank page. And she'd know she had arrived at the beginning again, and it was a new day.

89

John Yossarian *added Likes*
Sweden and conditions of utmost ease and luxury

Lucy Pevensie *added Likes*
Cair Paravel

Ah, Sweden—land of utmost ease and luxury. Is that where you've been hiding? Haven't heard from you in a while, Researcher 101.

Maybe that's because you insist on living in a castle. I imagine the cell service must be quite spotty at Cair Paravel. Did you take your husband to the Daniel Craig movie?

I did.

I took my wife, too.

Did she like it?

She liked it, although she gets annoyed by the way DC is constantly pursing his lips.

I agree with her. It's irritating.

Maybe he can't help it. Maybe his lips just go that way.

So the *effort* is going well with your wife?

We're a work in progress, but yes, slow progress.

Do you still think about me?

Yes.

All the time?

Yes, although I'm trying not to.

I think that's a good idea.

What?

That you try not to think about me.

What about you?

Are you asking if I think about you?

Yes.

I'm going to take a pass on that question. Is the survey over?

It can be if you want it to be.

Do I still get my $1,000?

Of course.

I don't want it.

Are you sure?

It just seems wrong given what's happened.

I wasn't lying, you know.

About what?

I did fall for you.

Thank you for saying that.

If I hadn't been married . . .

And I hadn't been married . . .

We never would have met.

Online.

Yes, online.

90

Bunny and I are sitting at the kitchen table, working our way through a bowl of pistachios and a pile of scripts, when Peter walks in with a friend.

"Do we have any pizza rolls?" he asks.

"No, but we have Hot Pockets."

"You're kidding," he says, his eyes aglow.

"Yes, I am," I say. "Do you think your father would allow that kind of junk food in the house?"

I extend my hand to his friend.

"I'm Peter's mother, Alice Buckle. If it was up to me we'd have a freezer full of Hot Pockets, but since we don't, I can offer you Wasa crackers with almond butter. I'm sorry, I wish I had Skippy, but that's on the blacklist, too. I think there are a few hard-boiled eggs in the fridge if you're allergic to nuts."

"Should I call you Alice or Mrs. Buckle?" he asks.

"You may call me Alice, although I appreciate you asking. It's a West Coast thing," I explain to Bunny. "All the kids call adults by their first names out here."

"Except for teachers," says Peter.

"Teachers are called 'dude,'" I say. "Or maybe 'du.' Is the 'de' silent these days?"

"Stop showing off," says Peter.

"Well, I am Mrs. Kilborn and you may call me Mrs. Kilborn," says Bunny.

"And you are?" I ask the boy.

"Eric Haber."

Eric Haber? The Eric Haber I thought Peter had a secret crush on? He's adorable: tall, eyes the color of peanut brittle, obscenely long lashes.

"Peter talks about you all the time," I say.

"Stop it, Mom."

A look passes between Eric and Peter, and Peter shrugs.

"So what are you two up to? Just hanging out?"

"Yeah, Mom, hanging out."

I stack the scripts in a pile. "Well, we'll leave you to it. Let's go out on the deck, Bunny. Eric, I hope to be seeing more of you."

"Uh—yeah, okay," he says.

"What was all that about?" asks Bunny when we've settled out on the deck.

"I thought Eric was Peter's secret crush."

"Peter's gay?"

"No, he's straight, but I thought he might be gay."

Bunny takes some sunscreen out of her bag and rubs it on her arms slowly.

"You're very close to Zoe and Peter, aren't you, Alice?" she says.

"Well, sure."

"Mm-hmm," she says, offering me the tube. "Mustn't forget the neck."

"You say 'mm-hmm' like there's something wrong with that. Like you don't approve. Do you think I'm too close?"

Bunny rubs the excess sunscreen into the back of her hands.

"I think you're—enmeshed," she says carefully. "You're very intense with them."

"And that's a bad thing?"

"Alice, how old were you when your mother died?"

"Fifteen."

"Tell me something about her."

"Like what?"

"Anything. Whatever comes to mind."

"She wore big gold hoop earrings. She wore Jean Naté body splash and she drank gin and tonic all year round, didn't matter the season. She said it made her feel like she was always on vacation."

"What else?" asks Bunny.

"Let me guess. You want me to go deeeeeper," I sigh.

Bunny grins.

"Well, I know this sounds funny, but for a few months after she died I thought she might come back. I think it had something to do with the fact that she went so suddenly; it was impossible to process that she was there one minute and gone the next. Her favorite movie was *The Sound of Music.* She even looked a little like Julie Andrews. She wore her hair short, and she had the most beautiful, long neck. I kept expecting her to suddenly pop around a tree and sing to me, like when Maria sang that song to Captain von Trapp. What was the name of that song?"

"Which one? When she realizes she's fallen for him?" asks Bunny.

"So here you are standing there loving me. Whether or not you should," I sing softly.

"You have a lovely voice, Alice. I didn't know you could sing."

I nod.

"And your father?" asks Bunny.

"He was absolutely wrecked."

"Did you have help? Aunts and uncles? Grandparents?"

"Yes, but after a few months it was just the two of us."

"You must have been very close," Bunny says.

"We were. We are. Look, I know I'm too involved in their lives. I know I can be overbearing and intense. But Zoe and Peter need me. And they're all I have."

"They're not all you have," says Bunny. "And you have to start the process of letting them go. I've gone through this with three children already—believe me, I know. Fundamentally you have to make a break. In the end they'll turn out to be exactly who they are, *not* who you want them to be."

"Are you ready, Alice?" Caroline comes bounding out on the deck, dressed in her running gear.

"Speaking of," says Bunny.

Caroline frowns and looks at her watch. "You said two, Alice. Let's get going."

"She's a taskmaster, your daughter," I say, getting to my feet.

• • •

"Alice—that was a nine-minute mile!"

"You're kidding!" I gasp.

"I'm not. Look." Caroline shows me her stopwatch.

"How the hell did that happen?"

Caroline bobs her head happily. "I knew you could do it."

"Not without you. You've been a wonderful trainer."

"Okay, let's cool down," says Caroline, slowing to a walk.

I give a little hoot.

"Feels good, doesn't it?"

"Do you think I can get down to eight?"

"Don't push it."

We walk quietly for a few minutes.

"So how's Tipi going?"

"Oh, Alice, I couldn't be happier. And guess what? They offered me a full-time job! I start in two weeks."

"Caroline! That's wonderful!"

"It's all falling into place. And I have to thank you, Alice. I don't know what I would have done without your support and encouragement. You and William letting me stay here. And Peter and Zoe. Really, just incredible kids. Being with your family has been so good for me."

"Well, Caroline, it was truly our pleasure and our gain. You're a lovely young woman."

When we get home, I pick up a laundry basket full of clean clothes that has been sitting in the middle of the living room floor for days and bring it upstairs into Peter's room. I place the basket on the floor, knowing full well that it will now sit there for a week. He's been petitioning for a later bedtime. I told him the day he started to put his clothes away and take a shower without me asking him to was the day I'd consider a later bedtime.

"You have so much energy, Alice. Maybe *I* should start running," says Bunny, poking her head into the room.

"All thanks to your daughter," I say. "And congratulations, by the way, to the mother of the recently gainfully employed. It's incredible news about Tipi."

Bunny's eyes narrow. "What news?"

"That she's been offered a full-time job?"

"What? I just got her an interview at Facebook. I pulled major strings to get it. Did she accept the job at Tipi?"

"Well, I think so. She seemed deliriously happy." Bunny flushes red. "What's wrong? She didn't tell you? Oh, God, was it supposed to be a surprise? She didn't say that. I just assumed she would have told you."

Bunny shakes her head vigorously. "The girl has an advanced degree in computer science from Tufts. And she's going to blow it all away working for some nonprofit!"

"Bunny, Tipi is not just some nonprofit. Do you know what they do? Microfinance. I think last year they gave away something like 200 million dollars in loans—"

Bunny cuts me off. "Yes, yes, I know, but how is the girl going to support herself? She'll barely make a living wage at Tipi. You don't understand, Alice. Your kids haven't started to think about college yet. But here's a piece of advice. The liberal-arts education days are over. Nobody can afford to major in English anymore. And don't get me started on art history or theater. The future is math, science, and technology."

"But what if your kids are bad at math, science, and technology?"

"Too bad. Force them to major in those subjects anyway."

"Bunny! You can't be serious. You of all people, who's made a living in the arts all her life!"

"For crying out loud, you two," says Caroline, stalking into the room. "Yes, Mom, it's true. I've accepted the job at Tipi. And yes, it's also true, I'll be making basically minimum wage. So what? So is half the country. Actually, half the country would be lucky to be making minimum wage, to even have a job. I'm the lucky one."

Bunny staggers backward and sits down on the bed.

"Bunny?" I say.

She gazes blankly at the wall.

"You don't look well. Should I get you a glass of water?" I ask.

"You're living in a dream world. You cannot survive on minimum wage, Caroline. Not in a city like San Francisco," says Bunny.

"Of course I can. I'll get roommates. I'll waitress at night. I'll make it work."

"You have a master's degree from Tufts in computer science."

"Oh, okay. Here it comes," says Caroline.

"And you are absolutely crazy not to do something with it. It's your job, no, it's your responsibility to do something with it. You'd be making twice, three times the income right off the bat!" she yells.

"The money isn't important to me, Mom," says Caroline.

"Oh, the money isn't important to her, Alice," says Bunny.

"Yes, the money isn't important to her, Bunny." I sit down next to her on the bed. "And maybe that's okay for now," I say gently. I put my hand on Bunny's knee. "Look. She's young. She has nobody to support but herself. She has lots of time for the money to be important to her. Caroline's going to be working for an organization that really makes a difference in women's lives."

Bunny glares at both of us defiantly.

"You should be proud, Bunny, not angry," I say.

"Did I say I wasn't proud? I didn't say that," she snaps.

"Well, you're certainly acting that way," says Caroline.

"You are pushing me into a corner! And I don't appreciate it," shouts Bunny.

"How am I pushing you into a corner?" asks Caroline.

"You're making me out to be somebody I'm not. Some ungenerous person. I can't believe—I mean, what in the world? Me, of all people," says Bunny indignantly, then, suddenly, she covers her face with her hands and groans.

"What now?" asks Caroline.

Bunny waves Caroline away.

"What, Mom?"

"I can't speak."

"Why can't you speak?"

"Because I'm mortified," whispers Bunny.

"Oh, please," says Caroline.

"Be nice. She feels bad," I mouth to Caroline.

Caroline sighs heavily, her arms crossed. "Mortified over what, Mom?"

"That you're seeing this part of me," says Bunny in a muffled voice.

"You mean *Alice* is seeing this part of you. I see this part of you all the time."

"Yes, yes," says Bunny, her hands dropping to her sides, looking absolutely miserable. "I know you do, Caroline. Mea culpa. Mea culpa!" she cries.

Caroline starts to melt when she sees her mother's genuine distress.

"I think you're being too hard on yourself, Bunny," I say. "It's not that black and white. Not when it comes to your kids."

"No, I'm a hypocrite," says Bunny.

"Yep," says Caroline. "She's a hypocrite." She leans in and kisses Bunny on the cheek. "But a lovable hypocrite."

Bunny looks at me. "How pathetic am I? Not even half an hour ago I was lecturing you pompously about how you should let your kids go."

"There's only one way to let them go that I know of," I say. "Messily."

Bunny picks up Caroline's hand. "I *am* proud of you, Caro. I really am."

"I know, Mom."

She strokes Caroline's palm. "And who knows, maybe you could give yourself a little microloan, if you need it. One of the perks of working at Tipi. If you find it difficult to live on the salary, that is."

Caroline shakes her head at me.

"But, Alice, I have to tell you, if either Zoe or Peter shows any aptitude for math or technology, you really should—"

Caroline puts a finger on her mother's lips, silencing her. "You always have to get the last word, don't you?"

Later that afternoon I check Lucy Pevensie's Facebook page. There are no new messages or posts. Yossarian is not online, either.

I scroll through my Facebook news feed.

Nedra Rao
It's the 21st century. Is there nobody capable of making flattering bike shorts for women?
47 minutes ago

Linda Barbedian
Target! New sheets for Nick's dorm room.
5 hours ago

Bobby Barbedian

Target! Not on your life.

5 hours ago

Kelly Cho

Is afraid the chickens are coming home to roost.

6 hours ago

Helen Davies

Hotel George V Paris—ahhh . . .

8 hours ago

Lately when I read my feed I feel such a mixture of worry, irritation, and envy, I wonder if it's even worth having an account.

I'm antsy. I open a Word file. A minute goes by. Five minutes. Ten. My fingers hover over my keyboard. I nervously type "A Play in 3 Acts by Alice Buckle," then quickly delete it, then write it again, this time in caps, thinking capital letters might give me courage.

The sounds of Marvin Gaye's "What's Going On" drifts into my bedroom from downstairs. I look at my watch. It's 6:00. The cutting board will be pulled out soon. Peppers will be washed. Corn will be husked. And somebody, most likely Jack, will take his wife for a spin around the kitchen. Others of us—William and I—will be reminded of middle school dances and drinking cans of Pabst Blue Ribbon beer in the basement of the neighbor kid's house. And the youngest of us, Zoe and Peter, and perhaps even Caroline, will download Marvin Gaye onto their iPods, feeling like they are the first ones on earth to discover that earthy, sexy voice.

I put my fingers on the keyboard and begin to type.

91

William walks into the kitchen. "Are you hungry for lunch?" he asks.

I look at the clock. It's 11:30. "Not really."

He rummages around the cupboard, pulling down a box of crackers. "Do we have any hummus?"

"Second shelf. Behind the yogurt."

"So. News," says William, opening the fridge. "I got a job offer."

"What? William! You're kidding me. When?"

"They called yesterday. It's in Lafayette. Great benefits. Health. Dental."

"*Who* called yesterday? You didn't even tell me things were serious with anybody."

"I was afraid it would fall through. I didn't want to get your hopes up. It's an office supply company."

"Office supplies? Like Office Max?"

"No—not like Office Max. King's Stationery. It's a mom-and-pop shop, but they're growing. They've got two stores in the Bay Area and plan to open two more in San Diego this year. I would be direct mail marketing coordinator."

"Direct mail? As in flyers, postcards, and mailers?"

"Yes, Alice, as in what people usually throw in the recycling bin before even looking at it. I was fortunate to get it. There were dozens of applicants. The people seem nice. It's a perfectly fine job."

"Of course it is," I say. "But William, is this what you want?" Were office supplies his big dream?

"What I want doesn't matter anymore," he says quietly.

"Oh, William—" He holds up his hand and cuts me off.

"Alice, no. Stop. I owe you an apology. And if you'll just shut up for a second I can give it to you. You were right. I should have tried harder to make it work at KKM. It's my fault I was laid off. I let you down. I let the whole family down. And I'm sorry. I'm really sorry."

I'm stunned. Did William just admit to me he may have had something to do with being laid off, that it wasn't just all about redundancies? Did he just say it was his fault? He leans over the sink and looks out the window into the backyard, chewing his lip, and as I watch him I feel the last bits of anger over the Cialis debacle drain right out of me.

"You haven't let me down, William. And your 'not trying' wasn't the only reason you were laid off. I know that. A part of it was out of your control. Maybe it's my fault, too, somehow. All of this. Where we are. Maybe I let you down, too."

He turns to face me. "You haven't let me down, Alice."

"Okay. But if I did, and I probably did, I'm sorry. I'm really sorry, too."

He gathers his breath. "I should take this job. I like paper. And pens. And sticky notes. And highlighters."

"I *love* highlighters. Especially the green ones."

"And mailing supplies."

"And staplers. Don't forget staplers. Do you know staples come in colors now? And Lafayette has a great downtown. You can probably walk there for lunch from the office. Grab a Starbucks in the afternoon."

"I hadn't thought of that," says William, dipping a cracker in the hummus. "That will be nice."

"Have you formally accepted?"

"I wanted to talk it over with you first."

"When do you need to give them an answer?"

"I have a week."

"Well, let's just let it sink in. Really weigh the pros and cons."

I'm hoping this will buy me some time to find out what's going on with my job. I haven't heard anything back from Kentwood Elementary as to my query about going full-time in the fall, but I'm hopeful. Often the Parents' Association doesn't make decisions about how funds are being dispersed until the very last minute.

"Seeing that there are no other job offers forthcoming there are only pros, Alice. I can't think of any negatives," says William.

He's right. We don't have the luxury of choice. Nobody does. Not anymore.

92

The next day I wake with a headache and a fever. I spend the morning in bed, and at lunchtime William and Zoe bring me up a tray: a bowl of chicken noodle soup, a glass of ice water, and the mail: an envelope and *People* magazine.

I sniff the soup. "Mmmm."

"Imperial Tea Court," William says.

I pop a noodle into my mouth. "You drove to Imperial Tea Court? In Berkeley?"

He shrugs. "They make the best noodles. Besides, my days of bringing you noodles in the middle of the day are numbered."

"What are you talking about?" asks Zoe.

"Nothing," I say.

We haven't told the children about William's job offer yet. I know they've been worried and will be very relieved to hear he's employed again, but I don't want to say anything to them until we've made a firm decision. William and I glance at each other.

"Obviously not nothing," says Zoe.

Jampo comes running into the room and leaps on the bed.

William snatches him up. "You're not allowed up there. How about a run, you monster?" Jampo stares at him aggressively like he's a terrorist and then suddenly licks his face. William's really been making an effort with Jampo. Are they friends now?

"We need to have a discussion about *nothing* this evening," I say.

"Can you give me a ride to Jude's before your run, Dad?" asks Zoe.

Jude and Zoe are officially a couple again. The day after we caught the mouse, I heard Zoe on the phone with Jude, crying and apologizing. That night he came over for dinner and the two of them held hands under the table. It was so sweet and felt so right it stopped my heart.

"I guess so. Caroline and I have to talk to Nedra about the cake, anyway. Alice, are you two speaking yet?"

"I'm about to send her a smoke signal," I say.

"The wedding is in two weeks. Perhaps you should light the fire now."

After lunch I take another nap, and when I wake I swallow three more Advil. I can't seem to shake this headache. Everything aches. Even my rib cage. I listen for noises from downstairs but it's quiet. Nobody's home but me. I log on, but there's nothing from Researcher 101: no email and no Facebook messages. I'm almost relieved that's the case. I finish off the noodles. I rifle through *People*. Then I open the envelope that's come in the day's mail.

> Dear Alice Buckle,
>
> The Kentwood Elementary School Parents' Association regrets to inform you that we will not be renewing your contract as a drama teacher for the upcoming school year. As you know, the Oakland public school system is experiencing dire budget shortfalls, and it has been decided the funds that the Parents' Association previously dedicated to the Drama Program will have to be rerouted elsewhere. We appreciate your years of loyal service and wish you the very best of luck in your endeavors.
>
> Sincerely,
> The Kentwood Elementary School Parents' Association Board
>
> Mrs. Alison Skov
> Mr. Farhan Zavala
> Mrs. Kendrick Bamberger
> Ms. Rhonda Hightower
> Mrs. Chet Norman

A door slams downstairs and a few seconds later, I hear laughter. I lie there in bed, stunned. Why didn't I see this coming? I should have known something was up when I saw Mrs. Norman at Berkeley Rep. Clearly this was already in the works. She was so smug and her husband so apologetic; she most likely spearheaded my termination.

When William clomps up the stairs in his sneakers, I pretend to be asleep. He walks to the side of the bed and I can feel his eyes on my face. He gently touches the back of his hand to my forehead to see if I'm hot.

"You're a bad faker," he says.

"I've been fired," I whisper.

I hear the rustle of paper as he reads the letter. "Fuck them," he says.

"It hurts," I whimper.

William puts his hand on mine. "I know, Alice."

I'm sick for the next three days.

"It's a summer flu," says Bunny. "You just have to let it run its course."

Every morning, I get up thinking it will have passed. I go downstairs, pour myself a cup of coffee, feel nauseous at the smell of it, and go back upstairs.

"She's a very bad patient," says Jack.

"The worst," says William.

"Am I not sighing enough?" I ask.

"No. You're not moaning enough, either," says William.

"We need to talk," I say. "About *nothing*," meaning his job offer.

"When you're feeling better."

I watch bad TV. I spend a lot of time online.

KED3 (Kentwood Elementary Third Grade Drama Parents' Forum)
Digest #134
KED3ParentsForum@yahoogroups.com

Messages. in this digest (6)

1. I'm starting a *Get Alice Buckle Her Job Back* **group. Please join me!**
Posted by: Farmymommy

2. RE: I'm starting a *Get Alice Buckle Her Job Back* **group. Please join me.**
Yes! Count me in. I have to admit I feel terrible about the way this was handled. It was done so impersonally. Somebody (you know who I'm talking about, **Storminnormandy**) should have had the courage to tell her face-to-face. At the very least she should have been given a goodbye lunch, at Blackberries, or Red Boy Pizza. Yes, *Charlotte's Web* was a disaster. We all agree with that (sorry, mothers of the geese), but doesn't she deserve another chance? And if not another chance, at least appreciation for all her years of service? **Posted by: Queenbeebeebee**

3. RE: I'm starting a *Get Alice Buckle Her Job Back* **group. Please join me.**
Are you kidding me? May I remind you Alice Buckle basically had our kids do a striptease dance in the auditorium. All that was missing was the pole.
Posted by: **Helicopmama**

4. RE: I'm starting a *Get Alice Buckle Her Job Back* **group. Please join me.**
Please desist from starting this group. There are circumstances that none of you are aware of that led to Alice Buckle's termination. Circumstances that I cannot, unfortunately, reveal to you at this time. What I can tell you is that Ms. Buckle had some serious lapses in judgment. Let's just leave it at that and move on. **Posted by: Storminnormandy**

5. RE: I'm starting a *Get Alice Buckle Her Job Back* **group. Please join me.**
Alice Buckle is a very good friend of mine. She does not want her job back. Well, not anymore. When she first found out, she would have done anything to get her job back because she was panicked about how her family would survive on NO income (her husband is currently unemployed, too). But after sitting with it for a few days she's come to agree with **Storminnormandy**. It is time for her to move on. She wants to apologize for her mistakes. And she really hopes you will not terminate the performing arts program altogether.
Posted by: Davidmametlurve182

328 | MELANIE GIDEON

6. RE: I'm starting a *Get Alice Buckle Her Job Back* group. Please join me. I
have loved every single minute I've spent working with your children.
Posted by: Davidmametlurve182

My cell rings.

"Are we talking yet?" asks Nedra.

"No."

"I heard about your job. I'm so sorry, Alice."

"Thank you."

"Are you okay?"

"I've got the flu."

"Who gets the flu in the summer?"

"Apparently me. So did you decide on the lemon or raspberry cake?"

"Oysters."

"Oyster cake."

"No, for appetizers."

"I thought that was too obvious. Oysters being aphrodisiacs and all."

"That's a very nice apology," says Nedra. "Accepted. Potluck two
nights from now."

"You're still doing the potluck so close to your wedding?"

"Italian. We'll make it easy. Just bring a jar of tomato sauce."

"Nedra?"

"What?"

"Jude is an amazing kid."

"And so is Zoe. Kisses. I'll talk to you soon."

I end the call and log on to my Facebook page.

Nedra Rao
Misses her best friend.

2 hours ago

Nedra Rao
"unlikes" Kentwood Elementary.

3 hours ago

Linda Barbedian
Can't believe she's going to be an empty nester.

4 hours ago

Kelly Cho

Et tu, Brute?

5 hours ago

Phil Archer

Pawnshop—a time capsule. Who knew?

6 hours ago

Helen Davies

Wanted: VP Food and Beverage Division in Boston. Startle me. Sell me. Pitch me. See LinkedIn for more info.

7 hours ago

93

John Yossarian *is married.*

Lucy Pevensie *is married.*

I guess congratulations are in order?

You, too.

I take it things are going well then?

Things?

With your wife?

Things are becoming clearer with my wife. They are, however, becoming less clear in all other areas.

Like work?

Yes, like work. I've been looking for another job. It's time for me to leave the Netherfield Center.

Because of me?

No, because of me. I crossed the line. You didn't do anything wrong.

I'm very sorry to hear that.

Don't be.

Well, if it makes you feel any better it appears I crossed the line, too, at work. I definitely will have to look for another job.

Oh, no, Wife 22. : (

It's all right. It's my fault. I made the mistake of mixing up my love for

the kids with my love for the job. I was tired. I got sloppy. I should have quit a long time ago.

What now?

Now I make amends.

94

Still sick. Once again, the house is empty except for Jampo and me. William took the kids to the pool and Caroline and her parents went into San Francisco to look at apartments; she may have to get five roommates in order to afford living in the city, but she'll move out by the end of the month. I'm going to miss her terribly, but I take comfort in the fact she'll only be a BART ride away.

I can't stop thinking about Helen's Facebook posting. I go to her LinkedIn page to find out more about the job. After reading the detailed description for the VP of Food and Beverage (and having spent the last month being the lucky recipient of William's gourmet meals and various sundry food obsessions), I know this would be the perfect job for William—a job that would perhaps even qualify as his pipe dream—however, there are three big obstacles. One: William is far too proud to apply for it himself; two: the job is in Boston; and three: me. I'm sure Helen still hates me. But maybe, after all these years, I've finally been given the opportunity to set things right.

An hour later, I hold my breath, utter a quick "Please, God," and press Send.

From: Alice Buckle <alicebuckle@rocketmail.com>
Subject: A voice from the past . . .
Date: August 13, 10:04 AM
To: Helen Davies <helendavies@D&DAdvertising.com>

Dear Helen,

 I have owed you a real apology for years. Actually I owe you a few apologies, but first, the big one—I'm very sorry about William. I want you to know I did have standards. I believed in the sisterhood. Up until that point I had never been the "other woman" in a relationship and I never intended to become one. But something happened between William and me that was—well, it was unexpected. It just sort of carried us away. Neither one us was looking for it. I know that's a cliché, but it's the truth.

I'm sorry that I flirted with him behind your back. I'm sorry that I didn't invite you to our wedding (I wanted to, I knew it was the right thing to do, but I let myself be talked out of it). But mostly I'm sorry that it's taken me twenty years to apologize.

And now, in a strange bit of comeuppance, I find myself in the uncomfortable position of asking you for a favor. I'm writing to you on behalf of William. I saw your job listing for the VP of Food and Beverage: William would be perfect for it. He's too proud to apply himself, but I'm not too proud to ask you for a chance to throw his hat in the ring. I don't want any special favors, I only ask that you don't hold me against him.

I've attached William's CV.

All the very best,

Alice Buckle

95

Alice?

Hi Dad.

I have something 2 tell u.

I have something to tell u 2.

Been clning house. Dump runs. Salvation Army. Pawnshop.

Pawnshop? Why?

Wanted 2 buy Conchita some jewelry.

In a pawnshop?

Don't make fun. Pawnshop has many treasures. Asked Conchita move in w me.

You're kidding!!

U don't approve?

Of course I approve. I think it's wonderful!

I thought I done with all this.

With all what?

U know what.

Romance?

Sex.

Love, Dad?

Yes, love.

:'(

Why u sad, sweetheart?

:-#

I'm your father. U don't have to B embarrassed.

I haven't always told you the truth, Dad.

I know that, honey.

Things are kind of hard around here.

I had a feeling something was going on. U been so far away.

I'm really sorry. I'm feeling a little lost.

Do not give up. U be found soon. Good thgs on their way 2 u.

Oh, Dad. How do you know?

Becos I sent them in the mail.

96

Pat Guardia

Can't believe she almost didn't do this. Loves her husband so much.

1 hour ago

Pat Guardia

Somebody kill me now.

3 hours ago

Pat Guardia

Hates her husband with all her heart.

4 hours ago

Pat Guardia

Water just broke. Going to the hospital! Have never been more in love.

6 hours ago

"Hello, baby," I whisper, looking down at Pat and her newborn in the hospital bed.

"Go ahead," says Pat. "Take off his hat. I know you want to smell him."

I slip off the blue knit beanie and breathe in the sweet, milky new-baby-head smell.

"Oh, God, Pat. How can you stand it? He's gorgeous. And he's got a perfectly shaped head. How did you manage that?" I ask.

"Only twenty minutes of pushing," says Tita proudly.

"Only because Liam is my third," says Pat.

Shonda hands Pat a pink box wrapped in glittery ribbon. "I know I'm supposed to bring something for the baby, but tough. You're the one who needs a present right now. Miracle Serum of Light Complexion Illuminator. Not that you need it, sweetheart."

"It sounds like a church," says Tita.

"Oh, it is," says Shonda. "Once you start using it, you'll be worshiping at MSLCI's altar forever, trust me."

"You finally got your boy," I say.

"What am I going to do with a boy?" says Pat. "All I know is girls."

"Cover his wee-wee when you change his diaper," I tell her.

"And how long should she refer to it as a wee-wee?" asks Shonda.

"A month, two months tops," I say. "Then you can graduate to penie."

"None of this wee-wee and penie silliness. You should call it a penis from the beginning," says Tita.

"You feel very strongly about that, Tita, don't you," says Shonda.

"I hate it when people make up ridiculous names for their *hoo-hoos*," says Tita.

"Do you want to hold him?" Pat asks me.

"Could I? I already washed my hands."

"Of course. Go sit in the rocker with him."

She carefully hands me the baby. He's asleep, so I tiptoe over to the rocker. Once I'm seated, I take a good look at him: the perfect bow-shaped lips, the tiny fist curled up against his cheek. I sigh happily.

"You could do it again, Alice," says Pat. "You're only forty-four. My friend just got pregnant and she's forty-five."

"God, no," I whisper. "I'm done with all that. My babies are nearly grown. I'll just have a baby vicariously through you. I'll take him anytime you need a break. Day or night, you just call and I'll take him," I say. "I mean that, Pat. I'm not just saying it."

"I know you're not," says Pat.

"You're crying, Alice," says Tita.

"I know," I say. "Newborns always make me cry."

"How come?" asks Shonda.

"They're just so vulnerable. So defenseless. So pure."

"Uh-huh," says Shonda.

"You're crying, Shonda," says Tita.

"So are you, Tita," says Shonda.

"I'm not crying," says Pat, sniffling.

We're all in different parts of the room, but it feels like we've joined hands. This is what happens with the Mumble Bumbles—this sudden sort of swelling and gathering each other up.

"When I was young, forty-five seemed so old," I say. "My mother seemed so old."

Liam uncurls his fist and I slide in my pinkie. He grasps it tightly and brings it to his mouth.

"But now that I'm almost forty-five it seems so young. My mother was such a baby. She had so much life ahead of her."

"And so do you," says Tita softly.

"I've gotten everything all wrong. Zoe doesn't have an eating disorder. Peter isn't gay."

"Just because she passed away doesn't mean you can't speak to her, Alice," says Shonda.

"That marriage study was a stupid idea. I screwed up at work."

"The conversation never stops," says Tita.

I nestle my face into Liam's blankets. "He's so beautiful."

"She'd want you to pass her, Alice," says Shonda.

"Please, please let me take care of him sometimes," I beg, standing up.

"To not pass her would be a betrayal," says Pat.

"I feel like I'm saying goodbye," I say.

"Not just goodbye, but hello," says Tita. "There you are. Hello, Alice Buckle."

I walk to Pat's bedside, tears streaming down my face, and hand Liam back to her.

"Everybody dreads their tipping-point year," says Tita. "They think if they just don't pay attention to it, it'll go away. I don't know why you all make such a big fuss. Not when *this* is what's on the other side of it."

The Mumble Bumbles gather around me and soon we're a crying, hugging mob, one tiny human in the middle of us, the future, his finger pointed up toward the sky.

97

Festive Italian Potluck at Nedra's House

6:30: Standing in Nedra's kitchen

Me: Here's the pasta sauce. I brought two kinds. Mushroom and three-cheese.

Nedra: That's very nice, but you're an hour early.

Zoe: Is Jude home?

Nedra: In his room, darling. Go on in. What time does the movie start?

Zoe: Seven.

Nedra: Have fun!

Me: I thought we could go over the maid-of-honor responsibilities.

Nedra (*watching Zoe walk away*): This makes me very, very happy. The two of them back together. Does it make you happy?

Me: Did you hear what I just said?

Nedra: Show up.

Me: I'm right here.

Nedra: On my wedding day—show up. That is your responsibility.

Me: Done. I'll even wear a hideous Queen Victoria dress.

Nedra: I bought you a beautiful dress.

Me: You did?

Nedra: A halter-top. Very flattering. You've got great shoulders and arms. You should show them off.

Me: I have something to tell you. About Researcher 101.

Nedra: You don't have to tell me anything, Alice. In fact, I'd rather not hear it. La-la-la-la-la.

Me: I think it's over.

Nedra (*sighing*): It wasn't over before?

Me: He's going to try and make it work with his wife.

Nedra: He has a *wife?*

Me: Stop, Nedra. Please. I just told you it's over.

Nedra: So you're going to try and make it work with William?

Me: Well, that's the funny thing. It doesn't seem like work right now.

Bobby (*walking into the kitchen*): Ladies! I know I'm early. I hope I'm not interrupting. But look at this gorge-o bread. Smell it. Here (*ripping off the end*). La Farine. Just out of the oven. Have a bite.

Nedra: Where's Linda?

Bobby: She's not going to be able to make it.

Me: Well, looks like we'll all be partnerless. William and Kate can't make it either.

Nedra: What's Linda's excuse?

Bobby: She's divorcing me. I got the potluck. She got everything else.

7:30: In Nedra's living room

Nedra: I hate to say it, but I knew the twin master suites were the beginning of the end.

Bobby: I want to get high. I deserve to get high. Do you have any pot, Nedra? Alice, you don't have to sit so far away. Divorce is not contagious.

Nedra: Actually, you're wrong. Divorce *is* a sort of contagion. I see it all the time. A man comes in looking for representation and then a few weeks later another man comes in, a friend of the first man, just wanting to know his rights and all, but just in case, he's brought along a comprehensive list of all the marital assets, the last three years of income tax returns, and a recent pay stub. Alice, you stay right where you are.

Bobby (*starting to cry*): She wants to move to New York to be closer to the kids.

Nedra (*getting up*): Bloody hell. Hold on.

Me (*sitting next to him on the couch*): Don't cry, Bobby B.

Bobby: I love it when you call me that. You're such a nice woman. Why didn't I marry *you?*

Me: I'm no prize, believe me.

Bobby: I've always envied William.

Me: You have?

Bobby: Even after twenty years together, the two of you are still so connected.

Me: We are?

Bobby: It used to drive Linda crazy. She thought you guys were faking it. I told her you can't fake passion like that.

Nedra (*walking back into the room, holding a joint*): Success!

Me: Jude smokes?

Nedra (*lighting the joint and inhaling*): Of course not. It's mine.

Me: *You* have your own supply?

Nedra (*handing the joint to Bobby*): Here you go, darling. It's the good stuff. Very clean. I have a medical condition.

Me: What's your medical condition?

Bobby (*taking a big toke, and then another and then another*): Oh, Jesus, that's good.

Nedra: You don't believe me?

Me: No, Nedra, I don't.

Nedra: It's in the *DSM*. It's an actual disorder.

Me: What's it called?

Nedra: Middle age.

Bobby (*coughing*): I have that, too.

Nedra: There's only one known cure.

Bobby: What's that?

Nedra: Old age.

Bobby (*cackling*): Is it the Mary Jane, or is Nedra suddenly really funny?

Me: *Mary Jane?* Just how old *are* you, Bobby B?

Nedra (*inhaling deeply, then looking at the joint*): I'm getting married. Can you believe it? Me? A bride?

Bobby: Will you represent me in the divorce?

Nedra: I wish I could, darling. But I know the both of you. It wouldn't be fair. I can recommend somebody very good.

Zoe (*walking into the living room with Jude*): Quick, get the camera so we can take pictures of them and they'll be so embarrassed and horrified they'll never touch the stuff again.

Me: Oh, my God, Zoe! What are you doing here? I am not smoking, for your information. I haven't taken one hit.

Nedra: This is very rude of you. To just walk in on us and invade our privacy. I thought you went to the movies.

Jude: Do you think this is a rave?

Zoe: You do realize pot is much stronger these days than it was when you were growing up?

Jude: Frequently it's dipped in embalming fluid.

Zoe: One puff could trigger schizophrenia.

Nedra: In a teenage brain—with an unconnected frontal lobe. Our frontal lobes have been connected for decades now.

Bobby: Blame it on me.

Nedra: Blame it on Linda.

Jude (*reaching for his guitar*): Well, since you're all high and everything, would you like to hear a song?

Me: I'm not high. And I would. I would really like to hear a song, Jude.

Zoe (*blushing*): It's called "Even Though."

Bobby: Hold on. I have to lie on the carpet for this.

Me: Me, too.

Nedra: Move over.

Me: I feel like I'm in high school.

Bobby (*starting to cry again, softly*): There's something about being stoned and lying on the floor.

Me (*reaching for Bobby's hand*)

Nedra (*reaching for Bobby's other hand*)

Jude (*strumming the guitar, looking at Zoe*): I wrote it for Zoe.

Bobby (*moaning*): Ohhh!

Jude: Is he okay? Should I stop?

Bobby (*clutching his heart*): Ahhhh!

Jude: What? What is it?

Nedra: He means play, darling. He means the world needs more love songs. He means *bonne chance* and *glück und den besten wünschen* and *buona fortuna*. He means "how wonderful it is to be young."

Bobby (*sobbing*): That's exactly what I mean. How did you know?

Me: Nedra is fluent in moans.

98

From: Helen Davies <helendavies@D&DAdvertising.com>
Subject: Re: A voice from the past . . .
Date: August 15, 3:01 PM
To: Alice Buckle <alicebuckle@rocketmail.com>

Alice,

I knew I was in trouble the day you interviewed for the job at Peavey Patterson. I'm sure you aren't aware of this, as you practically ran out of William's office that day, but he watched you go. It was involuntary. He couldn't help himself. He stood in his doorway and watched you walk down the corridor. Then he watched you stand by the elevators, nervously punching the down button over and over again. And then, even when you were gone, he still stood there in the doorway. You knew each other even before you knew each other. That was the look on his face the day he interviewed you. *Recognition.* I didn't stand a chance.

As far as the position, even though William is certainly qualified, I'm not sure I can help. Give me a few days to think about it. I assume you don't want to move to Boston. And I assume he doesn't know that you've applied for him and you'd like to keep it that way. He's always been a proud man.

Apology accepted.

HD

99

"I took the job," says William.

"What job?"

"The direct mail job, Alice. What other job would I be talking about?"

It's been two days since I got the email from Helen, and—nothing.

"But *we* didn't talk about it."

"What's there to talk about? We're both out of work. We need the income, not to mention the benefits. It's done. To be honest, I feel relieved."

"But I just thought—"

"No. Don't say anything else. It's the right thing to do." He leans back against the kitchen counter, his hands jammed in his pockets, and nods at me.

"I know. I know it is. It's really great, William. Congratulations. So when do you start?"

William turns around and opens the cupboard. "Monday. So, interesting news. Kelly Cho was let go from KKM."

"She was let go? What happened?"

"I guess they did a major restructuring," says William, grabbing the flour. "I was only the first round."

It's Friday. Tonight, Nedra is throwing a celebratory dinner (for friends and colleagues that won't be at the ceremony—she even invited Bunny, Jack, and Caroline), and tomorrow is the wedding.

"What are you prepping?" I ask.

"Cheese puffs."

"Sorry—I overslept," says Caroline, walking into the kitchen.

Bunny follows her in, yawning. "Please tell me there's coffee."

Caroline pours two cups of coffee and sits down at the table with her pad, frowning.

"We're never going to get all this done."

"Delegate," says William.

"I'll help," I say.

"Me, too," says Bunny.

Caroline and William glance at each other.

"How I can put this nicely?" says Caroline.

"Right," I say. "Our services are not desired. Bunny, should we retire to the deck?"

"I'm really very happy to peel something. I'm an expert peeler," says Bunny.

"Fine, Mom, I'll call you when we get to the potatoes," says Caroline.

Bunny takes a sip of her coffee and sighs. "I'm going to miss this."

"What? My nearly dead lemon tree? Living with the constant threat of earthquakes?"

"*You*, Alice. Your family. William. Peter and Zoe. Having coffee with you every morning."

"You really have to leave?"

"Caroline's found an apartment. She's got a job. It's time for us to go home. Promise me we won't fall out of touch again."

"That won't happen. I'm back in your life for good."

"Marvelous. That's just what I wanted to hear, because I'll imagine we'll be going back and forth quite a bit on this."

"On what?"

"I read your pages. There's some really good stuff in there, Alice, but I'll be honest. It needs work."

I nod. "Let me guess. *People don't talk that way in real life,* right?"

Bunny chuckles. "Did I really say that to you? Oh, goodness, that was a long time ago, wasn't it?"

"Is it still true?"

"No. You have a good ear for dialogue now. Now the challenge will be disclosure. Moving past your vulnerability. Your work is autobiographical, after all."

"Some of it." I make a face.

"I'm being too nosy? I'm sorry."

"Oh, don't be. I need a kick in the ass."

"A kick in the ass is the opposite of what you need. What you need is a cupping of the chin," says Bunny, turning to me and cupping my chin. "Listen to me. Take yourself seriously. Write your goddamn play already."

"You're not going to believe it!" says William, an hour later.

I'm in my bedroom closet, attempting to figure out what to wear tonight. I rifle through my clothes. No, no, no. Too fancy, too outdated, too matronly. Maybe I could get away with wearing the Ann Taylor suit.

"I just got an email from Helen Davies."

"Helen Davies?" I try and look surprised. "What does she want?"

"Do you remember she posted her firm was looking for a VP of Food and Beverage?"

I shrug.

"Well, I didn't pay any attention to the posting because the job was in Boston, but she just wrote to me and asked if I'd be interested. They've decided to move the division to the San Francisco office."

"Seriously?"

"Yes, seriously. She thinks I'd be the perfect person to head it up."

"I can't believe it."

"Me either."

"It's unbelievable timing."

"Eerie, isn't it? It feels like fate. Like everything that happened twenty years ago is just circling back around. It feels good, Alice. Good!" He twirls me out of the closet and waltzes me around the room.

"You're crazy," I say.

"I'm lucky," he says, dipping me.

"You're a kook," I say. He swings me back up and our eyes find each other.

I bury my face in his shirt, suddenly feeling shy.

"No, you don't. You're not allowed to hide," he says, pulling me away from him. "Look at me, Alice."

He gazes down at me and I think *it's been so long,* I think *there you are,* I think *home.*

"We're going to be okay. I have to admit I was worried. I wasn't sure," says William, tucking my hair behind my ears. "But I think we're going to be okay."

"I hope so."

"Don't hope so. Believe it. If there was anytime you needed to believe, it's now, Alice."

He takes my face in his hands and tilts it up. His kiss is tender and sweet and doesn't last a second longer than it should.

"Whoa. I'm dizzy." I untangle myself from him and sit down on the bed. "All that twirling." And kissing. And gazing. And being gazed at. I feel breathless.

"I'll need to make a few hires. I was thinking about Kelly Cho."

"Kelly? Wow. Well, I guess that would be a really nice gesture."

William goes on, musing out loud. I haven't seen him so animated in months. He does a two-step around the bedroom. He doesn't notice when I open my laptop.

From: Alice Buckle <alicebuckle@rocketmail.com>
Subject: VP Food and Beverage: William Buckle
Date: August 17, 10:10 AM
To: Helen Davies <helendavies@D&DAdvertising.com>

Dear Helen,
    You are one class act.
    Thank you. From the bottom of my heart, thank you.
    Alice

100

John Yossarian

Adrift on a little yellow raft

10 minutes ago

Lucy Pevensie

Mothballs and fur

15 minutes ago

You're back in the wardrobe?

I'm afraid so.

Time passes differently in Narnia then IRL.

Look at you, using acronyms like IRL.

You'll only have been gone for five minutes when you return.

A lifetime on the Internet.

Your husband won't even know that you left.

That's the hope, anyway. I'll miss you, Yossarian.

What will you miss?

Your paranoia, your complaining, your salty brand of sanity.

I'll miss you, too, Lucy Pevensie.

What will you miss?

Your magic cordials, your bravery—your ridiculous blind faith in a talking lion.

Do you believe in second chances?

I do.

I can't help thinking it was fate that brought us together.

And fate that kept us apart. Forgive me for complicating things, for falling for you, Wife 22.

Don't apologize. You reminded me I was a woman worth falling for.

GTG. I see land.

GTG. I see light through the crack of the wardrobe door.

101

I'm about to close my Lucy Pevensie account for good, but before I do, I poke around on John Yossarian's wall one last time. It's been such an intense couple of months and Researcher 101 has played such a big part in my daily life. Even though I'm ready to say goodbye, and I know it's the right thing to do, I still feel bereft. It's a last-day-of-camp feeling. I'm bittersweet, but ready to pack it up and go home.

On Yossarian's information page, I see a link to a Picasa album, which contains his profile photos. Suddenly I wonder if he's disabled his geotag function. I open the album and click on the yeti photo. A map of the United States pops up with a red pushpin stuck smack in the middle of the Bay Area. No, he has not disabled his geotag function. I zoom in on the pushpin. The photo was taken on the Golden Gate Bridge. I exhale with pleasure. This is dangerous. This is titillating. There's a part of me that's still curious, that will always be curious. Even though we had a certain kind of intimacy, in truth I know nothing about him. Who is he? How does he spend his days?

I repeat the same process with the photo of the horse and once again the pushpin is stuck in San Francisco, but the location is Crissy Field. He's got to be athletic. He probably runs and bikes. Maybe he even does yoga.

I click on the photo of the dog, but this time the red pushpin appears on Mountain Road in Oakland. Wait a second. Is it possible he lives in Oakland? I just assumed he lived in San Francisco, based on the Netherfield Center's proximity to UCSF.

I click on the photo of the labyrinth and the pushpin again shows his location as Oakland. But this photo was taken minutes from my house. In Manzanita Park.

I click on the photo of his hand, my heart thudding. *Stop this, Alice*

Buckle, stop it right now. You extracted yourself. You just said goodbye. A map of my neighborhood pops up. I enlarge the map. It zeros in on my street. I drag the icon of the little yellow man onto the pushpin, wanting more detail, and an actual photo of an actual house appears. 529 Irving Drive.

My house.

What? The photo was taken from my house? I try and process this information.

Researcher 101 has been inside my house? He's been stalking me? He's a stalker? But this makes no sense. How could he have gotten into my house? Somebody is always home, between school being out and Caroline working only part-time, and Jampo would have barked his head off if somebody broke in, and William never—William . . . Jesus.

I zoom in on the photo of the hand. And when the familiar details of that hand come into focus—the big palm, the long, tapered fingers, the little freckle on the top of the pinkie, I feel sick because—*it's William's hand.*

"Alice, can I borrow some conditioner?" Bunny stands in the doorway wrapped in a towel, clutching her toiletry bag in her hand. Then she looks at my face. "Alice, dear God, what happened?"

I ignore her and go back to my computer. *Think, Alice, think!* Did Researcher 101 somehow hack into our family's photo library? My brain feels folded over, like an omelet. Researcher 101 is a stalker, Researcher 101 has been stalking me, has been stalking William, William stalking, William is a stalker, Researcher 101 is a stalker is William is Researcher 101. *Oh, my, God.*

"Alice, you're mumbling. You're scaring me. Did somebody get hurt? Did somebody *die*?" she asks.

I look up at Bunny. "William is Researcher 101."

Bunny's eyes widen, and then, to my surprise, she throws back her head and laughs.

"Why are you laughing?"

"Because *of course* it's William. Of course! It's too perfect. It's—delicious."

I shake my head in frustration. "You mean duplicitous."

Bunny steps into the room and peers over my shoulder as I frantically scroll back through our emails and chats, seeing them in an entirely different light this time.

Me: I can have the weather delivered every morning to my phone by weather.com. What could be better?

101: Getting caught in the rain?

"I can't believe it. The nerve of him. The Piña Colada song?" I shriek.

"My God, that's clever," says Bunny. "I guess he was tired of his lady; they'd been together too long." She winks at me and I scowl back at her.

Me: You're very lucky. He sounds like a dream dog.

101: Oh, he is.

"Oh, yes, very funny, so funny, so terribly funny, William, ha-ha," I say.

"Do you recognize that dog?" asks Bunny.

I look at the photo more closely. "Goddammit. That's our neighbor's dog. Mr. Big."

"Your neighbor is Mr. Big?"

"No, the dog is Mr. Big."

"How could you have missed that?" asks Bunny. "It's almost like he wanted you to know, Alice. Like he was giving you clues."

Me: Yes, please change my answer. It's more truthful. Unlike your profile photo.

101: I don't know about that. In my experience, the truth is frequently blurry.

"That son of a bitch," I say.

"Mmm. Sounds like he's been reading a bit too much Eckhart Tolle," says Bunny.

Me: If we had met? If you had showed up that night? What do you think would have happened?

101: I think you would have been disappointed.

Me: Why? What are you keeping from me? Do you have scales? Do you weigh 600 pounds? Do you have a comb-over?

101: Let's just say I would not be what you had expected.

I groan. "He was toying with me the entire time!"

"One person's toying is another person's dropping clues and waiting to be discovered. Maybe you were just slow on the uptake, Alice. Besides, I have to tell you that so far, I haven't read one thing he's written that wasn't true."

"What? *Everything* was a lie. Researcher 101 was a lie. He doesn't exist!"

"Oh, but he *does* exist. William couldn't have made him up if Researcher 101 wasn't somehow a part of him. Or a *him* he wanted to be."

"No. He played me. He just told me what I wanted to hear."

"I don't think so," says Bunny, chuckling.

"What is wrong with you, Bunny? Why do you seem so delighted about all of this?"

"Why *aren't* you delighted? Don't you understand, Alice? You can carry on with both Researcher 101 and William. Forever. Because they're one and the same!"

"I feel so humiliated!"

"Again with the humiliation. There's no reason to feel humiliated."

"Of course there is. I said things. Things I never would have. Things he had no right to know. Answers he cheated out of me."

"Well, what if he had asked you those things to your face?"

"William never would have asked me."

"Why not?"

"He wasn't interested. He stopped being interested a long time ago."

Bunny tightens the towel under her arms. "Well, all I can say is that he went to an awful lot of trouble for a husband who wasn't interested in knowing what his wife thought or wanted or believed. And now I just have one question for you." She gestures to the Ann Taylor suit that I've spread out on the bed. "You aren't planning on wearing that to dinner, are you?"

• • •

"You got something from your father," says William, walking into the bathroom. "I had to sign for it."

I've been upstairs for an hour, stewing, and avoiding William, trying to will myself into a positive frame of mind for dinner. But the sight of him infuriates me all over again.

"You look great," he says, handing me an envelope.

"I don't look great," I snap.

"I've always loved that suit."

"Well, you're the only one, then."

"Jesus, Alice. What's going on? Are you mad at me?"

"Why would I be mad at you? Should I be mad at you?"

My phone chimes. It's a text from Nedra. *Hope you're getting that toast ready! Practice, practice, practice. So excited about tonight. Xoxoxo.*

"Damn toast," I say. "That's the last thing I want to do."

"Oh—that's why you're so snappish. Nerves," says William. "You'll do fine."

"No, I won't do fine. I can't do it. I just can't do it. I can't be expected to do everything. You do the toast!" I cry.

"Are you serious?"

"Yes, I am. You're going to have to do it. I'm not doing it."

William looks at me aghast. "But Nedra will be so disappointed. You're the maid of honor."

"It doesn't matter who gives the toast. You. Me. It just has to be somebody from this family. Get Peter to do it. He's good at those sorts of things."

"Alice, I don't understand."

"No, you don't. And you never have."

William shrinks away from me, as if I've hit him.

"I'll come up with something," he says softly. "Let me know when you're done in here so I can take a shower."

After William's gone, I don't know what to do with myself, so I open the envelope. There are two items inside: a card from my father and an old hankie folded carefully into a square. The hankie belonged to my mother. There are three little violets embroidered on the white cotton along with my mother's initials. I press the hankie to my nose. It still smells of her Jean Naté body splash. I pick up the card.

> *Sometimes things we lose come back to us. Not usually, from this old man's experience, but sometimes, they do. I found this in the pawnshop in Brockton. The owner said it's been sitting in the case for over two decades, but that won't be a surprise to you. I know you've made some mistakes and done some things you wish you could take back. I know you're feeling lost and you're not sure what to do. I hope this will help you make up your mind. I love you, honey.*

I carefully unfold the handkerchief and there, nestled in the white cotton, is my engagement ring: the one I threw out the car window when William and I had the argument about inviting Helen to our wedding. Somebody must have found it and brought it to the pawnshop. The jewels have darkened with age and it needs a good cleaning, but there's no mistaking the tiny diamond flanked by two even tinier emeralds—the ring that my grandfather gave to my grandmother so many years ago, the ring that I so cavalierly tossed away.

I try and make out the engraving on the inside of the ring but the type is too small. I can't think about what it all means now. If I do, I'll lose it. We have an hour before we have to leave for dinner. I slip the ring into my pocket and go downstairs.

The dinner is being held at a new trendy restaurant called Boca.

"Is that Donna Summer playing?" asks William, when we walk in the door.

"Jude told me Nedra was hiring a deejay," says Zoe. "I hope they don't play seventies music all night long."

"I love this song," says Jack to Bunny. "I sense your dance card will be full tonight, 'Bad Girl.'"

"Did you take your baby aspirin?" Bunny asks.

"I took three," Jack says. "Just in case."

"In case of what?" asks Bunny.

"This," he says, kissing her on the lips.

"You two are cute," says Zoe.

"You wouldn't think it was cute if that was your mother and me," says William.

"That's because between the ages of thirty and sixty, PDA is gross," says Zoe. "And after sixty it's cute again. You're older than sixty, right?" Zoe whispers to Jack.

"Just a squidge," says Jack, pinching his thumb and forefinger together.

"There's Nedra," says William. "At the bar." He gives a low whistle.

Nedra is wearing a forest-green silk wrap dress with lots of cleavage showing. She rarely shows décolletage; she thinks it's déclassé. But tonight she made an exception. She looks stunning.

"We should probably tell her," says William. "Do you want to or should I?"

"Tell her what?" asks Peter.

I sigh. "That your father is doing the toast, not me."

"But you're the maid of honor. You have to do the toast," says Zoe.

"Your mother isn't feeling well," says William. "I'm standing in for her."

"Right," says Zoe, whose face tells me everything she's thinking: her mother is running away—*once again.* I should care, I'm setting a very bad example for my daughter, but I don't. Not tonight.

"Darling! Have a Soiree," cries Nedra, when she sees me approaching. She holds out a martini glass filled with a clear liquid. Little purple flowers skitter across the surface.

"Lavender, gin, honey, and lemon," she says. "Give it a try."

I summon the bartender. "Chardonnay, please," I say.

"You're so predictable," says Nedra. "That's one of the things I love about you."

"Yes, well, I predict you're about to not love my predictability."

Nedra puts the martini glass down. "Do not put a damper on my evening, Alice Buckle. Do not even think about it."

I sigh. "I feel terrible."

"Here we go. What do you mean you feel terrible?"

"Sick."

"Sick how?"

"Headache. Stomachache. Light-headed."

The bartender gives me my wine. I take a big sip.

"That's just nerves," says Nedra.

"I think I'm having a panic attack."

"You are not having a panic attack. Stop being so dramatic and just say what you need to say."

"I can't give the toast tonight. But don't worry, William's going to take my place."

Nedra shakes her head. "That is a hideous suit."

"I didn't want to upstage you. But I shouldn't have worried. All this—" I say, waving at her breasts. "Wow."

"I asked one thing of you, Alice. One thing most women would be thrilled about. For you to be my maid of honor."

"There's a reason. I'm a mess. I can't think straight. Something's happened," I cry.

"*Really*, Alice?" She looks at me incredulously.

"I got some bad news tonight. Some really, terrible, horrible bad news."

Nedra's face softens. "Christ, why didn't you open with that? What's happened? Is it your father?"

"Researcher 101 is William!"

Nedra takes a dainty sip of her Soiree. She takes another little sip.

"Did you hear me?"

"I heard you, Alice."

"And?"

"Are you about to get your period?"

"I have evidence! Look. This is one of Researcher 101's profile photos." I take out my phone, go to Facebook, click on his photo album, and then click on the photo of his hand. "First of all, it's geotagged."

"Hmm," says Nedra, looking over my shoulder. I drag the icon of the little yellow man onto the red pushpin and when the photo of our house pops up on the screen, she claps her hand over her mouth. "Wait, it gets better." I zoom in on the photo. "It's his hand. He could have used any hand. Any hand from the Internet. A clip art hand, even. He used his own."

"That bloody, fucking idiot," says Nedra, grinning.

"I know!"

"I can't believe it."

"I *know*!"

She shakes her head in disbelief. "Who knew he had it in him? That is the single most romantic thing I've ever heard of."

"Oh, God, not you, too."

"What do you mean not me, too?"

"Bunny had the same reaction."

"Well, that should tell you something, then."

I finger my engagement ring in my pocket. "Oh, Nedra, I don't know what to feel. I'm so confused. Look," I show her the ring. "This came today in the mail."

"What is it?"

"My engagement ring."

"The one you threw out the car window fifty million years ago?"

"My father found it in a pawnshop. Somebody must have turned it in." I hold the ring up to my eye and squint. "There's an engraving, but I can't read it."

"Your refusal to deal with your adult-onset presbyopia is becoming a real problem, Alice," says Nedra. "Let me see."

I hand the ring to her.

"*Her heart did whisper he had done it for her,*" she reads. "Oh, for God's sake."

"It does not say that."

"Yes, it does."

"You're making that up."

"I promise you, I'm not. That sounds familiar. Give me your phone." She types the quote into Google search. "It's Jane Austen. *Pride and Prejudice*," she squeals.

"Well, that's just ridiculous," I say.

"Completely ridiculous. Over-the-top ridiculous. You have got to forgive him. It's a sign."

"I don't believe in signs."

"Oh, that's right, only romantics believe in signs."

"Wimps," I say. "Saps."

"And you go right on believing you're not one of them, darling."

"What are you two whispering about?" asks Kate, popping up behind Nedra. Kate is wearing a yellow dress that I'm sure Nedra picked out for her. Together they're a sunflower: Kate is the blossom, Nedra the stem.

"My God, you look beautiful," says Nedra, reaching up and stroking her cheek. "Doesn't she, Alice? She looks like an Irish Salma Hayek."

"Okay. I think that's a compliment. Listen, I think we're getting close to sitting down," says Kate. "Maybe fifteen minutes? Alice, when do you want to do the toast? Right before we eat? Or after."

"She's not giving a toast," says Nedra.

"She's not?" says Kate.

"William's going to do a toast in her place."

Kate raises her eyebrows.

"I'm sorry. I'm really sorry, but I'm just not up to it tonight. But William will be brilliant. He so good at these sorts of things. Much better than me, actually. I'm terrible in front of a crowd. I get all sweaty and my legs—"

"Enough, Alice," says Nedra. "Let's circulate, darling," she says to Kate.

I take my chardonnay and go sit at an empty table in the back of the room. I see Zoe and Jude in a corner, holding hands, staring intently into each other's eyes. Peter is out on the dance floor, doing the robot all by himself and by the looks of it having a grand time. Jack, Bunny, and Caroline are sitting at a table. And William is at the bar, his back to me. I grab my phone. John Yossarian is still online. William must have forgotten to log out.

I've changed my mind. I want to meet you, Researcher 101.

Uh—I can't really chat right now. I'm sorry. I'm in the middle of something.

When can we meet?

I thought you went through the wardrobe, back into your real life.

Real life isn't all it's cracked up to be.

I don't understand. What happened?

When can we meet?

I can't meet with you, Wife 22.

Why?

Because I'm with my wife.

She can't hold a candle to me.

You don't know her.

She's a wuss.

That's not true.

You're a wuss.

Possibly.

Tell me the truth. You at least owe me that. Are you happy in your marriage?

That's not a small question.

I had to answer it. Your turn.

I watch as William puts the phone down, then picks it up again, then puts it down again and takes a big sip of his drink. Finally he picks the phone up once more and begins to type.

Fair enough. Okay. Well, if you had asked me a few months ago I would have said no. She was unhappy and so was I. I was troubled over how far we had grown apart and how distant we had become. I had no idea who she was anymore, what she wanted or what she dreamed about. And it had been so long since I had asked her. I wasn't sure I was capable of having that conversation, at least not face-to-face. So I did something I'm not proud of. I went behind her back. I thought I could get away with not telling her, but now I think I'm going to have to confess.

Do you remember you said that you thought marriage was a sort of Catch-22? The very things that made you fall in love with your spouse became the very things that made you fall out of love with him? I'm afraid I'm finding myself at a similar Catch-22 moment. I did something out of love, in order to save my marriage. But the thing I did might be the very thing that ends it. I know my wife. She's going to be very upset when she finds out what I've done.

So why confess at all?

Because it's time for me to show up.

"Excuse me, everybody, excuse me," says Nedra. She's standing at the front of the room, holding a wireless microphone. "If everybody will please go to their tables now."

I watch William slide off the bar stool, his phone in his hand. He sees me and waves me over, pointing to the table where Bunny, Caroline, and Jack are already sitting. Unbelievable. He doesn't look rattled in the least bit.

When I get to the table, he pulls my chair out for me. "How did it go with Nedra?"

"Fine."

"She's okay with me giving the toast?"

I shrug.

"Are *you* okay with me giving the toast?"

"I have to go to the bathroom."

In the bathroom, I dab my face with cold water and lean over the sink. I look horrible. Under the fluorescent light my suit looks pink, almost cartoonish. I take a few deep breaths. I'm in no rush to get back to the table. I open my Facebook chat.

I'm heartbroken.

Why are you heartbroken, Wife 22?

You did this to me.

That's not exactly true. We both played a part in this.

I was vulnerable. I was lonely. I was needy. You preyed on me!

I was vulnerable, lonely, and needy too, did you ever think of that?
Look, this is not productive anymore. I think we should stop chatting.

Why do you get to make that decision? You're just going to leave me hang—

The little green button next to his name turns into a half moon. He's gone. I'm furious. How dare he log off on me! I walk out of the bathroom and nearly collide with a waiter. "Can I get you anything?" he asks.

I look out into the room and see Nedra approaching our table. She hands the mike to a clearly flustered William, kisses him on the cheek, then returns to her table, where she slides her chair as close as she can to Kate's.

William stands up and clears his throat. "So, I've been asked to give a toast."

"I don't want anything, but you see that man with the mike? That's my husband. He'd like a piña colada," I whisper to the waiter.

"Of course. I'll bring it to him after he's done speaking."

"No, he's desperate for one now. He's parched. So parched. See how he keeps swallowing and gulping? He needs it to get through the toast. Can you put a rush on it?"

"Absolutely," says the waiter, scurrying to the bar.

"I've known Nedra and Kate for—let's see—thirteen years," says William. "The first time I met Nedra—"

I hear the whir of the blender. I watch the bartender pour the drink into a glass. I watch him garnish the drink with a piece of pineapple and a cherry.

"And I knew," says William. "We all knew."

The waiter crosses the room with William's drink.

"You know how you just know? When two people are right for each other?"

The waiter begins wending his way through the tables.

"And Kate—Kate, my God, Kate. What can I say about Kate," blabs William.

The waiter is waylaid by a couple asking for drinks. He takes their order and moves on.

"I mean, come on. Look at the two them. The bride and—well, the bride."

The waiter arrives at William's table and slides the drink in front of him. William looks down at the drink, confused. "What is this? I didn't order this," he whispers, but everybody can hear him because he's holding the mike.

"It's a piña colada, sir. Your throat is parched, sir," says the waiter.

"You've given me somebody else's order."

"No, it's for you," insists the waiter.

"I'm telling you I didn't order it."

"Your wife did," whispers the waiter, pointing to me.

William looks across the room at me and I give him a little wave. Dozens of micro-expressions flit across his face. I try and catalog them: bewilderment, vulnerability, shock, shame, anger, and then something else, something I'm entirely unprepared for. Relief.

He nods. He nods again, then he takes a sip of the piña colada. "That's good. Surprisingly good," he says into the mike and then promptly spills the glass all over his white shirtfront. Bunny and Caroline leap to their feet, their napkins in hand, and begin dabbing at William's shirt.

"Soda water, please!" yells Bunny. "Quick, before the stain sets."

I dart into the bathroom hallway. Thirty seconds later, William finds me.

"You *know*?" he whispers, pressing me up against the wall.

I glare at his wet, stained shirt. "Obviously."

He saws his jaw back and forth. " 'Real life isn't all it's cracked up to be'?"

"You toyed with me. For months. Why shouldn't I toy with you? Just a little."

He takes a deep breath. "William had a very bad year. William is not trying to make excuses for himself. William should have told his wife about his bad year."

"Why are you talking about yourself in the third person?"

"I'm trying to speak your language. Facebooking you. To your face. Say something."

"Give me your phone."

"Why?"

"Don't you want to know how I found out?"

William hands me his phone.

"Every time you take a photo, your longitude and latitude is tagged. Your last profile photo—the one of your hand—it was taken at our house. You left me a trail that led right back to you."

I turn off the location services setting on his phone's camera. "There. Now nobody can track you."

"What if I want to be tracked?"

"In that case you should seek professional help."

"How long have you known?"

"Since this afternoon."

William runs his hand through his hair. "Jesus, Alice. Why didn't you say something? Does Bunny know?"

I nod.

"Nedra, too?"

"Yes."

He grimaces.

"Don't be embarrassed. They adore you. They thought it was the most romantic thing they had ever heard of."

"Is that what you thought?"

"Why, William? Why did you do it?"

He sighs. "Because I saw your Google search. The night of the FiG launch? You didn't clear history. I saw it all. From 'Alice Buckle' to 'Happy Marriage.' You were miserable. *I* made you miserable. I made that stupid comment about you having a small life. I had to do something."

"And the Netherfield Center? That was an invention? Its connection to UCSF?"

"I knew you wouldn't take part in the survey unless it was properly credentialed. Setting up the website wasn't hard. What was hard was when it took on a life of its own. I was planning to confess. The night we were supposed to meet at Tea & Circumstances? Then Bunny and Jack came. I never intended to stand you up. I begged you not to go, remember? I didn't think it would end like this."

"But why did you have to sneak around? You could have just asked me the questions to my face. You didn't even try."

"What do you mean? I stalked you. I solicited you. I opened a fake Facebook account. I pinged you, alerted you, and notified you. I read the goddamn *Chronicles of Narnia* and *Catch-22*."

"Is this on? Is this working?" We hear Nedra testing the mike. "William? Are you out there? It's terribly bad form to not finish a toast. To be a toast dangler. At least in the UK, it is."

"Oh, Jesus," groans William, uncharacteristically flustered. "Save me."

"Fine," I say. "I'll give the damn toast."

As I make my way across the room, I try and clear my head. I should say something about love, obviously. Something about marriage. Something funny. Something sweet. But my mind is swimming with thoughts of William. The lengths to which he went to reach me.

When I get to the table, Zoe hands the microphone to me. "Go, Mom," she whispers.

I bring the microphone slowly up to my lips. "Do you know how you know you know?" I sputter.

I did not just say that. My knees are shaking. I stare out into the crowd nervously and clutch at my throat.

"Head high," Bunny says under her breath.

"When things are right."

"People don't talk that way in real life," Bunny whispers.

"There's just no stopping lovers from being together."

"From the heart, Alice. From the heart," she urges me.

"I'm sorry. Hold on." I search for William but I don't see him anywhere. "Let me try this again. Nedra. Kate. My sweetest, dearest friends." A hush settles over the restaurant. I look out at the room.

"My God, look at all those phones. Do you realize there are phones on everybody's table? Is there anybody here without a device? Raise your hand. No, I didn't think so. You know, it's crazy. It's really crazy. We live in such connected times. It's so easy to become addicted to having access to everything and everybody in a split second, but I'm not so sure that's a good thing."

I pause, take a sip of my water, and stall, hoping clarity will come to me. Where the hell did William go?

"Someone once told me waiting was a dying art. He worried that we had traded speed and constant access for the deeper pleasures of leaving and returning. I wasn't sure I agreed with him. Who doesn't want what they want when they want it? That's the world we live in. To pretend otherwise is ridiculous. But I'm starting to think he was right. Nedra and Kate, you are a perfect example of what waiting brings you. Your partnership inspires me. It makes me want to be better. You have one of the strongest, most stalwart, loving, and tender relationships I've ever seen, and it will be my privilege to bear witness to your marriage tomorrow."

I try and unobtrusively wipe my sweaty palms on my skirt.

"Now, I know I'm supposed to give you some advice now. Sage advice coming from somebody who's been married for two decades. I'm not sure what wisdom I can offer, but I can say this. Marriage isn't neutral. Sometimes we'd like to think it is, but listen, hiding out in the infirmary waiting for the war to end is no way to live."

I look out at a sea of confused faces. Uh-oh.

"What I'm trying to say is don't have a Sweden of a marriage. Or a Costa Rica of a marriage, either. Not that I don't like Sweden or Costa Rica; they are perfectly lovely places to live and visit and I appreciate their neutrality, politically anyway. But my advice is—have the courage to let your marriage be some fiery country in the throes of revolution where each of you speaks a different dialect and sometimes you can barely understand each other but it doesn't matter because, well, each of you is fighting. Fighting for each other."

People start to whisper. A pair of women get up from their table and make their way to the bar. I'm losing them. What was I thinking? I am the least equipped person in the world to be giving advice about marriage. I'm a fake, I should sit down, I should shut up, and just when I'm getting ready to bolt from the room, my phone chimes. I ignore it. It chimes again.

"This is embarrassing, I'm so sorry. It might be an emergency. My father—you see. Let me just take a peek."

I put the microphone down and pick up my phone. I have a message from John Yossarian.

18. What did you used to do that you don't do now?

I look up, and in the corner of the room I see William smiling at me. *You son of a bitch,* I think. *You sweet, dear, son of a bitch.*

I pick the microphone back up. "Listen, all I have to say . . . all I have to say is—run, dive, pitch a tent. Spend hours on the phone with your best friend."

Nedra pops up and gives a Queen Elizabeth wave with a cupped palm. Laughter ripples through the room.

"Wear bikinis."

More than a few groans from the women in the over-forty group.

"Drink tequila."

Hoots of appreciation from the under-forty group.

"Wake up in the morning happy for no good reason."

People are smiling. Faces are soft. Eyes are glistening.

"You've got them, Alice," whispers Bunny. "Reel them in slowly now."

I take a deep breath. "Lie in the grass, dream of your future, of your one imperfect life and your one imperfect marriage to your one imperfect true love. Because what else is there?" I lock eyes with William. "Honestly, there's nothing else. Nothing else matters. To love." I raise my glass. "To Nedra and Kate."

"To Nedra and Kate," the room echoes back.

I plop down in my chair, wiped out.

"Mom, you were awesome," says Peter.

"I didn't know you could just wing it like that," says Zoe.

Nedra blows me a kiss from across the room, tears in her eyes.

"Where's Dad?" asks Zoe.

"There," says Peter, pointing. He's leaning against the wall watching us, holding his phone in his hand.

I get my phone and quickly type.

Lucy Pevensie *invited John Yossarian to the event "Proposal"*
The Bathroom Hallway, August 17, Now.
RSVP Yes No Maybe

An instant later I get a message.

John Yossarian *has responded Yes.*

"Back in a minute," I say.

I'm standing near the bathroom door and William steps forward, into the dim light of the hallway.

"Wait. Before you say anything, I'm sorry," I say.

"*You're* sorry? For what?"

"I didn't make it easy for you. I was hard to find."

"Yes, you were hard to find, Alice. But I made you a promise a long time ago that no matter how far you wandered, how far you went off trail, I would come after you, I would find you and I would bring you home."

"Well, here I am. For better or for worse. And you're probably thinking for worse right now."

"No, I'm thinking we have got to stop meeting in the bathroom hallway," he says, inching closer.

I pull the engagement ring out of my pocket. I wave it in his face and he stops short.

"Is that—?"

"Yes."

"What? How?"

"It doesn't matter."

"Of course it matters."

"No, it doesn't. What matters is this," I say, sliding the ring on my finger.

William inhales sharply. "Did you just do what I think you did?"

"I don't know. What do you think I did?"

"Made me obsolete."

"Oh, pah! It's the twenty-first century, not the nineteenth. Women can put their engagement rings on their own damn fingers. Now I need to know something and you need to tell me the truth. And may I suggest you answer without thinking about it too much? If you had to do it all again, would you marry me?"

"Is that a marriage proposal?"

"Answer the question."

"Well, that depends. Is there a dowry involved? Give me the damn ring, Alice."

"Why?"

"Just give it to me."

"You still owe me a thousand dollars for participating in the study. Don't think I've forgotten," I say, taking the ring off and handing it to him.

He looks at the engraving and a smile creeps across his lips.

"Read it out loud," I say.

He gives me that dark, brooding, trademark stare of his. "Her heart did whisper he had done it for her."

I had no mother for twenty-nine Christmases, Easters, and birthdays. No mother for college graduation. No mother sitting in the front row at the opening night of my play. No mother at my wedding or the birth of my children. But I have a mother today. Here she is, speaking to me as if no time has ever passed, telling me exactly what I need to know.

"My father found it in a pawnshop in Brockton. It's been there for twenty years. Nedra said it's a sign."

"If you're a person who believes in signs," he says.

"I am."

"Since when?"

"Since—forever."

William reaches down for my hand.

"Not so fast. I'm a married woman."

"And I'm a married man."

"You never answered my question."

"*Yes,* Alice Buckle," he says, sliding the ring onto my finger.

"You showed up," I whisper.

"Shush, you nutty ho ho," he says, as he pulls me into his arms.

April 30

GOOGLE SEARCH "Happy Family"
About 114,000,000 results (.16 seconds)

15 Secrets to Having a Happy Family
Experts fill you in on a few of the secrets of happy families. You too can experience some of the domestic bliss that seemed previously reserved just for TV . . .

HAPPY FAMILY
After realizing that chore charts were too hard to keep up with, and were not practical for the types of behavior I was wanting to recognize . . .

The Happy Family . . . Hans Christian Andersen
"And the rain beat on the dock-leaves to make drum-music for their sake, and the sun shone in order to give the burdock forest a color for their sakes; and they were very happy, and the whole family was happy; for they, indeed were so."

GOOGLE SEARCH "Peter Buckle"
About 17 results (.23 seconds)

Peter Buckle
. . . president "Oakland School for the Arts" Creepy Thriller and Romantic Comedy Club. Tonight's double billing . . . *Annie Hall* & *The Exorcist*!

Peter Buckle . . . YouTube . . .

Lead singer, Peter Buckle, for *The Vegans* . . . singing "Breast or Thigh: Why I Stopped Eating Chicken and Why You Shouldn't Eat Chicken Either."

GOOGLE SEARCH "Zoe Buckle"

About 801 results (.51 seconds)

Zoe Buckle is on Twitter . . . Go Girl

Zoe Buckle's Go Girl is THE site for vintage clothing . . . Liberty of London on sale today!

Zoe Buckle U Mass

Alumna Alice Buckle touring the University of Massachusetts, where daughter Zoe Buckle will attend in the fall . . .

GOOGLE SEARCH "Nedra Rao"

About 84,500 results (.56 seconds)

Nedra Rao of RAO LLP on maternity leave . . .

Nedra Rao and her wife, Kate O'Halloran, are pleased to be expecting their second child . . .

GOOGLE SEARCH "Bobby B"

About 501 results (.05 seconds)

BobbyB Move and Groove

. . . the Premiere Door-to-Door College Moving Service. We take care of EVERYTHING—from lugging fifty-pound suitcases up five flights of stairs, to putting clean sheets on the bed. All that's left for you to do is make the breakfast reservation.

GOOGLE SEARCH "Helen Davies"

About 520,004 results (.75 seconds)

Helen Davies . . . Elle Décor
It took Helen Davies three long years to renovate the Oxford Street manse, but finally the founder of D&D Advertising has the dream home she's always wanted . . .

GOOGLE SEARCH "Caroline Kilborn"
About 292 results (.24 seconds)

Caroline Kilborn . . . Tipi Stories from the Field
I'm on my way to Honduras, where I'll be spending the next year seeing firsthand how microfinance works . . .

GOOGLE SEARCH "Bunny Kilborn"
About 124,000 results (.86 seconds)

Bunny Kilborn . . . in memory of my husband
Bunny Kilborn, renowned Artistic Director of the Blue Hill Theater . . . that's why I established The Jack T. Kilborn Scholarship for Emerging Play-wrights . . . Jack was always such a huge supporter of the arts. He would have been thrilled to know . . .

GOOGLE SEARCH "Phil Archer"
About 18 results (.15 seconds)

Phil Archer . . . Conchita Martinez
Phil Archer and Conchita Martinez were married in St. Mary's Church in Brockton, MA. Alice Buckle, daughter of the groom, gave Archer away . . . reception . . . Irish American Club on 58 Apple Blossom Road.

GOOGLE SEARCH "William Buckle"
About 15,210 results (.42 seconds)

William BUCKLE
William Buckle D&D Advertising—nominated for a Clio for his spot "Geotag" for Mondavi Wines.

William BUCKLE

Oakland Magazine: SEEN—William Buckle and Alice Buckle: Celebrating their 22nd wedding anniversary at FiG . . . sharing a rhubarb kumquat compote.

GOOGLE SEARCH "Alice Buckle"

About 25,401 results (.55 seconds)

ALICE BUCKLE

Ms. Buckle's play *I'm Protracting Our Goodbye* debuts at the Blue Hill Playhouse . . . *Boston Globe,* "The emergence of a bright new talent. A true original, poignant, witty, sophisticated and sweet," "a modern-day comedy of manners . . . misunderstandings and misinterpretations, underpinned with the sting of truth."

GOOGLE SEARCH "Netherfield Center"

About 0 results (0 seconds)

Netherfield Center for the Study of Marriage . . .
We're sorry but this page can no longer be found.

APPENDIX—THE QUESTIONNAIRE

1. How old are you?

2. Why did you agree to participate in this study?

3. How often do you have a conversation with your spouse that lasts more than five minutes?

4. How well does your spouse participate in the running of the household?

5. What would your spouse say your favorite food is?

6. When is the last time you ate your favorite food?

7. Tell us something you do that your spouse doesn't know about.

8. What medications are you taking?

9. List three things that scare you.

10. Do you believe love can last?

11. Are you still in love with your spouse?

12. Do you ever think about leaving your spouse?

13. If so, what would stop you?

14. List five positive things about your spouse.

15. List three negative things about your spouse.

16. What is your favorite book?

17. How well do you think you know your spouse?

18. What did you used to do that you don't do now?

19. What do you do now?

20. List your jobs chronologically.

21. Are you religious? Do you believe in God?

22. List your favorite part of your spouse's body when you were in your twenties.

23. List your favorite part of your spouse's body now.

24. Describe your first impression of your spouse.

25. Where did you go on your first date?

26. List some little irritations of marriage.

27. How many credit cards do you have?

28. How often do you Google yourself?

29. How does your marriage compare to your parents' marriage?

30. What is the last anniversary gift you received from your spouse?

31. Describe your spouse when you first met him/her.

32. What do you wish you had known/been warned about regarding marriage?

33. Is your spouse a good listener?

34. Have you ever been ashamed in front of your spouse?

35. Do you and your spouse exercise together?

36. Is it okay for spouses to keep secrets?

37. Does your spouse do a good job communicating his/her needs to you?

38. What do you consider flirting?

39. What's the last mean thing you said to your spouse?

40. What's the last mean thing your spouse said to you?

41. Would your friends say you are happily married?

42. Would you say you're happily married?

43. Describe your first kiss with your spouse.

44. What do you believe should NOT be done in public?

45. What's the worst emotional state a person can be in?

46. Do you fake things? If so, give examples.

47. How many times a week do you exercise?

48. Finish this sentence: I feel loved and cared for when . . .

49. Whose marriage do you most admire?

50. If your spouse gave you one free pass to have sex with another person, whom would you choose?

51. If you gave your spouse one free pass to have sex with another person, whom would your spouse choose?

52. Do you and your spouse find the same things funny?

53. What is the most memorable place you ever had sex?

54. Do you and your spouse agree on how to educate your children about issues such as drug and alcohol use?

55. Do you get along with your in-laws?

56. What's the last loving thing you said to your spouse?

57. What's the last loving thing your spouse said to you?

58. What's your favorite movie?

59. How often do you quarrel with your spouse?

60. What's the sexiest book you've ever read?

61. Describe the moment you knew your spouse was "the one."

62. Did you participate in any secular premarital counseling? If so, give an example of a question you were asked during counseling and your answer. Does it still hold true today?

63. Where did you get married?

64. Describe a situation when your spouse let you down.

65. What do you think about the current trend of couples divorcing based on spouses feeling more like roommates than lovers?

66. When is the last time you flirted with a person other than your spouse?

67. What does it mean to be good?

68. Describe how your marriage changed during your first pregnancy.

69. Write a letter to your daughter telling her what you can't say in person.

70. Describe something you wouldn't admit to your best friend.

71. List some things you wish you could stop doing but can't.

72. Describe a cliché of parenthood that took you by surprise.

73. Was your second pregnancy different from your first?

74. Was your marriage adversely affected by the addition of another child?

75. Write a letter to your second child telling him what you can't say in person.

76. How much money would it take to be happy, and does money make it easier to stay happily married?

77. Is marriage a dictatorship or a democracy?

78. If you had to explain marriage to an alien who had just arrived on earth, what would you say?

79. If somebody asked you to share a life lesson that you learned in your forties, what would it be?

80. Define passion in one sentence.

81. What did you imagine falling in love would be like when you were young?

82. Knowing what you know now, what advice would you give to your children about romance?

83. Give three reasons people should stay married.

84. Give one reason people should get divorced.

85. Have you had romantic feelings in the last year for a person other than your spouse?

86. Have you had sexual fantasies in the last year about a person other than your spouse?

87. Are you an advocate of gay marriage?

88. Has your life turned out the way you hoped it would?

89. List three things a spouse would do that you would find unforgivable.

90. Write a letter to your spouse telling your spouse what you can't say in person.

ACKNOWLEDGMENTS

My deepest gratitude goes out to my agent, Elizabeth Sheinkman, who never stopped believing in this book. Abiding thanks to Jennifer Hershey, Jennifer Smith, Lynne Drew, and Sylvie Rabineau, as well as Gina Centrello, Susan Corcoran, Kristin Fassler, Kim Hovey, Libby McGuire, Sarah Murphy, Quinne Rogers, Sophie Baker, and Betsy Robbins—a writer couldn't ask for a more crackerjack team. I'm very thankful for the keen insights and editorial acumen of Kerri Arsenault, Joanne Catz Hartman, and Anika Streitfeld, who were in the trenches with me right from the beginning. I'm also indebted to the readers who were kind enough to muddle through the first draft and give me honest and helpful feedback: Elizabeth Bernstein, Karen Coster, Alison Gabel, Sara Gideon, Robin Heller, and Wendy Snyder. A loud shout-out to my colleagues at the San Francisco Writers' Grotto. And as always, none of this would be possible or mean anything without the two Bens.

Wife 22

MELANIE GIDEON

A Reader's Guide

A Conversation with Melanie Gideon

Random House Reader's Circle: *Wife 22* is such a high-concept novel, with so many moving pieces that inexorably come together in the end. How did you manage to keep the details in order? How did this guide your writing process?

Melanie Gideon: Yes, writing *Wife 22* was a bit of a narrative high-wire act, to say the least! I am a firm believer in outlining. In fact, I spend three to four months before I even start writing coming up with a blue-print for the book. Also, I discovered this wonderful software called Scrivener. The best feature is a digital corkboard which allows you to move scenes and chapters around in your manuscript willy-nilly. And it also gives you a view from forty thousand feet up; you can see the entire book at once. That was invaluable.

RHRC: You've said that the catalyst for writing your memoir, *The Slippery Year*, came about after your husband purchased a camper van in an attempt to rekindle your family's sense of spontaneity and adventure, both of which had dwindled somewhat in the face of parenthood and responsibility. Can you recall whether there was an equally poignant moment that served as the impetus for writing *Wife 22*?

MG: Well, after I wrote *The Slippery Year* I knew I wasn't done with the themes of that book. I wanted to continue to write about marriage, but not my own! I needed the freedom to go places I wouldn't have gone in a memoir. So—I needed material. I took one of my best friends out for a drink and when we were on our second glass of wine I put on my little researcher cap and started to ask her questions about her marriage. After she invoked a tone of confidentiality I was amazed at how forthright she was willing to be about everything: love, sex, aging, security, happiness, and parenting. That's when I knew I was on to something. What if an ordinary wife and mother had the opportunity (and, most important, the anonymity) to admit what she really thought, felt, wished for, dreamed, regretted, and longed for in her life and marriage? Thus *Wife 22* was born.

RHRC: You met your husband in the early 1990s while working at a progressive company that manufactured supercomputers, which enabled many of your early exchanges to occur through email before this was a widespread means of communication. You credit this technology for allowing you to continue your relationship once it became long-distance, with your husband leaving to attend Wesleyan University and you staying on as a full-time employee in Boston. Now, of course, it's commonplace for relationships to be cultivated online without the parties ever having met in person, as is the case between Wife 22 and Researcher 101. What do you think is to be gained or lost in these types of paradoxically isolated, though intimate, modern-day connections?

MG: Maybe it's my age—I'm in my forties—but, unlike Alice, I've never started an intimate relationship with a stranger online and suspect I never will. In fact, I'm a bit of a Luddite when it comes to technology. I resisted Facebook and Twitter for a long time, and I confess I still find it challenging to post, tweet, or blog. I get incredible stage fright trying to think of something clever to say. People will see it or—worse—ignore it. What if nobody "likes" it? What if nobody comments? It's like middle school all over again! Part of what I wanted to explore in *Wife 22* was if social media brought us closer together or pushed us farther apart. I think it does both. I long for the old days when my husband and son and I would watch a TV show together. I mean really watch it, without our attention constantly flickering to the devices on our laps. Watching TV in my household is not a passive act. We're always talking back to the TV, commenting, laughing. On the other hand, I learn things about my husband every day through Facebook—new things: what he's thinking, what he's reading, what's making him laugh, what moves him. Social media allows us to be strangers to one another, to be voyeurs, but in a safe way. There's something about that distance that's titillating, especially when you've been married for twenty years.

RHRC: You've said that the influx of devices in our lives has spawned a phenomenon known as "the waiting obsession"—the inability to completely sign off technology and the 24-7 anticipation that someone, somewhere will reach out to us. Similarly, in *Wife 22*, Alice is so fueled by the feelings of expectation and exhilaration underlining her online exchanges with Researcher 101 that she essentially suspends the relationships she has in "the real world." Can Alice be held accountable for this behavior or, in some ways, do you think we have become hardwired to thrive off the thrill of suspense, as opposed to the steadier, long-lasting relationships that we might take for granted?

MG: Like her namesake, Alice in Wonderland, our Alice Buckle falls through the rabbit hole of the Internet. She does live almost her entire life online, and is usually putting off real life while she's waiting to hear from Researcher 101. I don't think this behavior is hardwired. I think it's evolutionary. These are the times we live in now. The truth is, it's difficult, almost impossible, to live an unconnected life. And once you're connected (email, Facebook, Twitter, etc.), how do you shut it off? I think of myself as being old-school about technology. I still leave my house sometimes without my cell phone. I can go for hours without checking my email. But you can be sure every morning as soon as I wake, before I've even taken a sip of my coffee, I am firing up my laptop. I don't like this addiction, but I don't see any easy answers. We've opened Pandora's box. There's no going back.

RHRC: The structure of *Wife 22* is unique—it's partly told through Alice's responses to Researcher 101's questions, though the full questionnaire is only revealed in the appendix. Which question would you say was most difficult for Alice to answer and why?

MG: I think the hardest question Alice has to answer is less of a question and more of an exercise: "Write a letter to your spouse telling your spouse what you can't say in person." In doing this she finally has to face the truth about her marriage, about how they've lost each other and, really, how she's lost herself. It's a turning point for Alice.

RHRC: The anonymity of the survey is so appealing to Alice—"the most powerful aphrodisiac." If you could revisit Alice and William in ten years, do you see them having maintained the openness they've managed to revive, or does this fall away with the ambiguity that enabled Alice to be so candid with Researcher 101?

MG: I am a believer in happy endings, so I would hope that both Alice and William have learned their lesson and will work hard to maintain their relationship IRL. In real life!

RHRC: *Wife 22* is currently in development with Working Title Films. Who do you envision being cast as Alice? As William? Did you have any particular muses for them in mind as you were writing?

MG: Well, I'm not sure I should give out any names, because you never know what's going to happen, and I'm superstitious and I wouldn't want to jinx anything, but I will say there are so many amazing actresses in their forties who would be perfect for Alice. As for William, hmmm—I'll just give initials: GC. And no, I didn't have any muses in mind when I wrote the book. I tried that tactic, but Alice and William became so real for me—so flawed and lovable. I really thought of them as average, ordinary people. Now, however, that I have some distance from *Wife 22*, I'm happy to reimagine them as actors.

RHRC: Your memoir, *The Slippery Year,* explores many of the same themes as *Wife 22*—marriage, motherhood, the banalities of everyday life that somehow manage to consume our existence, and the loss and rediscovery of oneself both as an individual and in the context of a relationship. How did you broach these subjects differently from a firsthand perspective and from that of a fictional character whose life stands utterly apart from your own? Did you ever find yourself consciously or subconsciously imparting pieces of yourself into Alice's personality, or were you mindful to distinguish her in her own right?

MG: I tried very hard to make Alice's life and marriage as different from mine as I could. Of course, being a similar age, having a son, and being married for twenty years certainly provided a foundation for the book. I know this world intimately. But most of the stories and scenes were either fictional or composites of experiences relayed to me by my friends and family. I got to play journalist with this book and it was incredibly fun.

RHRC: Reviewers have applauded your appealing voice, which rings with such a signature blend of hilarity and quick wit. This lightness seems a bit of a departure from your fantasy novels for young adults, which tend to skew on the darker side and deal with thornier subject matter. Did you know that you could be so funny? Was it more or less challenging to tap into this writing style while composing *Wife 22,* as opposed to your memoir?

MG: I didn't know I could write funny until I wrote *The Slippery Year.* I think there was something about being in my forties that really freed me up. I wasn't embarrassed to talk about my neuroses and fears. I was able to laugh at myself, and the voice just flowed out of me. *Wife 22* was a very similar experience. It was a much more challenging book to write than my memoir, but all in all it was a liberating and joyful experience.

Questions and Topics for Discussion

1. Consider the epigraph by E. M. Forster: "Only connect." How did this inform your interpretation of the novel before and after reading? What is the significance of this quote in a book that so often satirizes our reliance on technology to achieve immediate and constant connectivity?

2. What do you make of the fact that the novel unfolds in part through Alice's narrative and elsewhere through Google searches, Facebook status updates, and email and text messages? Did you find that this made for an organic reading experience, considering how much social media is enmeshed in our daily lives?

3. What did this unconventional mode of storytelling reveal about the characters that you might not have learned otherwise? How about the effect of seeing the answers to the marriage survey without first having read the questions? When you arrived at the appendix, did you match any of the inquiries to their responses, and did you find anything surprising?

4. Of her marriage, Alice says that she and William are "floating around on the surface of our lives like kids in a pool propped up on those Styrofoam noodles." She longs for a deeper connection to her husband, yet struggles to move beyond the monotonies apparent in everyday life. Why, then, does she find it so natural to be candid with Researcher 101? Do you think it's that much easier to confess truths about ourselves under a veil of anonymity?

5. Researcher 101 writes, "Waiting is a dying art. The world moves at a split-second speed now and I happen to think that's a great shame, as we seem to have lost the deeper pleasures of leaving and returning." Do you

agree that our access to people and information comes at the expense of developing meaningful connections over time, through patience and commitment? Is it possible to cultivate this kind of slow-budding relationship in a digital age, or are we too primed for instant gratification?

6. Alice's answer to the question of what she used to do—"Run, dive, pitch a tent, bake bread, build bonfires"—is much at odds with what she does now—"Make lunches, suggest to family they are capable of making better choices, alert children to BO." Why is it that Alice, in William's words, insists on keeping herself from the things she loves? How does she go about reclaiming these pieces of her former self throughout the novel, and in what ways do you think she's transformed by the end?

7. Alice struggles with crossing the threshold into her tipping-point year, when she will turn the same age as her mother when she died. She sees this as having to say goodbye, as facing the fact that her mother will never age, never meet William, never watch Zoe and Peter grow. When, if ever, does she begin to perceive this milestone as not so much leaving something behind as moving into a new future?

8. At one point, Alice recognizes that she "can be overbearing and intense" when it comes to parenting. In what ways do you think her relationships with Zoe and Peter have been affected by her mother's untimely death? How does Alice's realization that she has more than just her children enable her to take responsibility for her own life?

9. The relationships between mothers and daughters—particularly between Alice and her mother, a relationship Alice discusses with Bunny and the Mumble Bumbles, and between Alice and Zoe—are a principal theme of the novel. What do the Mumble Bumbles teach Alice about what it means to be a parent, and how does this uniquely constituted group function in her life in general? Did you detect any instances in which Alice was invited to assume the role of a daughter? How does she apply the lessons learned from these moments to her relationship with Zoe?

10. How does Melanie Gideon use humor to address the challenges inherent in love, marriage, parenthood, friendship, and life?

11. Alice admits that she hopes for a richer life with William—"rich in the ability to feel things as they're happening, to not constantly be thinking of the next thing." Do you think she's achieved this after all?

12. If you could answer one question under a veil of anonymity, what would it be?

MELANIE GIDEON is the bestselling author of *The Slippery Year: A Meditation on Happily Ever After,* which was named an NPR and *San Francisco Chronicle* best book of the year. She is also the author of three young adult novels. Her work has appeared in *The New York Times,* the *San Francisco Chronicle, More, Shape, The Times,* the *Daily Mail,* and *Marie Claire.* She was born and raised in Rhode Island. She now lives in the Bay Area with her husband and son. *Wife 22* is her first novel for adults.

ABOUT THE TYPE

This book was set in Garamond, a typeface originally designed by the Parisian typecutter Claude Garamond (1480–1561). This version of Garamond was modeled on a 1592 specimen sheet from the Egenolff-Berner foundry, which was produced from types assumed to have been brought to Frankfurt by the punchcutter Jacques Sabon.

Claude Garamond's distinguished romans and italics first appeared in *Opera Ciceronis* in 1543–44. The Garamond types are clear, open, and elegant.